MADAME

ANTONI LIBERA is a literary critic, translator and theatre director, noted especially for his collaborative work with Samuel Beckett. *Madame* is his first novel.

AGNIESZKA KOLAKOWSKA was born in Poland in 1960, brought up in England and educated at Yale and Cambridge. She has translated works from Polish and French into English, as well as working as a freelance editor and journalist. Books translated include: *Them: Stalin's Polish Puppets* by Teresa Toranska (Harvill) and *Freedom, Fame, Lying and Betrayal* by Leszek Kolakowski (Penguin).

Praise for *Madame*

'Masterfully constructed, the tantalizing pace builds to a mystifying and heart-wrenching climax. Libera writes with a wit worthy of Nabokov . . . this epic fantasy is deeply satisfying, heartbreaking and enthralling.' *Publishers Weekly*

'*Madame* has everything: poetry, politics and love . . . Libera has scored a beautiful victory for the better half of human nature.' *San Francisco Chronicle*

'Essentially a vision of a life-changing teenage crush, Libera's debut novel . . . captures the frustrations of grasping for anything of the world from behind the Iron Curtain and of battling or passion of any kind.' *Scotsman*

'When the copyright expires, expect this novel to sit on the classics list of every major publishing house . . . *Madame's* tantalizing pace, its moving climax, the vital eloquence of its protagonist . . . create what must be one of the novels of the year.' *Big Issue In The North*

'Every detail in this brilliantly constructed novel rings true, and anybody who wants to know what the Soviet empire was really like should read it.' *New Statesman*

'At their heart, the best works usually have a simple story and *Madame* is no exception . . . *Madame* is that wonderfully rare achievement: a book for adults who understand that questions and answers are interchangeable.' *Los Angeles Times*

'A sophisticated coming-of-age tale that's also delicious high entertainment.' *Kirkus Reviews*

'Libera writes with wit and élan, capturing the boy's gauche self-absorption and adoration. As his obsession escalates, so the narrative becomes increasingly feverish, until we too are seduced by the elusive *Madame* and her story . . . Libera's playful first novel is an unusual rite of passage story.' *Independent on Sunday*

'Brilliantly narrated, cleverly structured and always entertaining . . . this is the novel of the year because it is steeped in an unshakeable belief in the beauty of art.' *Die Welt*

'*Madame* will be read and remembered with affection for its young protagonist's blundering charm, which eventually shines through despite his clumsy pseudo-intellectual pretensions. Its simple, central themes – longing, coming of age and the search for wisdom – make it an important literary milestone.' *Sunday Herald*

MADAME

Antoni Libera

Translated from the Polish by
Agnieszka Kolakowska

CANONGATE

First published in Great Britain in 2001
by Canongate Books Ltd
14 High Street, Edinburgh EH1 1TE.

This edition published in 2004.

Published simultaneously in the United States of America
by Canongate U. S.,
841 Broadway, New York, NY 10003.

Published in English in the USA by
Farrar, Straus and Giroux.
First published in 1998 by Wydawnictwo Znak, Poland.

10 9 8 7 6 5 4 3 2 1

The publishers gratefully acknowledge general subsidy from the Scottish Arts Council towards the Canongate International series

British Library Cataloguing-in-Publication Data
A catalogue record for this book is available on request from the British Library

ISBN 1 84195 520 5

Typeset by Palimpsest Book Production Limited
Polmont, Stirlingshire
Printed and bound in Denmark by
Nørhaven Paperback A/S, Viborg

www.canongate.net

for Pawel Huelle

Contents

Say not thou, What is the cause that the former days were better than these? For thou dost not inquire wisely concerning this.

Ecclesiastes 7:10

A novelist should aim not to describe great events but to make small ones interesting.

Arthur Schopenhauer

ONE

Those were the Days!

For many years I used to think I had been born too late. Fascinating times, extraordinary events, exceptional people – all these, I felt, were things of the past, gone for good.

In my early childhood, in the 1950s, the 'great epochs' for me were above all the 1930s and the years of the war. I saw the latter as an age of heroic, almost titanic struggle when the fate of the world hung in the balance, the former as a golden age of carefree oblivion when the world, as if set aglow by the gentle light of a setting sun, gave itself up to pleasure and innocent folly.

Later, some time in the early 1960s, I realised I had come to see the Stalinist period, only just over, as another such 'great era'. True, I had lived through part of it myself, but as a child too young to appreciate its malevolent power; and although I was well aware that, like the war, it was a nightmarish time, a time of degeneration and crime and collective madness, still it imposed itself on my mind – just because it *was* so extreme – as something unique, almost out of this world. And I felt a strange regret that I had been denied the chance to experience it in full, had scarcely brushed against it, confined as I was then to a view from the pram, the nursery and the little garden on the edge of town. The wild orgies of slaughter indulged in by the authorities of that time, the demented trances that gripped thousands of people, the tumult and delirious ravings – all this reached me only as a distant echo, faint and quite beyond my comprehension.

My sense of late arrival was not limited to the sphere of history. It had occasion to emerge in a rich variety of contexts, on a smaller, almost miniature scale.

Take, for example, my first piano lessons. My teacher was a dignified elderly lady, her family landed gentry, her own student days spent in Paris, London and Vienna in the 1920s. And here I am, on day one, already listening to reminiscences about the glorious past, the days of great talents and great masters, the speed at which pupils used to learn, the delight taken in music, how splendid it all was then and now how hopeless.

'Bach, Beethoven, Schubert . . . and above all, above all, that wonder of nature, that example of perfection incarnate, that divinity – Mozart! The day he came into the world should be celebrated like the birth of Christ. The twenty-seventh of January, 1756: remember that date! There are no geniuses like that now. And music nowadays – oh, it's not even worth discussing. Waste of breath. It's finished. A barren wasteland, a desert.'

Or take chess. The game caught my interest, and after a few years of solitary practice I joined a club to develop my skills. There were just a few of us – a little group of teenage enthusiasts. Our instructor, a degenerate pre-war intellectual partial to the bottle, had us practise various openings and endgames, and showed us how such-and-such a game should be played. Sometimes, after making a move, he would suddenly interrupt his demonstration and ask, 'Do you know who thought up this move? Who was the first to play like this?'

Naturally, no one knows. This is just what the instructor has been waiting for, and he launches into a so-called educational digression: 'Capablanca. In 1925, at a tournament in London. I hope you all know who Capablanca was . . .'

'Umm . . . he was a Master,' someone mumbles.

'A *Master*!' He sneers at the hopeless inadequacy of this response. 'I'm a Master, too. He was *the* Master, the absolute Master! A genius! One of the greatest chess players the world has ever known. A virtuoso of the positional game! They don't make them like that anymore. They don't have tournaments like that anymore. Chess has gone to the dogs.'

'But what about Botvinnik, Petrosian, Tal?' someone ventures; these were the stars of Soviet chess at the time.

Our instructor's face twists into a scowl of unutterable disapproval. Then he lapses into a gloomy reverie. 'No, no,' he says finally, with an expression of distaste verging on disgust, 'that's not the same thing at all. Not compared to the way chess *used* to be played, to what chess players *used* to be. Lasker, Alekhine, Reti – now *they* were true giants. *They* had the divine spark. Capricious, spontaneous, full of wit and flair and *élan*: true Renaissance types. In their day chess was still the game of kings! But now . . . it's just a waste of time. Competitions between clockwork robots.'

Or take another example: mountain climbing. I must have been about thirteen when a friend of my parents', a seasoned mountaineer, took me up into the Tatras for what was to be my first real climb. I'd been to Zakopane before, but my experience there as a tourist had been confined to stays in comfortable *pensions* and lowland walks in the valleys and pastures. This time I was to stay in a real mountain shelter and climb real mountains.

And here I was at last, with my experienced guide, in the very heart of the Tatras, in a hostel of almost legendary fame. Our lodgings weren't too bad, as we'd had the foresight to reserve a double well ahead. But the food situation was worse: queues for meals were endless. Trips to the bathroom involved similar difficulties. These obstacles and indignities overcome, we finally set off. There, ahead of us, is the trail, and there, at last, the long-awaited encounter with the majesty of silent peaks and vast empty spaces. But the longed-for peace and emptiness are disturbed at every turn by hordes of screaming schoolchildren, our contemplation of surging peaks and plunging abysses made impossible by the singing and collective clamour of tour groups going down 'Lenin's trail'. And my seasoned guide, in his dark-green windcheater, thick brown cords tied at the knees with special bindings, thick woollen checked socks, knee-high and tight, and well-worn, lovingly cared-for French hiking boots, perches himself gracefully on a rock and launches into this bitter lament:

'So much for the mountains! So much for mountaineering! Even this they've managed to wreck. Everywhere you go, you come up against these damn pests. Mass tourism – whoever heard of such a thing? What's the point of it? It was different before the war. You arrived, and the first thing you did after you got off the train was to stock up: buckwheat, noodles, bacon, tea, sugar, onions – not very refined, perhaps, but cheap and dependable. Then you went on to Roztoka or Morskie Oko, either on foot or in one of those small open-roofed vans that made the trip whenever enough people wanted to go – never by coach! There was a family atmosphere about that shelter at Roztoka, and the best thing was that nobody was there – fifteen people at most. That was the base camp; you'd strike off from there, sometimes for a few days, sleeping rough in shepherds' huts and, higher up, under the rocks. That's what it's about, after all: silence and solitude, being alone with Nature and with your thoughts. You feel as if you were alone in the world, in a place where earth meets sky, touching the heavens, the cosmos . . . floating somewhere above the rest of civilisation. But just try and do that now, with these idiots all over the place. Tours; coach trips; "guides", they call themselves. Lowlanders! A circus, that's what it is – a travesty. It's sickening.'

For years this kind of sneering at the hopelessness of the present and nostalgic sighing for a glorious past rang in my ears as an almost daily refrain. So when I took my place, at the age of fourteen, in the classroom where I was to spend my last four years of school, I was not surprised to hear variations on the same theme. Now they took the form of paeans of praise to former pupils.

During lessons the teachers would sometimes stray from the subject to reminisce about some of these old students and their doings. The personalities were invariably very colourful and their antics quite fantastic. But one would be wrong to suppose that these accounts took the form of edifying parables about exemplary pupils or cautionary tales about rogues miraculously reformed: nothing was further from the truth. The protagonists may have been exceptional, but they could hardly be called sweet or angelic; the features that made them exceptional did not rank high in any catalogue of student virtues. They were intractable, unruly and insubordinate, occasionally insulting and provocative; they had an inflated sense of their own worth; they exuded boldness and independence. They were headstrong, wilful and proud, and they went their own way. But they all dazzled with their talent – a stupendous memory or a beautiful voice, brilliance or wit or a first-class brain – they all had something extraordinary. It was hard to believe, listening to those stories, that the events described had really taken place, especially since the teachers, in recounting their charges' outrageous antics, not only failed to allow so much as a note of condemnation to creep into their narratives but, indeed, seemed to find in the retelling, and in the whiff of scandal that often tinged it, a kind of nostalgic relish, even a certain pride, as if fortune had singled them out for a special honour in allowing them to witness something so far removed from the ordinary.

But of course there *was* a moral. In all these piquant, apparently iconoclastic tales of nonchalant bravado lurked a far less pleasant message. It was a warning, and it went more or less like this: 'The fact that such things once happened does not mean they will continue to happen. In particular, it does not mean that anything of the sort can be allowed to happen in *this* class. Those years, those people, were exceptional, unique. Now they're gone, and nothing about them has anything to do with you. Remember that: don't even think of trying to emulate them. You'd come to a dismal end.'

This attitude was one with which I was all too familiar, but in this case I could not come to terms with it. Yes, the world was once a richer, more interesting, more vivid place – of that I had no doubt. I was also prepared to believe that musicians, and artists in general, were greater in the past. I could concede, although less willingly, that mountain climbing was once a nobler activity than it is now and that the royal game of chess had masters more worthy of it. But *school*? Was I really supposed to believe that even *pupils* were better in the past? No – this idea I could not accept.

It's just not possible, I thought, that all this greyness and mediocrity around me is irrevocable; it can't be entirely beyond redemption. After all, the way things are also depends on me: I can influence reality; I, too, can create it. In which case, it's time to act. Time to launch myself into something. Let something happen: let something start, once again, to happen! Let the old times return, and with them the great heroes, in new incarnations!

The Modern Jazz Quartet

One legend that inspired me in those days was the legend of jazz, especially Polish jazz. Its heroes were teddy boys, daring challengers of the Stalinist morals of the day; the notorious and fascinating writer 'Leo' Tyrmand, 'renegade' and libertine, indefatigable promoter of jazz as the music of freedom and independence; and the leaders of the first Polish jazz ensembles, with their rich, colourful lives, their often brilliant careers, their trips to the West, even, sometimes, to the mecca itself – the United States of America. This was the world that made up the legend. My head teemed with images of smoke-filled student clubs and cellars, of heady all-night jam sessions, and beyond them, in a Warsaw still in ruins, still not rebuilt, of deserted streets at dawn, when the jazzmen emerged from their underground lairs as if from bomb shelters, deathly tired and strangely sad. There was a magical quality to these visions, an obscure, haunting charm that made me ache to experience something similar.

I didn't hesitate long. I rounded up some friends who, like me, took music lessons and were competent on some instrument, and persuaded them to form a jazz band. We put together a quartet – piano, trumpet, percussion and double bass – and began to rehearse. We met after classes, in the school gym. Alas, our rehearsals had very little in common with the stuff of my dreams. Instead of intoxicating clouds of cigarette smoke, alcoholic fumes and French perfume, we were wreathed in a sickly fug of adolescent sweat, lingering from the last PE session; instead of the bohemian atmosphere of half-lit, crowded cellars, redolent of decadence, we had the ambience of a dingy gym in the harsh light of early afternoon or the cadaverous glow of the ceiling lights. Rows of ladders fixed to the wall, barred windows and a bare and endless stretch of floor, wobbling in places underfoot because some of the boards had come loose, and ornamented only by a lone leather vaulting-horse – these were our stage and backdrop. Our playing, too, fell short of the artistry of the famous ensembles: we experienced no legendary trances, no Dionysian frenzies, none of that divine fluency and blind improvisatory exhilaration. The most you could say was that we had more or less mastered a skill; we were competent at best.

I told myself not to worry: it was always like that at the beginning; our time would surely come. And to boost my morale I imagined us dazzling the audience at some future concert or school party, bringing them to their knees in admiration, my own brilliant solo greeted with storms of applause and cries of enthusiasm as I, without taking my hands from the keyboard, turned confidently to the audience to nod a nonchalant thanks and in that brief second saw all the school beauties raptly gazing at me with adoring eyes.

After a few months of rehearsing we had a big enough repertoire to play for well over two hours, and decided the time was ripe for our first performance. But here we encountered an unexpected obstacle. It turned out that the idea of a school jazz club, performing on weekends, say, was one the school authorities would not even consider: to permit such a thing would be tantamount, they were convinced, to colluding in the scandalous transformation of a respectable educational institution into a place of entertainment and from there, inevitably, into a den of iniquity. The students, for their part, refused to consider allowing the Modern Jazz Quartet, as we called ourselves, to play at the three annual school dances: at carnival, or the ball held a hundred days before graduation, or the senior prom. Rock'n'roll was by then a star in the ascendant, The Beatles and similar groups were in the early days of their triumph, and this was the only kind of music teenagers wanted to listen and dance to.

Given this state of affairs, our one chance of performing

(and even this the school authorities considered a magnanimous concession) was at school ceremonies – stiff, tedious, soulless affairs full of bombast and pompous rhetoric. To agree to such conditions was to accept a compromise that bordered on a betrayal of all our hopes and ambitions – especially since it was stressed that if we chose to accept the offer, we must play in a 'quiet and cultured manner': 'none of those barbaric rhythms' and 'none of that foul caterwauling'. Thus we were reduced to providing 'musical interludes' at official school functions – which rejoiced, among all of us, in the most dismal reputation.

In the end, our role in these events was more grotesque than ignominious, more farce than defeat. We played what we wanted, but the context was absurd. For instance, 'Georgia' came on the heels of a histrionic collective rendition of Mayakovsky's 'Left Forward', and blues followed the recital, in a series of hysterical shrieks, of verses depicting the horrifying plight of workers in America, where, it was confidently stated, 'each day some unemployed / jump headlong from the bridge / into the Hudson'. The whole thing, in short, was preposterous, and everyone, the audience as well as ourselves, felt this. How, in such conditions, could one even entertain the illusion that one was creating history or participating in momentous events?

Once a small flame of hope did briefly appear. But it flickered for only an instant, and the circumstances were exceptional.

We were indulged with various diversions in those days, and one of the most tedious was the annual festival of school choirs and vocal groups. It always took place, according to the rule, in the school whose group had won the first prize, the notorious Golden Nightingale, the preceding year. To our misfortune, it so happened that this particular year the pathetic trophy had gone to a group from our school – the ludicrous Exotic Trio, whose speciality was Cuban folklore. Their regrettable triumph meant that the task of organising the festival now fell to us. This was a monstrous headache, involving 'community work' after class and, most nightmarish of all, three days of auditions culminating in a concert given by the winners, at which attendance, as a sign of the hosts' hospitality, was obligatory.

The reality surpassed our worst expectations. This was owing principally to our singing instructor, the terror of the school. Known as 'the Eunuch' because of his reedy voice (a 'Heldentenor', by his own description) and his old-bachelor ways, he was a classic neurotic, with a tendency toward excessive enthusiasm and an unswerving conviction that singing – classical singing, naturally – was the most glorious thing on earth. He was the object of endless jokes and ridicule, but he was also a figure of fear. When something had enraged him beyond the limits of his endurance he was capable, at the height of his fury, of lashing out and doing us physical harm. Worst of all, he could utter threats so macabre that, although we knew from experience they would not be carried out, the very sound of them made the world go dark before our eyes. The one he resorted to most often went like this: 'I'll rot in prison for the rest of my days, but in a moment, with the aid of this instrument' – whereupon he would take a penknife out of his pocket and flick it open to reveal the blade – 'with the aid of this blunt instrument here, I'll hack off someone's ears!'

And this maniac, this raving lunatic, to put it mildly, was to be in charge of the festival. What this meant in practice may easily be imagined. For the duration of the affair he became the most important figure in the school. This was *his* festival; these were the days of his triumph. They were also, for him, as the person responsible for the whole thing, days of great stress. He prowled the corridors in a state of feverish excitement, observing everything, poking his nose into everything, wanting to choreograph our every move; after classes he proceeded, with relish, to torment the choir with hours of practice. Everyone was thoroughly sick of him and we longed for the day when this purgatory would come to a blessed end.

By the last day of the festival most of the students were showing symptoms of profound depression and went about in an almost catatonic stupor. The permanent, oppressive presence of the demented Eunuch, the constant flow of new decisions, the endless chopping and changing, the whole accompanied, for hours on end, by the dreadful howling of choirs in full flow – all this tried our endurance to its limit. At last, however, the blessed end arrived. The last notes of some exalted song performed by the winners of this year's Nightingale resounded and died away; the honourable members of the jury made a grand exit in stately procession; and the students, left to their own devices, with just the chairs to be put away and the stage to be swept, gave way to uncontrollable euphoria.

I had been about to close the piano lid when for some reason I began instead to sound out, rhythmically, four descending notes in a minor key, a simple arrangement that was the typical introduction to many jazz classics, among them Ray Charles's famous 'Hit the Road Jack'. My unthinking, barely conscious, repeated action had a spectacular and quite unexpected effect. The crowd of students milling about cleaning up the room immediately took up the rhythm; people started to clap and stamp their feet. After that, events took their unstoppable course. The three other members of the Modern Jazz Quartet, feeling the call of blood, launched themselves upon their instruments. The double bass was the first, plucking out the same four notes, eight quavers in quadruple time. Next on stage was the percussionist; with lightning speed he threw the covers off his instruments, flung himself at his drums and, after a few energetic drumrolls and strikes on his cymbals as an *entrée*, began, in an attitude of great concentration, his head to one side, to pound out a four-four *basso continuo*. Then – at first distantly, still from within the instrument cupboard – the trumpet came in, joining us in several repeats of those first four electrifying notes; and when the trumpeter at last appeared on stage, to screams of ecstasy and whoops of joy, he sounded the first bars of the theme.

Everyone went berserk. People began to sway, twitch, twist and contort themselves to the music. And then someone else, a boy who had been looking after the technical side of things, leapt up onto the stage. He pulled up a chair for me (thus far I'd been playing standing up), stuck a pair of sunglasses on my nose to suggest a resemblance to Ray Charles, pushed a microphone up to my lips and said in a passionate whisper, 'Let's have some vocal! Come on, don't be shy!'

Who could resist such an enticement, a plea so eloquent with yearning, brimming with the will of an inflamed crowd? Its urgency was stronger than the choking shame in my throat. I squeezed my eyes shut, took a breath and rasped out into the microphone:

Hit the road Jack,
And don't you come back no more . . .

And the frenzied, dancing crowd came in with perfect timing. Like a well-rehearsed ensemble they took up the words, endowing them with new meaning and determination:

No more no more no more!

English was not our school's strong point, and hardly anyone understood what the song was about, but the force of those two words, that '*no more*' so sweet to the Polish ear, advancing rhythmically up the rungs of a minor scale in a row of inverted triads at the fourth and the sixth, was clear to all. And the crowd took up the chant fully aware of its significance.

No more! Enough! Never, never again! No more howling; no more having to sit and listen. Down with the festival of choirs and vocal groups! To hell with them all! Damn the Golden Nightingale, damn the Exotic Trio, may they vanish from the face of the earth! Damn the Eunuch, may he rot in hell! *Don't let him come back no more . . .*

No more no more no more!

And as the crowd was chanting these words for the umpteenth time, in an unrestrained, ecstatic frenzy of hope and relief, there burst into the room, like a ballistic missile, our singing instructor – puce with rage and squawking in his reedy voice, 'What the bloody hell is going on here?!'

And then a miracle happened – one of those miracles that usually occur only in our imaginations or in a well-directed film, one of those rare things that happen perhaps once in a lifetime.

As anyone who remembers Ray Charles's hit knows, at the last bar of the main thematic phrase (its second half, to be precise), on the three syncopated sounds, the blind black singer, in a dramatic, theatrically breaking and swooping voice, asks his vocal partner, a woman throwing him out of the house, the intriguingly ambiguous question, '*What you say?*' This question-exclamation, most likely because it ends on the dominant, is a kind of musical punchline, one of those magic moments in music for which we unconsciously wait and which, when it comes, evokes a shiver of singular bliss.

Now it so happened that the Eunuch's blood-curdling scream fell precisely at the end of the *penultimate* bar. I had less than a second to make up my mind. I hit the first two notes of the last bar (another repeat of the famous introduction) and, twisting my face into the mocking, exaggerated grimace assumed by people pretending not to have heard what was said, crowed out with that characteristic rising lilt, in the general direction of the Eunuch, standing now in the middle of a stunned and silent room, '*What you say?!*'

It was perfect. A roar of laughter and a shiver of cathartic joy went through the room. For the Eunuch it was the last straw. With one bound he was at the piano and had launched himself at me. He kicked me roughly off my chair, banged shut the piano lid and hissed out one of his horrifying threats: 'You'll pay dearly for this, you little snot! We'll see who has the last laugh! You'll be squealing like a stuck pig by the time I'm finished with you. In the meantime, I'll tell you right now that you've just earned yourself an F in singing, and I really don't see how you can change that before the end of the year.'

That was the last performance of the Modern Jazz Quartet. The following day it was officially dissolved by the school authorities, while I, as an additional reward for my brilliant solo (and it *was* brilliant, whatever else could be said about it), was favoured with a D in discipline.

All the World's a Stage

The brief life of our ensemble, like the incident which brought it to a definitive close, seemed to confirm our teachers' warnings against attempting to emulate former pupils. Here was a tale strikingly like their reminiscences of the past, full of potential colour and spice, just waiting to be brought out in the telling; but the reality was flat, and then silly, and finally, after one moment of glory, when for an instant it sparkled and shone, abrupt and ignominious in its ending.

Yet I didn't give up. The following year I tried again to forge some magic from the drab reality around me.

It was the time of my first fascination with the theatre. For several months I'd had no interest in anything else. I knew what was playing in every theatre in town; I even went to some plays twice. Like a professional drama critic, I never missed an opening night. I also read endless numbers of plays, devoured all the theatrical magazines I could lay my hands on, and studied the biographies of famous actors and directors.

I was captivated. The tragic and comic fates of dramatic heroes, the beauty and talent of the actors, the *élan* with which they threw themselves into their scenes and recited their soliloquies, the mysterious half-light and the dazzling glare, the darkness, the backstage secrets, the gong that rang before the act began, and then the joyful conclusion – the audience applauding, the actors, including those whose characters had just died, taking their bows – this whole world of illusion had me under its spell. In those days I could have stayed in the theatre forever.

I decided to see what I could achieve. I wanted to know what it felt like to be up there on the stage, captivating the audience, mesmerising them with eyes and voice and force of expression: what it was like to act, to put on a show. Heedless of the still recent fate of the Modern Jazz Quartet and the troubles it had entangled me in, I set about organising a school drama circle.

The path I was taking wasn't strewn with roses. On the contrary, it bristled with difficulties and pitfalls far more treacherous than those I'd encountered playing jazz. Playing an instrument, at any level, presupposes certain well-defined and measurable skills; the very possession of them is a guarantee of results, however basic. But the art of theatre is deceptive. While ostensibly much more accessible, it requires, if it is to bear its magic fruit, enormous amounts of work and skills of a very particular kind; otherwise it becomes, insidiously, a source of ridicule. So I had to keep a tight hold on the reins if the spirit of disenchantment was not to paralyse me, for I was involving myself in something which, while diverging considerably from my hopes and dreams, exposed my love for the divine Melpomene to the harshest trials.

Anyone who has ever been in a play knows how rehearsals, particularly walk-throughs, can sap morale: how easily every shortcoming – lack of sets and costumes, absence of lights and props, lines imperfectly learnt and woodenly rendered, clumsy movements and artificial gestures – can breed discouragement. When one considers that in the present case these elements were supplemented by two further factors, namely the amateurishness of a school production and a lack of real motivation on the part of the participants, the full extent of my torment becomes apparent. On the one hand, the cast seemed to believe I knew what I was doing: I fed them the illusions they needed, and they appeared to trust in our ultimate success. On the other hand, when they saw what I saw, they would lose faith and relapse, which meant that standards fell and the temptation returned to give up then and there.

'We're wasting our time,' they would say, 'we'll never get anywhere. We'll only end up looking ridiculous. And even if we do get somewhere, how many performances will we have? One, maybe two. Is all this worth it for just one performance?'

'Of course it's worth it,' I would reply. 'If it works, it would be worth it just for one moment. Trust me, I know what I'm talking about . . .' (I was thinking, of course, of the Quartet's swan song.)

'Oh, that's just talk,' they'd say, shaking their heads and dispersing in mute resignation.

Sometime near the end of April, after months of preparation, endless reassessments, substitutions and changes of mind, countless nervous breakdowns and moments of feverish exhilaration, the play assumed its final shape. It was an hour-long collage of selected scenes and monologues from famous plays – Aeschylus to Beckett. *All the World's a Stage* was characterised throughout by the darkest pessimism. It began with the monologue of Prometheus chained to his rock and went on with the dialogue between Creon and Haemon from *Antigone*; then came a few bitter passages from Shakespeare, among them Jaques's soliloquy from *As You Like It* about the seven ages of man, beginning with the words we had adopted as our title; then the concluding soliloquy of Molière's *Misanthrope,* followed by Faust's first soliloquy and a fragment of his dialogue with Mephistopheles. Lastly, there was a fragment of Hamm's soliloquy from *Endgame.*

This script, submitted to the school authorities for inspection, was rejected.

'Why is it so gloomy?' the deputy headmaster wanted to know, eyeing it with disfavour. Tall, thin, with a sallow complexion and a slightly tubercular look, he was generally known as the Tapeworm. 'You feel like killing yourself after reading this. We can't tolerate defeatism in this school.'

'But these are classics, sir,' I ventured, trying to defend my creation. 'They're almost all in the syllabus. I'm not the one who drew up the syllabus.'

'Don't you try to hide behind the syllabus,' he replied, frowning as he shuffled through the pages. 'There's a reason you've selected these particular passages: it's a deliberate attempt to question every decent value and discourage people from study and work. Here, for instance,' he said, pointing to the page with Faust's monologue. He read out the first few lines:

The books I've read! Philosophy,
And Law, and Medicine besides;
Even (alas!) Theology.
I've searched for knowledge far and wide.
And here I am, poor fool, no more
Enlightened than I was before.

'Well? How else should this be read, in your opinion? It says that studying is worthless and won't get you anywhere. Doesn't it? And you expect us to applaud such a message?!'

'We had it in literature class,' I retorted impatiently. 'Are you saying that it's all right in class or at home, but not on stage?'

'It's different in class,' the Tapeworm replied, unruffled. 'In class there's a teacher to tell you what the author intended.'

'Well, then, sir, what, in your opinion, did Goethe intend here?' I asked.

'Isn't it obvious?' he snorted. 'He was talking about pride: excessive, overweening pride. And arrogance. Just like yours, in fact. Once you start thinking you know everything, you're bound to come to a bad end. Here you are,' he said, pointing to a passage further down, 'it says so here.'

To Magic therefore have I turned
To try the spirits' power and gain
The knowledge they alone bestow;
No longer will I have to strain
To speak of things I do not know.

'Well? There you are. Magic, evil powers, pacts with the devil – that's what happens to the swollen-headed and the proud. But that's something your script somehow fails to mention. And in any case,' he said, suddenly changing the subject, 'why is there no Polish literature represented here? This is a Polish school, after all.'

'This is a selection from the greatest works in the history of drama –' I began, but the Tapeworm cut me off in mid-flow and said, in tones of heavy sarcasm, 'Ah. So you consider, I take it, that our own literature has no drama worthy of note. Mickiewicz, Slowacki, Krasinski – for you they're small fry, third-rate, second-rate at best . . .?'

'I didn't say that,' I replied. This was an easy thrust to parry. 'Nevertheless, on the other hand, you must admit that the works of Aeschylus, Shakespeare, Molière and Goethe are performed the world over, while our own classics tend to be appreciated mainly on their home ground.'

'That's right – "Exalting the foreign, dismissing your own", as the saying goes,' he mocked.

'Strictly speaking, it's not a saying; it's from a poem by Stanislaw Jachowicz, another of our great poets. You know, the one who wrote, "Poor pussy was ill and lying in bed",' I supplied helpfully. 'I'm sure you know it . . .'

'All right, that's enough, Mr Know-it-all,' snapped the Tapeworm, cutting off my show of erudition. 'Do you realise your attitude is a typical example of "cosmopolitanism"? You know what that means, don't you?'

'It means "citizenship of the world".'

'No,' said the deputy headmaster. 'It means indifference to or even contempt for one's own culture and traditions. You worship the West; it's a form of idolatry.'

'The West?' I repeated, feigning surprise. 'As far as I know, Greece, especially before Christ—'

But the Tapeworm didn't let me finish. 'It's a curious thing,' he said, 'that in your script you have also omitted Chekhov, Gogol and Tolstoy. Why this strange oversight? You surely don't intend to claim that their plays are produced only in Russia – I mean, in the Soviet Union. Or do you?'

I could see that further discussion was fruitless. 'So, what's the decision?' I asked. 'Can we do it or not?'

'Not as it is, no. Not unless you incorporate the changes I've suggested.'

'I'll have to think about that,' I said diplomatically; inwardly I made a gesture expressive of what he could do with his changes and snarled, Not on your life, you bastard.

Insulting the Tapeworm, especially in one's imagination, was no great feat. Finding a solution was harder. After all the months of rehearsals, after all our hopes and dreams, I couldn't bring myself to tell the cast about the deputy headmaster's decision. Yet concealing it, playing for time and making promises I couldn't keep, was also out of the question.

With nothing more to lose, I made my way, that very afternoon, to the offices of the Warsaw section of the Amateur and School Theatrical Events Board, housed in one of the city's theatres. I went there intending to enter our play in the competition; but I did not do so lightly. The idea was tempting: to participate in the festival organised by the Board, the most prestigious event of its kind, and at the same time to defy the Tapeworm – but what if it ended in disgrace? What then? Our experience of the stage was very slight; never having faced a live audience, we did not know how we would react. Would stage-fright paralyse us? Would we forget our lines? How would we cope with the unexpected? The idea of making a hash of it was terrifying. And then the competition itself was another unknown factor: perhaps, regardless of how well we acted, our compilation would seem puerile or, worse, boring, or simply ludicrous in its tragic intensity. Failure in these circumstances meant utter humiliation. I felt I was taking an enormous risk.

A sleepy calm reigned in the festival offices. Behind the desk a young secretary sat languidly painting her nails.

'I'd like to enter our group in this year's competition,' I said, a touch uncertainly.

'On whose behalf?' inquired the secretary, without looking up from the task on which her attention was bent.

'What do you mean, on whose behalf?' I asked, surprised. 'On *my* behalf. I mean, on behalf of the group I represent.'

She looked me up and down. 'You don't look like a teacher or an instructor to me.' She returned to her nails.

'And indeed I'm not – neither one nor the other,' I admitted, with a pretence of chagrin. 'Does that mean I can't enter our group?'

'The deadline's passed,' she replied, noncommittal.

Something in my heart contracted in a spasm of dismay, yet I felt a kind of relief. I'd tried and failed, and perhaps it was for the best. My prospects of victor's laurels had vanished, but so had the spectre of shame and defeat.

'The deadline's passed . . .' I repeated dully, like an echo. 'Do you mind telling me when?'

'At noon today,' she announced, exuding false regret.

I looked at my watch. It was a quarter past three.

'I had classes until two . . .' I said, as if debating with myself.

She spread her hands in a helpless gesture, taking the opportunity as she did so to inspect the results of her work. 'You should have come yesterday.'

'Oh, well,' I muttered, and began to shuffle about resignedly, preparing to leave. But at that moment the door opened, admitting none other than S. – one of the most popular actors of the day – himself, in person. The secretary leapt up to greet him with an ingratiating smile.

S. had distinguished himself not only on stage but also as something of a character: he was known to be moody and capricious, and was generally considered a fascinating personality. Anecdotes about him abounded: how difficult he was to work with, how he would play practical jokes on his fellow actors on stage and yet take pains to make himself agreeable to the theatre staff and, particularly, to his fans. His self-absorption and delusions of grandeur were legendary; his disingenuousness, his transparent attempts to cloak these weaknesses in a veil of false modesty and to portray himself as a timid naïf, were an ever-reliable source of amusement. He craved applause and admiration, and liked to be surrounded by young people, who could be relied upon to provide both; he taught at the drama school and patronised a variety of theatrical events, the festival among them. His latest triumph had been as Prospero in *The Tempest*, a production for which tickets had been sold out weeks in advance. I had managed to see it several times, and knew it almost by heart.

Now, as he strode in with an arch '*Buon giorno, cara mia*' for the secretary, I was seeing him close up for the first time. For a moment I was all but struck dumb with the thrill. But when he magnanimously offered me his hand and with his typical disingenuousness hastened to introduce himself, I recovered my wits and hazarded a gambit in which I suddenly perceived the glimmer of a chance: I addressed him in the words of Ariel:

All hail, great master! grave sir, hail! I come
To answer thy best pleasure; be't to fly,
To swim, to dive into the fire, to ride
On the curl'd clouds, to thy strong bidding task
Ariel and all his quality.

Whereupon, sizing me up with a keen glance and finding me apparently to his approval, he assumed his Prospero's severe and haughty look and, taking up where I'd left off, replied:

Hast thou, spirit,
Performed to point the tempest that I bade thee?

'*To every article*,' I said, and went on:

I boarded the king's ship; now on the beak,
Now in the waist, the deck, in every cabin,
I flam'd amazement . . .

He took a step toward me and threw an arm around my shoulders:

My brave spirit!
Who was so firm, so constant, that this coil
Would not infect his reason?

I galloped on:

Not a soul . . .

– but then I paused, as if hesitating, and, looking my extraordinary partner straight in the eye, found myself, to my astonishment, continuing in heroic iambics:

But stay, one such there was – alack, the same,
Indeed, who stands before you now, come hither
By dreams of everlasting glory driv'n,
My entry here to register. This pageant,

Liege, on which your justice will ere long pronounce
I would fain enter; but this dread Sycorax –

I gestured in the general direction of the secretary –

This monstrous hag, who here doth sit and paint
Her claws all day, informs me that the deadline
Now is past. It passed at noon, she says –

I glanced at my watch –

'Twas but three hours ago! Thus envious Fortune
Deceitfully hath pierced my hopes, and shot
Her arrows through my flesh. What now, my lord?
My hopes are spread before you, and my fate
In your good graces lies. I do beseech thee,
Give me your hand, and lend me your good favour.
For this, good sir, most humbly do I pray thee.

During this improvised tirade S. had been eyeing me with markedly increasing stupefaction. Now, as I declaimed my final line, he shook himself out of his stunned state and took up my challenge:

'Tis Sycorax, thou sayst, who bars your entry?
Nay, 'twill not do. I'll bind her with my magic:
Thus will she break. In such a one 'tis folly
To oppose me. She'll do my bidding.

With a mock-serious scowl he strode toward the secretary, stretched out his arms as if to draw her into the hypnotic coils of his magic, and declaimed:

Attendest thou, cruel queen? Dost thou not hear me?
This youth must be admitted. You'll see to it.

And she, melting with adoration under his gaze and falling unwittingly into the flow of the rhythm, replied in the same metre:

Yes, sir, at once, of course, I'll do it now!

At this S. also seemed to relax and lose some of his starchiness. He spread his arms in a rapturous gesture, a blissful smile on his face. And with grotesque sweetness he cooed his favourite phrase: 'Ah, how lovely!' Embracing her in a fatherly hug, he began to stroke her hair. At which she flushed and bared her teeth in a nervous smile, full of shame and sweet longing.

Going home, I walked on air. Within less than half an hour I had been subjected to a hail of experiences so remarkable that each one of them would take days to digest. I had met S., actually met him, in person! What's more, we had clowned about together, and played our parts as equals, for all the world as if we were on stage; and I had charmed him – I had enchanted him! Most important of all, I had succeeded in getting my group entered in the festival – and with what aplomb! I was bursting with exhilaration and pride. And I felt sure, felt deep in my bones, that here at last was the hour of my triumph; my time had finally come. After such a beginning, such a radical reversal of fate, things could only get better.

I hastened to round up the cast to tell them the good news and explain what it would mean for us. I felt as if I were addressing troops on the eve of battle.

'I know we'll win this competition; I can feel it,' I said as I concluded my morale-building speech. 'Just imagine how the Tapeworm will look when he finds out! You'll be covered in glory!'

For the first time they seemed genuinely convinced. Our performance, since it had been entered at the so-called last minute, was slotted in at the end of the festival, so we had a chance to assess the competition before our turn came. But in the end I decided that this was not an advantage. If the other performances were good, especially if they were very good, they might sow seeds of doubt and clip our wings; if, on the other hand, they were bad, and especially if they were hopeless, they would detract from the value and sweetness of a deserved triumph. I assessed my strategies like a general before a decisive confrontation with the enemy.

We arrived at the theatre where the festival was taking place a short time before we were due on stage. It was the interval, and one of the first people we bumped into was S. himself, surrounded by a garland of juvenile admirers, presumably festival participants, and basking in their reverent gaze. It was as if he had been waiting for our – or rather, my – arrival. He raised his hands in a gesture of greeting and (having manifestly prepared his lines) exclaimed:

Here's Ariel! Spirit, farest thou well? What magic,
My quaint bird, hast thou prepared for us?

A wave of heat flooded over me and my heart began to race. It was clear that much depended on what, and how, I replied. Without much reflection, therefore, and heedless of the dreadful risk involved – that of falling flat on my face in front of an unknown audience – I blurted out, making sure only to keep the metre:

'Twill be enough, good master, if I say
That you'll see all the world on stage anon!

Then, to avoid further complications, I gestured pointedly at my watch and turned energetically to the dressing-rooms. The remaining cast members, beaming with pride, followed joyfully on my heels. Just before the door closed I heard S. still casting his charms over his admirers. 'That's how we always talk,' he was saying.

Our performance went very well, as I'd been sure that it would. There was no question of anyone's forgetting his lines – not a single slip, not even so much as a stutter. Our acting was inspired, and we enjoyed it. One by one, the most sublime scenes from the greatest works of drama unrolled before the audience, each culminating in a monologue that fulfilled the function of a Greek chorus. But the force did not flow from our technique, our mastery of the texts or our confidence on stage. It flowed mainly from the fact that every line we uttered was imbued with truth – the truth of our own feelings and experience. In speaking the lines it was as if we were talking about ourselves. Just as the crowd of students had taken up that '*No more*' and endowed it with a meaning of their own, so now we were singing our own song, with the words of the classics as our text.

It was a song of anger and rebellion, bitterness and resentment. Not this, it said – youth should not be like this! School should not be like this, the world should not be like this! Prometheus chained to his rock was a young teacher we had adored, fired for 'excessive liberality' in the classroom. The unyielding, uncompromising Creon personified the narrow-minded Tapeworm. Every silly and pathetic Shakespearean creature represented the Eunuch or his like. But the Misanthrope I reserved for myself: Alceste was me. It was with special relish that I spoke the lines of his final speech:

May you always be true to each other, and know
All the joys and contentments that love can bestow.
As for me, foully wronged, maligned and betrayed,
I'll abandon this world where injustice holds sway
And retire to some tranquil and far-away place
Where honour's a virtue and not a disgrace.

But I put even more intensity into Hamm's monologue from *Endgame* – perhaps because these were the closing lines of our performance. I took a few steps forward, stared piercingly at the audience, in particular at the jury, seated at a long table with S., their chairman, in the middle, and began with tremendous calm:

Me to play.
You weep, and weep, for nothing, so as not to laugh,
and little by little . . . you begin to grieve.

I cast a long, lingering look around the room and went on:

All those I might have helped. Helped!
Saved. Saved!
The place was crawling with them.

Then I turned on the assembled company with a thunderous glare and launched with fury into the attack:

Use your head, can't you, use your head, you're on earth, there's no cure for that. Get out of here and love one another! Lick your neighbour as yourself! Out of my sight and back to your petting parties!

Having spat this out, I sank into a kind of gloomy apathy and spoke the final two sentences softly, as if more to myself than to the audience:

All that, all that!
The end is in the beginning and yet you go on.

I let my head sink slowly down, and then came the blackout, during which we all hurried offstage.

The storm of applause that broke out left no room for doubt as to the results of the competition. And, indeed, we were not left long in suspense. The good news, at that stage still unofficial, was brought to us about an hour later, in the foyer, where we ran into the members of the jury as they emerged from their deliberations. It was S., of course, who announced it – predictably, in the following form:

Most excellent, my spirit! Thou didst well
And worthily perform. The prize is yours.

'I don't believe it,' I replied, finally putting an end to this Shakespearean back-and-forth. 'It's too beautiful to be true . . .'

'You'll soon see for yourself,' he said, likewise reverting to prose. 'Prospero never lies. At most . . . he might play tricks,' he added with a roguish wink, and proceeded to honour us each in turn with a shake of the hand and a solemn 'Congratulations'.

I was happy. Here it was, granted at last – the thing I'd dreamed of so often. The reality of which I was a part, which I had in a sense created, was indeed on a par with the stuff of legend. I felt like a hero whose deeds would go down in history. I was not, however, allowed to feel this way for long.

A few days later, when official news of our victory reached the school, the Tapeworm ascended the stage at morning assembly (which on Saturdays always included a summing-up of the week) and proceeded to favour us with a speech. It went more or less as follows: 'It is my pleasure to inform you all, as well as the School Board, that our drama group has won first prize at this year's Festival of School and Amateur Theatres. We congratulate them; we are delighted.'

'There, you see, sir?' shouted our Haemon, unable to contain himself. 'And you didn't want to approve it!'

'You're mistaken,' replied the Tapeworm with a complacent smile. 'What I didn't want to approve was something quite different, something that certainly wouldn't have won you any prizes. Fortunately your leader' – his eyes sought me out and he pointed in my direction – 'turned out to be a sensible boy. He took my advice and made the necessary changes.'

'That's not true!' I couldn't let such a brazen lie pass. 'We played everything according to the script!'

'The *e-men-ded* script,' he enunciated, wagging a playful finger at me to defuse the tension in the air: I was, after all, publicly accusing him of lying. 'But enough of this squabbling over trivialities,' he concluded magnanimously.

The Tapeworm's move was not without effect. Although in principle people believed me, not him, seeds of doubt had been sown: the deputy head had his faults, but it was hard to believe him capable of such deceit. So we were constantly baited and teased – jokingly, but in an annoying way – with questions like, 'Well, was it censored or not?'

Listless and irritated, I waited for the prize-giving ceremony. Obviously, I thought, there's nothing to be hoped for from the school; I should have given up on that a long time ago. That's not where I'll get the appreciation I deserve. It was only a few days before events confirmed how right I was.

The prize-giving was scheduled for Sunday at five. It was to include presentations of brief extracts from the selected performances, and would take place not at the theatre where the competition had been held but at the municipal community centre, which, although fine as a public amenity, was not exactly a temple to art. It housed a variety of offices and workshops, a rather grungy café and a huge conference hall, used during the week for committee meetings and on weekends either for the depressing evenings put on to entertain the old-age pensioners who lived near by or for noisy dances, attended by the older representatives of the local youth and usually ending in drunken brawls. In short, it wasn't the most attractive locale; for me, with my aspirations, it was an affront, an outrage to my artistic soul. But perhaps it was the only possibility: at that hour theatres would be getting ready for evening performances and perhaps weren't available. Or so, at least, I told myself. A pity, of course: it would have been nice if such a pleasant ceremony could have been held in one of the temples at which I worshipped. Oh, well, I consoled myself, it's not all that important; no point in worrying about it.

But the sight that met our eyes when we arrived on Sunday turned my muffled resentment into serious anxiety. We seemed to have blundered into some kind of horrific nightmare.

The famous conference hall was done up as if for a carnival. On stage a bunch of teddy boys, members of a rock group idolised by the local youth and rejoicing in the name of The Firecats, were feverishly milling about. They all wore the high-heeled boots favoured by The Beatles, tight, narrow trousers and short jackets beneath which hideous folds of ruffled cloth could be seen, drooping unattractively. Thus attired, they were fussing about hooking up the cables to their electric guitars, tuning the converted radios that served as their amps and endlessly trying out the microphone with hoarse rumbles of 'testing, one-two-three', an activity which produced fearful whistles and caused the window panes to vibrate alarmingly.

Then there was the public. It was the most bizarre and fantastic assortment of people ever gathered in one room. The first few rows were filled by pensioners from the nearby Home of Tranquil Old Age. Behind them and on benches to the side sat the competitors, surrounded by numerous relatives, and representatives of various schools, come no doubt to cheer on their friends and make as much commotion as possible. The back of the hall was reserved for the rabble: overgrown students from technical schools, soldiers on leave and gangs of excitable teenagers, alert to every opportunity for dubious pleasantries and spoiling for a fight.

It was clear what all this meant: our ceremony had been incorporated into the community centre's normal programme, an item like any other on its list of activities. And, indeed, to the management it must have seemed providential: for the pensioners a more perfect form of entertainment could not have been devised, and for the rabble it was ideal as the medicinal dose of culture exacted by the Ministry of Education as payment for each rowdy dance.

I looked around desperately for S. and the other members of the jury, hoping that their presence, even if it didn't raise the standard of the proceedings, might at least lend them some measure of seriousness. But in vain. Prospero, having removed his mantle, had dissolved into thin air.

I did notice another actor, however, a smooth and foppish type best known not for his achievements on stage or screen but for his appearances on television shows of the vilest sort, such as *Quiz* or *Teatime at the Microphone*. Dressed in a black suit and shiny black patent-leather shoes, a white drip-dry shirt and a pretentious bow tie, he was nervously fussing about the stage, talking to the organisers and jotting things down in his notebook. Clearly he was to be master of ceremonies.

The thing began. The brilliantined buffoon gave a prancing leap onto the stage, seized the microphone and launched into his act. He postured, strutted and smirked; he gushed; he paid effusive compliments to the audience. It was all in the worst of taste. But the public loved it, and he was applauded.

The order of the proceedings was as follows: the master of ceremonies called the winners up on stage, beginning with the lowest prizes; then, with much consulting of notes, he introduced everyone in the group; finally, modulating his voice like an American television host, he announced each prize and the performance for which it had been awarded. The Firecats' percussionist crashed out a deafening flourish on his cymbals and drums, the master of ceremonies, having presented the certificate to a member of the group, withdrew, and the prizewinners were left alone to display their artistic skills. When this part of the ritual came to an end, there ensued a musical interlude (a notion familiar to me from another occasion), enthusiastically greeted by the back rows, in the form of some rock'n'roll number by The Firecats.

It was a ghastly spectacle. The most absurd school ceremonies, the most grotesque moments of the Festival of Choirs and Vocal Groups, were nothing compared with this travesty. To call it ludicrous, preposterous, a mockery, a farce, would not do justice to its monumental idiocy. Embarrassment and shame trickled down my back in rivulets of cold sweat.

Where am I? What am I doing here? Why did I let myself in for this? I wailed silently.

And all the while, ineluctably, our turn was drawing closer. I couldn't decide what to do. Refuse to go on stage? Refuse the award? Refuse to perform? I didn't dare; it would have made too much of a scene. In the end, I put my faith in the spirit of improvisation.

When the dreaded moment finally came, when the master of ceremonies, having reached the high end of his range of vocal possibilities, called us up on stage, one of my cast, to wit Prometheus, whispered into my ear: 'You can do what you like, but count us out. We're not coming.'

'I'll take care of everything,' I said through gritted teeth, like the captain of a sinking ship. 'You can leave the stage as soon as he's handed over the certificate.'

We stood there, in the glare of the lights, like a group of condemned men on the way to the scaffold. The master of ceremonies droned on, consulting his notes – some nonsense about the 'high artistic value' of our performance. And I was looking at the back rows, where the rabble was, and thinking, They're sitting there like good little lambs, just waiting for this farce to end so that they can finally have their dance and whoop it up. Just as we waited for the end of the Festival of Choirs. And they're right: now *I'm* the thorn in their side, the pathetic creep they have to listen to. As soon as I leave the stage and the public disperses, they'll clear away the chairs, make a dance-floor and throw themselves into the wild gyrations of some frenetic dance to The Firecats' music. And that will be *their* triumph: their '*No more*'.

These lugubrious thoughts suddenly revealed a challenge. No, I decided: I wouldn't give them the satisfaction. I wouldn't let them amuse themselves at my expense. Let them sneer, but not at me. Let them amuse themselves as they please, let them jeer – and quite rightly – at the Festival of Amateur Theatres; but they shall not mock me!

And then it occurred to me that they were the supreme judge here. To bring the thing off in front of people like myself, to win the hearts of the pensioners in the front rows, even, yes, to impress S. himself with my skills – none of that was so very hard. But to subdue the rabble, especially rabble itching for the brutish bacchanalia to come – now *that* would be an achievement. It was a challenge worth attempting.

'And now, ladies and gentlemen,' shrieked the master of ceremonies, 'the winners of this year's first prize, the Golden Mask! A big hand for them!' And he hurried offstage.

'A big hand for the end!' someone yelled from the back.

With a discreet but authoritative nod I signalled to the cast to leave the stage. Then I took a few steps forward and, shading my eyes dramatically against the lights, commanded with an edge of impatience, 'Lights, please.'

The old electrician in charge of the lights, whom I knew from the theatre, grasped at once what I wanted. He slowly killed every light but one, a spotlight on my face and the upper half of my body.

Then, in the most ordinary voice I could manage, as if talking to myself, I began my piece:

All the world's a stage,
And all the men and women merely players:
They have their exits and their entrances;
And one man in his time plays many parts,
His acts being seven ages . . .

I spoke these words with a kind of cold indifference, as if from birth I had been under no illusions as to the nature of this world and life in it, as if the only emotions I knew were disgust and contempt. There was also scorn in my voice, and a certain arrogance. One might have been forgiven for thinking that, instead of reciting verse, I was openly mocking my audience. At each successive age of man I sought out the appropriate age group where it sat in the hall and spoke to them; it was to them that I directed Jaques's wry little portraits. But behind all this there was a message, and it shone through clearly.

This, more or less, was its gist: Here you are; take a look. This is you. All of you, without exception. But not me. I may have a certain number of years, a certain age, but I fit none of these roles. I'm not a mewling and puking infant. True, no one here is. But neither am I a whining schoolboy with his satchel, creeping unwillingly to school. And the best proof is that I'm standing here now, doing what I'm doing. I'm not a lover sighing like a furnace or a soldier full of strange oaths; I'm certainly not a justice in round belly lined; still less am I slippered or in my second childhood.

Who, then, am I? And why don't I have a place in this picture?

I have no place in the picture because I am not here. I am merely a mirror that reflects the world: its pupil, its eye. I am pure Irony and Art. And that is something that lies beyond life.

The silence as I spoke the last lines was almost absolute. Not a cough, not even a rustle. I breathed a sigh of relief. I've done it, I thought. Whatever they're thinking, at least they've been silenced. Subdued by Shakespeare. I've won.

The applause may not have been thunderous (there had, after all, been something insulting in my performance), but it was sincere and respectful. I took a polite bow and was about to leave the stage when the master of ceremonies suddenly rushed in, seized me by the right wrist as if introducing a boxer before a fight, thus preventing my escape, and shouted at the already dispersing public, 'One moment, ladies and gentlemen, one moment! We haven't finished yet! There's still one more surprise, one more wonderful surprise to come!'

What has the idiot come up with now, I wondered, with horrible foreboding. What else does he expect from me?

'Our great Shakespearean scholar here,' the master of ceremonies ploughed on, 'had been awarded another prize – a special, individual prize – funded, ladies and gentlemen, by none other than the chairman of the jury himself, our beloved, incomparable Prospero!'

At this my heart began to beat at a brisker pace, and I even managed an inner smile. An individual prize from S.! Well, well. That was something, even in these miserable circumstances.

'Ladies and gentlemen!' the MC persisted, 'This is a rare and remarkable event, sure to go down forever in theatrical history. And the prize, ladies and gentlemen . . .' – he reached into the right-hand pocket of his jacket – 'the prize . . .' He paused dramatically, raising both hands, one still gripping my wrist and the other clasping the object extracted from his pocket, and screamed, 'The prize is a RUHLA WATCH!'

'*Rukhla, Rukhla!*' came gleeful shouts from the back of the room. With the heavy guttural consonants, absent from the accepted German pronunciation, the word becomes an obscene verb (in the third person singular, present tense, to be exact); the rabble, of course, exploited this for all it was worth. I felt my knees giving way. But the MC still held my wrist aloft in a tight grip, and this kept me from collapsing in a heap to the ground.

The reasons for my collapse, the full ghastly extent of this horrific, ultimate, murderous blow, will be plain to those who know something about Ruhla watches and their peculiar significance.

The Ruhla watch was manufactured in East Germany (Gee-dee-arse, as it was popularly known), and was distinguished in those days for being by far the cheapest watch available in Poland. By itself, this would not, of course, have been a point in its disfavour; but its suspicious cheapness went along with unbelievably low quality. Ruhla watches generally stopped working after just a few weeks of use, and during their brief span never once gave the right time: they were always fast or slow, from the moment you bought them. Their unfortunate owners were eternally having to set them forward or back, and to perform a series of complicated calculations whenever they wanted to determine the right time. This, however, was not enough to account for the Ruhla's reputation: there were a lot of shoddy goods on the market then, but not all of them became objects of ridicule. The Ruhla owed its unique status to the shrill advertising campaigns that insistently extolled its alleged virtues. Radio and television programmes were full of it; on game shows for the masses it was the most frequently awarded prize. A car with a loudspeaker could often be seen making the rounds of the city's streets, haranguing people with the following jingle, blared out at full volume:

Come and play on Guess-me-Kate;
Win a Ruhla and a date!!

People reacted to this insistent hard sell with verses such as:

A Ruhla watch is rotten luck;
It wouldn't buy a decent fuck.

To complete the picture, there was the name itself – or rather, its spelling. In Polish it could become a somewhat risqué *double entendre*, providing material for countless ribald jokes, to the further delight of the populace.

In short, the Ruhla watch was an inexhaustible source of hilarity, and the fact that this miracle of East German technology was now being presented to me in public (not even in a box, mind you; in a little plastic bag stapled at the top) was an unbearable humiliation. Burning with shame and embarrassment and wanting only to disappear from sight, I shoved the wretched thing into my pocket, left the stage and rushed for the exit. At the door, however, an unknown individual with a pockmarked face barred my way. Dragging me aside, he handed me a piece of paper and said, 'You have to sign for it.'

I scrawled a hasty signature and resumed my flight. As I escaped, I heard an impatient shout, 'Hey, you, come back here! You've forgotten the guarantee!'

I dragged myself home in a state of utter wretchedness, obsessively reliving those final moments. Just when I though the worst was behind me, when I was congratulating myself that by some miracle I had not come off too badly, the real blow had been delivered. It was like something out of a film: just when you think the hero is safe at last, something awful and unexpected happens and he dies after all, from a bullet shot by a bad guy lurking in a dark corner.

I also wondered about S.'s role. What had he intended? Did he consider that, having allowed me to dally with him for a moment on his Olympian heights, he was now duty bound to cast me into the abyss, so that I wouldn't get ideas above my station? Or was it revenge for that first improvisation of mine, when I had caught him off guard and briefly held the advantage? And did that roguish wink in the theatre foyer already presage the revenge he had in store? I lurched blindly from one wild surmise to another. In the end, I decided his motives had been much simpler. I think he genuinely liked me and, searching for the right gesture, considered that a watch would be a charming allusion to and fitting memento of my late entry for the competition. Moreover, being notoriously stingy, he naturally alighted on the cheapest solution: the Ruhla. It probably never even crossed his mind that his choice would wreak such havoc in my soul.

Whatever the truth of the matter, I still had to decide what to do with the thing. If I was to shake it off, cleanse myself of its polluting stain, as it were, *something* had to be done with it, and it seemed quite clear to me that a compromise would not do. Passing it on to someone else, giving it to the poor, even leaving it on the street for someone to find – none of these was a satisfactory solution. It had to be destroyed – returned to a state of nonbeing.

The place of execution was carefully chosen: it was to be Paris Commune Square (Wilson Square before the war), this being an intersection of three streets named after our three great national poets: Mickiewicz, Slowacki and Krasinski – the very same whose works, as the deputy head had pointed out, had been missing from my script. To them I now offered up the miserable Western (at least in the geographical sense) trinket bestowed on me as a result of my treacherous cosmopolitanism.

I took the watch out of its plastic bag, laid the straps flat and placed it, face up, on one of the tram tracks. It ticked loudly, showing (correctly) nine o'clock.

I took a few steps back and sat down on a bench. After a few minutes the number fifteen arrived, going in the direction of the city centre. There was a sharp crack, repeated like an echo as the wheels of each car went past. I rose and approached the gallows. On the track lay a crushed circle of metal, encrusted like a mosaic with tiny shards of glass; the cheap plastic straps, surprisingly stiffened, were still in place on each side. I picked up this dead, mummified thing and examined it curiously. The entire mechanism was one solid mass: no trace remained of the hands, the numbers on the dial, or the little screw on the side where you wound it up. One thing only survived: at the top, horribly disfigured and barely recognisable, but still discernible even in the dim light of the streetlamp, five silver letters glowed, triumphant and invincible. 'Ruhla,' they spelled.

I pondered them for a moment with a twinge of pity and turned my steps slowly towards the corner of Mickiewicz Street. There I wrapped the remains of the watch in the guarantee, enclosed them, thus enshrouded, in the casket of their plastic bag and deposited the whole in the gutter.

Our Daily Bread

My ruthless, even cruel act of severance from all that had happened brought a certain relief, but it could not bring about a complete cure. In the teenage boy that I was, something had broken and died, and the damage was irreparable. I came to doubt that anything extraordinary or wonderful, anything comparable to the kind of thing that happened in all those stories about the old days, would ever happen to me.

With the doubts came a sort of dull lethargy and a feeling of emptiness. I didn't sink into total apathy: I still adored the theatre, still went to concerts, still read avidly; but at school I simply lost interest. I withdrew from everything that wasn't obligatory: no drama circles or music ensembles, no extracurricular activities, nothing that wasn't absolutely required. Just lessons and then home, to loneliness and silence and sleep.

Paradoxically, this state of mind allowed me to look more closely at the world around me. When I had been actively involved, whether as pianist in a jazz quartet or acting or directing in a drama group, I hadn't noticed what went on around me, for in my thoughts I was always elsewhere – at an audition or on a stage, at a concert, in a dream. Now that I was free of all this, I began to concentrate my attention on the separate little world of school and its day-to-day life. What kind of thing absorbed the students? What mattered most intensely to *them*? The things that mattered usually belonged to the sphere of the forbidden: smoking, drinking, playing truant, faking signatures and the best ways of cheating in exams. Then there were more serious offences: sneaking into X-rated films, throwing parties and the clandestine exchange of information (more often than not false or wildly inaccurate) about sex or sexual organs, usually supplemented by dirty stories and unsavoury jokes.

These were the elements that made up the fabric of school life, and from them was woven an immensely rich folklore, with a private language of its own, full of bizarre private codes, odd nicknames and colourful expressions, and a store of anecdotes about students, teachers and incidents involving them. It was like a game comprehensible only to the initiated; the stories were endlessly told and retold, with the same relish and the same gales of helpless laughter. No one ever seemed to tire of them. Among the most popular of these stories was the one about the eggnog.

One day, Butch, the class troublemaker and tough guy, brought two whole bottles of the stuff to school, intending to drink them after class with his buddies. He smuggled them in in his satchel meaning to transfer them to the safety of his locker as soon as he got to school, but before he had time to accomplish this, he inadvertently banged the bottom of the satchel against a chair, smashing both bottles. Realising what had happened, he snatched up the satchel and at the last moment managed to flee to the cloakroom. In his wake dashed his two closest mates, loath to abandon a friend in need. When the three of them opened the satchel and surveyed its contents, an apocalyptic vision met their eyes: it was almost half full of viscous yellow liquid in which textbooks, notebooks and other paraphernalia of school life helplessly swam. A dramatic rescue operation began. One by one, carefully, with two fingers, Butch plucked the victims of the flood from the sickly ochre depths; he held them aloft and then with a nod signalled to his friends that he was ready. At this they tilted back their heads, opened their mouths and held them under the sodden pages to catch the stream of sweet eggy nectar. When everything had been fished out, including the glass from the broken bottles, the desperate feast began. The satchel with the remaining liquid, well over a pint and a half, was passed from hand to hand like a trophy cup or a cavalry boot filled with champagne; it continued its rounds until it was quite empty.

The results were not long in coming. Given the hour (between eight and nine in the morning) and the fact that the revellers had not breakfasted, the dose they had consumed was near murderous. First to succumb to the inevitable was Cass, thin as a rail and the slightest of the three; spasms of nausea seized him in the second period. White as a corpse, a wild panic in his eyes, he suddenly ran out of the classroom with his hand over his mouth and for a long time failed to reappear. The teacher became concerned and sent someone to have a look; the messenger duly returned with the news that Cass was draped half conscious over the lavatory bowl and throwing up . . . bile, which probably meant appendicitis, or possibly twisted bowels. The school doctor was sent for, but he wasn't yet in his office, and the unfortunate Cass was taken home.

The next victim was Zen, a refractory and difficult boy, often insolent to the teachers. He was struck down in the fourth period. For once, however, perhaps because he was so weakened, he behaved contrary to his usual manner: he meekly put up his hand, waited patiently for permission to speak, and then said he felt sick and asked please could he be excused. The biology teacher, a strict disciplinarian with a sharp tongue, known as the Wasp or the Viper, had already heard about the Cass affair and suspected she was being made a fool of. Determined to take no nonsense from anyone, she not only refused him permission to leave the room but called him up, perhaps as an act of revenge, to the blackboard. For some moments Zen attempted heroically to battle with nature, but the outcome was inevitable. Nature won: Zen heaved suddenly and in one graceful movement expelled a prolific, multihued fountain of vomit, liberally splashing the teacher's blue sweater. The class burst into loud guffaws. The Viper, however, retained her composure. She dabbed at her sweater with a handkerchief and then proceeded, like the good naturalist she was, to subject the handkerchief to a smell test.

'Well, well: so this is the famous bile that Fanfara' – for this was Cass's surname – 'was throwing up. Apparently this class favours alcohol as its morning drink. Well, you won't get off lightly for this one, I promise you that. Now, go and get a cloth and clean up this mess!'

Butch alone remained victorious until the end of the day. But it was a Pyrrhic victory. He went about in a befuddled daze, visibly struggling; more important, he got an F in every subject taught that day – a grand total of five. His lack of books and his complete inability to account for their absence were sufficient for that.

Another colourful story that made the rounds concerned Titch, a big, stocky youth who sat in the back row. He was blessed with a booming voice and was said to be prodigiously endowed, which made him the object of constant jokes and much daring speculation. This anecdote concerned the singular and inspired way in which he rescued a group of his friends from imminent discovery when they were enjoying a smoke in the lavatories – even though he himself disapproved of smoking.

Smoking was strictly forbidden, of course, and severely punished. The life of smokers was not an easy one. Subjected to pocket searches, breath tests and humiliating examinations of clothes for the odour of tobacco and fingertips for tell-tale nicotine stains, they had to resort to various complicated manoeuvres to conceal their habit and lived in perpetual fear of discovery. They smoked at every break, but only during the long lunch break could they do so in relative safety and with some enjoyment, for the teachers were too busy then to patrol the lavatories. From time to time, however, a spot-check was made even in the lunch break, and then the smokers, their vigilance lulled, would be caught red-handed. The consequences were dire: confiscation of the cigarettes and a D in discipline, which was one step away from expulsion.

The teachers sometimes stalked in packs and sometimes on their own. By far the more dangerous was the lone hunter: he would walk nonchalantly down the corridor, apparently minding his own business, wrapped in thought or perhaps conversing amiably with a student. Then, as he neared the cloakroom, he would suddenly bang the door open and there he would be, bursting through it and falling on his prey. There'd be no question of flight; everyone was caught.

On the day of the famed incident, the smokers were subjected to just such a raid. But on this occasion the lone hunter who marched fearlessly into the cloakroom like the legendary Commendatore was the least expected of people: it was the art teacher, a tiny, modest, delicate wisp of a thing who blushed terribly at the slightest provocation. Someone must have asked her to make the rounds; she would never have done it on her own initiative.

The lavatories were filled with smoke, and the smokers were enjoying a lively discussion about whether it was better to inhale through the nose or through the mouth, when someone shouted, 'Look out! It's a raid! They're coming!' Everyone rushed for the stalls, hoping to drown the evidence; but it so happened that all the stalls were occupied, and they were left with the instruments of their crime dangling helplessly in their hands. Someone tried desperately to open the window, but it was too late.

At that moment Titch, the disapproving non-smoker, rushed to their aid with an inspired counter-attack, worthy of Blücher at Waterloo; and it was this that broke the siege. Taking in the situation at a glance, he extracted his monstrous member and then, with the confident step of the experienced exhibitionist, strode straight towards the enemy, as if making for the urinal. From behind the clouds of smoke came a brief, muffled squeal of terror, and then Titch's deep booming voice, 'Oh, I'm terribly sorry, miss, but these are the men's lavatories.'

The art teacher beat a flustered retreat and everyone breathed a sigh of relief. Titch was the hero of the hour and the recipient of many appreciative pats on the back. 'He chased her off with his sprinkler,' was how the affair was popularly summarised.

Another story worth repeating concerned Roz Goltz and the unforgettable beginning of his essay about the lot of an oppressed serf, as described in Boleslaw Prus's novella *Antek*. Roz (his real name was Roger) was an unusual boy. Secretive and unapproachable, he moved in his own mysterious ways, made no close friends, and had an odd way of speaking. His habit of asking strange – but by no means stupid – questions in class, confounding the teachers and backing them into corners, had earned him the nickname 'the Philosopher'. He was an extreme rationalist: everything had to be explained from first causes and followed to ultimate conclusions, which often led to a *reductio ad absurdum*. His smart-aleck ways, sometimes verging uncomfortably on mockery, would doubtless long since have earned him a good talking-to were it not for his scientific gifts. He was very strong in physics and chemistry, and his maths was of university standard. He also knew a lot of things that weren't on the school syllabus. He had read dozens of popular books on natural science, history and medicine.

Despite his agile and receptive brain, Roz had an Achilles' heel: he was hopeless in literature. He couldn't fathom the set books and had no idea how to discuss them; writing essays was torture for him. He would usually copy them from friends during break, and repaid the favour in kind by letting them copy from his maths notebook; but when he tried to write anything himself it ended up full of linguistic and stylistic oddities, and, more important, strayed ridiculously far from the assigned subject.

The literature teacher, knowing he would have to pass him whatever happened, because of his brains, would sigh and shake his head. 'Well, there it is, your native language just isn't your strong point.' Usually he gave him a D minus.

On the day when the essays about the plight of serfs were due, Roz volunteered, for the first time in his life, to read his out.

The teacher couldn't believe his ears. 'What's this? Roz is volunteering to read? But certainly, by all means! How could one not applaud such a momentous event?'

So Roz got up and began to read. And his first sentence was as follows: 'After a hard day's work, Antek looked like male genitalia after intercourse.'

The boys whinnied loudly, the girls giggled, and then a deep hush fell on the room as the class held its breath, waiting for the teacher's reaction. The teacher, however, continued to sit there quite calmly, smoothing his goatee, as if nothing special had happened. 'Well, go on,' he said matter-of-factly.

But the rest of Roz's essay was not distinguished by anything of note. Perhaps the style was slightly more strained than usual in the effort at originality.

'Why did you volunteer to read?' the teacher asked when Roz reached the end.

'Because I wanted to get more than a D minus,' Roz unhesitatingly replied.

'And what made you think you would?'

'The liveliness of the style, which you're always telling me I lack, but mainly the fact that I took to heart what you're always saying about how *words should be surprised at themselves if the style is to be original.*'

The teacher's face reflected with painful eloquence his inner battle. He was clearly tempted to let it go and dismiss Roz as a hopeless case, but he knew he couldn't let that first sentence pass without comment.

'All right,' he said finally, 'I'll give you higher than a D, but only if you explain exactly what Antek looked like after a hard day's work.'

'How do you mean?' asked Roz, surprised. 'He looked the way I said he did.'

'Describe it, then. What did Antek look like, exactly?'

'He looked,' Roz stammered, 'like male . . . genitalia.'

'Ah! But surely that's not all?' insisted the teacher.

'Like male genitalia . . . after intercourse,' Roz mumbled feebly.

'Precisely!' The teacher mercilessly pinned Roz to the wall. 'And that means – what, exactly? Do tell us.'

A long silence fell, and the suspense in the room reached new heights. Would Roz dare to press on over such slippery ground? And if he did, wouldn't he sooner or later come out, willy-nilly, with some filthy monstrosity? And – perhaps even more urgently – would the teacher, with all his attention concentrated on tying the unfortunate Roz in knots, involuntarily reveal some of his own knowledge about the object of Roz's bold comparison?

'I don't know,' he muttered finally.

'Ah!' The teacher was triumphant. 'You don't know. Well, then, if you don't know, don't write about it. And the only reason you're not getting an F is that you volunteered to read.'

There were sighs of relief, but also disappointment. Not, of course, because Roz hadn't got an F, but because that rare thing, a discussion in class on such a fascinating topic, had come to an end.

Such, then, was the daily bread of our school.

Madame la Directrice

On this somewhat Lenten menu the figure of the headmistress occupied a prominent position. Or, rather, not so much the headmistress herself as the elaborate tangle of surmise and speculation that grew up around her person.

The headmistress appeared rather late on the scene – just as we were entering the sixth form – and taught French. She was a very good-looking woman of thirty-odd, and the contrast between her and the other teachers – a grey, boring and embittered lot, of whom the best that could be said was that they were nondescript – was a striking one. She was always well dressed, in clothes whose quality and cut made it immediately apparent that they were of Western manufacture; on her well-cared-for hands she wore a discreet number of elegant rings. Her face was carefully made-up, and her chestnut hair, cut short and styled by a skilful hand to display her long, graceful neck, was smooth and glossy. Her deportment and manners were impeccable; and there wafted about her, in delicious waves, the intoxicating aura of good French perfume. At the same time she gave off an icy kind of chill.

Beautiful and cold, splendid and unapproachable, proud and merciless – this was our headmistress. The Ice Queen.

Her arrival threw the school into a turmoil, and for a number of reasons. Her appearance and behaviour alone would have been enough; the senior teachers eyed her with suspicion and were a little afraid of her, while the younger lot either were jealous – of her looks, her clothes and her position – or tried to insinuate themselves into her good graces. But there was also a rumour, spread soon after she came, that she was planning a radical reform of the school, and planning it for the very near future. The alleged aim was to make the school into an early outpost of a new educational experiment: to use a foreign language – in this case, of course, French – as the language of instruction. Her efforts in this direction were said to be well advanced; some thought the change might even take place with the beginning of the next school year.

This prospect, on the face of it so beneficial, sowed terror throughout the school. For most of the teachers, some of whom had been there for years, it augured inevitable departure: in an experimental outpost of this kind, all subjects except history and literature had to be taught in both Polish and the other language simultaneously, and so they would have to be not merely fluent in the latter but capable of teaching in it as well. And for the pupils the thought of having to learn everything in two languages conjured up nightmares.

Another element in the consternation caused by the coming of Madame la Directrice was the disquieting tangle of emotions she stirred in the hearts of the students. At first – almost at first sight – she inspired an instinctive affection, bordering on worship; she was like something not quite of this world, a goddess who by some miracle had stepped down to earth from Olympus. Then her coldness, her superciliousness and her peremptory ways began to make themselves felt, sometimes painfully, and the enthusiasm waned somewhat. The ensuing disappointment, however, transformed itself not into hostility or a thirst for revenge, but into something quite different: a classic case of sadomasochistic love, fuelled by humiliation and pain on the one hand and images of filth and violence on the other.

In other words, worship of the headmistress continued, but in a very particular form. In secret she was the object of fervent prayers, in which all past cruelties and humiliations were forgiven; in public – in the lavatories, in corners of the school-yard – of coarse ale-house gossip and obscene and brutal fantasies. These acts of sacrilege, in which the object of worship was verbally humiliated and abused beyond all bounds of shame, helped to deaden the stings of unrequited love, but they were also degrading to the desecrators themselves, so that, when they returned to their inner sanctuary to prostrate themselves before their idol, they paid for their profanities with further pain and self-inflicted torment.

It was some time, however, before we experienced for ourselves the stifling atmosphere of heated passions generated by Madame la Directrice, for when she first came she did not teach our class; all this was gossip and hearsay that filtered down to us from other classes. I myself was too busy with theatre at the time to pay much attention. It wasn't until I abandoned my extracurricular activities that I became interested.

The main topic of discussion in school was, of course, Madame's private life. This was a fertile and highly rewarding subject of speculation, for Madame la Directrice was unmarried. How, when and by whom this fact had been established no one knew, but it was considered incontrovertible. And indeed she wore no wedding ring, had never been seen in the company of a man who might have been her husband, and had never once, it was claimed, mentioned her family – an eloquent omission, for all the teachers spoke of their families at some point, for one reason or another. And then there was something the Tapeworm had allegedly let slip: on one occasion, carried away on a stream of effusive praise for her talents, her energy and her organisational abilities, he is supposed to have added, 'And her lack of family ties, too, is important, for it allows her to devote herself entirely to her work here at school.' In short, we devoted most of our time to a minute analysis of the implications of the headmistress's single state. The permutations were endless.

She was unmarried, yes . . . but was she single or divorced? (The possibility of widowhood was not even considered.) And if divorced, who had her husband been and why had they separated? Had she left him or had he left her? And if she had been the one to leave, why had she left? Incompatibility? Of habits, of temperament? Was he too macho or too much of a wimp? Or perhaps they had split up because of someone else. Was there someone else? Had he found someone or had she? How, where? And so on and so forth. We went over every conceivable possibility.

But if she was single . . . ah, then the possibilities were even more exciting. Single, and thirty years old. No, over thirty! Could she still be a virgin? Hard to believe. So when was the first time? Where, and with whom? When she was at university? During the holidays? In a student dormitory? Unlikely. Well, then, perhaps in more luxurious surroundings – in some hotel, or a suite of rooms, or an elegant apartment? And what about now? How often does she do it? And what's the arrangement? Is she living in sin with one person? Or is it a series of brief encounters, each time with someone new? In other words, does she sleep around? And isn't she worried about getting pregnant? Does she take precautions? What are they? *Dear God, what are they?*

Another urgent issue, and the subject of much lively debate, was her membership of the Party. Of this, as of her single state, we had no evidence, but it was virtually unheard of for a school head not to belong to the Party; Party membership was almost a *sine qua non* for such a post. And here another series of pressing questions presented itself. Had she joined the Party from true conviction or for the good of her career? If it was for her career, what did she expect to get out of it? Money? Position? Or privilege – the main privilege of Party membership being the chance to go abroad, to the West, to France perhaps, to Paris, where she could stock up on good clothes?

These questions naturally led to others. Did she have anything on her conscience? Any past act of shabbiness, anything shameful or base? (It was the general opinion that membership of the Party inevitably entailed such things.) Had she ever denounced anyone, informed on anyone, done anyone an injury? Turned away from a 'politically unsound' colleague?

Then there was, of course, the all-important question of how she behaved at Party meetings – in particular how she spoke. How did the word *comrade* sound on those gorgeous lips? *Listen, comrades . . .; Comrade Tapeworm has the floor . . .; Comrade Eunuch, would the comrade summarise the essentials of his speech . . .? Has comrade Viper ensured the provision of coffee?* No, it was unimaginable that such sentences should issue from such lips. And yet she must have pronounced them, or others like them; that was how people spoke at such meetings.

All these speculations, fantasies and wild surmise were at first no more than games of the imagination, still in the realm of the theoretical, so to speak. Until the moment when Madame began to teach our class. Then it all changed.

It happened quite suddenly, at the beginning of our final year. Our previous French teacher, Mrs W., an elderly and decent soul, decided unexpectedly to retire, and on the second of September, with no prior warning, Madame la Directrice strode energetically into our classroom, struck an imposing attitude at the teacher's desk and announced that she herself would be responsible for our progress in French until our graduation at the end of the year.

The news came like a bolt from the blue; it was the last thing we had expected. When she was making her way down the corridor and our lookouts, stationed as usual behind the pillar to track the movements of enemy forces and warn of imminent danger, announced the joyful news that *she* was coming, we thought it must be just one of her brief, routine visits. The idea that she would actually *teach* us – that from that moment on we would experience the joys of her presence, feast our eyes on her divine form, inhale her scent, speak to her and suffer delicious torture at her hands – three times a week! – was one we had not considered even in our wildest dreams.

That was when it began, almost from the first lesson. All the things we'd heard about suddenly became concrete and very real. Her private life, her single state, her Party membership – subjects which up to that moment had evoked no more than a vague, theoretical curiosity – suddenly became burning issues. The last of these, for example, was now seriously disturbing. How could a creature so splendid, so breathtakingly gorgeous, belong to a workers' party? That voice, those manners, those alabaster hands, those Venus de Milo legs – in a party of miners and peasants, a party of the proletariat? Everyone knew what they looked like: you could see them in the socialist-realist sculptures around the Palace of Culture and within the arcades of that other lugubrious 1950s monolith, the Young People's Housing District; in the gallery of portraits on the banknotes, which displayed archetypal images of prominent national representatives: the Miner, the Worker, the Fisherman, the Peasant Woman in a headscarf; in the hundreds of propaganda posters that littered the city. They were creatures of monstrous size, with hard, brutal faces and trunklike legs, their feet rammed into hideous clumpy boots, their huge, clumsy paws clutching pickaxes, hammers and sickles.

Could one imagine *her*, so delicate and petite, so fragrant, in her Parisian silk blouse, in such company? We imagined the things that might happen to her there, and the thought of them was terrifying. For we knew what these marble heroes turned into once they stepped down from their plinths into the real world. We knew because we saw them in the street, in crowded trams, in canteens and on construction sites. They looked quite different then, and far more threatening: thickset and blubbery, with tiny porcine eyes, filthy and stinking of sweat, dressed in shapeless quilted jackets and caps, coarse and aggressive and always looking for a brawl.

She must have known what kind of people her 'comrades' were. Didn't they disgust her? And wasn't she afraid of them? Didn't it ever occur to her that they might turn on her and demand their right to . . . her body? Dreadful thoughts, all of them, and the cause of many sleepless nights.

And then we got our first taste of that legendary pride of hers. The reality was far more painful than we had expected. It wasn't that she was cruel or that she treated us badly; our experience confirmed none of the reports. It was something else: her air of complete, utter indifference. She seemed impregnable, impervious to everything, without human weakness of any kind. Nothing moved her, one way or the other; nothing angered or pleased her. She never shouted at anyone; indeed she never displayed any kind of emotion at all. When someone gave an unsatisfactory answer she never commented on it, far less ridiculed it; she corrected it in a businesslike way and silently entered an F in her book. Nor did we ever hear so much as a single word of praise. You could have learnt the assignment by heart or rephrased it in your own words as fluently as if you were reading from a book; you might flawlessly conjugate, at lightning speed and without a stammer of hesitation, the most difficult irregular verbs in every possible tense – and still, for your pains, you would get only a matter-of-fact '*bien*', accompanied by the silent entry of a good mark beside your name. Nothing more. In treating us this way she was, in a sense, the ideal of justice: the same towards everyone, industrious or lazy, gifted or not, well behaved or recalcitrant. And that's just what was so unbearable.

She never allowed herself to be drawn into conversation of a personal kind, despite the natural opportunities that French lessons afforded, for the first quarter of an hour was always devoted to 'conversation'. Madame would pick a topic and begin to talk – in French, of course; then she would throw out a few simple questions. From this a so-called conversation was supposed to emerge. This was the moment for the approach. But what usually happened was that a pupil would launch into some supposedly fascinating story, get stuck in the middle for lack of vocabulary, and suddenly switch to Polish, whereupon Madame would interrupt with a sharp '*Parle français!*'

'I can't speak in French, it's too hard, please let me finish in Polish,' the desperate dreamer would plead.

'*Mais non!*' she would reply, '*si tu veux nous raconter quelque chose d'intéressant, tu dois le faire en français.*'

And the unfortunate hopeful, so eager to 'tell us something interesting' but unable to do it in French, would sink back into his seat, deflated like a punctured balloon.

But for those who could manage the French, things were no better. One of Madame's worshippers once prepared an entire speech with the purpose of snaring her in a net of questions and extracting some personal detail. In vain. When she realised there was something a little suspect about his fluency, she interrupted him every few words to correct grammatical mistakes; then, when he had somehow surmounted these obstacles and succeeded, against all odds, in reaching his first question, namely where and how had she spent her holidays, she said she was sorry, but *elle n'a pas eu de vacances cette année*: she hadn't gone anywhere.

Thus Madame turned out to be not so much a cruel and imperious monarch, merciless in her treatment of her subjects and relishing the humiliation they suffered at her hands, as a heartless angel – a sphinx. She seemed to exist in a different dimension. Her impregnable aloofness, formality and icy calm were so unshakeable that she was impervious even to the primitive measures adopted by her worshippers in the first row, who in their desperation resorted to dropping pencils or books so that, in reaching for them, they might look up her skirt. She must have seen the point of the exercise, for it was ridiculously transparent, but she did not react. She merely made it impossible for them to succeed. Her sitting posture was impeccable: you could have spent the whole lesson lying under her desk peering up through binoculars, and still you would have seen nothing. Another time, when a dropped pencil rolled out of the perpetrator's reach, she simply picked it up and, without pausing in what she was saying, put it away in a drawer. To the mute signallings of the victim, trying desperately to communicate that he had nothing to write with and would she please give him back his pencil, she paid not the slightest attention.

In short, there was nothing she needed to do to make us suffer; the abyss that separated us from her was enough. Beside her, the girls in the class – plump, sallow-skinned, sweaty-palmed, their features still undefined – felt ugly and smelly and flustered; even the prettiest of them couldn't compete. As for the boys – pimply and fuzzy-faced, uncertain of voice and clumsy of movement, their chins unattractively sprouting the first wisps of beard – her presence threw them into agonies of shame and embarrassment. She was a rose in full bloom, a butterfly, while we – we were not even buds, with their promise of opening one day to reveal the beauty of fully formed flowers; we were weeds that grew wild by the roadside, or ugly, misshapen larvae, bunched up in ungainly positions in their cocoons.

The entire class lived only for the French lessons; between them we merely existed, in a kind of hypnotised daze. The boys wandered about gloomy and sullen, with flushed cheeks and dark circles under their eyes, leaving no doubt as to the activities to which they devoted their spare time; the girls crept around listlessly, scribbling in their diaries, where they scrupulously wrote down every detail of Madame's appearance each day: her skirt, her dress, the colour of her scarf; her make-up, and whether it seemed heavier or lighter than on the previous day; her hair, and whether it looked as if she had recently been to the hairdresser's. These notes were then compared, cross-referenced and compiled, so that the girls, like secret agents or archivists for the Security Services, were in possession of almost all the facts concerning Madame's use of cosmetics and the contents of her wardrobe. They knew such arcane details as the brand of mascara she used and the number that corresponded to the exact shade of her lipstick; they had evidence that she wore tights (an almost unobtainable rarity in those days) rather than stockings, and that one of her bras was black. (Once, when she raised her arm to write something on the board, I did indeed get a fleeting glimpse of a black strap.)

The pent-up tension was relieved by chatter. Each discussion gave rise to some new idea or hypothesis. According to one of the most popular of these, Madame was . . . frigid. Of course, no one was quite sure what this term meant, but that was precisely its main attraction. Opinions on the matter differed; they could, however, be reduced to three basic lines of thought.

According to the first – let us call it the radical line – a frigid woman was one almost entirely lacking in reproductive organs; her genito-urinary system was limited to a urethra. This view was adopted by the most primitive boys, the so-called extremists.

Exponents of the second line of thought, more moderate but vastly richer in possibilities, claimed that a frigid woman was merely one whose sexual and emotional needs were undeveloped or repressed. Such a case, they insisted, was not incurable; indeed, according to them, it was quite simple to remedy. Perhaps the essential and certainly the most interesting aspect of this theory was an unshakeable conviction on the part of those who held it (known for this reason as the romantics) that, of all possible therapists, they were the ones most competent to treat such a complaint. If only Madame were to place herself in their hands, she would be cured in no time.

The third view, perhaps strangest of all and held by some of the girls, could be summed up in the claim that to be frigid was simply to be in love with oneself. According to its exponents, Madame was so perfect that she had no need of men, indeed found them repulsive. She loved only herself, and in consequence was physically intimate only with her own body. This intimacy was supposed to consist mainly in the incessant cultivation of that body and to involve ministrations so intense that they bordered on the sexual: prolonged bubble baths, face masks, the anointing of her skin with creams and unguents, long, caressing massages of her stomach and breasts, and, finally, parading naked around her flat and examining herself lovingly in the mirror. In short, she was supposed to represent a rare case of female narcissism.

And then, in addition to all this, there was *that book* – Zeromski's *Ashes*. It was firmly established as part of the canon and a prominent item on the school syllabus. Now Andrzej Wajda's film version had been released – with some entirely unexpected effects.

We were already supposed to have 'done' this particular item on our reading list. The novel, a hefty three volumes, had aroused little interest, and hardly anyone had bothered to read it through; Roz Goltz hadn't even glanced at it. So the film did not generate much excitement. Since we had already spent tedious days ploughing through *Ashes* in its written form, it was too late to exchange them for a few hours at the cinema, and in this case no one was much interested in comparisons between literature and screen. Nor did anyone pay attention to the heated press and television debates in which Wajda was, as usual, accused of desecration and cheap effects. And yet people went to see it, and more than once.

They went for three short scenes. In the first, Helena, the young and pretty heroine, is shown in her room at the manor preparing to retire for the night; as part of these preparations she apparently finds it necessary to warm her bare legs at the fire, and this she does in the most attractive way, her night-dress riding high up on her thighs as she shamelessly thrusts her body towards the flames. The second scene takes place in the Tatra mountains, against a picturesque background of splendid rugged peaks; in it the heroine, by then a few years older, is raped by a gang of highland robbers, and this provides another opportunity for a close-up of her legs, bare and flexed at the knee. Finally, in the third, some savage and degenerate Polish soldiers, fighting at Napoleon's side in the unfortunate Spanish campaign, indulge their lust with a group of swarthy nuns against the background of the conquered city of Saragossa.

There was nothing all that extreme about any of these scenes – they contained little nudity and not even much cruelty – but by Polish standards their audacity was breathtaking. It helped that the violated Helena was played by Pola Raksa, at that time a young star and, with her piercingly clear eyes and thrillingly, dramatically breaking voice, the object of thousands of teenagers' lustful sighs. She was known for her appearances in a number of films aimed at young people, in which she played coltish, innocent girls who tempted men and boys with her charms but never allowed them so much as a kiss. So to see her now being savagely raped by highland robbers (perhaps in revenge for her shameless flirting) was a pleasure of a rare kind. And there was a similar, though slightly different, pleasure to be derived from identifying with Polish soldiers who fought on Spanish soil in such an ignoble cause.

Butch claimed that in one cinema the projectionist would, for a small fee, put on a special treat for aficionados after the last showing and screen just the three all-important scenes, over and over again, freezing the film on the right frames – for example, just at the moment where Pola Raksa stands by the fireplace with one lifted leg exposed almost to the hip. (This, incidentally, gave rise to a long and completely pointless discussion about whether it was possible to freeze-frame with a film projector; Roz Goltz, who knew all about everything, insisted it wasn't, because it would burn the frame, and a fight nearly broke out.)

In any case, it seemed that the rather singular interest generated by the film had one beneficial result: a national classic once dismissed with a shrug and a yawn now had young people reaching for it unprompted. What they did with it, however, could not exactly be called rereading, nor could the longing it satisfied be described as a thirst for literature. It was dipped into mainly for the mountain rape scene, in the hope that the written description might supply more detail than the brief shot in the film. And this, for the reader, was the beginning of the most remarkable experience of all, for it turned out that in the book, the scene to which the film devoted less than a minute was preceded by an introduction of epic proportions – three whole chapters – and could be read as an independent whole: the story of the brief passion that flamed between the two protagonists and of its tragic end.

It begins with the 'lovers', sick of the world, escaping into the mountains (the chapter entitled 'There . . .'). Here they proceed to spend a sort of honeymoon, living in a hut on the edge of the woods in a state of almost permanent ecstasy (a chapter eloquently entitled 'Hills and Valleys'). Finally, as a result of their reckless decision to spend the night in a cave high up the mountain ('Window in the Rocks'), they are set upon by highland robbers. It is at this point that the rape scene occurs, followed by the despairing heroine's suicidal leap from a precipice.

Among the pupils this episode became immensely popular. It was obsessively read and reread, whole chunks of it were quoted by heart and every detail was minutely discussed. No other text on the syllabus had ever kindled so much passionate debate or inspired such in-depth analysis. Special attention was, of course, devoted to anything that could conceivably have a connection with sex; but since the language was so flowery, so full of metaphor and so richly studded with bizarre turns of phrase, it was not always evident what did and what didn't.

Take, for example, the following sentence: 'Exhaustion tore the passion from their bodies.' The intended significance of this became the subject of endless speculation and analysis: did it mean that the protagonists' exhausting climb had *weakened* their sexual desire or, on the contrary, *strengthened* it? Some believed, with Roz Goltz, that the enigmatic verb could be interpreted only in its negative sense, implying a drop of sexual vigour, and that anything else was absurd. Others, mainly the romantics, insisted that the controversial verb 'tore' was to be taken in the sense of 'intensified' or, better still, 'wrung' or 'squeezed', as one squeezes the last of the toothpaste from a tube. In this case, it was the protagonists' capacity for sexual arousal that was being wrung or squeezed out of them – a capacity they had exploited to excess, one might even say plundered. In support of this theory they adduced – from memory – the following two sentences:

> Erupting onto these summits, they not only thrust away water and thirst, and shook the dust of the earth off their feet, but also separated in spirit from their flesh, their veins, their blood, their bodies. Then they acceded to the highest bliss, and it seemed the beginning of eternal happiness, the limit of that other world, a heavenly passion.

'There you are,' the romantics insisted, 'it says that they *separated in spirit from their bodies.* That means they became pure body: pure, naked animal instinct, shameless and uncontrolled. Isn't it obvious?'

Another scene that was interminably discussed was the one where the pair, intoxicated with happiness, decide to kill themselves by jumping off the precipice. The fascinating attraction of this passage lay not in the dramatic or lofty subject matter but in two or three sentences (underlined in almost everyone's copy) of a universal and quite independent significance. The first of these is uttered when the hero, urging his beloved to make the desperate leap that will take them to the 'land of happiness', suddenly utters, in tones that brook no denial, the following surprising command: 'Well, take off your clothes!' It soon transpires that his intention is simply to suggest that they should use her dress to tie themselves together before the leap, so as not to be separated during their fall; but the first impression these words made on the reader was so strong that it 'tore' them irretrievably from the context in which they were embedded.

The next sentence was descriptive: 'Slowly, as if in her sleep, she rose and with a calm smile began to tear at her bodice.' Here, again, the final words were underlined, usually twice, and further stressed by an exclamation mark in the margin.

The dramatic suspense was happily broken in the third sentence: 'But when, from within the folds of black silk, there flashed an arm that was whiter than a pure cloud, he pressed his lips against it.' Here the crucial phrases were 'from within the folds of black silk' and 'he pressed his lips against it'.

And then there was the final, tragic sequence: the attack, the rape and the leap from the precipice. This, too, was endlessly pored over. Oddly enough, here the attraction lay not in reading about the base pleasures of the robbers, clad in 'red trousers and black shirts smeared with grease', but in the passage which precedes this most dreadful event and describes the circumstances of the attack.

The text makes it quite clear that the attack comes at dawn, when the lovers are still lying asleep, 'covered by a coat'. The hero, however, awakens only when he is already fettered and bound in four places – at the elbows, wrists, knees and ankles – and tied to the trunk of a spruce tree; in the cave a huge fire, lit by the robbers, is burning brightly. The question naturally arises why he did not discover this sooner: how could he possibly have slept through all that tying and binding and fire-lighting, not to mention the noise, to be woken at last only by what, in the text, was described as a 'terrible feeling'?

Roz Goltz poked merciless fun at this passage. 'What a load of rubbish!' he would exclaim. 'You've got to be out of your mind to write something like that. I'm woken by the slightest creak of a door, the buzzing of a fly, the tiniest ray of light – but he, oh, no, *he* manages to sleep through seven bandits running around, tying him up, undressing him, tying him to the trunk of a tree and leaping over the fire. It's ridiculous! It just defies plain ordinary common sense!'

'You may be good at physics,' one of the romantics would counter, 'but you don't know anything about what it's like to live with someone in a physical relationship. It was because all that sex had exhausted him. There he was, banging away at her day and night without a break – it's no wonder he was like a corpse afterwards. Just like your Antek after a hard day's work. It's perfectly natural. Anyway, Zeromski was a sex maniac, so he knew what he was talking about.'

This lively interest in the mountain scene in *Ashes* was not kindled by a thirst for knowledge about the still mythical sphere of sex, still less by any appreciation of the qualities of the prose. It sprang, quite simply, from hopeless love for Madame la Directrice. All that debate and literary analysis was mere camouflage, an attempt to pretend to oneself that the issues discussed, while interesting and amusing, had absolutely nothing to do with oneself personally. But the truth was that the story embodied all the secret dreams and longings connected with the person of Madame. In the imagination of the readers, *she* was the beautiful Helena, and the reader himself the cause of her ecstasies. No one ever admitted this out loud, of course, but it was perfectly plain.

For my part, I'd finished with *Ashes* a long time before. The book had bored me to death as it had everyone else, and the mountain episode, with its insufferable pathos and purple prose, was more than I could stomach: after a few pages I simply skipped it and went on to where the main story line resumed. Now I was torn: seeing what was going on around me and feeling the tension building up around Madame, I was tempted to take a look and find out for myself what all the fuss was about, what exactly was supposed to be the connection between the book and our own lives. But pride prevented me. I didn't want to be one of the sheep, didn't want to stoop, even in my own eyes, to the level of my friends, panting with a mixture of sentimentality and lust. And, of course, there was the fear that it would come out – for it was generally acknowledged that whoever was reading *Ashes* must secretly be harbouring a burning passion for the icy Madame.

So I thrust away the temptation and refused even to look at the book. Except once, and that was largely by accident. But I paid for it dearly.

It was during a biology lesson. I was sitting on my own at a double desk in the back row, terribly bored. At some point I noticed that on the unoccupied half of the desk someone had left a book, wrapped carefully in brown paper. To while away the time I picked it up and looked inside. The title page was missing and most of the pages were uncut. I took a look at the text. Yes, this was it: *Ashes,* volume two – the one with the mountain episode. It didn't take long to find it: it was the only part where the pages had been cut, and their bottom corners were sticky from much thumbing. I placed it on my lap, assumed an attitude of deep concentration, right hand on forehead (the left was needed for turning the pages), and began to read.

What I saw surpassed my wildest imaginings. I knew it was kitsch, full of rapturous moans and heaving sighs, but I hadn't expected anything like this. It was mind-boggling. How could Zeromski have written this stuff? And, having written it, consented to its publication? Why had no one prevented him? It was also hard to believe that this was part of a book on the school syllabus – and that people actually liked it. Loved it! And then there was their reason for liking it: this – *this!* – is what they wanted to take as their model for their imaginary love affair with the headmistress!

On the other hand, perhaps it wasn't so odd after all. For this prose, with its ridiculous style, its lofty idealism, its thick tangle of euphemism, symbolism and innuendo, and its improbable plot, contained something that the overly sensitive, excitable adolescent, struggling with hormones run amok, immediately picked up on. That something was perversion, and a fascination with perversion. It was clear that in these passages Zeromski was giving vent to some private obsession, some secret, deeply buried longing; the most exalted prose could not conceal this. It was a classic 'sign of exhibitionist excess', to use a phrase once coined by a certain philosopher.

Mostly, though, the thing was screamingly funny. Reading all those descriptions of 'virginal fields like lovers, flowing with milk and honey', all those stiff, artificial dialogues full of exclamations like, 'How manly you are, how strong and how terrible!' and poetic invocations of an 'eternity long past', it was a struggle not to laugh out loud.

Then I had an idea. Wouldn't it be fun to take some of the most ridiculous phrases and put them together in a sort of romantic prose poem, which I would then present in literature class, poker-faced, as the work of some newly discovered poet, unanimously hailed by literary scholars as an unknown genius on a par with our greatest classics? The idea was immensely appealing, and exerted such a pull on my imagination that from then on I read with only this in view, concentrating on the expressions, metaphors and sentences I would use, how I would put them together, which of them would come first and which I would keep for last.

I was so absorbed in my fury of creativity that I didn't even notice the Viper's approach. She had crept up from behind and was now standing over me, looking over my shoulder. Like the hero of the novel waking up to find himself fettered and bound, I was unaware of the threat until her bony hand came down, like the claw of some huge crustacean, and whisked the book from my lap.

'So, what's this we're reading in the biology lesson?' she began, launching into one of her typical disciplinarian acts. 'I'm sure it's fascinating, but is it relevant?' She glanced at the beginning of the book. 'Title page missing . . . pages uncut . . . just this bit in the middle here . . . look at these pages, they're filthy from use. Well, let's take a look – maybe *we'll* find it interesting, too?' And she read out:

> Here, on your breast, was a wolf – here, next to your beating heart! But you killed it. Oh, my lord and master! That terrible snout, those white fangs, they were here, next to your throat. Its curved claws slashed at your ribs, its eyes looked into yours. How manly you are, how strong and how terrible! How invincible! You are stronger than winter, stronger than the ice and the wind! Nothing can frighten you, nothing on earth, neither man nor animal. How terrible you are! How beautiful! I tremble at the thought . . . I am your slave . . . Oh, my love . . . There . . .

The class settled down to enjoy itself. It was clear that a lengthy break could be expected, further enlivened by the entertaining spectacle of a student being held up to mockery and ridicule. This kind of thing could always be counted on for amusement.

'Well, no, I see that it isn't quite relevant,' pursued the Viper, 'the wolf isn't our subject today.'

Out of the corner of my eye I caught a few people in the act of discreetly slipping their copies of *Ashes*, volume two, into their satchels. The Viper, in the meantime, effecting a slight change of tone, launched into the main part of her pedagogical act.

'So this is what our proud Shakespearean, the pride of our school, the winner of last year's Golden Mask, is reading! Sentimental tripe for schoolgirls, bilge for the masses! Romantic rubbish!'

She was right, of course. But I had to defend myself. 'This is Zeromski's *Ashes*,' I muttered in an undertone, as if wanting to save her further embarrassment. 'It's on the syllabus.'

The Viper was not in the least put off. 'Zeromski's *Ashes*,' she pointed out, 'is required reading for pupils in the year below you. I may teach biology, but for your information I am not entirely unacquainted with the literature syllabus. So you're a little late with your reading. That's point number one. And two, since you're so industrious and conscientious that you're catching up on your reading in the time reserved for biology, perhaps you'd be kind enough to tell us why the only cut pages are here in the middle and the rest hasn't been touched. Here you are,' she said, displaying the book, 'just here, on these moans and sighs . . .'

The class burst out laughing. I was furious. 'It's not my copy,' I blurted out, searching for a means of escape, but this only made things worse.

'Not your copy?' asked the Viper, surprised. 'Whose is it, then?'

'I don't know,' I snarled, 'it was just there.'

'I see. It was just there . . . so I suppose you just picked it up and began reading from the middle?'

'That's where it fell open.'

'Indeed! It fell open.' She wouldn't give an inch. 'Not only do you have the tastes of a besotted schoolgirl, you're a hypocrite as well – trying to disown them. And I suppose next you'll be telling me you just wanted to see what it is the others like so much about it?'

But it's true, I wanted to say, that's exactly right! But I couldn't prove it, and no one would believe me. I had to find another line of defence. As if I had reached the end of my tether, I snapped, 'What would you have preferred? Would you rather I'd cut the pages here in class? Why all these insinuations?'

This was a good move. Naturally, it infuriated the Viper even more. 'Very well,' she said drily. 'Let's leave it at that. But tell us, in that case, what we've covered in today's lesson.'

'The rabbit . . . the anatomy of the rabbit,' I stammered out, noticing on the blackboard a huge poster with a picture of this mammal, its stomach open to reveal a colourful tangle of entrails.

'Excellent! Very good,' said the Viper. 'But what about it? Which organs, which functions, which internal system?'

'Reproductive,' someone prompted in a whisper, but I took this to be a joke at my expense, intended for the amusement of the class.

'I don't know,' I admitted, defeated. 'I wasn't paying attention.'

'That's what I thought,' acknowledged the Viper in tones of false regret. 'So you won't hold it against me if I give you an F.' She entered it in the book with a flourish. 'And now, it's my pleasure to inform you that today we've been learning about the sex life of the rabbit. A subject right up your street – odd you didn't notice. In any event, you will please learn it thoroughly and present it to us in the next lesson, so that no one can doubt your competence in the matter.'

This stung, and the prospect of the rabbit was a dark one. But the worst thing, of which the Viper was quite unaware when ridiculing me in class, was the implication that I was secretly reading the notorious episode, just like everyone else. And there could only be one reason for that: Madame had broken my heart, too.

TWO

In the Beginning was the Word

The effects of my unmasking were not slow to make themselves felt. I had barely sat down after my mauling at the hands of the Viper when I heard the first whispers and felt the first covert glances. I had no doubt the whispers were about me: my downfall was being rejoiced at, and a mean kind of consolation derived from the discovery that I, too, worshipped the Ice Queen, and shared in the general suffering. It was unendurable.

After school I made my way, as I always did at life's difficult moments, to the nearby park (called, ironically, Zeromski Park), where I could think things through calmly and try to find some sort of solution. I sat down on a secluded bench and began to analyse the situation.

I had been imprudent and had been held up to ridicule as a result. But the episode had also forced me to face facts: I, too, had fallen for Madame la Directrice. I was not immune; in refusing to admit it I had simply been deceiving myself.

My act of self-analysis, however, failed to produce its usual salutary effect: instead of making me feel better, it made the wound fester. I would now suffer not only all the tortures that went with the disease but also the humiliation of being, in my own eyes and everyone else's, another victim. This was too degrading a prospect to be borne.

No, I thought as I gazed at the changing colours of the leaves in the October sun, I can't allow this; I can't abase myself like this. I've got to do something. If I don't, I'll soon be like all the rest of them – pathetic, oblivious to all sense of shame, stooping to anything for the slightest scrap of attention.

I was eighteen years old – at least twelve years younger

than she was. I was also her subordinate, and of the lowest rank. I knew that in these circumstances I could seek consolation only in words: to hope for anything more was ridiculous and would lead to agonies of embarrassment and humiliation. By 'words' I didn't mean 'literature'; I didn't intend to behave in accordance with Shakespeare's description of the third age of man and take to composing 'woeful ballads' or – God forbid – besieging her with love letters. What I had in mind was something else: a kind of game in which words acquired a plurality of meanings and also a new strength. A game in which words became more than just a means of communication; they became, in a sense, facts. In this game, language, within a certain domain, *became* reality: ephemeral sounds with conventional meanings became things of flesh and blood. It was to be a kind of fulfilment through words.

I had already experienced the magic power of words; I knew what they could do, how much they could achieve. Not only could they change reality, they could *create* it and in some cases supplant it. It was through words that I had reversed, in the offices of the ASTB, a decision that had seemed without appeal; it was through words that, later, I had subdued the rabble. Words had been the true source of that unforgettable moment after the Choral Festival: it was the magic 'No more', that cry of 'What you say?' which had transformed our relief into an ecstatic Dionysian frenzy and brought catharsis.

And weren't words always mightier than facts, even in the underground life of school? Of the dozens of incidents engraved forever in the collective memory of our class, Roz's notorious essay was unquestionably the one that held first place. It even beat Titch's inspired, uncompromising siege-breaking manoeuvre, which faded somewhat over time and lost some of its sparkle.

Not without reason was the book which proclaims that all things began, and always begin, with the Word known as the Holy Book!

I decided to make use of what I had learnt. I would not rely on Providence for opportunities to exploit the magic power of words. I would create them. I would deliberately pave the way and prepare the ground.

This, like the jazz ensemble and the theatrical performance, involved a certain amount of work. But this time, creating the necessary conditions for future rapture would consist mainly in amassing concrete and detailed knowledge about Madame and her life. The matter had to be approached scientifically. No more absurd fantasies, no more guesswork or wild surmise: it was time for some serious research. And the information had to be substantial, not useless facts like the shade of her lipstick. If I was to initiate the game I was planning, I needed a good hand, with a few aces. In short, an investigation was called for.

This bold plan, if I was not to dismiss it the next morning as some ridiculous fantasy conceived in a moment of gloom, had to be quickly anchored in reality. Immediate action was required. What was there I could do at once? Of course! The telephone book! I could find out her address.

I rose and set off with a determined step for the post office.

It was unlikely that a school head wouldn't have a home telephone. But that didn't mean the number would be in the book. It might be ex-directory, or in someone else's name; if the phone had been recently installed, it might not figure in the last edition, for a new phone book only came out every two or three years.

My fears turned out to have been needless. Only three people with the same surname as Madame were listed, and of these only one had a woman's first name. Furthermore, it was Madame's. In addition, there was an academic title after the comma: 'MA', it said. This seemed to settle the matter: it could only be She.

The easy, swift success of my first stab at detective work had a dual effect. It evoked a shiver of excitement and strengthened my faith in my plan, but it also brought a sense of deception. For I was now back where I had started, facing a blank wall, and this in turn revived all my doubts.

Subjecting these feelings to a thorough analysis, I concluded that they were symptoms of a subconscious fear. Instead of getting on with it, I was stalling. While I longed for the day when, armed with the necessary knowledge, I could finally begin my Great Game, I also feared it; so I looked for reasons to procrastinate, even to give up altogether.

I've got to overcome this, I thought; I have to play an attacking game. And before I could change my mind I set off for the address in the phone book.

The street – more precisely, the housing estate – to which it led me was roughly halfway between the school and my own house. When I got off the bus and plunged into the maze of paths that wound around the buildings, my heart beat faster. What if I ran into her? It could happen at any moment. Wouldn't she think it odd? Of course, I might have any number of perfectly good reasons for being there, but still . . . What should I do if it happened? Utter a polite greeting and walk on? Or say something? Act surprised, make some comment, try to engage her in conversation?

None of these answers was satisfactory. A chance encounter just now would upset my plans and was definitely to be avoided. I put myself on guard. As soon as I spotted her, I decided, I would change direction or turn away; if the worst came to the worst, I could pretend to be wrapped in thought and pass by as if I hadn't seen her. As long as I was outside this presented no problem; but what if I met her at the entrance to her building, or – even worse – on the stairs? I'd have to say something then.

Luckily, the list of tenants was displayed on the outside of the building. Having found her name, I looked at the names of her neighbours and memorised a couple of them just in case. Armed with this knowledge, and slightly relieved, I began to walk slowly towards the entrance. Now I could run into her right at the door and I had an answer ready: however surprised or suspicious she was, I could say, 'I'm going to see Mr So-and-so,' giving the name of one of the upstairs neighbours. 'What's so extraordinary about that?'

The building had four storeys; she lived on the second floor. In front of her door I was engulfed by another wave of emotion. So it was here! This door! This doorknob! This doorframe! Having made sure that there was no spyhole in the door opposite through which someone might see me, I put my ear to the cold surface of the door. Silence. No one seemed to be in. I went upstairs and checked the names on the doors there, just in case. Then I ran downstairs and outside into the courtyard, and counted the windows.

This wasn't difficult, as all of them clearly gave onto the courtyard, and there were only three on each floor. The one nearest the staircase proved, after a glance at the clearly visible interior of the ground-floor flat, to be the kitchen window; the other two, a big one with four panes and a smaller one with two, belonged to a room, or perhaps two rooms – here the ground floor brought no enlightenment, for the curtains were drawn.

I surveyed the building opposite, identical in every feature, and made for the entrance directly across from hers. There I began my observations – first from the second-floor landing and then from the third.

Despite the short distance between the buildings, it was hard to tell whether there was an interior wall between the two main windows. I thought there wasn't, but I couldn't be sure; and this uncertainty, in a matter apparently quite trivial, gave me no rest. For the possession of two rooms implied a great deal.

In those days, because of the housing shortage, a certain number of square feet was assigned per person; if one had no special privileges, one was condemned to the existence of a bee in a hive. If, for one reason or another (for instance, because someone had died), there was a bit more space, the other family members lived in perpetual fear that one fine day an eviction notice would come through the letterbox and send them off to a smaller flat, since their own now exceeded the permitted norms. Every square foot of extra space also cost a fortune in rent (a means of exerting additional pressure on tenants), and few people could afford this. So it rarely happened that a single person had more than a so-called a-1 (a studio) or at best an a-2 (a kitchen-cum-bedsit).

So if the flat I was now straining to glimpse, mentally and visually, from the third-floor landing of the building opposite had two rooms, its tenant either shared it with someone, or enjoyed special privileges, or paid a king's ransom in rent. Of these three possibilities I would have preferred the second, which also seemed the likeliest; and I wouldn't have minded the third. The first, although perfectly possible, was more disturbing. But why should it be? After all, if she lived with someone and I found out, sooner or later, who that someone was (a family member? a male friend?), I would have some good material for my 'siege'.

Then, in one moment, all this conjecture was dispelled, for dusk was falling; it fell early in the autumn. A light came on in the flat above hers, and it lit up the *entire* space behind the two windows, clearly showing that there was no wall between them. This was further confirmed when the tall figure of a man appeared at one window to draw the curtains and reappeared to perform the same action at the other literally no more than a second after disappearing from view at the first.

I breathed a sigh of relief. So it was one room after all! A large one, certainly, but only one. Such a humble, unobtrusive little detail, but so uplifting! It improved her reputation (she may still have privileges, but more modest ones); it eliminated once and for all the possibility of a flatmate; and it radically reduced the rent she paid for extra space, or perhaps cancelled it altogether.

In my excitement I forgot all about the debacle with the Viper and the prospect, looming darkly on the horizon and bristling with traps for the unwary, of being grilled about the anatomy of the rabbit. Ebullient, I walked along the dark streets and summed up my achievements for the day.

Although there was nothing very remarkable about the knowledge I had acquired, it brought things into sharper focus. Within less than two hours I had reduced the distance between us by light-years. From a tiny point, flickering somewhere in the vastness of the cosmos with a mysterious, pale-blue light, she had become a solar disc seen from a nearby planet. I was no longer just one among dozens of her pupils, kept at a businesslike distance; I had become a singular kind of acquaintance. I knew where and how she lived; I could phone her; I could send her a letter, and on the envelope, after her name, I could put the academic title I had found in the phone book.

And then the significance of that title, or rather of its presence in the phone book, hit me. Of course, it was there as an additional distinguishing feature, in case someone else shared both her names. But the possessor of such a title must be able to produce the document establishing his right to use it – in this case an MA certificate. Which meant she had been to university and had finished her degree. It seemed so simple, and yet it had taken me so long to think of it.

Today's Subject: All Saints' Day

The conversations with which Madame began her lessons were always on some topic of current interest: a headline event, something to do with the life of the school, the approaching holidays, things of that kind. It turned out, accordingly, that the topic of our next lesson was All Saints' Day, which was drawing near. The conversation was funereal: tombstones, coffins, wreaths, candles, obituaries and gravediggers – the point being, as always, to familiarise us with some of the vocabulary connected with a given subject.

This was inconvenient for me. Nevertheless, when my turn came I stuck to my plan, and began as follows: '*Quant à moi, je n'ai pas encore de morts dans ma famille*, no one in my own family has died. But,' I continued, 'I still intend to go to the cemetery with a group of other pupils, to tend to the neglected graves of some university professors.'

'*C'est bien louable*,' she observed. Commendable. But instead of elaborating on her compliment or at least asking me about my plans, which is what I'd been counting on to help with the next step in my vertiginous climb, she said, 'The graves are mossy, and ivy covers the crosses.'

One could only agree with this observation. It did not, however, get me very far. I made another attempt. '*Oui, en effet*,' I conceded, a tinge of melancholy in my voice. 'Unfortunately it also covers the names on the gravestones. That's why we're going to clear it away.'

She seemed quite indifferent to this. '*Les tombeaux où*

rampent les lierres sont souvent beaux,' she went on. 'Ivy-covered gravestones have a certain beauty. You must make sure you don't spoil anything.'

What extraordinary taste the woman had! The dubious beauty of a grave was more important to her than the person buried there. She was inhuman.

'Naturally,' I agreed and then, not wanting to get stuck on this shoal, rushed on: 'But perhaps you know of some neglected grave we could tend? We'd be glad to do it.'

She considered this for a moment. '*Non, rien ne me vient à l'esprit.*'

Nothing occurred to her?

'*Tous vos professeurs sont toujours en vie?*' I hazarded, unable to keep the disappointment from my voice. Surely all her teachers couldn't still be alive?

'*A vrai dire, je n'en sais rien*; I've no idea,' she replied coldly, impenetrable as a slab of granite.

I looked about desperately for some crack in this smooth surface, anything that would give me a handhold, for I felt in danger of falling off at any moment. 'Well, then, perhaps you remember some names, at least? Maybe some of the older ones?' I blurted out. 'We could check where their graves are, or try to find them.'

This wasn't the most felicitous of remarks, and I wasn't surprised when she riposted by dismissing my enthusiasm as morbid. '*Tout cet intérêt pour les morts me paraît quelque peu exagéré.*'

Exaggerated? '*Mais pas du tout!*' I said indignantly. Feeling this was my last chance, I launched a frontal attack: 'It's for my friends. They asked me to find out, so that's what I'm doing. It occurred to me that you might know.'

'Me?' She shrugged in puzzled inquiry. 'Why should I know anything about it?'

But her position was now hopeless: 'Didn't you get your degree at Warsaw University?'

'*Si, bien sûr.* Where else?' She had given up a pawn – she had said what I wanted to hear. And yet her voice still vibrated with a kind of regal petulance.

'Well then!' Emboldened by my triumph, I plunged on: '*C'était quand, si je peux me permettre?*'

But asking what year she had earned her degree was of course too much, and she let me know it at once. '*Je crois que tu veux en savoir un peu trop*,' she pronounced grandly. 'And anyway, what difference does it make?'

'Oh, none at all,' I said, backing off – and immediately regretted it. The move had been thoughtless; I had lost a good strategic position. I compounded the error by adding, even more foolishly, '*C'était seulement une question pour entretenir la . . . dialogue.*'

She could not let such an advantage slip away. '*Pas* la *dialogue*,' she corrected immediately, '*mais* le *dialogue; dialogue est masculin*. In this case, however, you should have said *conversation*, not *dialogue*. That's one point. And the other is that the subject today is cemeteries and gravestones, not higher education, and particularly not mine.'

It was a classic move. Whenever anyone exceeded some limit, especially if they began asking questions, she would first tell them off for bad grammar and then put them firmly in their place.

But this time her thrust hardly touched me. I had what I wanted, and the mess I'd made of my bold, indeed frankly insolent, last charge – after all, asking when she got her degree was tantamount to asking her age – left scarcely a scratch. The only bothersome thing was the way I'd bungled it; that stung a little, and to appease the sting I decided to turn it all into a joke. 'If I used the word *dialogue* instead of *conversation*,' I said, 'it was just to avoid the rhyme.'

'*Comment?* What rhyme?' Her face twisted with regal displeasure. I pursued calmly, '*Si j'avais dit: "c'était seulement une* question *pour entretenir la conver*sation," *ça ferait des vers*. Can't you hear it?'

'*Qu'est-ce que c'est que ces bêtises!*' she said impatiently and, waving me away, told me to sit down.

Material for the Report

That same day, straight after school, I presented myself at the Department of Romance Languages at Warsaw University. There I said that I was a pupil in my final year at a school that the Ministry of Education, in its wisdom, had decided to transform into a bold experiment with French as the language of instruction, and that I had been delegated to approach the department with a certain request. The circumstances of this request I explained as follows.

I had been entrusted with the task of writing a report about the study of Romance languages at the university. It was to be mainly about the entrance exams and programme of study for each year, but was also to contain a so-called historical sketch – this had been stressed – outlining the department's work over the years and supplying brief portraits of its most distinguished figures, including some of its former students who had excelled in some way or gone on to interesting careers.

Now, while I had succeeded in obtaining the data for the main part of the report (the entrance exams and programme of studies), as well as for its historical part (the history of Romance language studies and the famous professors), and indeed on these subjects had more material than I knew what to do with, I had no information, absolutely none at all, about any interesting or distinguished students, and God knows I had done my best. I'd pestered everyone with questions, I'd tried to find the right contacts – nothing. I was directed straight back to the department, every time – here to this very office, where all the records were. So I would be most obliged, and naturally my superiors would also be grateful, if the department would kindly make the relevant records available to me.

The secretaries in the dean's office gazed at me with such concentration that their faces contorted with the effort, as if I were speaking some exotic language. But my *exposé* sounded so convincing, and the cause so worthy, that they couldn't bring themselves to send me away empty-handed; they merely remarked that they weren't sure they had quite understood and asked what exactly they could do for me.

'I don't want to put you to any trouble,' I said politely. 'Perhaps if I could just see the lists of graduates? That shouldn't be too much of a problem, should it?'

They gazed at me in blank astonishment.

'I just want the basics,' I said, conciliatorily. 'The year of graduation, the title of the MA thesis, that sort of thing.'

'For which years?' one of them, presumably the senior, finally asked.

I performed a rough mental calculation, and decided that Madame couldn't have finished university before 1955. 'Well, let's say from the mid-1950s.'

'From the mid-1950s!' the Senior One gasped. 'Do you know how much of it there is?'

'It can't be helped, I'm afraid, that's the task I've been set,' I replied, and spread my arms in a gesture intended to express helpless devotion to duty.

She rose, went up to an enormous cupboard, placed a ladder against it and ascended. Reaching up to the top shelf, piled with stacks of bulging folders, she extracted an unimposing-looking file, shook the dust off it and came back down.

'There you are,' she said, handing it to me. 'From 1955 to 1960.'

Struggling to contain my excitement, I sat down at one of the desks and began to peruse the documents entrusted to me.

The pages were divided into five columns, headed 'Name', 'Date of birth', 'Title of thesis', 'Supervisor' and 'Final mark'. I took a notebook out of my briefcase and slowly, page by page, began to go through the list of graduates. From time to time, when I felt the eyes of the secretaries upon me, I made a show of copying something down in my notebook.

Madame's name was not on the lists for 1955, 1956 or 1957. This wasn't seriously disturbing; indeed, in a sense it was a relief, for it also delayed her date of birth: she was younger than I'd thought, and that could only be in my favour. In this situation, every year that reduced the age difference between us was worth its weight in gold.

The tension did not begin to mount until I had gone through the list for 1958 and still hadn't found her name. The chances of finding her now were swiftly diminishing: there were only two years left. If she wasn't in those, I would have to ask for lists from the following years, and the secretaries might find this suspicious; besides, I didn't want to abuse their patience, already sorely tried.

I turned over the page with '1959' inscribed on it in an elaborate calligraphic style. And there it was, finally, on the very first page. A shiver of relief and anticipation ran through me. I took in at a glance the data entered in the five columns, and became the possessor of the following knowledge:

– that in addition to the name by which she was known, a graceful but popular one, she also had another, much rarer: Victoria
– that she was born on the twenty-seventh of January, 1935
– that her thesis was entitled *La femme émancipée dans l'oeuvre de Simone de Beauvoir*
– that her supervisor had been Dr Magdalena Surowa-Léger
– that her final mark had been the highest and rarest: an A

A little dazed and slightly overwhelmed, I stared at this information and wondered what to do next. I had what I wanted; I had made progress. But this only whetted my appetite. I was still in the woods: my new knowledge gave rise to a whole new series of unanswered questions, and made me realise how much more there still was to find out. In fact, of the things I had discovered one alone was entirely satisfactory: her date of birth. I now knew that she was thirty-one years old, and that in three months she would be thirty-two. Everything else cried out for further inquiry and explanation. Why 'Victoria', for instance? And what had she written in her thesis? And why that topic in the first place – had she chosen it herself, or had it been assigned? I'd heard that students usually chose their thesis topics themselves. But if she had chosen it herself, *why* had she done so? Because of her literary tastes? Her views? Her personal experience?

Simone de Beauvoir had been translated into Polish, and I had read several of her books: the first two volumes of her autobiography, *Memoirs of a Dutiful Daughter*, and *La Force de l'âge*. I hadn't been very taken with them: I'd found them long-winded and overwritten, in some places grotesque in their extreme rationalism, in others effusively over-emotional. Nevertheless, I couldn't deny that they gave me some insight into a woman's psychology, and in particular into the morals and intellectual life of the Paris existentialist set.

The general impression I got was of a sort of learned twittering. Beauvoir tells us how she rejected compromise and 'bourgeois' values in favour of intensity of experience, and resolved to lead what was known in existentialist terminology as an 'authentic' life. But the 'authentic' life, contrary to what one might suppose, was not one of decadence and extravagance. It consisted, first, in a fanatical and ridiculous politicising of every conceivable sphere of existence: one had always to be in opposition to something, to protest and to rebel against something or other. This protest was usually indulged in at little cost to oneself – indeed it tended, if anything, to be quite profitable – and always made a horrendous din. Secondly, it involved interminable and relentless self-analysis: every single experience, reaction and desire had to be subjected to rigorous intellectual scrutiny and then interpreted psychologically and philosophically. That, at least, is what it looked like. Reading these fat, bloated tomes full of verbiage, one got the impression that from her earliest childhood Simone de Beauvoir had lived in a state of permanent self-vivisection. She treated herself as an object of scientific inquiry, and her internal eye was alert to the slightest reaction. Every detail of every emotion was immediately noted down; nothing was overlooked, nothing left unanalysed.

What was there in all this that could have interested Madame? Did she like it or was she repelled by it? Did Beauvoir's personality, views and way of looking at the world seem foreign to her, or did they strike a familiar chord? Was her choice of thesis topic prompted by approval and admiration, perhaps even by a feeling of kinship? Or was it, on the contrary, the result of profound disagreement, irritation and disgust? She was, after all, the head of a socialist school, and as such was unlikely to feel much sympathy, let alone approval, for anything written by the (admittedly unofficial) consort of the author of *L'être et le néant*. For however enlightened this reigning deity of artistic and intellectual life in Paris in the 1940s and 1950s might be, however left-wing and fervent in her dreams of world revolution, however slavish in her devotion to the French communists and outspoken in her support of movements of national liberation throughout the world, the fact remained that she was connected with existentialism. And existentialism, from the Marxist point of view, was a 'nihilist', 'fundamentally bourgeois' and even 'fascist' doctrine. (After all, Martin Heidegger – 'Hitler's right-hand man in Nazi higher education' – had been one of its co-founders!) Marxism, of course, as 'the only truly scientific system', had long ago exposed, with childish ease, the intellectual poverty and moral rottenness of this 'pseudo-philosophy'. Nevertheless it continued to proliferate, as weeds do, and to poison people's minds. It was still necessary, therefore, to oppose it.

After 1956, opposition to existentialism assumed a new form. During the early years of the Cold War it had been simply taboo; with the 'thaw', however, it was allowed some expression, although mainly in order that it might be ridiculed and condemned. That, at least, was the official ritual, and numerous journals, magazines and academic conferences acted accordingly. This being the case, what could one expect from an MA thesis, especially an MA thesis supervised by someone with such a sinister name?

Surowa-Léger: the name was not just sinister but dubious. The woman had connections with bourgeois France! She had probably married a Frenchman. So she must be interested in trips abroad. And that meant she must be ideologically untainted – or at least very careful. She must have seen to it that Simone de Beauvoir's famous 'emancipated woman' turned out to be 'incorrectly' or at best 'superficially' emancipated.

'Do you know how I could get in touch with Dr Surowa-Léger?' I asked.

'Dr Léger,' replied the Senior One, neatly omitting the first barrel of the name, 'left the department a long time ago.'

'She's at the Academy, I suppose?' I asked in tones of respectful gravity.

'She left the country,' the other secretary hastened to explain. 'Five years ago. She went to France. For good.'

'Oh, I see . . .'

My head began to spin with new questions. Gone! Left for good! Stayed in the West! It was like some kind of malevolent curse. People who went to the West and stayed there were considered 'traitors' or 'renegades'; at best they were seen as people with no 'moral fibre', so tempted by Western trinkets – clothes and cosmetics, cars and nightclubs – that they succumbed to the shameful lure of consumerism. Of course, Dr Léger had probably left in order to join her French husband – but perhaps she had planned the whole thing in advance, in cold blood? Perhaps Magdalena Surowa had married M. Léger not for love or even because of a common interest in things French, but only because she hoped that sooner or later, through him, she would get to the West? In any event, that wasn't the important thing. The question was who she was while she was still in Poland. An ideologically pure Marxist, critical of existentialism and other Western novelties? Or someone who approved of it, even admired it, along with other forms of Western decadence?

On the answer to these questions depended the interpretation of Madame's final mark. What was the significance of that A? Had it rewarded a devastating critique or a sympathetic analysis? Or perhaps the thesis was no more than a pretence at criticism, a mask, assumed in order to wallow safely in forbidden ideas? How on earth was I to find out?

'Where could I find out more about these people?' I asked, gesturing towards the open file.

'Which people, exactly?' inquired the Senior One, an edge of impatience in her voice.

I almost said, 'Well, for example, about Miss . . .' but at the last minute I thought better of it. I began leafing nonchalantly through the file, as if the choice were a matter of complete indifference to me, until I came to 1959 again.

'Oh, well, let's say these, for instance,' I said offhandedly, 'the ones from '59.'

'Fifty-nine,' the Other One repeated, 'let me see, whom have we there?' She got up and came over to look at the list. Once again I was on the verge of supplying Madame's name as an example, and once again I held my tongue. The Other One went down the list of names with her finger. About halfway down she stopped.

'There you are!' she cried in a joyful voice, 'Dr Monten. He'd be perfect for you. He's a lecturer in our department, in seventeenth-century literature.'

Monten, Monten . . . wasn't that the name of my mountain *cicerone,* the man who had taken me to the Tatras, the friend of my parents' from before the war? Could it be the same man? Could this 1959 graduate of Warsaw University and possessor of that seldom-found combination of first names, Frederick Bonaventure, have any connection with my friend? Was he perhaps a relative, even his son?

I knew there was a son, but I had no idea what his name was, how old he was or what he did. Somehow we'd never talked about it, and I had never met him. Now, excited by this extraordinary coincidence, which might turn out to be priceless for me, I feverishly began to calculate whether it was possible.

Indeed it was. My guide had been around sixty when he took me to the mountains; he could easily have a son of thirty-two. All I needed now was some confirmation.

'Would that be the son of Professor Constant Monten?' I inquired, knowing full well that my Tatras guide possessed no such title.

'*Professor* Monten?' asked the Senior One. 'I don't know anything about that.'

'But surely,' I insisted, 'surely you know who I mean? That famous geologist – you know. And he's a well-known mountaineer, too.'

'I've no idea, I assure you,' she said, shrugging, and cast an inquiring glance at the Other One. The Other One just goggled.

'Well, never mind,' I said lightly, then added, poker-faced,

'On the other hand, it would be quite simple to check.'

'You could just ask,' said the Other One, her tone clearly implying that if it was so important to me I could take the trouble of going to the source and inquiring about it myself.

'Oh, there's no need to bother him with questions,' I said. 'Couldn't we just check the name?'

'*What* name?!' snapped the Senior One, barely controlling her impatience.

'His father's,' I explained equably. 'If it's Constant, he must be the one. It's not a very common name.'

'And where do you expect us to check it?' inquired the Other One, equally impatient.

'Surely you must have a record of it somewhere? In this country you have to give your father's name on every form you fill in.'

'We'd have to call administration . . .' mused the Other One, half to herself and half to her superior.

'Yes, why not do that?' I agreed enthusiastically.

'Yes, all right, but what's it got to do with anything, anyway?' said the Senior One, giving way to her irritation. 'What's the purpose of all this? What does it matter whether Dr Monten is or isn't the son of this professor of yours?'

'Oh, but it does, it does,' I sighed enigmatically, 'it matters a great deal. You have no idea how much depends on it!'

The Senior One cast a martyred glance at the heavens, reached for the telephone and began to dial. 'It's me again, from the dean's office,' she announced. 'Could you please check Dr Monten's first name for me?'

'His *father's* name!' I hissed desperately at her.

'I mean, Dr Monten's *father's* name,' she corrected, drumming her fingers on the desk. There was a pause, during which I shut my eyes and crossed my fingers. 'Thank you, thank you so much,' I finally heard her say, and the receiver came down with a crash. 'Yes, his name is Constant. And that's the last thing I'm doing for you today. We have work to do, you know.'

'I'm so terribly grateful, I don't know how to thank you,' I said, jumping up and kissing her hand. 'And you, too, of course,' I added, bounding toward the Other One. 'And now

I'll take myself off. I won't bother you any more. I'm gone!' I said, rushing for the door. '*Au revoir, mesdames!*'

Outside in the corridor, just as I was letting go of the door-handle, I heard the muffled voice of the Senior One exclaim, 'Good heavens, what an odd creature! Where in the world did he come from?'

Freddy the Professor

In the bus, I took up my usual position near the rear door, facing the back window, so that I had a view of the street and not of the crowd of passengers inside, and began to arrange my spoils into some sort of order in my mind.

The information that a student from Madame's year, someone who had studied with her, was almost certainly the son of my Mountaineer made everything else I had learned pale in comparison. Her date of birth, the title of her thesis were dry, official facts, a poor second-best beside the juicy first-hand knowledge undoubtedly in the possession of Frederick Bonaventure, to whom Fate, in her magnanimity, was now directing me.

The directions supplied by Fate, however, were no more than an opportunity, and it was up to me to make good use of it. Constant Monten's son might be a rich source of information, but I couldn't assume he would reveal everything he knew about Madame as soon as he saw me or heard my name. I had to lead up to it. The question was how. I couldn't just ask him straight out. It seemed I was going to have to play more games, give another one of my performances; but I had no idea at the time of the sort of comedy this would turn out to be. All I knew was that I had to start with the Mountaineer.

That evening, after supper, when my parents were listening to Radio Free Europe in the dining-room, I took the telephone from there into my room (so as not to disturb them), plugged it in and, having closed all the doors behind me, dialled Constant's familiar number.

'I have an unusual favour to ask,' I began after we had exchanged greetings.

'Go ahead – what can I do for you?'

Even at that moment I wasn't sure how I would open my game. It seemed sensible to begin by making sure that the precious Dr Monten from the Department of Romance Languages was indeed his son. In the end I chose a somewhat bolder opening move.

'Does Professor . . . um, that is, Frederick, does he still work at the university?' I asked, promoting the son as I had recently promoted the father.

'Professor? Frederick?' he repeated.

I froze. It wasn't him after all! How awful! 'Your son, I mean,' I stammered.

'Oh, you mean *Freddy*!'

I breathed again.

'For a moment I couldn't think who you meant, you made it sound so formal. Yes, of course, he's still teaching at that little school.'

'School?' I repeated, with a return of anxiety.

'Well, what else would you call that university of theirs nowadays? A kindergarten – not even a high school! Before the war it was a university, but now . . . it's a joke.'

'Seriously? Is the standard so low?' I asked in a worried tone.

'I'm telling you, it's a waste of breath even to discuss it.'

'Well, I'm glad you told me, because that's actually what I wanted to talk to you about. I don't know if you remember, but this is my last year of school. Soon I'll have to decide what I'm going to study at university, and I've been thinking about Romance languages. But I haven't quite made up my mind; I'm still hesitating. So I thought Professor . . . Freddy, I mean . . . might be able to give me some advice, since he lectures there, and he got his degree there as well. Do you think that might be possible?'

'I would even say it was advisable,' he replied wryly.

'That's wonderful. Thank you so much. There's just one thing . . .'

'Yes, what?'

'If you could keep it all to yourself. Especially as far as my parents are concerned. You see, they're quite irritated by my leanings toward the humanities. They'd like me to do some sort of science.'

'Well, actually, they're right.'

'Yes, I know you agree with them, but still, I'd be grateful if . . .'

'Yes, all right, I won't tell them. But I'm warning you in advance, I'll do my best to make sure Freddy puts you off the idea. That won't be difficult, anyway: he'll do it himself without any prompting from me. He has a very low opinion of the whole enterprise.'

'I'll listen carefully to what he has to say, and I'll take it to heart. I'd especially like to hear anything he has to say about his own student days – that would be important in making up my mind, more than anything else, I think. In fact, it might be crucial. So – when and where?'

'Freddy's coming over for lunch next Sunday. Why don't you come around at about five? He'll be all yours.'

'Thank you. See you then.' I put down the receiver and fell exhausted onto my bed.

Over the next few days, like a chess player preparing for an important match, I practised over and over in my mind every possible variant of every conceivable strategy I could use in the conversation that awaited me, so that I would never be at a loss for the next move. There was no doubt that the subject that interested me would come up sooner or later: at some point he was bound to ask who my French teacher was, indeed it seemed quite likely that he'd start off with that very question. But even if it didn't arise, it would be easy enough to provoke it. The problem was, what then? What if Madame's name evoked no reaction at all? If Frederick Monten, for whatever reason, just ignored it, as if he had never heard of her? Of course, I could always throw out a casual question like 'I don't suppose you know her, by any chance?' But that would be a last resort. The main thing was not to expose my design;

he mustn't have the slightest suspicion of what I was after. The thought that someone might find me out, might discover that I was in thrall to Madame, was terrifying.

It was shame – shame, the enemy of experience. That was the tyrant that held me in its grip, forcing me to act undercover, always pretending, always in disguise.

Wouldn't it be wonderful if the very sound of the name overwhelmed Dr Monten with an uncontrollable flood of memories, so that he fell into a sort of narrative trance and began, unprompted, to recount tale after tale from the life of the young Madame? And I would sit there and listen to him with feigned indifference, interjecting the occasional 'Well, well,' or 'Really? How extraordinary!' This, however, seemed highly improbable.

The Song of Virgo and Aquarius

As I waited for Sunday, I was also waging an inner battle, for I was tempted to make some use of the things I had already learnt, and while I tried to resist the temptation, I also spent much time reflecting on how this might best be done.

At the next French lesson, the time usually devoted to conversation was given over to reading aloud from an article in a glossy magazine devoted to popular science about the structure of the universe. Madame would write some of the basic concepts up on the blackboard – 'Solar System', 'Milky Way', 'Big Dipper' – and we were supposed to copy them down into our notebooks. We ended up with some dozen new phrases to learn and, to extend our vocabulary in this domain, were set an essay on any subject connected with the universe or the celestial dome.

This time the nature of the assignment accorded well with my aims. The idea came to me during the lesson, and by the time I got home, all I had to do was put it into good French. This is what I wrote (I give it here in translation, for the convenience of the reader):

When we talk about the sky, the stars and the planets, we are naturally led to think also of astrology – the older sister of the Queen of Sciences, as the study of the universe was once known. Astrology is based on the assumption that the celestial bodies in our stellar and planetary system have an influence on the earth, and in particular that they influence us – our character and our destiny.

The basic concepts of astrology are the horoscope and the Zodiac. The Zodiac is a stellar ring on the celestial sphere, consisting of twelve constellations, along which our sun wanders in the course of a year. Each of these constellations has its own name and sign. Their origins are lost in the mists of time, in the myths and strange legends of the ancient world.

In the light of modern science the domain of astrology tends to be dismissed as poetry or childish fantasy. However, there are still people – and by no means only the uneducated – for whom it is a genuine area of knowledge. For astrology represents a sort of challenge for modern science. It is synonymous with mystery; it is a different path toward knowledge.

The best and most famous expression of scepticism about the value of science, and of fascination with Magic, is to be found in Goethe's *Faust*. At the very beginning Faust talks about how, despite all his learning, he is no further forward than when he began:

To Magic therefore have I turned
To try the spirits' power and gain
The knowledge they alone bestow;
No longer will I have to strain
To speak of things I do not know.

A moment later, on picking up a volume of the predictions of the sixteenth-century doctor Nostradamus (a Frenchman, incidentally), considered to be the greatest astrologer of the modern era, he says:

What secrets lurk in this old book
In Nostradamus's own hand?
Perhaps it's here I need to look
To grasp the stars' mysterious flight;
I'll learn what Nature has to teach;
I'll hear, endowed with magic's might,
The spirits whisper, each to each.

My own attitude towards astrology and horoscopes was always extremely sceptical until one day I, too, like Faust, picked up the 'mysterious book of Nostradamus' – his *Centuries Astrologiques,* written in 1555 – and began to read. I studied it thoroughly; in particular, I checked my own horoscope very carefully to see how accurate it was. I was astonished at the result: everything fitted, everything was confirmed.

I was born in September. On the tenth of September, to be precise. Which makes me a Virgo.

Virgo – the Virgin – is an earth element, and earth represents certainty and stability. People of this element have a clear aim in life and are unwavering in their progress towards it. They are logical and rational, precise and industrious. They never give up before they find a solution to a problem; they think everything through and approach it methodically. Their love of order can be excessive, even pathological; in such cases Virgos become slaves to their own principles. Finally, Virgos have excellent memories and are good at music and chess.

Is this not the perfect portrait of me? Let those who know me well be the judge.

I know, I know: you'll say a portrait like this is easily coloured to suit. All right. But what if there is more than just this vague portrait – what if there are other things that fit, traces of deeper connections?

What I am about to tell you shook me profoundly when I first came upon it.

Up to now the thing more or less held together. From here on, however, it became unadulterated drivel:

We must start with the myth of Virgo and Aquarius.

Each of us must surely have wondered why the signs of the Zodiac are mostly animals, and why these particular animals and not others; and why Libra – the Scales – is among them, and then why two humans are also among them. Most important, we wonder why these two people are not just a man and a woman but the Watercarrier and the Virgin.

The ancient legends that lie at the source of this intricate construction tell the story of the Cosmic Division.

In the beginning there was Monos, a homogeneous entity, closed and infinite like the surface of a sphere. But the defining principle of his existence was flawed: Monos, in his monomania, folded in upon himself, sank deeper and deeper into his Monosity, and sought his own destruction. Finally, when he reached the critical moment, he spoke. It was the last instinct, perhaps, of his fading will to exist. He said 'I': 'I am.' Having spoken, he heard himself; and, having heard himself, he ceased to be a monolith: he became Hearing and Voice. He split himself in two. In short, by his act of speech he became Heteros.

This new principle of existence remains the foundation on which the world is built.

The Zodiac is an ingenious expression of this dualism. Everything that is, is a duality: it has its 'thesis' and its 'antithesis', and these, in their eternal conflict, cause the world to oscillate. All forms of life embody this duality. Hence we have *two* Fish (Pisces) and the Twins (Gemini). Nearly all the animals exhibit some sign of it: the Ram (Aries), the Bull (Taurus) and the Goat (Capricorn) have two horns; the Scorpion (Scorpio) and the Crab (Cancer) have two front pincers.

The most perfect embodiment of this dualism is to be found in the human pair: the Virgin (Virgo) and the

Watercarrier (Aquarius). Alone, each is incomplete; together, they form a unity and a whole. And while Leo (the Lion) and Sagittarius (the Archer) form a hostile pair, expressing man's conflict with the beast that lurks within him and his desire to destroy it, the Virgin and the Watercarrier together express love; they are the 'north' and the 'south' of the universe, its two poles, which, bound by the force of mutual attraction, create a magnetic tension.

This beautiful idea was echoed as early as the fourteenth century, in the work of the divine Florentine. This is how Dante ends his *Divine Comedy*:

The love *that moves the sun and the other stars.*

But that isn't all the ancient legends have to say about the Virgin and the Watercarrier. It turns out that these two figures, which move the world by the force of their mutual attraction, have other, deeper and more complicated meanings. They appear to be the figures of a young girl and a mature man, but when we look at what they are doing, it turns out that each of them represents an element that contradicts this embodiment.

Aquarius, the Watercarrier, is presented in a desert landscape, giving water to fish. He pours it out carefully from a jug that is always full. The Virgin, meanwhile, sits or kneels gazing dreamily into the distance, a goose-quill pen in her hand.

What is the significance of these objects, these poses and these occupations?

Let us note, first of all, the fundamental difference between the two figures: while Aquarius is clearly busy with something (pouring water from a jug), Virgo cannot be said to be doing anything much. She dreams, she gazes – perhaps she wants to write? – but this cannot be called work.

Next, let us recall what water symbolises. Water invariably signifies a source, a beginning. It is the *materia prima.* In the Indian tradition, for instance, water is the source of the Cosmic Egg; in the Hebrew Genesis, at the dawn of all things, the spirit of God moves upon the face of the *waters.* For this reason water is always associated with the female element, with fertility, with dark, unknown depths and life-giving powers.

And indeed, did life not begin in water? Did it not creep out to land from the dark womb of the sea?

Aquarius, then, although embodied in the form of a man, actually represents all that is female. By giving water he gives life; he watches over life's creation. And at the same time, with the sound of splashing water, he beckons, he tempts.

And what about Virgo? We have already observed that she sits idle, lost in thought, holding a goose-quill pen and gazing off into the distance. The goose-quill pen symbolises the art of literature – originally a male domain. Our word *poetry* comes from the Greek *poiein,* which means to make, to produce or create. The ability to create – especially out of nothing – is a divine attribute, and God as a causative force is always male. (Woman does not create out of nothing; she transforms what there is.) Thus the poet is essentially male, even if physically a member of the fairer sex. Look at Sappho, for instance – we know what she was like.

Virgo, then, although embodied in the form of a woman, actually represents all that is male.

This is also expressed in her name, associated with virginity, purity and innocence. These may appear to be female characteristics, but in the sphere of ideas virginity is a male attribute. Womanhood, in fact, is *never* a state of virginity: Woman is always initiated. The Male, on the other hand, cut off from blood – menstruation, defloration, giving birth – not only *is* in a state of virginity but *cannot be otherwise.* Maleness is by its very nature *always* inexperienced, always uninitiated.

That virginity and maleness are indissolubly linked is a truth so glaringly obvious that it hardly needs stating.

It even finds expression in some Romance languages, especially in French: the French *virginité* and *virginal* come from the Latin *vir,* which means man, or male. What further proof could one want?

Virgo and Aquarius, then, the royal pair united by love, only appear to be a young woman and an older man. In fact they are a *young man* and a *mature woman.* It is he who gazes into the distance, innocent and inexperienced, daydreaming and composing poetry; while she, experienced and knowing, well aware of what is important, beckons to him enticingly with the splashing sound of water. 'Come, here is the source,' she seems to be saying, 'come to me and I will let you drink; I will quench your thirst.'

Let us now leave these celestial heights and descend from the firmament to the earth.

Since the day I discovered this myth and learnt the deeper significance hidden in the signs of the Zodiac, I have been testing it, checking how much of it is confirmed in practice, and whether Virgos really are in some way connected with Aquariuses. Naturally, I began with myself. To whom am I drawn? Who, I asked myself, dazzles *me*? Who has the power to captivate me, to charm and beguile me like the Erl King? Is there such a person? Yes – Mozart, the greatest genius who ever lived. His music enthrals me, enraptures me; I could listen to it forever. He is the love of my life, the altar at which I worship.

And what is his sign? On which day of what month did he come into the world?

The date of his birth is engraved in my memory like holy writ; my music teacher drilled it into me from my very first lessons:

the twenty-seventh of January

The sun on that day was in the first decade of Aquarius.

And I am not alone. My case is a common, even classic, one.

Take, for example, the greatest of the Virgos – Goethe. (Goethe, let us recall, was born on the twenty-eighth of August.) As we all know, Goethe had a rich life. He knew hundreds, even thousands of people, and to many of them he was bound by some special circumstance or connection. But three people stand out particularly on this list: Mozart, Mendelssohn and Franz Schubert.

Goethe saw Mozart just once in his life, at a concert in Frankfurt-am-Main. He was fourteen and Mozart was seven. The child prodigy played the most difficult compositions on the piano and the violin and then, without looking, gave a musical definition of the pealing of bells and the chiming of clocks. He made such an impression that Goethe couldn't get him out of his mind; he is said to have mentioned him even on his deathbed. 'I see him, I see him clearly,' he is supposed to have whispered through withered lips. 'Little man with the sword . . . don't go! . . . More light!' And when he was younger he listened constantly to Mozart's music, with wonder and adoration. When he became director of Weimar's famous theatre, Mozart's operas were the main ones staged there. He was so taken with the beauty of *The Magic Flute* that he spent many years trying to write a sequel. He also couldn't get over his disappointment that Mozart hadn't set *Faust* to music. 'Only he could have done it,' he is supposed to have remarked in his old age. 'He could have done it, and he should have done it! The music to my *Faust* should be like the music to *Don Giovanni*!'

Then there is the story of Goethe and Mendelssohn. Mendelssohn appeared fairly late in Goethe's life, when the latter was seventy-two and the former eleven – barely older than Mozart. And the result of this first meeting? Within an hour the cocky little imp had the mighty Jove at his feet, ecstatic with admiration, devouring him with his eyes and ears, utterly captivated.

But what role was the child playing? What was it, exactly, that little Felix was doing when he performed before the Master? Why, yes, of course – he was *teaching* him! Opening his eyes and ears, playing Beethoven and Bach, whose music Goethe had never heard, initiating him into the mysteries of harmony and technique. Educating, instructing, enlightening. In short, the child was teaching the old man. Extraordinary! Unbelievable!

Unbelievable? It might have been if the child hadn't been an Aquarius. But Felix, too, like the divine Mozart, was born under that sign (on the third of February). He was thus a female element, older by definition.

And so we come, finally, to the story of Goethe and Schubert: not quite like the others, but equally significant.

This time it is Goethe who is the object of fascination. Schubert falls in love with his poetry. He reads it, he recites it, he is overwhelmed with admiration. And one passage in *Faust* affects him so strongly that he is moved to tears. Which passage is it? Of course: it is Margaret's monologue, spoken as she sits at her loom. Those unforgettable first four lines:

My peace is gone
And my heart is sore;
My soul is heavy,
There's no calm any more.

They resound in Schubert's head, they obsess him. He cannot sleep. Finally he understands that he will get no rest until he sets them to music. And thus is born the most famous of his songs, *Gretchen at the Spinning-Wheel*. It is the beginning of a new chapter – a new era! – in musical history. *Gretchen* is followed by one masterpiece after another; all in all, Schubert sets about sixty of Goethe's poems to music.

Need one add when Schubert was born? Could this passionate lover of the inspired verses of a Virgo have been anything other than an Aquarius? The thirty-first of January was the date he came into the world.

This last example is perhaps the most significant of the three. It is a kind of archetype.

When Goethe, greatest of the Virgos, wrote that extraordinary poem, the song of a virgin in love, he was giving expression to his deepest self, to what he was because of the stars. I am Margaret, he might well have said (anticipating Flaubert, who many years later was to say the same of his Madame Bovary). For indeed, is this a woman's experience of love? Does a woman in love lose her mind, give way to madness, long for death? Of course not. A woman who loves is calm and controlled, for love is her realm and her natural state. A woman in love knows perfectly well what she wants, and she strides boldly towards her goal. She wants to conceive and give birth; she wants life, not death.

But the male element, when pierced by Love's arrows, behaves just like Goethe's Margaret. Let us listen to his lament:

My thoughts spin round,
My poor head aches;
My poor mind reels
Till I think it will break.

His face alone
From my window I seek;
It's him alone
I run to greet.

O to embrace him,
To clasp him at last!
To touch and enfold him
And hold him fast!

And kiss him till
I've no more breath,

And kissing brings
A blissful death.

And what does the Watercarrier do, moved by the desperate cry of the wounded Virgin? What does a *mature woman* (in the person of Franz Schubert) do when she hears the lament of a *young man* (the eternally young Goethe)? She goes towards him; she stretches out her hand to him. She swallows her ambition and pride, forgets her fear of humiliation and speaks to him. She lends him her voice: she composes music and transforms words into song. She turns the savage cry into sweet melody.

For song brings harmony and reconciliation. It is through song that opposites are united and dissonances resolved; it is through song that the ultimate synthesis is reached, and the spirit reconciled with the flesh.

In the song of Virgo and Aquarius, the Stellar Victoria is realised.

I long for that victory with my Aquarius!

It was well after midnight when I put down my pen. I had written almost twenty pages. Feeling strangely dazed, I closed my notebook and went to bed.

The next day I paid another visit to the university, this time to the departmental library, to find a French translation of the passages I had quoted from *Faust* and look up a few words and phrases I wasn't sure of in Larousse, Robert and various other dictionaries. This done, I made the appropriate corrections and then read the essay through from the beginning, marking all the *liaisons* with a pencil and underlining the words to stress when reading it out loud.

As soon as I got home, I took advantage of my parents' absence to have a sort of dress rehearsal: I read the whole thing out loud. And while up to that point I'd been rather pleased with it, I now began to have serious misgivings. It wasn't that I read badly; I stumbled over the occasional word, but not so often, and this could easily be corrected with practice. The problem lay elsewhere: the thing was just too long. I couldn't possibly hope to get through it all in one lesson. Knowing Madame, I could be sure she would stop me after the first few minutes, whether or not I had made any mistakes. If she didn't find anything wrong with it, she might let me read on for about six paragraphs, say, before cutting me off with that soulless '*bien*' and entering the mark in her book; and if my *art d'écrire* turned out to be less than sound, she would interrupt with constant corrections, thus distracting from the content, and finally say that was fine, I needn't go on, and tell me to sit down. And then there was her suspicion of people who volunteered; that, too, had to be taken into account.

Leaving all that aside, and assuming that by some miracle Madame let me read on to the end, uninterrupted, I still had serious reservations. The rest of the class was bound to realise that something was up: over half an hour! Twenty pages instead of the usual three or four! An essay of that length couldn't fail to arouse suspicion. And the content! All those fantastic stories, connected loosely at best with the subject; all that suspect erudition; all those transparent allusions and obvious hidden meanings – 'young man', 'mature woman', 'virginity', 'initiation'; even an outsider would smell something fishy, and it certainly wouldn't take the class long to figure out where the author was headed and what his true purpose was. Even the ones at the bottom of the class in French and the ones who never paid attention would rouse themselves from their lethargy and prick up their ears, intrigued by this reading that went on and on. And they'd probably wake up just when I got to the second half, where the layer of hints and allusions was thickest.

It was absurd to imagine that anyone would interpret this extravagant linguistic performance as an effort to improve my marks in French. Nor would it be dismissed as some bizarre flight of fancy, a laboured whim meant to dazzle the teacher and earn the gratitude of the class for taking up most of the lesson. It would be taken solely as proof that despite my ostentatious displays of indifference I, too, was in thrall to Madame; that I, too, like dozens of others, was utterly, helplessly smitten.

'It's not just *Ashes* under the desk any longer,' they'd say.

'Now he's volunteering to read! Look at him, fawning on her, insinuating himself into her good graces, stooping to anything for a bit of attention!'

Awakened to this prospect, imagining the sniggers and jeers, I relinquished all thoughts of volunteering to read. Now I wouldn't read even if I was called. I would simply refuse, explaining enigmatically that I had allowed myself to get carried away and wouldn't like to take up the class's precious time with my scribblings, but, of course, she could see my essay any time she liked, here it was, *voilà, regardez mon cahier, j'ai écrit presque vingt pages* – I've written almost twenty pages; but if for some reason she didn't want my notebook, if it was too heavy, for instance, then – and here an entirely new idea came to me – then she could have a copy, a clean copy that I'd made, on just a few pages of foolscap.

Yes, that wasn't a bad idea at all: copying it out so that I could hand the copy to Madame if need be. Suddenly it seemed the best solution; none of the others was quite so satisfactory. I abandoned my attempts to perfect my recitation, took up my pen and carefully copied the whole thing onto several sheets of cross-ruled writing paper.

But on the day of the lesson new doubts assailed me. Even if everything goes as planned, I reflected as I left the house that morning, going over it all for the hundredth time, even if I give her the copy and manage to make it look casual, almost as an afterthought, is this a good move? What will it achieve? I'll only be revealing myself, exposing my position. It's far too early for that – it's the last thing I need. It's a gambit that might cost me a great deal.

By the time I got to school the thought of any ploys with the copy could not have been further from my mind, and when the lesson began I was praying I wouldn't be called.

Per Aspera ad Astra

Madame was in a remarkably good mood that day. She was cheerful and relaxed, and more talkative than usual; she spoke more freely, less formally. During the conversation period she strolled about among the desks, which she rarely did, stopping here and there to strike up a conversation. At one point she even permitted herself a little joke: when someone was describing how, during a terribly hot summer in the country, he'd cooled off with a plunge into a clay-pit, she observed with a smile, '*On peut dire que tu as joui de la vie comme un loup dans un puits*: one might say you had as much fun as a wolf in a well.' Her interlocutor seemed to have missed some of the implications of this remark, for he appeared enchanted with it, agreeing happily and vigorously nodding his head.

'And how did your essay about the stars go?' she asked finally, proceeding to the next stage of the lesson. 'All done? Would someone like to read theirs?'

This was unheard of. Never before had she asked for volunteers. The class was stunned, and Madame continued in a teasing tone: '*Quoi donc? Il n'y a personne?* No one wants a good mark? What's the matter with you today?'

I felt my pulse quicken. Perhaps I should volunteer after all? In the circumstances . . . She did ask for volunteers, and no one seems very eager . . . No, definitely not. It's out of the question.

'*Bon, alors,* since there don't seem to be any volunteers, I'll have to pick on someone. Mademoiselle Swat, then, please.'

The plump, tapir-like Adrienne Swat heaved herself to her feet and launched, crimson-faced, into her essay. It wasn't exactly thrilling. Indeed, it didn't even meet the criteria for a *composition*; it was more of a collection of sentences strung together, like a definition, or something out of a children's book:

'*Quand il n'y a pas de nuages, nous voyons le ciel, le soleil et la lune . . . Le ciel est bleu ou bleu pâle . . . Les étoiles sont loin . . . des millions de kilomètres d'ici.*' And so on in the same vein. Luckily it didn't last long.

Madame did not interrupt the reading at any point, but she was displeased, and said so. '*Je ne peux pas dire* that I'm dazzled by your originality. Frankly, I expected more of you. It's a pity. Not very satisfactory. However. It's worth a C – at most.' She entered the mark carefully in her book. 'All right. Who's next?' She ran a manicured finger down the list of names. The nail was a polished, pale pearl. '*Qui va me stimuler . . . qui va m'exciter?* I'd like to get something out of this too . . . some pleasure . . . *plaisir* . . . from the fact that I've finally managed to teach you something.'

I don't know about the others, but on me the effect of these words was electrifying. This was what I had meant, that day in the park when I'd sat on the bench in the afternoon sun and thought out my plan, by a game in which words acquired a plurality of meanings. Her words were meant quite innocently, spoken in good faith and intended at face value. But to me they sounded different – as if spoken in a different key. Only one element of the game was lacking: the initiative had not been mine. The words her lips had pronounced had been prompted by the circumstances – circumstances in which my role had been passive; she had not spoken them to me, or not only to me. Their value was thus diminished. Was there anything I could do to obtain more?

'*Bon, alors*,' the manicured finger halted at a name near the bottom of the list; 'what does Mademoiselle Wanko have to offer us?'

Agnes Wanko, the daughter of a wing-commander in the air force for whom every official memorial day or anniversary was an opportunity to descend upon the school and lecture us about the defence of Poland or reminisce about the war, was the class swot, with all the characteristics typical of the breed. Respectful, ingratiating, her hand eternally raised (fingers straight, head up), she sat in the front row and kept well away from anyone and anything that could conceivably be viewed with disapproval. She could not be said to dazzle with her looks, nor was she distinguished by any eagerness to be helpful to others. She was always one of the first to arrive, spent her breaks in exemplary fashion, strolling in the corridor, always ate her sandwiches in the canteen the way you were supposed to and not, like most of the others, wherever she happened to be (even in the lavatories), and after school invariably went straight home. In short, she was a model of good behaviour; she might have been a robot instead of a human being. No loitering about, no insubordination, and, of course, no question of ever playing truant. As for clothes, boys and other amusements of that kind, she seemed to have no need of them. She cared only about her results: everything else – including Madame – was a matter of complete indifference to her. She was, of course, assiduous in her efforts to get good marks, but she pursued this goal with none of the slavish idolatry some of the others displayed.

Madame's picking on her now seemed to me – especially since for once, and despite the appeal for volunteers, Agnes had not raised her hand – to be an act of warning from an angry goddess whom someone had neglected to propitiate. She was demanding a sacrifice. I can see, she seemed to be saying, that you don't worship me, and I am not pleased. But don't imagine you can get away without offering me homage. The fact that I usually ignore your raised hand does not mean that you may cease to raise it. It is your duty to raise it, since you deny me love.

The diligent Agnes Wanko rose, picked up her notebook and read out, with excessive care over her accent, the title of her essay: '*De Copernic à Gagarin.*'

Titters and stifled guffaws came from somewhere in the back of the classroom. Madame glared repressively at those dark, forgotten regions and said politely, '*Bon, alors, on t'écoute.*'

Agnes Wanko's essay had as its epigraph *Per aspera ad astra*, and consisted of selected examples of man's progress in his struggle to free himself from the earth's restraints and soar ever higher into the celestial regions. It began with Copernicus, went on to the Montgolfier brothers and their balloon flight, and proceeded, by way of Lomonosov and his many discoveries (most prominently the helicopter in which he was alleged to have flown over the mountains of the Caucasus with a certain Georgian, who went on to live for another hundred years and tell the tale), to the final and longest part, namely the countless extraordinary achievements of Soviet aviation, the greatest of them being, of course, Yuri Gagarin's triumphant space flight.

Listening to this, one could be in no doubt as to who had suggested the essay and provided the material for it: Wing-Commander Wanko's little talks left an indelible mark on the memory. The work now being read out was characterised by the same way of thinking, the same arrangement and the same emphasis. First came the ritual bow in the direction of Polish scientific achievement (the patriotic touch); next, given the language in which the essay was written, a polite gesture of acknowledgment towards the French (the international touch); these tributes made, the balance was immediately restored with an impressive example from the inexhaustible treasury of Great Russian Science (the political touch); finally, there was a paean of praise for the technical and scientific achievements of our Brother the Soviet Union, Motherland of the Proletariat and Land of Progress (the faithful ally touch). The choice of material, its use and its arrangement were all exemplary.

However, before Agnes had waded through to the end, an incident occurred that disturbed her grave and reverential recital. Its instigator and protagonist was none other than the infernal Roz Goltz, that irrepressible *enfant terrible* who let nothing and no one stand in his way. At the very beginning of her essay, in the part about Copernicus, Agnes was quoting the following popular couplet about our greatest scientist:

He moved the Earth, he stopped the Sun,
Of Polish soil he was the son.

(which in her translation, although it lacked both rhyme and rhythm, sounded even more pompous:

Il a arrêté le Soleil, il a remué la Terre.
Il tirait son origine de la nation polonaise.)

when Roz Goltz suddenly burst out, in Polish, '*Polonaise*? What does she mean, *polonaise*?! He was a German, not a Pole! And he wrote in Latin.'

'*Calme-toi!*' Madame intervened, but Roz paid no attention.

'His mother's maiden name was Watzenrode – that's not a Polish name. And he studied in Italy – in Bologna, Ferrara and Padua.'

'So what?' retorted one of the romantics, traditional enemies of the insufferably objective Roz. 'He was born in Torun, and he worked and died in Frombork.'

'Those were crusader settlements,' Roz interrupted immediately, 'built by the Germans. You can still tell, even today.'

'You don't know anything about Polish history!' shouted the 'romantics'.

'*Silence, et tout de suite!*' commanded Madame, stepping in firmly between the opposing sides. 'What's the matter with you? You can discuss it later, at the end of the essay. And in French, not in Polish!'

'*Je préfère en polonais*,' Roz replied, undaunted. Whenever he let himself be drawn into a skirmish of this kind, he would get excited, lose his temper, and dig his heels in. 'Of Polish soil he was the son!' he jeered, mimicking Agnes Wanko's pompous tone. 'What's that supposed to mean, anyway? That if he hadn't been Polish he wouldn't have been what he was, or what? Or that his scientific genius is a source of rightful pride for the whole nation? Either way it's an incredibly stupid statement. You have to be out of your mind to think that belonging to a particular nation can be the cause of an astronomical discovery. And all this pride just because a countryman of yours did something interesting and became famous for it is an admission that you yourself are a worthless moron, and with an inferiority complex to boot. One's just as bad as the other. If Poland had produced thousands of scientists like Copernicus instead of just poor old him, and other countries just one or none at all, then it would be different. But even then all I'd say is that *statistically* there were more great discoverers born in Poland than elsewhere.'

At this the romantics sniggered loudly, Agnes Wanko continued to stand placidly where she had stood, and Madame, for the first time, seemed to be at a loss.

'There's nothing funny about it!' said Roz, offended. 'And since you're so cheerful, I'll tell you something else. The reason the Poles are so sensitive about their achievements as a nation is that they're insecure. If they were as good as they want to appear, their history would be quite different, for one thing;

and for another, they wouldn't go on and on about all their great achievements. Do the Italians go on about Leonardo, or the English about how terribly English Newton is? But in this country you hear that kind of thing all the time. And that's also because the nationality of most of its greatest figures tends to be a bit hazy – a bit of a sore point. Chopin, for instance: he was half French. So was Gallus Anonimus, the first Polish historian. Even the author of the first dictionary of the Polish language, Samuel Linde, was German. And the only writer of Polish origin who ever made it, and is read all over the world, unfortunately didn't write in Polish. I mean Conrad, of course. And thank God for that! Because if he'd written in Polish, he would probably have written like that precious little wonder of yours, Zeromski. Well, isn't that right?'

'You talk as if you weren't Polish yourself,' one of the romantics said.

'He's not,' muttered another: 'Goltz isn't a Polish n—'

'That's enough!' Madame cried. 'I will not listen to this any longer! You're to stop it right now!'

But Roz could never let anyone else have the last word. 'Whether or not I'm Polish remains to be seen. If I ever amount to anything, and especially if I become famous, then I'll turn out to be more Polish than any of you. I'll be treated like a king! And you'll all go around boasting that you went to school with me. Unfortunately that's how it works. And that's how it'll always work here. The best people either aren't really Polish or get the hell out.'

Then something extraordinary happened: Madame strode energetically up to Roz and said, in Polish, 'One more word out of you and you'll be sent out of this classroom.' A deathly hush fell. 'Stand up when I'm talking to you!'

Roz got to his feet, visibly subdued.

'You're to come to my office after school, at two o'clock. And now I'm warning you: if I hear one more interruption, if you disrupt my lesson one more time, you'll regret it. No one ever wins with me. Remember that.'

She returned to the blackboard, and Roz meekly subsided onto his bench.

'*Continue, s'il te plaît*,' she said to the bloodless Agnes Wanko, still standing there patiently, unmoved, notebook in hand. She spoke quite calmly, as if nothing untoward had occurred. And that inhuman creature, like a machine that had been switched back on, resumed her recital.

The silence in the classroom was absolute. Agnes's voice seemed to come in waves, breaking the stillness like ripples on the surface of a pond. For the first time, something had shaken the imperturbable Madame. Roz had succeeded in upsetting her balance, even if only for a moment, and putting her on the defensive; he had even made her speak Polish rather than French. And he had profited from it, too: summoned to her office, to see her alone, after school! Who had not dreamed of such a thing! What would they not stoop to for the glimmer of a hope of such punishment! People looked at Roz with mingled envy and admiration. How lucky could you get! The cunning little fox! In summoning him for a 'talk', she had acknowledged him as an equal – a partner.

But there was another, perhaps more important aspect to the incident with Roz. It was Madame's counter-attack – the way she had quelled the revolt, and that spectacular finale – that had stunned the class into silence. Just when it seemed that she was helpless, that unleashed forces of anarchy had spread beyond her control and would turn on her at any moment, she, like some dominatrix of wild and dangerous beasts, had with one crack of the whip brought them to heel; one word, one gesture from her had been enough to restore order. In that fraction of a second she was like a proud lioness who with one swipe of her paw dashes to the ground the insolent upstart who has dared to oppose her, or has merely drawn too much attention to himself. She shone. Her dark eyes threw out sparks. Her slim, delicate figure glowed with a radiance that dazzled. It was beautiful and terrible. You wanted to die from it. And then that final warning: 'No one ever wins with me!' It was like a challenge – a call to arms.

Artemis. An Amazon. Brunhilde.

I admit that I, too, was impressed. I was even tempted to pick up the glove she had thrown down. And so I began once more to consider how I might attract her attention and gain her respect, even if it was a respect born of anger. I had long abandoned any idea of reading my essay aloud, and after Roz's performance it seemed like pure madness. I had come to doubt the soundness of my aim in writing it, and I now perceived another danger, far greater than that of casting off my disguise and exposing my true face. Roz – the infernal Roz! For even if Madame indulged me and let me read, and even if the class was too sleepy or too bored by my interminable prose to recognise it for the 'love song' it was, I hadn't a hope of getting past the clear-headed, all-knowing, ever-vigilant Roz. Insensible to jokes, unappreciative of farce, ever the guardian of common sense and scientific truth, he was sure to kick up a row and set upon me – for the myth about Virgo and Aquarius, for the invented Monos, and for all the other nonsense. As soon as he heard the first of my outrageous fabrications he'd interrupt me in mid-sentence as he had interrupted Agnes, and start jeering. 'What's the idiot talking about? It's a load of utter rubbish! Either he's really out of his mind or he's taking the mickey!' I imagined his mocking voice and a cold wave of terror went through me.

Just as the final judge at the AST festival had not been S. or the other participants but the 'rabble' at the back of the hall, so here, in this classroom, Roz Goltz was my distorting mirror. If I hoped for victory here, if I wanted to conquer the heart of the Iron Lady, my strategy had to take account of his presence. He was the dragon guarding the castle gates; he was the three-headed Cerberus I had to get past.

Did Madame really not see that Roz was a potential ally? Or perhaps she saw it perfectly well – perhaps that was why his punishment had not been harsher. After all, any other teacher (notably the Tapeworm) would have made him pay much more dearly. He'd have been sent out the door to cool his heels in the corridor and reflect on his two new Fs (one for the subject and one for discipline), and the next day at least one of his parents would have had to appear at school with him. He would have ended up with a D in discipline for the whole term, and on top of that he'd have been treated to a public reprimand at Saturday assembly. For his offence had been of a particularly horrendous kind. The fact that he had disrupted the lesson was trivial. His crime lay not in his actions but in his words – not in the fact that he'd stirred things up but in *how* he had done it, and *why*. If he had confined himself to making fun of Agnes, sneering at her incapacity for independent thought and insinuating that her father was her co-author, it might have been within the bounds of the tolerable. But no – he had dared to poke fun at Polish national pride! He had disparaged Polish achievements and denigrated Polish history; he had tried to deprive Poland of her greatest progeny. Copernicus not a Pole! Heavens, what an outrage! Chopin a Frenchman on his father's side! Intolerable. And then that last remark of his, about how the best people either weren't really Polish or left the country!

And yet, in spite of this, the headmistress had not tailored the punishment to the crime. She had merely made Roz settle down and had told him to come to her office after classes. Why? What did she intend to say to him? What further punishment, what tongue-lashing did she have in store? Or perhaps there wasn't to be a tongue-lashing at all; perhaps she only wanted to instruct him in the execution of his duties? Warn him against making an unnecessary fuss? Wasn't that how you treated your most loyal subordinates? You hauled them over the coals in public, dragged them through the mud, but in private, with just the two of you, you said well done and patted them on the head, with maybe just a small reminder that they shouldn't overdo it.

Whatever the truth of the matter, this strange and colourful incident suggested a strategy I hadn't so far considered: namely, to ally myself with Roz, discreetly, against Agnes Wanko. In this way I would endear myself to him (which might come in handy) while showing Madame I wasn't afraid of her anger (which would gain me her respect).

I forced myself to pay attention and listen to the rest of Agnes Wanko's essay. When she finished, Madame turned to the class and, as if taking her side, remarked wryly that since reactions to the essay had been so vehement, 'breaking all the accepted rules of debate', she was sure there were still many who were eager to have their say, and she'd be very interested to discover whether any of us were capable of rational remarks, or if all we could do was shout and jeer and sow anarchy. Furthermore, she was eager to see if anyone could manage to give us the benefit of their wisdom in a foreign language, on even the most elementary level, not in some kind of pidgin. *Voilà!* She was waiting. She was all ears. Let them show her what they could do.

This scathing speech, which, of course, assumed that no one would volunteer, gave me my opening. As soon as Madame had finished, and had been received with the predictable eloquent silence, I raised my hand and declared that I did indeed have something to say, and was capable of getting it across in the language of the lesson.

'*Ah, notre poète*,' Madame observed with a sarcastic smile. 'Excellent. By all means, go ahead. What do you have to tell us that's so interesting? Do give us the benefit of your observations.'

'Why "*poète*"?' I asked coldly, assuming an offended air.

'*Et qui divaguait, tout récemment,* about rhymes?' she shot back instantly. 'Who spoke of rhymes and pointed out that I wasn't hearing them? "*Question*", "*conversation*", "can't you hear it?" Well, didn't you?'

So the shot *had* gone home! And now she was throwing it back at me! Excellent! I hadn't missed! Now if I could just keep it up!

'*Ah bon, c'est ça*,' I sighed, as if it were only with the greatest difficulty that I recalled my words and was amazed she should have taken them amiss. Oh, so *that's* what you mean! Goodness, is that all? It's scarcely worth discussing.

'*Ce ne sont pas des traits* of the poetic soul?' she asked, still teasing.

'Perhaps they are poetic traits,' I replied, 'although I don't think they're sufficient for poetry. In any case,' I added, as a good phrase occurred to me, '*si je vous ai blessée, pardonnez-le-moi, c'était sans intention.*'

'*Blessée?*' The suggestion that I had hurt her could not be allowed to pass. '*Tu voulais dire "offensée"*.'

'*Est-ce qu'une offense n'est pas une blessure?* When we offend, do we not also hurt?'

'*Mais finis-en avec ces subtilités,*' she said impatiently. 'Enough of your hairsplitting. Get on with whatever it is you want to say.'

'I'd like to put a question to the writer of the essay.'

'Very well, put it, *s'il te plaît,* as long as it's relevant.' She didn't let up for a moment.

'*Je ferai de mon mieux,*' I replied, coldly polite. I would indeed do my best. I turned to Agnes Wanko. 'What do you take to be the meaning of the Latin phrase you used as the motto for your essay?'

'*D'accord, ça peut aller,*' Madame conceded, and to Agnes she said, 'Please explain it to him.'

'*Par les aspirations . . . par les espérances aux étoiles,*' Agnes recited smoothly, getting up from her seat.

'*Bon,*' Madame acknowledged the answer in her usual way and turned back to me. 'Satisfied?'

'*Oui, ça confirme bien,*' I replied, 'that my suspicions were right.' And I made as if to sit down.

'*Attend!*' She gestured at me to remain where I was. 'What do you mean? What suspicions?'

'Only that she doesn't know what it means. *Aspera* in Latin doesn't mean "aspirations", let alone "hopes". It means . . . it means . . .' Here I got stuck, for suddenly I couldn't remember the French for 'thorn'.

'*Mais quoi?*' she asked, with an elaborate courtesy which failed to conceal her amusement and left me uncertain whether she honestly didn't know what it meant or was, as I'd thought, only pretending.

'Umm . . .' I couldn't seem to emerge from the hole in my memory. '*Alors . . . ce qui nous blesse parfois.* Something sharp that hurts.'

'*Tu veux dire "offense", peut-être?*' she suggested helpfully.

'Why all the sarcasm?' I shot back. '*Les roses en ont . . . les roses . . . quand elles sont mûres et belles . . .*'

'*Ah, "les épines",*' she said, and the corners of her mouth twitched in a mocking smile.

'That's it! Exactly. I wanted to say "stings", but I knew that wasn't quite it. Thorns.'

'Well, what's your answer, Agnes?' asked Madame, turning back to the pale Miss Wanko.

'*Oh, je ne sais pas encore*,' Agnes replied coolly, paying no attention to me. 'I'll have to look it up in the dictionary.'

'*Ce n'est pas nécessaire*,' I observed, reminding her of my existence. 'Even a child knows what *aspera* means. And anyway,' I added, still on a wave of inspiration, 'you can ask Madame, she'll tell you. Surely you trust *her* . . .'

Now, let's see what you have to say to that, I thought, pleased with myself, and looked straight into Madame's dark eyes. You can't possibly wriggle out of this one.

But she did – although not with the happiest of results. '*D'accord*,' she said, with a hint of the conditional in her voice, 'let's assume you're right, and *aspera* means "thorns" and not "aspirations". What relevance does that have to this essay?'

This was a rash move: she had exposed herself badly. I rushed to the attack.

'*Oh, tout à fait essentielle*,' I replied, indignant. 'If *aspera* means thorns, then we're talking about difficulties – obstacles, setbacks. But is there anything about them in this essay?' I asked, pausing dramatically. 'Nothing at all! Not a word! On the contrary: from her examples you'd think it was just one long string of successes.'

I perceived out of the corner of my eye that Roz was silently applauding me under his desk. Encouraged, I gave him a discreet nod of acknowledgement (without, however, looking in his direction), signifying that his action had been noticed and appreciated, and continued: '*Quand j'ai entendu cette phrase,* I expected at least some mention of the opposition to Copernicus, and then maybe something about a plane crash, or at least about Icarus – who is, after all, the symbol of the dangers that await those who would conquer the skies. You'd think he'd naturally spring to mind. But what am I saying? If she doesn't know what *aspera* means, how can I expect her to have heard of Icarus?!'

This was too strong. Carried away by my own rhetoric, I

had overdone it. But the results weren't bad. Agnes Wanko, purple with rage, shrieked in her squeaky voice, 'For your information, I know perfectly well who Icarus was! I know more about it than you do! I got first prize in the mythology competition.'

I arranged my features into an expression of shocked astonishment and said to Madame, '*Mais elle parle polonais! C'est inadmissible!*'

This was too much. Agnes burst into tears, and Madame snapped, '*C'est moi qui décide de ce qui est admissible ou non!* Please don't lecture me.'

'That wasn't my intention,' I began, backing off, for I saw that I'd gone too far. But it was too late.

'*Assez!*' she cut in. 'Enough! I've had quite enough of your little games. And I'm very curious to see what you've come up with yourself, since you're so clever. Let's see if there's any substance behind your eloquence. Perhaps we'll find there's nothing there?'

Merde! I thought. (By now even my mental curses came out in French.) What a mess! Now what?

I glanced at the clock on the wall. Another ten minutes until the bell. Perfect – all was well. As long as I read slowly, I wouldn't get beyond the fourth or fifth page, which was where the thing really began.

'As you wish, Madame,' I said politely, and began to read.

She stopped me almost as soon as I'd begun. '*Le titre!* What is the title of your *oeuvre*? Even a child,' she added, in vicious mimicry, 'knows that you have to start with the title.'

I was floored. I had no title: I simply hadn't thought about it. Better not admit it now. There wasn't much time for reflection. I cast an offhand glance at the page in front of me and announced, as if I were reading it out, '*L'astrologie: Magie ou Science?*' And then, certain there wouldn't be time for me to read the thing even halfway through, let alone to the end, I gave way to a sudden temptation and added, after a pause, the intriguing subtitle, '*Le mystère du 27 janvier*'.

I looked up at Madame. Her face was inscrutable.

'Well, go on! *Lis, vas-y, on t'écoute.*' She seated herself sideways at her desk and propped her head on her hands.

I began again.

I read clearly and audibly, taking care over my accent and aiming for a cool, neutral tone. I was modest and matter-of-fact, entirely concentrated on my reading: not once did I raise my eyes from the page to check the reaction of the audience. The only thing that might have spoilt the coolness of my presentation was the occasional furtive glance at my watch, which I had managed at the last minute to twist over to the back of my wrist, but this was so discreet that it couldn't have been visible: with my notebook open in my hand, the face of the watch was right there in front of me.

When I reached the first of the quotations from *Faust* I saw there were still another five minutes to go. Not good: too long. I paused for a moment, and on the words, 'My own attitude towards astrology . . .' slowed down even more.

When I had plodded my way past the words 'I was born in September. On the tenth of September, to be precise. Which makes me a Virgo,' Madame could bear it no longer and demanded impatiently, '*Ne pourrais-tu pas faire un peu plus vite?!*'

Faster? Dear God! When I'd been searching for ways of provoking her into saying things that sounded ambiguous or suggestive, I hadn't dreamed I would be granted a morsel as tasty as this. I was stunned.

'*Plus vite?*' I asked softly, with an abstracted air: I wanted to hear her say it again.

'*Oui, plus vite, bien plus vite!*' she said emphatically, 'if you don't want me to fall asleep.'

And what if I do, it occurred to me to reply – but of course I didn't. Instead, in a more considered move, I shrugged and agreed. '*Bon, j'essaierai*, I'll try,' and then, just for fun, I added, 'but it might be risky.'

'Oh, stop all this clowning around and get on with it, please,' she snapped, drumming an irritated tattoo on the desk with her fingers, and rose from her chair.

Only two or three minutes now remained. In accordance with Madame's wishes, I read faster. Another six paragraphs went by, and then at last I heard the bell. It sounded just as I was reading out the words 'We must start with the myth of Virgo and Aquarius.'

I raised my eyes from the text and lowered my notebook, implying by gesture and expression my complete powerlessness in the face of these circumstances. I've done my best, it's not my fault, there's nothing I can do about it.

'*Combien il y en a encore?*' asked Madame coolly, her tone implying that she was prepared to sit there for the whole break if necessary, regardless of the bell.

I pretended to make a rough count of the pages. 'Oh, quite a bit, quite a bit,' I said with false concern. 'I wouldn't get through it even if I went on reading until the end of break, I'm afraid.'

And then another unexpected thing occurred. Madame came up to me, swivelled my notebook around the other way and began to turn over the pages one by one. On the last page, with Margaret's lament and the final sentence ('I long for that victory with my Aquarius'), she paused.

'*Bon*,' she said finally, '*on verra ce que tu as écrit*: we'll see what you've written.' And she went, taking my notebook with her.

What Then? What Then, My Lad?

I was exhausted – drained, dazed and on edge, my nerves jangling, as if I'd just finished some important, difficult exam. So much had happened! First Roz's astonishing outburst, then the mess with Agnes Wanko, then, most important, my duel with Madame. And then being called on to read, and finally, as if that were not enough, having my notebook confiscated. It was a lot for one lesson.

The seizure of my notebook was unprecedented. Madame never took away our notebooks, even for routine inspections, let alone for a special inspection like this, and so selective! Something must have aroused her suspicions, but I couldn't pinpoint what it might be. She hadn't raised an eyebrow at the subtitle with her date of birth; but then she had been bored, or at least had succeeded in giving that impression. And later, when she was standing over me leafing through my notebook, her face had expressed nothing but amused surprise at how much I had written. There was the moment when she had paused for a longer look at that final, crucial page, where her name appeared woven into the last sentence – but even then it was no more than a slightly prolonged look, not a definite reaction.

When I got home I shut myself in my room and lay down on the bed, hoping for sleep. But I couldn't switch off; my head was still spinning with the day's events. Obsessively I went over every detail in my mind. For instance, Madame's attack on Roz after his bitter remark that the best people in Poland 'weren't really Polish' or 'got the hell out'. I ran and re-ran this episode in my mind, examining it as if I were inspecting a reel of film, back and forth, frame by frame, and the more I did so the more certain I was that when Madame heard those words her angry features had contorted, just for an instant, in a kind of involuntary grimace or spasm. Something had tugged at the nerves and muscles of her face. Strange. I couldn't explain it. What was it that had stung so much? And why that in particular, and none of his other remarks? Why hadn't she put Roz in his place long before then?

Or the moment when she had asked me to read faster . . . But now I was no longer thinking of her suggestive phrase – '*Ne pourrais-tu pas faire un peu plus vite?* Can't you go a little bit faster' – and its possible interpretations or the exchange that followed. I was wondering whether she had hurried me on because she really was irritated and bored by my plodding delivery or because she wanted to hear how it went on – because the subtitle I had hit upon at the last minute had aroused her curiosity. After all, people do tend to notice their date of birth. And in that context you could hardly fail to be intrigued: 'mystery', 'enigma' – hard to believe that she had been entirely uninterested. The fact that she had shown no curiosity, had remained her impassive self, meant nothing: that was just how she was. Yes, that must have been it: she had hurried me on and then taken my notebook because she had sensed something else going on and wanted to find out what it was.

Then it occurred to me that she might by now have read it, or perhaps was actually reading it at that very moment. I leapt up, hunted down my satchel, which I had left lying about somewhere in the hall, and took out my copy of the essay – the clean copy I had written out on sheets of lined writing paper. Back in my room, I flung myself back on the bed, this time half lying, half sitting, and once again began to read it through, slowly and carefully, trying to see it through Madame's eyes.

At what point had she caught on to my subtle game? When had she realised what I was doing and why? And what did she think of it? Did she believe any of my nonsense? Did she even believe that such myths and legends, and such interpretations, existed? Or did they strike her immediately as transparent inventions? And if she knew it was all pure fantasy, if she had seen through my plan and discovered my true intentions, what was her response? Anger? Amusement? Scorn? Or perhaps respect, after all? Perhaps she was even a little touched? Here I had been set a simple essay to practise French composition, and I had produced – this!

It's hard to believe he went to all this trouble, she might think. Good heavens, what a romantic! He clearly didn't do it just to get good marks or to show off – he didn't volunteer, he didn't draw attention to himself: he just happened to be called on. Well, well – he must adore me.

On the other hand, she might be thinking more along the following lines: What a sly customer! Sly and untrustworthy, and too clever by half. All that clever rhetoric, all those erudite speeches, and an answer to everything. On top of that he makes suggestive remarks – flirts with me! But most of all, how does he know?! Where did he get the information? Did he dig it up himself? Did he spy on me? Or did he get it from someone else, steal it from somewhere? How dare he do such a thing, how dare he! And then to boast about it! The impudence! Insolent creep!

I had a feeling the second reaction was the more likely one.

In any event, I thought, putting aside the copy and closing my eyes, it has to end somehow . . . Yes, but how? Will she give me back my notebook without a word, without comment or correction, and pretend that she hasn't read it or didn't find it interesting? That she took it because I'd provoked her and because she was angry anyway, but later calmed down and after that just forgot about it? Oh, it simply went out of my mind – so many things to think about! Here it is, you can have it back, let's forget about it, pretend it didn't happen.

But there was another, much worse possibility:

She comes into the classroom. She puts my notebook on the edge of her desk, very deliberately, to make it clear that at the appropriate moment it will become the object of a spectacular trial, and begins the lesson. Conversation. Exercises. She appears not to notice me. Finally, a quarter of an hour before the bell, she makes her move. She reaches for the *corpus delicti,* opens it and begins to read. She picks out the juiciest bits and reads them aloud, torn out of context. And laughs at them, makes fun of me, pours out bucketfuls of scorn. To make me forever abandon the thought of flirting.

'This,' she thunders from behind her desk, 'this is the true face of our great thinker – our philosopher, our poet and God knows what else! Superstition. Obscurantism. The dark ages. This is the kind of thing he really likes, this is what he secretly admires. Yes, he can talk, he can go on for hours, but what good is it when he talks such rubbish? I've never seen such nonsense. Woman – initiated! Man – eternally a virgin! A virgin is really a young man! A man is really a woman! What other profound truths does our venerable guru have to tell us? What other wisdom, what depths of knowledge will he reveal? Perhaps he'll say he's not really a boy but a timid young girl . . .'

Well, perhaps she wouldn't go that far, but the thought of even a milder version froze my blood. Hoping to chase away this nightmarish vision, I gave myself up to daydreams.

There's no reason it should end so badly, I thought, no reason for her to be so cruel. After all, what did my crime amount to? It was only a joke. But how inspired, how original, how subtly and gracefully done! She had no grounds for feeling offended or thinking she'd been made a fool of. On the contrary, she should be flattered – both as a teacher and as a person. So much effort! And such writing! So why shouldn't she respond quite differently? Like this, for instance: She comes in. She begins the lesson. She doesn't give me back my notebook, doesn't even mention my essay. But after class – when everyone is leaving the room, say – she stops beside me for a moment and says, as if she'd just remembered something, '*Ah, oui, ton cahier!* Your notebook. *Viens le chercher dans mon bureau. Après les cours, à deux heures*. Come and see me after school, at two.'

And when I present myself at her office, she reaches into her desk for the essay, but then, instead of handing it to me with her usual businesslike '*voilà*' and leaving it at that, she opens it and leafs through it again. Then she turns to me. 'So you say, do you,' a teasing smile on her lips and in her eyes, 'that Aquarius is written in your stars? That you long for the victory with your Aquarius? Have you ever met anyone born under that beautiful sign? Apart, of course, from Mozart, Mendelssohn and Schubert?'

How was such a question to be answered?

'Why don't you answer? Have you nothing to say? First you do your best to arouse one's curiosity, and then you're as silent as the Sphinx. Well? Have you? Met an Aquarius?'

'If I'm not mistaken, Roz Goltz is an Aquarius.'

Not bad. What would it achieve? She might respond like this: 'So? Is he really the one your soul longs for? Your ideal, your other half?' Her voice vibrates with feigned interest. 'I can see all too well that you want to endear yourself to him. But does *he* see it, can *he* appreciate it? Or is he deaf to it?'

I could then say, 'I don't think so. I saw him applauding me recently, when I was criticising the essay that Agnes –'

Whereupon she should stop me and say, 'No, you don't understand, that isn't what I mean. I mean, are you certain that the one your soul longs for will come towards you? That he'll return your feelings or even respond to them? What if he doesn't? What if it turns out that he isn't, after all, the Schubert who will write the music to your virgin's song? What then? What then, my lad?'

On this last question she would look me in the eye. And I would say, 'That, of course, would be painful, and rather a pity. On the other hand, it might be a blessing. For happiness' – and here I could neatly insert a quotation from a story by Thomas Mann – 'happiness lies not in being loved; that merely gratifies one's vanity, and is mingled with disgust. Happiness lies in loving, and perhaps snatching brief, illusory moments of closeness to the beloved object . . .'

Yes, such an exchange in the seclusion of her office would be a beautiful thing. It would be a kind of fulfilment – at least within the small area of hopes and dreams connected with my essay.

I need hardly add that not the faintest shadow of such an eventuality was cast within the cave of our school reality. Nor were any of the other scenarios I'd imagined played out. The whole affair ended with a whimper, blandly and unexcitingly – and yet at the same time unexpectedly. One might say it didn't end at all, or ended only because it didn't go on, like a game abandoned by the players.

For Madame never alluded to the subject again. She gave me no mark, she made no comment, she said not a single word about my essay. Moreover, she failed to return my notebook. *She simply did not give it back.* She gave no reason. She simply kept it and went on as usual, behaving as if nothing had happened.

Why did I allow it? Why did I not insist on an explanation, at least on the return of my property?

When she failed to return the notebook at our next lesson with her, I thought it odd, but to tell the truth I preferred to let sleeping dogs lie. Besides, I had decided to adopt a strategy of provocative passivity: when she dictated something or told us to write something down, I'd simply sit there, motionless and impassive, staring at her insistently and ready to shoot out the challenge: '*Mais je n'ai pas de cahier, vous ne me l'avez pas rendu.* I've got nothing to write on.' I got the impression she was trying to avoid my eye. In any event, she ignored my mute display and said nothing. No reaction. And later, in the lessons that followed – but let us not run on ahead. For before the next lesson I met Dr Freddy Monten at his father's house, and this meeting made me see everything from a different perspective.

THREE

What is the Meaning of the Word 'Philology'?

It was exactly five o'clock when I pressed the white porcelain knob of the pre-war bell in its decorative surround recessed in the right frame of the door. The door was opened by Constant, in his usual tweed jacket with leather elbow-patches, a pale blue shirt, a small, elegant red-spotted bow tie, dark-green trousers of good thick corduroy and a leather belt with a chrome buckle. On his feet he wore a pair of highly polished brown lace-ups, neatly tied. The left lapel of his jacket bore the purple satin rosebud of the Légion d'honneur.

'Swiss punctuality,' he observed, looking at his watch (a gold Longines).

'I'm told it's not done to be too punctual,' I objected, sparing a melancholy thought for the poor Ruhla. 'Apparently the proper thing is to be a few minutes late.'

'That depends,' said Constant, 'on where you're going and why. If it's a party of some kind, then yes, you might indeed arrive a little late. But if you're going to see someone you've already had occasion to visit, especially on business, then punctuality is nothing to be ashamed of. On the contrary, it's a sign of the best habits.'

From the sitting-room to the right a slim man with a smooth and gloomy face slowly emerged. His hair was brushed flat, with a visible parting, and beneath his shirt collar he wore a carefully tied cravat of wine-coloured silk.

'And here is your expert,' said Constant. 'The Professor. Freddy, that is. Let me introduce you.'

Freddy approached and, piercing me with an intense look, clasped my hand firmly. 'How verrry nice to meet you,' he said in a melodious voice. His *r*s were guttural, rolled in his throat the French way.

'How do you do. Good evening.' I shook his hand, a delicate hand with long, agile fingers.

So that's what he's like, I thought, searching for a resemblance to Constant but not seeing one. An overbred fogey? A spoilt dandy? A blasé neurotic? What had he been like ten years ago, when he'd studied with Madame?

'Let's go in here,' commanded Constant, turning right into the room from which Freddy had just emerged.

The curtains on the tall windows, which gave onto the courtyard, were already drawn, and the interior of the room was dim. The gloom was dispelled only by a faint yellowish light that came from two small bracket-lamps on the wall above the two armchairs. Between the armchairs stood a low bow-legged table.

'Sit down,' said Constant, indicating the armchair on the right, while he himself sank comfortably into the other. Freddy, meanwhile, had vanished silently into the kitchen. 'How are your parents? Everything all right?' He crossed his legs, revealing dark plum-coloured socks, smooth over his calves.

'They're fine, thank you,' I said with a polite smile and a slight inclination of the head, conveying that I appreciated his question not merely as the usual gesture of courtesy but as a sign of his loyalty to me: he had kept my request to himself, as I'd asked.

'Freddy knows all about it,' he said. 'But don't worry, I didn't give him any instructions. I was a completely neutral, entirely loyal intermediary. I simply told him that you're about to finish school, are thinking of Romance languages as one of your options, and would like some advice.'

'Thank you, I appreciate it. And did you happen to mention, by any chance, that I'd also be grateful for some stories from his own days as a student?'

'No, I didn't mention that.'

Damn, I thought, clenching my teeth. With a hint of regret I said, 'Oh . . . that's too bad. It's important to me,' and, thinking that there might still be time to accomplish something before Freddy returned from the kitchen, began to elaborate on the theme. 'You've known me for a long time, and you know how much importance I attach to tradition – to an awareness of what came before, as a point of reference for the present. In fact, to some extent you're responsible for it. After all,' I said, with a note of teasing defiance, 'you're the one who really awoke in me this tendency to be always . . . testing things against the past.'

'Testing things against the past?'

'How else can I put it?' I looked up at the high ceiling, seeking inspiration there. 'I mean that whenever you undertake something, you want to know what it was like before. So that you can see yourself against that background, and know where and at what point you're making your entry on the scene; so that you can judge whether things are on an upswing or a downswing, whether you're entering some kind of golden age or a twilight of the gods, a period of rebirth or one of decline. Think of our mountain expeditions, when you used to talk about what climbing was like in the past and what modern tourism had done to it. That was an important lesson for me. It made me realise I was living in poor, miserable times and in a rotten world. So I had no illusions, and that meant I couldn't be disappointed. But you have to look at these things on different scales. The post-war period – especially here, in this country – seems to be a time of decline, regress and degeneration compared to the pre-war world. But even the bottom isn't entirely flat: there are bumps and concavities, hills and dales. Surely there's a difference between the dark night of Stalinism, a time of real terror, and what we have now, which is just grey and bleak and miserable? That was the "great purge"; this is "our little stabilisation". It may be nasty and brutish, but it's liveable. It's a normality of sorts. And when I think of this, it occurs to me that now, for the first time, I may have a chance of surpassing the past. Your son, if I'm not mistaken, began university in '53 – the declining days of the "cult of the individual". That was a terrible time: draconian laws, informers, denunciations, police surveillance – a nightmare. And they had another way of getting at you – blackmail about your personal life. I've heard dozens of stories about how lives were wrecked because of things they ferreted out, poking about in people's private affairs. Today at least there's none of that. But I'd like to hear some reminiscences from those days, a few stories – and the gloomier the better. It sounds strange, I know, but it would encourage me. Because it would make me feel that I'm starting from a better position, that for once, "now" is better than "then". And that would be precious.'

'It's funny, what you say,' said Constant after a moment of silence. 'But I still don't quite understand what it is you want to know. What sort of stories?'

My God, I thought, why is he doing this to me? I would have thought I'd made myself clear. 'Well, you know . . . just stories . . . from his student days, about his friends, what they were like . . . what they did, how they spent their time . . . their social life . . . you know, that kind of thing.'

'Oh, that!' He laughed, throwing back his head. 'Of course, you can ask him. I'm sure he'll tell you about it, but I doubt whether it'll be what you seem to want to hear. As far as I know, his memories of those days are quite pleasant. It was a difficult time, of course, but for him it was a happy one. He was soaring then. Everything went well for him in every way, academically and otherwise. The troubles and disappointments came later. *Now* he's disillusioned and complains all the time, but *then* . . . no, things were different then. But if it interests you, go ahead, ask him. I don't see why not.'

I was about to say, 'Couldn't you do it for me?' when Freddy appeared in the doorway, holding a tray with a porcelain teapot, two cups and a silver sugar bowl with a little lock. This put me off my stride.

'I don't suppose *you* . . .?' I muttered, but trailed off lamely in mid-sentence, for Constant no longer seemed to be listening. He leapt energetically to his feet, cleared some odds and ends off the little table, extracted from a drawer a large, white, starched linen napkin, and arranged it with fastidious care on the shining mahogany.

'*Voilà!*' he pronounced. Brushing an invisible speck of dust from the napkin, he moved back a step to make room for

Freddy, who, balancing his tray on the edge of the table, transferred the objects on the former to the linen-covered surface of the latter. Among them, in addition to teapot, cups and sugar bowl, were two small, delicate Meissen china plates which held, respectively, nuts and French biscuits, and a dainty little jug (also Meissen) with milk. Constant relieved him of the empty tray, put it under his arm and made for the door.

'Well, now, I'll leave the two of you alone,' he said. 'I wish you a fruitful discussion.' He sketched an imperial gesture of farewell to the assembled crowds and was gone.

In silence, Freddy poured out tea and offered sugar.

'Thank you, no sugar,' I whispered.

'Ah, you like bitterrness, then,' he remarked, turning the bowl towards him and plunging the sugar spoon into its depths. 'I used to like it myself, once.' He took two heaped spoonfuls of sugar and stirred abstractedly, gazing lugubriously into his cup.

I sat motionless, observing him. A strange man. I couldn't figure him out. Was this some sort of act put on for my benefit? Was he playing some kind of part? Or was this what he was really like? Gloomy, shut up within himself, with an absent gaze? I didn't know what to do – charge ahead regardless and try to break through his defences? Offer him something, sacrifice a pawn, in the hope that it might speed things up and allow me to manoeuvre myself into a better position? Or wait, and leave the field to him? Let him speak, let him expose himself? I chose the defensive strategy.

'So,' he said finally, taking a sip of tea, 'you say you'd like to study Rrromance languages. Rrromance philology.' He looked at me. 'In our splendid deparrtment.' His voice dripped with irony and his face contorted into an elaborate scowl of disgust.

'I'm thinking about it,' I said evenly.

'And may I ask why?' he pursued, still scowling.

It was hardly a difficult question, but I couldn't seem to find a quick answer. 'Well, how shall I put it . . .?' I tried desperately to gather my thoughts.

'Brriefly and simply would be best,' he advised.

I shrugged. 'I like French. I'm fairly fluent. You may find it hard to believe, but in our school the standard is quite high –'

'You misunderstand me,' he interrupted wearily. 'I don't mean *why* do you want to study in that deparrtment, I mean *to what end*?'

'How do you mean, to what end?'

'I mean, what do you want to do with it? What are your plans for the future?'

Once again he had me backed into a corner. ('As early as the fourth move Alekhin is already taking Capablanca by surprise,' I thought, remembering the commentary on one of the tournament games in which the great José had lost his world title.) Good God, man, I groaned inwardly, have a heart! I didn't come here to be interrogated, I came to find out something about that woman!

'I can't answer a question put like that,' I said finally. 'I can only tell you what I'm interested in and what I'd like to learn more about.'

'Very well,' he agreed with long-suffering reluctance. 'Go on.'

'Well, French culture, generally speaking. Literature, theatre and also philosophy – especially the intellectual current that began with Sartre's existentialism. You know: *Les Temps modernes*, Aux Deux Magots, the café at Saint-Germain-des-Prés, *L'Imaginaire*, *Le Mur*' – I threw out the first titles, names and catchwords that came to mind – '*Les Chemins de la liberté*, Camus's *Mythe de Sisyphe*, *L'Homme révolté*, *La Chute*, the theatre of the absurd, Genet, the *nouvelle vague* in film . . . that whole legendary intellectual and artistic world, which Simone de Beauvoir describes in such detail in her autobiography. And, since I've mentioned her . . . I might, for instance, do a study of her manifesto about the liberated woman, *Le Deuxième sexe*. For some reason it hasn't been translated into Polish yet, and as far as I know no serious study of it has ever been undertaken here – except perhaps in university seminars, or in a lecture . . . or someone might have written a thesis on it . . .'

Your move, I thought, and took a sip of tea. If you know

something, now's the time to speak. Take the damn pawn! Accept the sacrifice! And bring out your queen!

Unfortunately he did no such thing. Instead he clicked his tongue disapprovingly three times, frowned and shook his head. 'That's bad. That's verry bad.'

'Bad?' I put down my cup, missing the saucer and hitting the edge of the table. 'What's bad about it?'

'Everything, my frriend, everything, from start to finish.'

'I give up, in that case. Tell me.' I nibbled a few nuts from the Meissen plate. 'Tell me why I'm wrong.'

'You're wrong for a number of reasons. Let's start with the simplest.' He sat up in his armchair and clasped his hands together like an opera singer before an aria. 'Why is it, when you have so many fine, worthwhile, prrecious things to choose from, that you insist on the tawdry and the shoddy? Tinsel and glitter and plastic jewellery, when you could have genuine pearls and diamonds? You don't look completely uncivilised, so why, with the whole rrich, glorious trreasury of Frrench culture open before you, overflowing with trrue masterpieces and rreally splendid achievements, do you choose kitsch, junk, the rrotten frruit of decline? Si-mone-de-Beau-voir, I ask you!' He raised his hands in shocked disbelief. 'You couldn't do worse! You've hit bottom with that! The drregs! Don't you feel it? Can't you see it? Can you tell me just what it is that you see in her? I don't understand how you can even rread the stuff!'

I felt myself flush. I'd been snared in my own net. I cast about desperately for a way to disentangle myself. 'You misunderstood me,' I said, raising my hand in mild protest. 'But it's my own fault.' I waved my hand in the air and briefly put my fingers to my brow. 'I didn't make myself clear enough, I should have explained it better. The fact that I might consider doing a study of Beauvoir's *Second Sex* doesn't mean I admire her. On the contrary. I find her work incredibly irritating, boring – absurd, even. She's affected, garrulous and patronising, and she lectures you.' At each of these words Freddy nodded, as if to say, Exactly! 'But what does strike me as interesting is how such trash came to be so popular – and not just here, but in France. I can see how people here might like it: it's Western, after all, so it must be good. But over there, in the free world?! So what I meant when I said I might write about her was that I'd write a critique, a thorough one, and also analyse the sociological causes of her regrettable success.'

But after this neat U-turn Freddy's face still bore its frown of disapproval. If anything, it had deepened. 'No, no, you're wrong again.' He shook his head. 'Quite wrong. From the frrying pan into the fire, as it were. Do you have any idea where you'd end up if you trried something like that? With what sort of people? You'd find yourself in the company of rrepulsive, illiterate, backward crreatures who want to stamp out culture or trrade in it like shopkeepers, rready to do anything to get access to the rrotten West and all the nice things it has to offer. They'll drrag it thrrough the mud, rrevile it, heap calumnies on it, write any disgusting lie about it you ask them to. Is that the sort of company you want to keep? Is that how you want to be seen – as one of them? Along with the censor, the political commissar and the informer?'

'Ah, but you see –' I ploughed on, hating this nonsense but feeling I had no choice, and consoling myself with the thought that it might lead somewhere in the end, 'my critique wouldn't be anything like those blind, unthinking attacks on "bourgeois culture". It wouldn't be a "fundamental Marxist critique", far less an act of opportunism or moral prostitution, performed cynically for this or that privilege –'

'It doesn't matter,' Freddy broke in roughly. 'Objectively you'd be serving the interests of the rregime. You'd be prroviding arrguments for the claim that the West is wrong and its culture worthless and degenerate.'

'So there's no way out,' I said, half to myself.

'Why not? Of course there is, and it's verry simple.' He plucked a French biscuit from the plate and crunched it with relish.

'Namely?'

'Do something else.'

Well, yes, I thought, easy to say. But what if that was what Madame happened to like?

'Do you know of anyone who made that kind of wrong

choice?' I asked, grasping firmly at the thread slipping through my fingers. 'Not necessarily someone now,' I added hastily, to show I had no wish to pry into the current business of the department. 'It could be an example from any time – from your own student days, for instance.'

'Do I know of anyone who made the wrong choice!' He snorted sardonically. 'Do I know of anyone who didn't!'

'What do you mean? Are you implying that everyone made bad –'

'Listen,' he broke in. 'Rrremember, when you asked me to explain why you were wrong in your choice of studies, I told you there were a number of reasons, not just one. I'll tell you what I meant. The idea of working on Simone de Beauvoir is an absurd one *per se,* rregardless of your motives and aims. It's rreprrehensible in its own right. But let's assume you're interested in something else, something of genuine value – like, oh, I don't know, Pascal, for instance, or Racine, or la Rochefoucauld. Don't imagine I'd rrush in with enthusiastic support. No, I'd still try to dissuade you from Rrromance languages. I'd be just as strongly opposed.'

'Is the standard really so low?' I asked, falling back on the question I'd put to Constant on the phone.

'It's not a question of the standard,' he replied impatiently, 'although that, too, leaves much to be desired.'

'What, then?' I asked. Now I was genuinely curious.

'It's a discipline for which there's no place in this country. If you decide to work in that field, or even if you trry to study it, at the verry least it'll rreduce you to a nerrvous wrreck.'

He spoke with such fierce conviction that I shivered, but my curiosity had been piqued. What was all this supposed to mean? Why should choosing to study French literature, and later to make it one's field of professional research, lead to madness or nervous breakdowns? Why was it unhealthy and inadvisable, and what was so treacherous about it?

I took another sip of tea and a nibble of biscuit. 'You intrigue me,' I said. 'Could you elaborate? I confess I'm surprised and a little perplexed.'

A long silence ensued.

'What is the meaning of the word "philology"?' he asked finally, in a perfectly calm, matter-of-fact voice, as if he were launching into a Socratic inquiry and proposed to get to the truth by elenchus.

'Is that a rhetorical question, or do you expect an answer?' I still wasn't quite sure where he was headed.

'Yes, please, I'd like an answer.'

'Well,' I said, as if I were giving a definition at an oral exam, 'in this country the word "philology" is still used in the old, general sense to mean the study of the language and literature of a particular nation. And –'

'What does *philo* mean in Greek?' he broke in.

'It means liking or loving something,' I replied, 'or being friendly or well inclined towards something.'

'Good,' he said approvingly. 'And what about *logy*? What is the meaning of the Greek *logos*?'

'*Logos*,' I replied, 'can mean a great number of things, but in this case it means "word". However, in the word "philology" as we use it, it means "that which is composed of words": language and literature in general.'

'Very good. And *neo*? As in *neo-philo* –'

This time I interrupted. '*Neo* means new or recent, and neophilology is the study of the languages and literatures of modern nations.'

'Excellent. Now then, tell me, if you would, what is meant by the term "modern nations". Which nations, exactly, are these?'

I knew the answer, but I had some difficulty in formulating it clearly. 'Well,' I said after a moment's hesitation, 'it means nations . . . which have survived in more or less unchanged form . . . since the end of the Middle Ages . . . the time of the great discoveries . . . the fifteenth century.'

'Would you count India or China among them?' He was slyly probing.

I shrugged. 'No, I wouldn't.'

'Well, then?' He gazed at me expectantly.

'The term refers to the nations of our continent . . . to European nations,' I said finally, more decisive now, even with a slight edge of impatience.

'Ah!' He feigned surprise. 'Rreally? So *that's* what you mean! And that would include . . .?

'The English, the French, the Germans,' I rattled off, 'the Italians and the Spanish . . .'

'And the Rrrussians, surely,' he added, gazing at me in mock defiance.

'The Russians?' I smelt a trap. He was testing me.

'What, you mean you wouldn't include the Rrrussians?'

'The Russians are a Slavic nation.'

'Does that mean they're not modern?'

'No, but I had the impression that the term "neo-philology" referred to *Western* languages and literatures. The study of Russian language and literature belongs to the field we call Slavic philology.'

'Aaah, there we are!' he drawled triumphantly. 'So that's what you mean. Well, at least that's clear now.'

'I'm sorry,' I said. This excruciating tooth-pulling process had gone on long enough. It was time to speed things up. 'I don't quite understand what you're getting at. What's the point of all these laborious definitions?'

'Patience, young man, patience! We'll get to that in a minute.' He was clearly enjoying his role of classical mentor. 'We're agrreed, then, are we not, that neo-philology, as the term is popularly understood here, is that brranch of philology concerned with the languages and literratures of modern Western nations. But there's a deeper sense to the word. If you go back to the source and look at the orriginal meanings, you'll find it means love for those Western languages and the whole culture connected with them. And the question arrises of how one can love something in a country that is hostile to it, a country that in its political system, its ideology and its defence doctrine looks with extrreme disfavour upon anything from the West, a country that treats any citizen connected with things Western with pathological suspicion. Well, do you think it's possible? How do you imagine it can be done?'

'I think you exaggerate,' I said with a smile. 'Put that way, it sounds absurd. If things were really as bad as you make out, there wouldn't *be* any departments of modern languages – or philology, if you prefer – at our universities. But there are, and Western languages are even taught in schools. At my own school, for example, French –'

It was so neat, this latest manoeuvre. I'd come so close! But Freddy cut in again, and again my path was blocked.

'I think,' he observed, 'you can't have listened carefully to what I said. Did I say that the state forbids the teaching of forreign languages, that it persecutes Frrench, rreprresses English, trries to stamp out German? Surely not. I merely asked what you imagined it's like to work in a field where the subject of study belongs to a world that our People's Rrrepublic of Poland, and the Party that watches over us with such benevolence, trreats with suspicion and dislike – as an evil empire, a hostile power longing only for the chance to leap down our thrroats, to destroy us.'

'I understood you perfectly well, I assure you! It just seems to me that your description of the state of affairs is a little exaggerated, or perhaps . . . perhaps a little out of date. Of course, I don't deny that's how things *used* to be, under Stalinism, and when *you* were at university. But now, today? The Cold War is all but over. The struggle against imperialism is more a kind of ritual than something actively pursued – at least in the cultural sphere. Western books get translated, Western films are screened, Polish jazz musicians travel all over the world. I can't imagine they'd make problems for someone working on Racine, or Pascal, or Rochefoucauld, or similar classics. And anyway, how? What would they do? And what on earth for?'

'How and what for!?' He gave a great hoot of laughter. 'No, honestly, your naïveté is disarming.' He rolled his eyes heavenwards. Then his face suddenly stiffened: some invisible muscle seemed to pull on his upper lip, for it narrowed and tightened in a sort of spasm. At the same time something pulled the corners of his mouth downwards, and his lower lip was thrust out in a grotesque sneer. 'For your information,' he said, '*I* work on Racine. *I* work on Pascal and Rochefoucauld. And I have prroblems all the time. At every turrn.'

'Why?' I asked. I was genuinely surprised. 'What kind of problems?'

'Oh, for God's sake. I see we'll have to start with the basics.' He sighed. 'Your eyes have evidently yet to be opened to some elementary trruths. It's time you came down to earth and saw what it's like. Forgive me, but you sound as if you've been living on another planet, instead of in the reality of our "prrogrressive system".'

He leapt energetically to his feet. Then he entwined his arms behind his back, so that his right hand was wedged in the crook of his left elbow, and in this curious posture, his head now lowered, now tilted up towards the ceiling, began a slow diagonal pacing of the room. His steps were soundless, muffled by the thick, geometrically patterned, claret-coloured carpet. In this way he silently paced back and forth two or three times.

Wer den Dichter will verstehen, Muss in Dichters Lande gehen (Freddy's Story)

'What does one need,' he said at length, 'what do you think is the one thing that's absolutely essential if one wants to study, and rreally get to know, a nation's culturre – its language, its habits, its way of thinking? Clearly,' he pursued, without waiting for an answer, 'one needs to have dirrect contact with that country: its climate, its florra, its people, its monuments, its national trreasures. *Wer den Dichter will verstehen,*' he chanted, '*Muss in Dichters Lande gehen.* Do you know what that means, and who said it?'

'Of course,' I said. 'It's Goethe. "If you want to understand a poet, you must go to his country."'

'Corrrect.' He spoke like a pedantic old schoolmaster. 'Of course, Goethe was talking about the Orrient, but it makes no difference. What's important is that little word *muss.* If you want to understand, you *must* – you *must!*' he cried with a sort of sob, 'go and *see* the land where the poets lived and were born. Otherwise the whole thing's pointless: you'll know as much as a blind man knows about colour. You'll be a prrovincial amateur, all your knowledge drawn from books, like a schoolboy. Now, in the case of Rrromance languages, that means going to Frrance. And did you happen to notice, by any chance, where Frrance is located? That's rright – in the West. Behind the Iron Curtain.' He halted in front of my chair, stooped slightly and glared at me. 'Do you understand what that means? "Polish jazz musicians travel all over the world"! . . . Do you have any idea what that actually involves? The things you have to do before you're allowed to leave? Do you? Besides, a jazz musician isn't quite the same as a scholar studying a forreign culture, especially a forreign language. We're not exactly popular in our People's Rrrepublic. They watch us like hawks, and they keep us on a tight rein. Can you imagine what it's like to work in such conditions? Not verry prropitious for the free flow of ideas, let alone for access to forreign sources. Would you like to know what it's rreally like here? What *I* had to go thrrough when *I* went to the West?' Before I could express any desire one way or the other, he said magnanimously, 'All rright, I'll tell you,' and resumed his diagonal pacing across the carpet.

The monologue on which he now embarked lasted a good half hour, perhaps longer, and was the sort of impassioned tirade one typically hears from people with an obsession. In Freddy's case the obsession was with his superiors. He was in permanent, bitter conflict with every figure in authority he encountered, from the dean to the chairman of the department. He particularly loathed the director of the university Office of Overseas Co-operation, to whom he referred as 'our own dear little police grass'.

Life in the department was intolerable ('and it's like that everywhere'). Mediocrities were promoted and genuine scholars passed over; every decision was the result of intrigue and power play; you had to be 'in' with the right people in order to get anywhere or to get anything done. Scholarship, intelligence, general culture were irrelevant. The only things that counted were enough gall to bulldoze your way through to what you wanted and faithful submission to the regime: services rendered when required, Party membership, connections at the ministry. Without that you didn't have a chance; you'd be reduced to being a provincial schoolteacher or drudge. And you didn't have to make a fuss or show contempt in order to be cut out of a share in the distribution of goods and privileges; it was enough if you were independent and went your own way, especially if your work was good. In fact, this last by itself was sufficient to isolate you. Did I want an example? Certainly, there were plenty. *Voilà* – here's one:

About three years earlier Freddy had written, in French, an article about Racine's *Phèdre*. He had sent it off to a certain Professor Billot in Strasbourg, one of the world's greatest Racine scholars. In reply he had received an extremely friendly letter, full of praise for his *discours excitant*, and an offer of publication in the prestigious journal *Le Classicisme français*. Naturally, he had accepted. The article was published, and a few months later came an invitation to a conference at Tours. His article had been very well received among French scholars in the field; they wanted to meet this unknown author from Poland, talk to him, exchange ideas with him, even collaborate with him on projects of mutual interest. The *colloque*, which was to take place in a beautiful château in Tours, was a perfect opportunity for this. Hence the earnest plea that he accept the invitation and let them know as soon as possible the title of his talk. All his expenses would of course be met: hotel, local transportation and full board, along with the return train fare from Poland (first-class sleeper). He needn't worry about a thing: it would all be taken care of.

He needn't worry about a thing! If you didn't know the French really believed this, you might think it was some kind of cruel joke. For what did this stroke of wonderful luck involve in practice? What kind of trials did it condemn one to?

Never having been abroad, and being therefore unfamiliar with the procedure and the many formalities required, Freddy sought advice from his friend Professor M., an old humanist of the pre-war school. Professor M. was an independent man with an ironic outlook on life and just a touch of cynicism: he observed with perfect equanimity and stoic calm the multi-layered absurdities of the socialist regime, but at the same time refused to be ignored or shunted aside. He read the letter of invitation from Tours, shook his head sadly and explained succinctly what Freddy could do with it.

The best thing would be to frame it and hang it on the wall, because from an official point of view it was worthless. No government functionary, no official at the passport office would even glance at it. For one thing, it was in French. If an invitation was in a foreign language, the first thing you had to do was get it translated into Polish. And not just by anyone: it had to be by a *notarised* translator. In this case, however, obtaining such a translation would be a waste of time and money, for the invitation lacked literally every single basic requirement: it had no stamps or endorsements, no corroboration of any kind from the French *préfecture* of police, the Polish consulate or other vital organs of state. It was a completely worthless scrap of paper, good only for the bin. It's written on the official stationery of the University of Tours, you say? So what? Everyone has access to university stationery; it doesn't come in numbered sheets. What? It's signed by the conference chairman and by Professor Billot? What's that to us? Who are these people, anyway? Do they really exist? He might have invented them. How is the passport office supposed to know? The passport office can believe only what it's told by the appropriate organs of state administration, namely the *police* of the country issuing the invitation and the *consulate* of the People's Republic of Poland. Nothing else will make the slightest impression upon them. So if this sweet, carefree little *billet-doux* was to be of any use to him, he must apply at once to its sender for the appropriate endorsements from the Polish consulate and from the French *préfecture*. And this, of course, takes time and money. But since the hosts seem so eager to have us, let them pay – *let them pay*! It's only through paying that they can prove the sincerity of their interest in us.

In this case, however, Professor M. advised against such a move. For even if Freddy were to explain to Professor Billot the demands of the Polish passport authorities, and even if Professor Billot then obtained the required endorsements, the trip remained highly doubtful. In fact, Freddy probably wouldn't even get as far as the application stage. Why? For the simple reason that a passport application also had to be endorsed at one's place of work. This meant, in effect, that Freddy would have to obtain leave (paid or unpaid) for the duration of the conference. And who was going to give him that? The chairman, with whom he was at loggerheads? His superior, the envious professor who held the chair in seventeenth-century literature? Not likely. How's that? Just for a week, even less, a mere five days? Oh, but unfortunately that was just the time when his presence would be essential. Quite indispensable, in fact.

Was there no solution, then? Was there nothing to be done?

Oh, no, it wasn't that bad. There were things one could do. They were made possible by the Office of Overseas Co-operation, the administrative section of the university created for that very purpose. Before grasping at this hand of assistance, however, one had to be aware of certain principles governing 'exchanges abroad'.

It must be stressed, first of all, that it is not up to the West to decide who is to represent our People's Republic. That would be a deplorable interference in our internal affairs. The duty of the West, if it desires a Polish presence, is to supply grants, send invitations to lectures and conferences and request experts in the field. But the choice should belong to us. We're the ones who know best who the appropriate candidates are; only we can decide who it's safe to send, who we can rely on not to embarrass us. How on earth is the West supposed to know things like that?! Of course, there are 'special cases': people who can be trusted, reliable people who are politically mature. *Those* kinds of people *can* receive invitations in their names. But that's a different story. The point is that this simple system has a loophole, a tiny little crack, and this crack can be widened into a tunnel which may, if you dig in the right direction, get you through to the other side.

The loophole exists because the West is petty and mean, and deplorably stingy with its invitations and offers of collaboration, which come extremely seldom. As a result, the smallest grant, the tiniest subsidy, even for just a few days' visit, is worth its weight in gold. That's because people who are trustworthy and politically mature long to go to the West: a trip to the West is their most cherished dream, and if they don't get it they are inconsolable. It's just how they are. Out of concern for their welfare, therefore, our sensible People's government has worked out a clever compromise: it will agree to let out the people on whose presence the West, for obscure (and generally suspicious) reasons of its own, seems to have set its heart, in exchange for a second invitation, with the understanding that this time the choice of who is to have the honour of representing Polish learning is to be left to us. This is a splendid arrangement, beneficial to all concerned: the wolf (i.e., the West) is sated – it gets its dinner, and more than it asked for. And the lamb (i.e., ourselves) is safe – we send someone who really needs and deserves it (a trustworthy and politically mature individual), and the West's protégé (a suspicious and quite unreliable individual) gets invaluable support in the form of a guardian angel.

In other words, if Freddy wants to go to Tours he must write at once to Professor Billot and explain the situation in a suitable way, the suitable way being, in this case, to set out the basic truths: namely, that Poland is a subjugated country and a police state where a professional trip beyond the Iron Curtain can be made only in the company of a 'guardian'. Then some purely technical instructions on how to word the invitation to the conference, what kind of information to include (the amount of the *per diem* and the promise that all expenses will be met), and to what address to send it (Warsaw University, Department of Romance Languages).

A letter of this kind cannot be sent by post in the ordinary way, of course: our correspondence, especially our foreign correspondence, is watched and controlled like everything else. The consequences for Freddy if such a letter got into the hands of the secret police did not bear thinking about. He could say goodbye once and for all to trips abroad, maybe even to his university post. No, a confidential letter like this must be sent through 'reliable channels' by a 'courier'. The diplomatic bag would be the best solution.

If Freddy wanted to avail himself of Professor M.'s help,

the latter was at his disposal. He had the appropriate contacts. He could also help in the crucial matter of how to word the invitation, for he had a tried and tested model: it fulfilled all the requirements and also precluded the possibility of manipulation. For Freddy should be aware that such a transaction was complex and delicate. The invitation must contain no hint of blackmail (blackmail would never succeed anyway, for reasons of principle), but it must be made quite clear that it was addressed to one specific person and to that person alone. This was essential, for otherwise the 'other' might go without you or, worse still, in the company of someone else entirely.

It was all very difficult. Western academics, with their fine ideas and their heads in the clouds, hadn't a clue what it was like, and in their innocent naïveté they could cause trouble. God knows it had happened often enough: the conditions hadn't been spelt out clearly or firmly enough, the necessary provisos had been missing, and the person who had ended up going was someone entirely different from the person intended, and specified by name, in the invitation. So one had to be very careful. And the best way of making sure that the instructions got across was . . . simply to dictate the invitation, word for word.

Well, that was the picture. Now it was up to Freddy to make up his mind.

He struggled all night. Write the letter? Or just forget about it? It was a nightmare, a disgusting, humiliating, degrading process. On the other hand, if he didn't write it he wouldn't go to Tours. Was that not, in the end, too high a price to pay? What would he gain? Only the knowledge that he had submitted to principle, the satisfaction that he had asked nothing of anyone, the pride of having shown he didn't care. Cold comfort. Moreover, it wasn't entirely honest: he did care. And what would he lose? Invaluable experience, the chance to meet and exchange ideas with inspiring people, access to books and sources, a chance of furthering his career. Quite a lot to give up. Wouldn't it be a pity? After all, let's not exaggerate. The task before him – explaining to the French 'in a suitable way' what they must do to enable him to fulfil their wishes and lecture in Tours – wasn't so horrendous. It wasn't an abomination. He wouldn't be doing anything contemptible, denouncing anyone or selling out. He had only to provide a few instructions. The circumstances, after all, were such as they were; he wasn't responsible for them. And when they were being created the West hadn't lifted a finger. Who had sold off Poland at Yalta? Who had washed his hands of Poland like Pontius Pilate? Let them see what they've condemned us to!

He wrote the letter.

Professor M. helped him as promised. The letter was whisked off to France in the diplomatic bag and shortly found its way to its intended recipient. The answer was not long in coming. Yes, they understood, they would do everything required. There was just one problem: their budget was limited. Consequently they begged Freddy's indulgence, but he must understand that since there were now two people coming instead of one, they were unable to offer the same conditions as before. The train could unfortunately no longer be first class – alas, the budget would not even run to a couchette; there would be one double room at the hotel, and the *per diem* would have to be split between the two of them.

This was not cheering news. But what did it matter if it made the trip feasible, if it meant he could go to France? Very little – almost nothing at all. If anything mattered, it was the question of whom the department would send as the 'other'. Obviously it would have to be a Party member – but who? The head of the department? The chairman? That cunning old opportunist Professor Levittoux? Actually, he wouldn't be so bad. He had pre-war manners and quite a good brain, and his Party membership was pure opportunism. But he was unlikely.

Not long afterwards the director of the Office of Overseas Co-operation, a certain Gabriel Gromek, MA, summoned Freddy to his office for what was known as a 'little talk'. He began by asking him how he came to be acquainted with '*Mr*' Billot and through what channels he had established contact with the university in Tours. He then proceeded to upbraid him, quite severely, for publishing his work in a foreign journal without prior approval, indeed without even trying to obtain such approval or so much as consulting anyone ('quite unacceptable behaviour!'). Finally, indicating that the matter was a mere formality, he asked Freddy to sign a brief promise of loyalty to the Polish government during his trip abroad. This well-known trap was the means whereby pressure was later exerted to draw people into collaboration with the secret police. Freddy was speechless. But he concealed his consternation and, knowing full well that if he did not go, neither would anyone else, replied poker-faced that in that case, thank you very much, but if these were the conditions he would rather not go at all. Too bad, but never mind, he could live without it. It wasn't so important. And he rose to leave.

'Good heavens, Dr Monten, there's no need to take it like that!' exclaimed the director of the Office of Overseas Cooperation, furiously backpedalling; 'No need to take offence. No one's forcing you. If you don't want to sign, fine, we'll just take your word for it. All these precautions are for your own good, you know. You haven't yet been to the West, you've no idea what it's like. Conferences and symposia are just the bait – the carrot they dangle in front of you to get you there. It's your collaboration they're really after: they want you to become their agent. They'll take you out for coffee or to dinner in a restaurant, and before you know it you'll be betraying your country. Oh yes, they have their ways! They'll flatter you and fawn over you, and then they'll offer you money to sweeten the deal – just to open you up. Literature, classics, Racine' – he pronounced it *Rah-sign* – 'my aunt! All they want is to squeeze information out of you and to get you to slander and defame our people's democracy. They'll be lying in wait for you in the corridors during the breaks. We know what they're like! That's how they operate. So I'm warning you: be vigilant!'

Freddy listened to these ravings with an utterly bland expression, as if he hadn't quite grasped what they were about. Assuming an air of studied distraction (the young scholar absorbed in his books, head in clouds), he asked, with seeming irrelevance, whether he would be going alone or accompanied on this 'delegation'.

'You will be accompanied by Dr Dolowy,' he heard in reply.

Dolowy! Unbelievable! The last person he would have expected. Although perhaps it wasn't so surprising: assistant professor Dolowy was, after all, secretary of the Party Organisation and the dean's right-hand man. Still, there were limits. The man was a blockhead. He didn't even speak proper French! Of course the only reason he was going was to keep an eye on things, but even so . . . they might at least have sent someone with *some* knowledge of something. All *he* knew about was Louis Aragon and his precious Soviet Union. It was ridiculous. Who had suggested him? Who had approved it? Don't they realise they're making fools of themselves? They'll be the laughing-stock of the academic world. But perhaps they don't care . . . After all, sooner or later someone else will be invited and then some other Dolowy will get to hitch a ride on his coat-tails.

In the event, his fears proved unfounded, or at least excessive. Not that Dolowy suddenly revealed an unsuspected side to his nature, but his presence at the conference in Tours proved less burdensome than Freddy had expected. In fact, the man was hardly ever there. He put in an appearance just three times: once at the beginning, when he came to pick up his *per diems* and his meal vouchers for the cafeteria; once on the third day, for Freddy's lecture; and at the final banquet, given by the hosts in an elegant restaurant. If it hadn't been for his snoring and smoking and his habit of eating tinned sprats in oil (an impressive stock of which he had brought with him) off a sheet of newspaper, he would have been quite harmless.

What did he do all day? Visit museums and monuments? Unlikely. Go shopping, sit around in cafés? Likelier, but still doubtful. He was on a tight budget and counted every penny. Perhaps, then, he was carrying out some secret mission for the Polish secret police?

One night Freddy was awakened by curious noises coming from the other side of the room – a sort of muffled clanking sound, like something knocking against something. He raised an eyelid and saw a light: the lamp on Dolowy's bedside table. Dolowy himself, crouched in an ungainly pose, was rummaging around in his suitcase. Feigning sleep, Freddy continued to observe him through half-closed lids. But he failed to determine what the fellow was doing, and couldn't identify the source of the mysterious clanking sound emanating from the bottom of the suitcase.

The following morning, when Dolowy was in the shower, Freddy crept out of bed and with beating heart risked a peek at the man's luggage. There, under a pile of dirty linen – socks, handkerchiefs, underwear – were rows and rows of little glass jars with blue lids. Ossietra caviar. On each lid was a picture of a sturgeon against a background of grains of roe. There were dozens of them.

Now the light dawned: Dolowy was dealing on the black market. In Poland, Soviet caviar was a fraction of the price it cost in the West. The profit on one jar was mind-boggling, even if you sold it for half its usual Western price: some ten or fifteen dollars. It was a fantastic business operation – and with almost no risk. No one was much bothered if you took caviar out of Poland: since it was imported from the Soviet Union to begin with, it wasn't subject to duty, at least not in retail quantities. And was anyone in the West going to rifle through your bags to see what you were bringing in? Once in France, there was no lack of eager punters to take it off your hands: elegant restaurants would buy as much as they could and be grateful for it. It was a sweet deal all round.

Freddy later calculated that the total value of the caviar stashed in the depths of Dolowy's bags came to at least three hundred and fifty dollars. In Poland that was enough for the cheapest car: a second-hand Syrena or a Fiat 600.

Dr Dolowy had higher aspirations, however. Or so, at least, one could be led to believe by his unstinting efforts to increase this miraculously obtained capital still further. For the secretary of the Party Organisation, having coolly liquidated his stock of caviar, proceeded, not being one to rest on his laurels, to invest some of his newly acquired funds in several thousand ballpoints – not the pens themselves, just the little ball attached to the cartridge. In France, the realm of the Bic, they were of no use to anyone, but in Poland, a country of titanic enterprise and construction on a vast scale, where there was no room for such unimportant details, they were priceless. Those concerned with the production of pens – private entrepreneurs whose task it was to fill the various gaps in Poland's light industry – were ready to pay any price for basic parts like this. And so – more profit. Enough, perhaps, for a second-hand Wartburg?

At the final banquet Freddy did all he could to stay as far away as possible from his colleague, and especially to avoid being seated next to him at dinner. His efforts were vain. Dolowy somehow always contrived to manoeuvre himself into a nearby position. When they sat down he slyly insinuated himself into the seat just opposite Freddy, who was on Professor Billot's right. Freddy clenched his teeth and briefly closed his eyes. His enjoyment had been spoilt. Now he wouldn't be able to relax; instead of relishing the *délicieuse ambience* of the evening, talking freely and animatedly, he would be tense and embarrassed. And things could get worse: the boor might start talking himself, joking and showing off. And what if he drank too much? The very thought made Freddy break out in a cold sweat. He felt weak with shame.

This time, alas, his fears proved well founded, although Dolowy's performance was not the nightmare he had envisaged. It began with his assuming the role of benevolent protector or devoted impresario, in which part he launched, for Professor Billot's benefit, into an importunate and effusive torrent of elaborate praise. The object of his excesses was Freddy.

'He's the best we have!' he insisted, as if Freddy were some competitor or object for sale. 'He's our pride and joy. Respected by specialists in the field and adored by his students. It's thanks to him that our department has been enjoying such fame and popularity. Young people from all disciplines flock to us in droves. And that's why French culture, especially seventeenth-century French literature, so dear to all of us here, has found thousands of admirers in our country. It's all his doing; he's absolutely priceless. I, who specialise in Louis Aragon, can't compare with him. No one else in Poland has done so much for France. He's more than just a spokesman for France – he's a veritable ambassador! So you see he must, he absolutely must, remain in constant touch with his spiritual homeland. His visits to France are invaluable, not just for him, but for all those who draw, and wish to go on drawing, from this well, this inexhaustible treasure-house –'

'Please, please,' Freddy moaned in Polish, 'please stop.'

'*Quoi? Qu'est-ce qu'il a dit?*' asked Professor Billot.

'*Il est très modeste*,' Dr Dolowy hastened to explain, with a protective smile. 'He wants me to stop praising him. But you should listen to me, Monsieur le Professeur. His visits to France will benefit us all. I'm relying on you.'

Freddy was saved from further torment by a waiter bearing the first course: blinis with caviar. Dolowy broke off in mid-sentence. '*Oh la la! Quelles délices!*' he cried. '*C'est un festin royal!*' And he inquired of the waiter what kind of caviar it was.

'The best. Ossietra,' the waiter proudly announced. 'And fresh – straight from Russia. We have our own suppliers.'

On Dolowy's thick, caviar-smeared lips, open in eagerness to admit another heaped portion, a faint and playful smile lingered and was gone.

Freddy returned to Poland in a high state of nerves. Things had gone well – indeed, more smoothly than he had expected – but he felt no elation. In fact, he felt awful: stifled, humiliated and somehow soiled. Those soaring flights of the spirit, that pure crystal which was the poetry of his beloved Racine, that whole world of subtle ideas and perfect forms had been curiously polluted. Here was harmony and grace, the beauty of ancient ideals, French *clarté* at its best – and obscenely in the middle of it was Soviet caviar under a pile of dirty underwear, peddled surreptitiously in some dingy, suspicious spot, and on top of that some smaller cargo – ballpoints for pens! – intended for illegal trade with Polish 'private enterprise'. It was ugly and sordid and defiling.

And that wasn't all. He had left for France like a proud aristocrat of the spirit subjected to the indignity of being spied on by a miserable wretch who would then write up a surveillance report about him. But who had been the one to poke about in other people's luggage? Who was now in possession of damaging information about a colleague? Against his will, *he* had ended up as the spy and the potential grass! Knowing what he knew, he was in a position to ruin Dolowy and certainly to blackmail him. 'So, my friend, how did it go this time with the caviar? No hitches? How much did you get for it? Make a good profit, did you? And those ballpoints, you seem to be on to a good thing there!' And he could go on tormenting him in this fashion, making it clear that an attack on his part would not go unrevenged. Revolting, wasn't it? Especially since Dolowy clearly had no hostile intentions. On the contrary, he seemed prepared to be supportive (albeit only in his own interests). Of course, Freddy wouldn't have dreamed of denouncing Dolowy, even in his own defence, let alone of resorting to blackmail as a preventive measure. But the very fact that such a possibility had even occurred to him made him angry and disgusted with himself.

The worst thing was the humiliation. He was acutely, painfully aware that he had been bartered in, like of a piece of goods. His person, his talent, his understanding of Racine were nothing but merchandise to be peddled. 'Scientific exchange', my foot! It was trade in human livestock! He had been the object of a transaction; he had been hired out, like a thing, like a slave. And for what? For a few hundred dollars' worth of shady dealing, so that Dolowy could earn a little extra on the side through a bit of semi-legal trade and get a bigger place or a car. It was intolerable.

When he got back to Warsaw, he decided he would never again agree to go abroad under such conditions. If those were the rules of the game, he wanted no part of it. He'd find other ways of getting out of the country. He'd show them yet.

Unfortunately this was not easy. Professor M. was right: there were very few chinks in the Iron Curtain that one could slip through. And Freddy, in his laborious attempts to exploit them, got himself hopelessly entangled in an interminable string of procedures, so that he was forever running about after forms, signatures, references, assurances, guarantees and all the other essential requirements for a passport. It was a never-ending battle, and the machine against which he was pitted was truly infernal. His life became one long obstacle course.

But Freddy's struggles were not in vain. Once a year, on average, they bore fruit, and he got his passport. It was a 'private' tourist passport – not to be confused with the 'special' passport you got through the university when you were sent abroad to a conference or on an exchange, still less with the subtly different 'professional' passport, also obtained through the institution you worked for, let alone the 'consular' and 'diplomatic' passports, which were a different kettle of fish. So roughly once a year Freddy got to go to France – usually in the summer, during the holidays, when academic life in both countries was at a standstill. Work-wise, therefore, he derived little profit from his visits, apart from being able to work in the archives and libraries. Sightseeing or taking advantage of the various specialties France had to offer in the way of material culture was out of the question. He was terribly hard-up. The amount of hard currency he could legally take out of Poland was all of five dollars. He supplemented it as best he could with the publication fees for his articles and the occasional small grant from some institution where a sympathetic French friend could exert influence, but it was barely enough to live on. If he wanted to stay for the full time allotted to him, he had to deny himself more or less everything: restaurants, cafés, even the most modest shopping. He visited museums only on the days when there was no entrance fee; theatres and cinemas were out unless someone invited him.

And yet, in spite of his poverty, he felt a different person. He felt free. Free from worry and tension and stress, from the sensation of being besieged, from the fearful knowledge that every encounter with the outside world meant another conflict, another battle, out of which he would come crushed, downtrodden, humiliated. In France he felt none of that. In France, even though he was nothing – a foreigner, and from Eastern Europe at that, without a penny to his name – he wasn't afraid. He was serene. He was normal. He was himself.

As the time of his return approached, his serenity began to crack. 'It's like the rreturn of some sickness!' Freddy cried in an anguished voice. 'With every day that passes it gets worse.

You feel weaker and weaker, you lose all your taste for life; everything starts to seem hopeless and you sink into a kind of lethargy . . . Wait, I'll rread you something.' He went up to a bookshelf and took down a volume in French. 'Listen,' he said (I give the passage in translation):

> When they come through here on their way to Europe they have a gay, free, happy air. They are like horses returned to pasture, like birds who have flown the cage – men, women, young, old, all are as happy as schoolchildren on a holiday. The same people, on their return, have long, gloomy tormented faces; they have a worried look. Their conversation is brief and their speech abrupt. I have concluded from this difference that a country which one leaves with so much joy and returns to with so much regret is a bad country.

'Did you get that, or shall I translate it?'

'No, that's fine,' I said quietly, dazed by the things I'd heard.

'What do you think this passage is about? Who are the people it rrefers to?'

I shrugged. 'I don't know . . . I've no idea.'

'It's about Rrrussians!' Freddy cried. 'Nineteenth-century Rrrussians! From the time of Tsar Nicholas the First. Do you understand what that means? It means we've become just like them! They've succeeded in *trrans-forrm-ing* us! The rreds have succeeded where the white tsars couldn't!'

'Who wrote it?'

'The Marquis de Custine. A Frrench arristocrat. In 1839. To be exact, it's his report of something he heard frrom an innkeeper in Lübeck, who often came in contact with travelling Rrrussians. Those were his observations.'

La belle Victoire

I decided there was no point in besieging Freddy any longer with insidious questions. I would not get the information I wanted. Besides, I'd lost my enthusiasm for the game. The thick and entirely unexpected hail of information with which I'd been pummelled during the past hour had distanced me from Madame. I wanted only to be gone, out in the street and alone with my thoughts, to digest in peace and quiet the things I'd heard and put them into some kind of order in my mind. So when Freddy at last paused for breath, I saw my chance and took it.

'Thank you for letting me take up so much of your time,' I said. 'I'm very grateful. And you've persuaded me: I'll find something else to study. I understand everything now.' And I rose to go.

'Pleasure,' said Freddy. 'I'm glad I could be of some use.'

When we came out and Freddy switched on the light in the hall, Constant emerged from his study and joined us. 'Well?' he asked.

'Well, your son did a good job,' I said, spreading my arms in resignation. 'He convinced me.'

'I'm pleased to hear it. Very pleased.'

'Why should he get caught up in it!' exclaimed Freddy, as if summing up the proceedings. 'It's a madhouse! All that frrenzied rrunning about each time you want to go abroad, the agitation, the parranoia about people trying to escape . . . And I've spared you the worrst,' he said, turning to me, 'the stories about people who start going mad because they can't take it any more and decide they really will get the hell out, and the consequences for them as well as for the ones who stay behind. The atmosphere of suspicion, the speculation – who's planning something on the sly, who's preparing the ground . . . And then, he's gone . . . Will he come back? . . . or will he stay? . . . Will he, won't he . . . he didn't! . . . Who will it be next? . . . This one asked for political asylum! . . . That one stayed! . . . That one got married to get a passport!'

'Do you mean,' I interrupted, 'Dr Surowa-Léger?' I seized upon his words without thinking, startling myself no less than him.

Freddy paused and looked at me carefully. 'How do you know about that?'

Fully aware now of the risk I was taking, I made the move that exposed my queen. 'From my French teacher,' I replied calmly. 'She was her thesis adviser. And once, when she was talking about it –'

'Surrowa-Léger was her thesis adviser?' Freddy broke in.

'I think that was the name. I'm pretty sure that's what she said . . .'

'And who is this Frrench teacher of yours?' he inquired. 'What's her name?'

Controlling my voice with difficulty, I delivered up poor Madame.

'What?!' Freddy cried in amazement, and then gave a nervous little laugh. 'So . . . La belle Victoire . . . is a *school-teacher*?!'

I caught my breath. *La belle Victoire* – so that was what they called her! Perhaps, then, 'Victoire' wasn't just a name for official or family use but was the name she was known by?

'She's not just an ordinary teacher,' I explained. 'She's the headmistress. And a fairly unusual one at that: she's supposed to reform the school and make it into one of those experimental outposts where everything is taught in French . . . Anyway, what's so strange about it?'

Freddy and Constant exchanged a meaningful look and a couple of knowing nods. 'So she rreally did it,' said Freddy, in a sad sort of undertone, more to himself than to us.

'What do you mean? What did she do?' I asked. The suspense was unbearable.

'Oh, nothing, nothing . . . *ce n'est pas important*,' he muttered dismissively. Then, clearly anxious to avoid further discussion of the topic, he turned to his father and said briskly, 'Well, I'll be going, too.' And reached for his coat.

I did the same. But when I realised that my gloves were not in their usual place in my anorak pockets but wedged behind the coat rack, I did not retrieve them. Instead, acting on some impulse, I stuffed them even deeper into their hiding-place and covered them discreetly with my host's hat, which hung on a hook just above.

On my way downstairs with Freddy I expected at any

moment to hear the rasp of a bolt being pulled back, the creak of a door opening and Constant's voice summoning me back for the forgotten gloves. But nothing happened.

We came out into the street and the November evening. It was wet, dark and foggy. Freddy was silent, absorbed in his thoughts; and I somehow couldn't bring myself to speak. In silence we approached the first crossroads.

'I'm going this way,' I said, slowing down. 'And you?'

'I go strraight, strraight on,' he said indifferently, as if woken abruptly from a deep sleep.

'Well, then, goodbye. And thank you again.'

''Bye,' he said, and shook my hand. 'And good luck.'

I went down the side street for about fifty yards, turned and retraced my steps to the corner. Freddy had vanished into the darkness and fog. I started back at a run.

It was exactly ten minutes past seven o'clock in the evening when for the second time that day I pressed the white porcelain knob of the pre-war bell in its decorative surround recessed in the right frame of the door.

Maximilian and Claire

'Yes?' came Constant's voice from behind the door.

'I'm sorry, it's me again. I forgot my gloves.'

I heard a brisk, matter-of-fact 'Ah . . .' in reply, and then the sound of the bolt being drawn back.

'Completely absent-minded, as you see,' I babbled as I came in. 'Freddy's stories affected me so strongly that I don't know what I'm doing.'

'I told you,' said Constant, shrugging and turning to the coat rack to look for my gloves. 'I warned you.'

'You know what struck me most about all this?' I went on, throwing out the question like a lasso, trying to rope him in and hold him back from his quest.

'What?' He stopped in his tracks. The loop had caught.

'That whole atmosphere of suspicion, and the paranoia about escaping. Honestly, I'd no idea things were as bad as that.'

'Alas,' he replied sadly, approaching the coat rack.

I decided there was no time to be lost. 'Still, what a small world!' I sighed. 'I just *happen*, in passing, to mention my French teacher, and it turns out that Freddy knows her . . . and you seem to know her, too . . . at least that was the impression I got.'

'Do I know her!' Constant exclaimed, laughing and once again interrupting his search for my gloves. 'I've known her from the day she was born!'

I froze. It was like suddenly finding a gold mine right in front of my door. 'Really?' I drawled in a thin, slightly bored, drawing-room-chitchat sort of voice. 'That's amazing!' And then, offhandedly, 'How is that?'

'I knew her father well,' he explained. 'We used to go climbing together. In '34 we did Mont Blanc –'

'In '34?' I broke in.

'Yes, that's right. Why?'

'Oh, no reason – I just wondered,' I said, desperately casting around for a plausible-sounding explanation. 'In summer, of course?' I added, in the knowing tones of one who was an expert in the matter.

'Naturally in summer,' he confirmed, 'but what does that have to do with it?'

'I just wanted to make sure I knew which expedition you were talking about,' I said, alighting on the only thing that came to mind. As an explanation it was not spectacular, but it would have to do. Meanwhile I did some rapid mental arithmetic; '34, I thought: so she was conceived by then.

'In '34 I went to the Alps only once,' said Constant, for the record.

'Do go on, it's very interesting,' I said, back to my drawing-room small-talk voice, as if I were more interested in Alpine adventures than in Madame's father. 'So you went up Mont Blanc . . .?'

'He was a strange man. Like two people combined in one: a pedant and a rationalist, and at the same time a romantic, a dreamer. Scrupulous and reliable on the one hand – more than reliable: absolutely infallible, like a Swiss watch. If he made an appointment or a promise, you knew he would keep it, come hell or high water. He wouldn't fail you even if the world was crashing down around his ears. And on the other, an idealist, full of the most extraordinary flights of fancy. Sometimes the two came together: for instance, he liked to make appointments a ridiculously long time in advance, sometimes in places that were completely unfamiliar to him – even though he had no idea what the future held, and knew full well that it usually held surprises. And, like Phileas Fogg, he would always turn up precisely at the stated time – no confirmation, no checking of details, nothing.

'I remember one occasion like that. One day in late November we bumped into each other in the street, here in Warsaw, and began talking. He said he was just off to the mountains, the Schwarzwald first and then Chamonix for some winter climbing. I said I was also planning a trip to the Alps, but to Switzerland, and not until the summer. He began asking me for details: he'd never been to the Swiss Alps and very much wanted to go. I told him what I knew at the time; my plans were fairly concrete by then, although of course I didn't yet have all the details.

'"So when and where can we meet?" he asked suddenly, out of the blue.

'I was taken aback: I didn't even know when I would get there, or where I would be staying. The only thing I knew was the name of the place I was going to, and that I had to be there at the latest by the fifth of August.

'"Well, then, let's say the sixth, at noon, in front of the train station. That suit you?" he asked, glancing at his diary.

'I thought he was joking. But he wasn't – he was quite serious. And of course I needn't add that he was there, on the dot of noon.'

'That *is* amazing,' I said. 'But tell me something about your Mont Blanc trip.'

'Yes,' he said. The search for my gloves had by now been abandoned. 'Now that's a story that illustrates the other side of his nature. It began with an older friend of his, a well-known mountaineer with a fanatical love of the mountains. This man had one obsession: he wanted his child to be born on Mont Blanc. Not right at the top, of course – that would have been too much – but as near to it as possible: in the famous Vallot refuge, just below the peak. And in the winter of '26, when his wife was seven months pregnant, he attempted to realise his dream: he dragged her up there. But nothing came of it. After a snowstorm that lasted a week and almost blew the refuge off the face of the earth, they decided to go back down and have the birth in the normal way. On the way down, in the blizzard, an ice-bridge collapsed. It was a miracle they survived and she didn't miscarry.

'In spite of this, or perhaps because of it, my peculiar friend became infected with the same bizarre idea: he, too, decided that he wanted his progeny to come into the world near the top of Mont Blanc. And as soon as he found out that he was to be a father, off he went to the Alps to see what conditions were like and prepare the ground. That was when we climbed Mont Blanc together.'

'In '34,' I put in, just to make absolutely sure.

'Yes, yes, in '34. When we were setting out he didn't say a word about any of this. It wasn't until we were almost at the summit that he confessed what his true purpose was. I thought it was madness – especially since his wife (unlike that other, who at least was an experienced mountaineer) had no qualifications for that kind of thing, quite apart from being pregnant.'

'And who *was* his wife?' I asked, in a tone of polite, offhand inquiry.

'Oh, she was a very interesting person. Out of the ordinary. A strong woman. Not physically – physically she was frail – but she had great strength of character.'

'No, but what did she do, I mean?' I insisted, as if I were not really very interested in what she was like, and thinking that sooner or later we were bound to return to the topic anyway.

'She worked for the Centre de Civilisation Française. Do you know what that was? – and still is, I suppose.' He gave a bitter little laugh, and added, 'Although only in a sense.'

'Yes, I've heard of it, but I don't know exactly.'

'It's an institution for the propagation of French culture and art throughout the world. Before the war it had the status of an academic institution: you could do a French university degree there. It was an élite place, very prestigious. They set up a branch in Poland in '24, I think . . . I remember they had their offices in Staszic House, where the Academy of Sciences is – you know, that building behind the Copernicus statue . . .'

'Yes, I know the one you mean: where the New World Boulevard ends and the Krakowskie Przedmiescie begins . . .'

'Yes, that's right. In the Gold Room, on the first floor, on the right.' He smiled a nostalgic smile and seemed to lapse into a daydream.

I waited politely until he might reasonably be considered to have had his fill of memories, and then plucked him delicately from his reverie with another question. 'Well? Did they go?'

'Go?' he repeated, lost for a moment. 'Oh, you mean my romantic and Claire!'

'Claire?' I asked, seizing upon the name.

'That's what he called her. Her name was Klara.'

'Was she French, then, not Polish?' My tone was still offhand, indifferent.

'What Frenchwoman would have agreed to go on an escapade like that!'

'So they did go, I take it.'

'Yes, indeed. In September – to give her a chance to acclimatise.'

'And did they succeed?' I asked with a smile of disbelief.

'Perhaps not quite in the way he would have liked . . . but still, the lady who is your French teacher today was indeed born in the Alps.'

'You mean out in the open air, in the second half of January?' I asked, involuntarily giving myself away. But Constant, if he noticed my slip, gave no sign of it.

'Well, yes, the time of year wasn't very propitious. Which, frankly, was just as well: I hate to think what would have happened if it had been summer. As it was, the whole thing was kept more or less within the bounds of common sense.'

'How do you mean?'

'I mean that she didn't give birth on a mountaintop, in the clouds, in temperatures of twenty degrees below zero, but in some village down in the valley, in an ordinary house, with a doctor.'

Pity, I thought: it would have been appropriate, given the icy cold that blows from her. A fitting birth for the Ice Queen.

'Your peculiar friend must have been inconsolable,' I remarked, wondering how to set the snare that would get me his name. '*A propos,* what was his name?'

'Max. Maximilian. Like Franz Joseph's brother. And Robespierre, too, of course. An ideal name for him.'

'Because he was so radical, or even fanatical?'

'Not quite,' Constant replied. 'He was a *maximalist.* In all sorts of ways. He wanted to take everything to its extreme, to carry things through to the end. I can see how that could be fascinating in a man. Perhaps that was why she was so much in love with him.'

'You mean his wife?'

'Mmm . . .' A strange sadness seemed to overtake him. 'Come, I'll show you something,' he said, turning and leading the way to his study. I followed, discreetly unzipping my anorak.

The study was small, about ten feet by twelve, and stuffed to overflowing with books and papers. Here and there, poking out of the disorder, were startling objects from another world: a pickaxe, gleaming silver in the light; some hooks; something that might have been a safety-lamp; blue-patterned climbing ropes and a green safety-helmet. On the floor under the window stood an enormous wireless set with a 'magic eye' in the middle, its white keys like teeth bared in a smile; along the shelves, in front of the piles of books stacked there, were dozens of stones and pieces of rock. The only real piece of furniture was a drop-leaf desk with a decorative shelf (which held the telephone) and rows of pigeonholes, drawers and little nooks and crannies. The desktop – that is, the inside of the leaf – was fitted with a leather-bound blotter, and in the upper right-hand corner, next to the border by the hinge, was a round recess, presumably for an inkwell.

On the desktop, supported from below by two extensible rods, sat a typewriter, its cover off and a sheet of paper with a carbon in the roller. In the light cast by the desk lamp that sat beside the telephone on the little shelf, the name Erika, in flowery script, gleamed on its black-lacquered surface. Constant pushed it aside, opened the middle drawer with the little key protruding from its lock, and from that tabernacle within the desk's altar took an old, dark, cloth-covered album with worn edges. He unwound the rubber band that held it tight, turned over a few pages and held the open book up to the light of the lamp.

'Look,' he said, 'here they are. It was taken then, up there.' I came closer and looked. 'It's signed: the fifth of November. Thirty-two years ago,' he added, and fell silent.

The old photograph, small and almost borderless, showed a slim man and a dark-haired woman against a background of snowy peaks. The man was wearing a windbreaker and an outlandish beret; she had on a thick sweater and sunglasses pushed up over her hair. He was gazing upwards, squinting slightly; she was looking at him and smiling. If it had been undated, if the paper on which it was printed had been newer, and if I hadn't been told in advance what it was, I would probably have thought it was a photograph of Madame. Those same intelligent eyes, the same line of the nose, the same shape of the lips. The one difference was that while Madame's features were sharp and severe (there was something birdlike about her), her mother's were soft and gentle, and her look was almost tender. It might have been because she was expecting a child, but not necessarily. Perhaps Madame had inherited her coldness and severity from her father?

'You said she had great force of character?' I asked, picking up the thread I had purposely left trailing during the earlier conversation.

'Oh, yes. She may have been physically frail, but in spirit she was tough and courageous. She bore hardships calmly and cheerfully – she could laugh and joke even when there was very little to laugh about. You know how women are afraid of labour . . . how nervous they are when they're expecting . . .'

'Umm, yes, I've heard something to that effect,' I muttered uncertainly.

'Well, then, imagine what it must have been like, on top of that, to be faced with a complete change of conditions: new surroundings, a different climate, being far from home, the uncertainty of an unknown place . . .'

'Yes, I can imagine,' I said earnestly, gazing at the bookshelves.

'Well, she didn't change at all. She was just as she'd always been: calm and serene, good-humoured, able to laugh at herself. I say that not just because of what he told me,' he said, motioning with his head at the photograph. He put aside the album and took a worn book with a brown paper cover off a small bookshelf above the lamp. 'This says something about her, too.' He opened it carefully at the title page. The words were printed in Gothic script and there was a faded inscription in pencil. The frontispiece showed a photograph of a building façade with steps leading up to a front door. '*Jugendleben und Wanderbilder*,' he read out, in a good German accent. Then he pointed to the bottom of the page. It said: Danziger Verlagsgesellschaft, Danzig 1922. 'This is the Gdansk edition of the memoirs of Joanna Schopenhauer,' he explained, and then glanced at me. 'Do you know anything about her?'

'I just know that she was Schopenhauer's mother,' I admitted.

'Well, that's better than nothing. And why do you think her memoirs were published in Gdansk?'

I shrugged. 'I've no idea.'

'Because that's where she was *born*,' he said with emphasis, as if my ignorance in the matter were some outrageous failing. 'Right here, in this house,' he said, pointing at the frontispiece, 'on the south side of Holy Spirit Street. Her famous philosopher son was also born there. Didn't you learn that in your philosophy lessons or whatever they're called now?'

'Propaedeu –' I began, but he didn't let me finish.

'That's right – propaedeutics!' He repeated the pretentious term with a sneer. 'Propaedeutics in Marxism!'

I was about to correct him (the subject was in fact called

propaedeutics in philosophy) but decided against it. He was right, after all.

His voice full of scorn, he went on: 'Of course, you can hardly expect them to teach you about Schopenhauer in an introduction to Marxism-Leninism – especially about where he was born and where his famous *maman* was born: in the supposedly pure-Polish city of Gdansk! How inconvenient for them! Better to talk about other things more deserving of mention – how, for example, the great Leader of the Revolution, Lenin, stayed in our little village of Poronin. Now that's a *real* reason for pride – much more interesting and significant! But never mind, I'm straying from the subject . . .

'So, this rare edition that you see here somehow found its way to France. And that's where they' – he motioned again at the old album – 'found it, at a second-hand bookseller's in Paris, when they were passing through. And later, when they were in the Alps, they sent it to me as a gift – or, rather, *she* sent it to me, with this inscription. Here, read it.' He held the book out to me.

I took it and gazed with concentration at the faint pencilling. The writing was neat and even, the letters small and gracefully formed. This is what I read:

> See chapter thirty-nine.
>
> My own peregrinations, compared with those, are child's play.
>
> There's no cause for anxiety: the philosopher won't be gloomy; whatever this person turns out to be, it won't be a misanthrope.
>
> *Denn*
> *Wie du anfingst, wirst du bleiben,*
> *So viel auch wirket die Not*
> *Und die Zucht, das meiste nämlich*
> *Vermag die Geburt,*
> *Und der Lichtstral, der*
> *Dem Neugebornen begegnet.*
>
> For Constant from C.
> 1 January 1935

I looked up from the book.

'There are probably some things you didn't understand,' said Constant, smiling mysteriously.

'Well, yes, I don't know German,' I said evasively.

'Oh, the poem fragment, you mean? That's not the most important thing here.' He came over to me and, keeping his finger on the words to show me the place, translated it for me: '"For as you are born, so will you remain. Stronger than hardship and education is the moment of birth, the ray of light which greets the newborn." That's Hölderlin: it's from the *Rhine,* one of his most famous hymns. You know where the sources of the Rhine are, I take it?'

My most extravagant speculations about this visit had not included the possibility of a geography test. 'Well, I know they're somewhere in the Alps,' I said. 'Somewhere . . . in Splügen, in the Alps,' I concluded, remembering the title of a famous poem by Mickiewicz.

'Close, but not quite. In fact they're in the Adula range and in the St Gotthard Pass.' He closed his eyes, tilted his head slightly upwards and proceeded, in beautiful, fluent German, to recite the poem from memory, stressing the rhythm (I give it here in translation):

But now, from within
The mountains' hidden depths,
Beneath silvery peaks
And joyful green spaces,
From the place at which trembling
Forests and crags high above
Look down, day by day,
There, from that icy abyss, came the voice
Of a youth, begging
For mercy . . .
It was the voice of the noblest of rivers,
The freeborn Rhine . . .

'It used to be my favourite poem in those days,' he explained. 'I knew the whole of it by heart. And she knew it because I taught her. That's why she quotes it: she's telling me that she has taken its meaning to heart. But, as I say, that's not the main thing. What's important is the joke – here,' he tapped the place with his finger, 'in this sentence.' The finger pointed to the phrase 'There's no cause for anxiety.' 'But in order to get the joke, you have to see . . . what's in chapter thirty-nine.'

Neununddreissigster Kapitel, one of the last chapters in the book, started on page 233. I found it and slowly turned the pages. The text was abundantly underlined, and the margins were a forest of crosses and dashes which sometimes, through the addition of a dot, formed an irregular sort of exclamation mark.

'She had no trouble reading Gothic script,' I remarked, intending at the same time to remind him that I myself understood neither the script nor the language.

'Oh, that's not so hard,' he said dismissively. 'And she knew several languages.' He pointed again at the album. 'She also spoke fluent Italian and quite good English.'

'Oh.' I nodded, waiting for further elucidation. At last he decided to provide it.

'This,' he said, 'is Joanna Schopenhauer's description of her journey from London to Gdansk in the year of Our Lord 1787. She was pregnant – with Arthur, the future philosopher.' Then he told me the story.

Her husband had wanted the child to be born in England, because that would have made him a British subject – an invaluable asset for the merchant prince he wanted his son to become. But in the end he got cold feet and decided to take her back to his home town.

Their journey took them through Dover, Calais and Lille to Aachen, then through Westphalia to Berlin and onwards from there. Today the trip takes a day and a half at most (unless, of course, you fly), but then it took more than four weeks and was not without its hardships and strange adventures.

In Dover they were summoned aboard ship in the middle of the night, at about three o'clock in the morning, because there was a good wind just then. They were half asleep when they got to the dock, and Joanna's husband didn't want her to go aboard in the normal way, which at that time meant a rickety, swaying ladder with no safety rails. He insisted that she be hauled up in an armchair, like a special kind of cargo, and furthermore that before this operation was attempted it should be tried out on him, to test the strength of the ropes. Ample remuneration reconciled the sailors to the idea, and following the anxious husband, the armchair with its pregnant cargo, blown about by gusts of icy wind, was duly hauled up a height of three storeys.

They had hardly left the harbour when a terrible storm blew up, and the ship, tossed about by the waves, rolled and pitched horribly all the way to Calais. They arrived after four hours, exhausted by hunger and seasickness.

In Aachen they had another adventure. The town was known among other things for its hot sulphur springs, and Joanna, who had been curious about this natural wonder ever since she was a child, was eager to try the waters. While attempting to fill her cup straight from the boiling source she scalded her hand and in the process lost a valuable ring.

The harshest trials, however, awaited them on the journey through Westphalia. The bumpy high road cried out to the heavens for vengeance: their carriage bounced and shook over the rough ground, and the axles were constantly getting stuck in the mud. In their night lodgings rats and mice ran riot, while the kitchen, the only place one could get warm, was thick with black smoke, for there was no chimney, and after a few minutes one began to choke. The sullen local peasantry, oblivious to this, enriched the atmosphere further with their pipes.

Then, after they'd passed Osnabrück, an axle broke and they found themselves stuck, in gathering darkness and pouring rain, in the middle of nowhere, nothing but fields as far as the eye could see. Assistance was summoned: it arrived in the form of half a dozen farmhands from a nearby estate who came to haul the carriage out of the mud, and the local giant, known for his huge strength, who was to carry the exhausted Joanna to safety in his enormous arms. The giant, sure enough, picked up the pregnant Joanna as if she weighed no more than a feather. Unfortunately he was also asthmatic, and in consequence had to stop and catch his breath every few yards, putting the unfortunate woman down each time he did so without troubling much about the nature of her landing place (and by then it was dark anyway).

As if this were not enough, God chose that day to summon into His presence the only blacksmith in the vicinity, and another, who lived much farther away, had to be sent for. He could not come until the next day; when at last he arrived and had succeeded in repairing the broken axle, the compensation he demanded was so extravagant that Joanna's husband refused to pay. The blacksmith insisted; a quarrel broke out. In the end they decided to refer the matter to the local court, which was just then meeting in a nearby village.

The judge, however, pronounced a verdict so feeble and equivocal that neither party was satisfied: he decided that repairing an axle was work of an 'artistic nature' and therefore could not be appraised without seeking the opinion of at least three other blacksmiths. Consequently, either the parties must wait for the professional assessment, which would take a few days, or the sum claimed by the blacksmith as his due must be entrusted to the court, which would dispose of it appropriately once the assessment had been rendered.

The debtor naturally chose the latter alternative, privately resigning himself to the loss of the entire sum, but the blacksmith was unconsoled. Either he did not believe the court would ever disburse even a portion of the money entrusted to its safekeeping, or he was simply angry at having to wait to claim what he thought was due him. In any event, he decided to take justice into his own hands – namely to destroy what he had just repaired. It was only with great difficulty that he was dissuaded from this course as, cursing horribly, he approached the carriage, axe in hand. But the benefit from this turned out to be slight, for a few hours into the resumed journey the repaired axle again came apart, condemning the unfortunate travellers to further misery, trouble and expense.

'Is everything clear now?' Constant concluded, raising his eyebrows.

'You mean that . . . as a result of all these mishaps . . . a philosopher was born?'

'Rather, what *kind* of philosopher. And what kind of person in general. Do you know anything about him?'

'I know that his view of the world was radically pessimistic,' I pronounced, in the formulaic style of Agnes Wanko.

'Exactly. And apart from that he was an unpleasant character. Irritable, eccentric and full of hate, a recluse and a coward.'

'But such a beautiful writer!' I exclaimed, letting him know I had caught on to the joke and joined in the game. 'And so talented! Why shouldn't we rather see *that* as a result of the sufferings he went through in the womb? In her place,' I went on, opening the book at the title page and putting my hand on the faint inscription, 'I would have made a different joke. After the sentence "My own peregrinations, compared with hers, were child's play," I would have written sadly, "Alas, it won't be a genius."'

'Aren't you pleased with your teacher?' He smiled enigmatically. 'She's very intelligent.'

Danger, danger! said a flashing red light in my head. Go back, go back at once!

'Indeed I am,' I conceded matter-of-factly, as if assessing a student. 'But she isn't a genius. Since you mention her, though,' I added, changing direction, 'didn't your son call her La belle . . . Victoire? Is that right?'

'Yes, that's right,' he said, still smiling.

'Well, why did he call her that?'

'Don't you know what *belle* means?' he teased. 'I can't believe you don't know the word, especially if you're her pupil.'

'You know perfectly well what I mean,' I said, returning his smile. 'I mean the name itself, not the "beautiful" sobriquet.'

'Well, the name's just a name, what's so odd about it?' He was playing with me; clearly he had something up his sleeve.

'Oh, nothing, nothing at all,' I said, closing Joanna Schopenhauer's memoirs and putting them on the desk next to the album. 'Except I wasn't aware' – and here I could not bring myself to look my interlocutor in the eye – 'that it was the name she was christened with.'

'Well, it's true it's her middle name, but what of it? If you knew why she was called that, I'm sure you'd consider it much more important than her first.' He picked up the memoirs and replaced them on the shelf.

'Do you mean why or after whom, in whose honour?'

'I mean why, as a result of what circumstances,' he said.

'Well? You've piqued my curiosity. In '35?'

'Who said it was '35?'

'That's when she was born.'

'Which doesn't necessarily mean that's when she was christened.'

'And when was she christened?'

'Not until two years later, in the autumn of '37.'

'Why so late?'

'Aha! That's the question.' Again he smiled his playful smile.

'How long are you going to keep me in suspense?'

'They wanted to have her christened in Poland, so they put it off until they got back here. But after that – after that, quite frankly I'm not sure what they were waiting for.'

'So what happened in the autumn of '37 that finally made them do it?'

'What happened?!' A kind of sadness seemed to overtake him, and for a long moment he was silent. When he spoke, it was in an undertone. 'He made a certain decision that involved great risk. So he wanted to put all his family affairs in order.'

'Another expedition? Into the Himalayas? The Hindu Kush?'

'No, no,' he said bitterly. 'Worse than that. Much worse.'

'Worse?' The suspense was unbearable. 'What was it, for God's sake?'

'I'm just wondering if I ought to tell you,' he said, gazing into the distance. He shook his head. 'I've talked too much. These aren't things you should hear.'

I was stunned. He'd spoken so freely, and now this sudden change for no apparent reason – after all he'd told me! I cast around for a way to break his resistance. I knew that if I didn't,

I would lose what was perhaps my only chance of learning the truth; if I didn't drag it out of him now, all my trouble would have been for naught. I closed my eyes for a moment and staked all my chips on one throw: *va banque.*

'That's not fair,' I said. 'You start telling me something, and then you stop halfway through . . . What have I done to deserve being treated like a child?'

'You're right.' (I breathed a sigh of relief.) 'It's true, that's no way to behave.' He put his right hand to his brow and, contorting his face into a time-of-painful-decision grimace, drew it down over his smooth-shaven cheeks. 'All right, I'll tell you. But you must promise me you won't talk about this to anyone. No one! Not a soul. Do you promise?'

'Yes, of course.'

'I'm counting on you to keep your word.' He raised a cautionary finger. 'All right. That autumn he startled everyone by suddenly deciding to go to Spain, which had been in the throes of civil war for a year and a half. Hence the middle name.'

After his enigmatic introductory remarks I had expected some extraordinary revelation, but this took me totally by surprise.

'Not as a tourist, I take it.'

'You take it correctly,' he said wryly.

'Was he a communist?'

'Have you ever heard of a communist who christened his children?'

'Well, yes, that's just it . . .'

'That's just it, that's just it!' he mimicked. 'I knew you'd start asking questions, that's why I stopped. It's a long story and I didn't want to get into it. But, oh, well, I've promised now – what's done is done.' (Another sigh of relief.) He concentrated his gaze on a distant point, gathering his thoughts.

'I'm sorry, but before you begin . . . would you mind if I took this off?' I asked, gesturing to my anorak and opening it slightly. Having taken the fort, I wanted to consolidate my position.

'Took this off?' he repeated absently, clearly elsewhere.

'I'm *hot*.'

He still didn't reply. He was obviously worried about something. The most prominent object in his line of vision was the telephone on the little shelf. Suddenly he seemed to rouse himself. 'You know what?' he said briskly.

'What?' I replied in an undertone, my vigilance heightened.

'What would you say to a walk? I haven't been out all day; I'd be glad of a bit of fresh air.'

Damn, I thought anxiously, what on earth can he be up to now? I mustn't let him slip away. I tried dissuasive tactics. 'It's cold and wet outside,' I said. 'Typical November weather. Horrible!'

'Well, but you have to go home in any case. Wouldn't you rather have company?'

'Of course. I'm just wondering if this awful weather will help our conversation. I rather doubt it.'

'Well, it won't hurt. And walls . . . well, you know . . .'

'Walls? I don't understand.'

'Walls have ears!' he enunciated with the emphasis one gives to a truth so obvious that it needs no saying, and strode toward the hall.

I followed, increasingly tense.

'Turn off the light in my study, would you?' he asked as he put on his coat.

I went back obediently and pressed the button in the wooden base of the lamp. In the dark, an image remained imprinted on my retina: the image of the sheet of paper in the typewriter. At the top, in the left-hand corner, it bore Constant's name and address, and below it, slightly to the right, the words 'Minister of Internal Affairs'. Below that, in the centre, was one word in capital letters: 'COMPLAINT'.

'I've found your gloves!' came Constant's voice from the hall.

'Where were they?' I called back, coming out of the study.

'On the hanger, behind the rail. They were hidden behind my hat.' He handed them to me.

'Well, shall we go?'

'Yes, let's go.'

The bolt rasped as it was drawn back.

¡No pasarán!

Although I had no reason to fear that the door to this Aladdin's cave would close suddenly – Constant's promise and the enigmatic wariness that followed it were guarantee enough of his intentions – prudence demanded that I mobilise what resources I had for the conversation that lay ahead. This meant reaching into my memory and summoning up any knowledge I might find it useful to draw upon, as a prop or even as a kind of incantation.

What did I know about the Spanish civil war? What had I heard about it? How was it presented in the propaganda?

In school we concentrated mainly on Polish history, straying from it seldom and mostly to episodes in the history of other nations that were somehow connected with our own. The Napoleonic campaigns, the Austro-Hungarian empire and the fall of the tsars in Russia were the main topics of general historical instruction; mention may also have been made of the French Revolution and the Paris Commune. As for modern history, our picture of world events was entirely dominated by the Russian Revolution and Hitler: two centres of the world, two monstrous nuclei around which everything else turned.

The Russian Revolution was a 'turning point in history', a miraculous event which cured Russia of her ills, transformed her, within a short space of time, from the most backward to the most progressive of societies and heralded the dawn of freedom for all the nations of the world. Thanks to it, the oppressed peoples of the world arose and began to fight for their rights, and Poland regained the independence she had earlier (and quite rightly) lost as a result of giving 'magnates' and 'the nobility' free rein to indulge their lordly whims and allowing the 'propertied classes' the run of the country.

But such is the way of this best of all possible worlds that all good is immediately countered by evil. The Promethean fire which the 'great Russian nation' had gone to such efforts to kindle at once became the target of vicious attacks from forces hostile to humanity. Unfortunately our own country, too, was among them, and played a truly despicable role in the drama.

'The Polish aristocrats, under the leadership of Joseph Pilsudski, a bourgeois nationalist and counterrevolutionary', instead of being grateful to the Soviet Union for overthrowing the rule of the tsars, waged a war against it, which by a regrettable stroke of pure luck they won – to the detriment of all: their own nation as well as the other nations of the world.

The greatest evil, however, took root in the West, especially in Germany. There, vile imperialism took the form of fascism, which was 'reversing the wheel of history' and returning the world to a state of slavery. The freedom, happiness and prosperity which reigned in the Motherland of the Proletariat were such irritants in the eye of Reactionary Forces that they took up arms against her. But the Great Land of the Soviets dealt firmly with the evil. First it occupied half of Poland, rescuing at least part of it from the invading barbarians; then, when the aggressor still dared to advance, it forced his retreat, drove the beast back into its lair and there felled and slew it.

Since then the world has been divided into two parts: the liberated part, where the system of popular democracy has brought peace, freedom and justice to all; and the enslaved part, where a system based on exploitation has brought poverty and war. We were lucky enough to find ourselves in the former zone.

Against this background, the Spanish civil war was seen as an expression of the vicious struggle between the forces of progress and the evil forces of reaction. Modern Spanish history was presented as follows: As a result of the proletarian revolution in Russia, the crumbling social order of the backward country that was Spain began to totter on its foundations. Confronted with the victory of the Left, the reigning monarch, the appropriately named Alfonso XIII, 'fled the country like a rat', and in 1931 the Republic was born. Unfortunately, and against Lenin's wise advice, building the most advanced form of society was not attended to at once; instead half-measures were resorted to, and the results were disastrous. 'The Hydra of bloodthirsty reactionism raised its foul head', and in 1933 the achievements of the revolution were erased. Then the workers and peasants joined together in a popular front, and in 1936 brought down the Right. But again, instead of slaying the 'malignant bloodsucker' at once, they took pity on him, and this was fatal. The 'reptile', set loose, revolted and 'leapt savagely at the throat of the infant Republic'. This was what the world's most rapacious beasts of prey, the German and Italian fascists, had been waiting for. 'Scenting slaughter and profit', they rushed to the aid of the monstrous *Caudillo* and, after three years of struggle, ripped Spanish democracy to shreds. From that moment on Spain was 'bleeding to death in the shackles of the Franco regime'.

Our picture of this chapter in modern history was further enriched by a so-called Polish Page, which was presented as follows:

In the mid-1930s our country was governed by a fascist band of Pilsudski's followers who, to our eternal shame and disgrace, sided almost openly with the Spanish reactionary rebels. Fortunately, under that hard, repulsive shell there burned an inner fire, embodied at that time in the radical Left – the Polish Communist Party. It was this formation, the precursor and germ of socialist Poland, that rescued our honour, allying itself at once with the forces of progress and, most importantly, organising generous armed assistance to the Spanish Republic. The 'best sons of our soil' hastened eagerly to the battlefields of Spain, there to create, under the banner of the 1848 revolutionary slogan *For Your Freedom and Ours,* tough and resolute battle units – the Dabrowski Brigades, named after the general who took part in the 1863 Uprising and later fought and died in the Paris Commune. They paid a high price for their courage. The band of Pilsudski-ites in power, instead of being proud of them, first heaped calumnies upon them and then stripped them of their citizenship.

The Polish Page was not an obligatory part of the syllabus; it was an 'optional' addition to our reading, and I can't say that it had ever stirred my interest. If, in spite of this, I knew slightly more than most about the subject, it was owing to a certain accidental set of circumstances.

* * *

They were fairly recent, dating back about six months to the time when, disillusioned after the AST festival, I had withdrawn into the shadows and abandoned all forms of social activity.

One day, during break, when I was standing by myself at a window in the upstairs corridor, gazing absently at the grey concrete of the schoolyard, I saw Roach, the school representative of the Socialist Youth Movement, coming towards me. Roach's real name was Jacob Boleslaw Kugler. He was short and ugly – hence his nickname – and about two years older than I was, even though he was in the same year: he'd started late, and in addition, because of his frequent absences from school (due to the unstable lives of his parents, Party officials with high government posts whose fortunes depended on the winds of political change that blew from the East), had had to repeat a year. He was in 10d, a class parallel to mine that took German as the additional foreign language.

Although I had few contacts with people from 10d, and even fewer with the SYM, I knew Kugler quite well from chess tournaments. I didn't like him much. He was arrogant and malicious and looked down his nose at everyone. And what a creature! A gnome with a huge head and the exophthalmic stare of a basilisk, with an almost permanent smile of contempt on his pinched, narrow lips. He was extremely bright, however, and a very good chess player – which was why I put up with him. One might even say I had a certain weakness for him. He intrigued me, and he represented a kind of challenge. I couldn't beat him, but neither could he beat me: our prolonged and relentless battles always ended in a draw. I remember one such duel quite well, for it was more colourful than the rest, and symptomatic of our feelings and approach towards each other.

We were playing in a 'lightning game' tournament at the club. Lightning games, as their name implies, are played very quickly: each game has to take no longer than, say, ten minutes, five for each player, and is won either outright or by the player who hasn't lost by the time his opponent's time has run out. Moreover, in a lightning game you don't say 'checkmate': if your opponent's king is unprotected, you may simply take it.

After a long, exhausting series of heats, he and I both reached the final. We sat down at the table and, surrounded by the other players, our instructor among them, began the game. The silence was absolute. Roach, even though he played black, soon had the advantage and controlled the centre of the board. I made an elementary mistake and lost a piece; Roach, sure of his victory, speeded up the pace, hoping for a quick exchange. Soon only the kings and four black pawns were left on the board. I didn't have a chance. It would take him ten or fifteen seconds to queen his pawn, and another thirty seconds or so to checkmate me. He had the time. I was helpless. Then I had an idea straight out of a Shakespearean tragedy: instead of fleeing with my king to the centre of the board (where the checkmate process took longest), I made straight for the enemy monarch, and when my opponent had advanced his pawn to the penultimate square, I placed my king next to his – face to face, as it were. Roach, his attention on promoting his pawn, didn't notice; he advanced to the last square and effected his pawn's transformation into a queen. At which point, poker-faced, I took his king with mine.

'That's an illegal move!' he objected.

'You should have said so when I made the previous one,' I replied with exaggerated politeness. 'Or just taken my king. I was aware of the risk when I put it there.'

'Well, let's see what the judge has to say.'

Our instructor stood for a moment in perplexed silence and then announced grandly, 'A loophole in the rules. I declare a draw.'

Kugler rose with a disdainful shrug for this verdict. But the expression on his face belied his apparent nonchalance. The emotions I was concealing were of a rather different kind. Like Roach, I tried to appear confident, but inwardly I felt I had been incredibly lucky. I was terrified of him.

This distribution of strength and sentiments characterised our relations both on and off the battlefield of chess. Our antipathy was mutual and we kept our distance, but we respected each other. On the rare occasions when we met, the air was thick with biting irony and sarcasm, but it was a game, not a real war. He provoked me (and amused himself) by deliberately exaggerating, often to the point of caricature, certain habits of speech and styles of argument typical of Party activists bred, like his parents, in the good old days of the Stalinist period; I replied with calm irony and insincere meekness. Neither of us was serious, and neither believed the other.

Now, when he came up to me as I stood by the window in the corridor, the conversation was no different.

'So, what's our noble spirit musing about, in such splendid isolation?' he inquired, propping up the wall with his arm. 'Doubtless planning some new piece of *théâtre* . . .' He smiled his sarcastic smile.

'Wrong, comrade, quite wrong,' I replied wearily. 'Just looking for a bit of peace and quiet, somewhere I won't be pestered. In vain, it seems.'

He tut-tutted in feigned concern. 'Withdrawal from life leads to alienation,' he pronounced sadly, 'and that can only bring trouble. Better turn back from that path.'

'I don't feel up to it,' I said in a resigned tone. 'I've gone too far.'

'We could help you,' he suggested eagerly.

'Thank you, don't bother. It's incurable.'

'That's just defeatism. It's worth a try,' he said encouragingly.

'Many have tried, and failed.'

'We have something particular we want to discuss with you.'

'No doubt. I didn't think you'd come to make conversation.'

Quite unperturbed by my hostile tone, he got down to business. 'Among the many talents with which God has seen fit to endow you –' he began.

'God?' I broke in. 'Aren't you ashamed to blaspheme in this way against Science and Truth and the Laws of Nature? Or have they discovered something? Perhaps there are new instructions from Moscow?'

'Your sarcasm is entirely wide of the mark,' he said with calm condescension. 'It was a figure of speech. If God doesn't suit you, fine, let's say Nature. We're flexible.'

'Like a police truncheon.'

'That's poor, really pretty poor. You can do better.'

'Alas, it's my level. You musn't expect better of me – you'd only be disappointed.'

'Your humility, comrade, is excessive. Excessive! Anyway, where were we?'

'God – or perhaps Nature.'

'Ah, yes.' His eyes narrowed. 'As I was saying, among the many skills you possess, you also, if I'm not mistaken, know how to tickle the ivories.'

'There must be some misunderstanding,' I said. 'I only know how to play.'

'Yes, I've heard it called that, too. The point is, comrade, your skills musn't lie fallow. They must be developed, so they can give you satisfaction.'

'I don't seek publicity.'

'Yes, so we have observed. Especially when I think of your fondness for the stage: the klezmer performances, the cabaret numbers . . .'

'A cabaret with Aeschylus doesn't get much applause,' I said elegiacally. 'It was community work: I was propagating culture. Pure devotion to duty.'

'So much the better. In that case we have a common aim. I, too, have the good of the community in mind. And the school community is eager to mark an anniversary that will shortly be upon us, namely the thirtieth anniversary of the outbreak of the Spanish civil war – a war, comrade, in which the Poles, or more precisely the Polish Left, played such a laudable and glorious role. It would therefore like to celebrate the occasion in a suitable way, and expects us to organise the event.'

'Excuse me – who, exactly, expects it?'

'I thought I'd made myself clear. I repeat: the school community.'

'And how can you tell?'

'First of all, by the atmosphere,' he replied. He was calm and assured, like an experienced doctor making a diagnosis. The role of radical Party idealogue, keeper of the Doctrine and guardian of the Faith, was greatly to his liking; it amused him to remind me of what life had been like in the good old days of real Party discipline. 'People talk,' he explained, 'I listen. And secondly, from the fact that a formal motion to that effect has been made by the appropriate representative bodies.'

'Meaning what? By whom, for example?'

'For example, by the advisory council of our organisation.'

'The advisory council,' I sighed. 'Fascinating. I'd no idea such a thing existed.'

'Well, now you know, comrade.'

'All right,' I said sharply, suddenly impatient, 'what, exactly, do you want? What has any of this got to do with me?'

'Let me hasten to explain. What we want is a musical touch. In other words, comrade, we want you to *play*,' he said, stressing the verb. 'To employ your talents for the good of the community.'

I smiled coldly. So that's what's eating them, I thought. 'And what is it, exactly, that you would have me play?' I tried to sound discouraging.

'Oh, nothing extraordinary. With your virtuosity, it'll be child's play.'

'Well?'

'Just a few Spanish melodies . . . some songs from those days.'

'I'm afraid they're not in my repertoire,' I replied grandly, with a tormented-maestro expression.

'We'll provide you with the sheet music, comrade,' he assured me.

His eagerness was genuine, I realised. I decided to see how far he was prepared to go to get what he wanted.

'It's not a question of the sheet music,' I said, with a petulant air. 'It simply isn't the sort of thing I play. I only play jazz or classical music.'

'Oh, come now, what are a few Spanish tunes to you!'

'Indeed, very little. However, my principles forbid it. A person of principle like yourself should be able to understand that. But I have a suggestion for you.'

'Yes?' He was wary now.

'Why don't you ask our Exotic Trio? They specialise in . . .

Cuban folksongs, after all – that should be perfect for your programme.'

'We already have,' he confessed, in a tone devoid of enthusiasm. 'They're practising,' he added importantly.

'Well, then, what's the problem? You've got your musical touch.'

'If we had, we wouldn't be talking to you.'

Then an idea for a really grotesque ploy came to me. I shot out an exploratory arrow. 'Well, since you seem so desperate . . . all right, perhaps I might be of some use to you.'

'Oh, there's no doubt of that,' he assured me, smiling with cold insincerity.

'If I understand you correctly, you want some musical interludes – a musical background, if you prefer. In the Spanish style and rhythm, so as to give the audience a better feel for the national character of the story.'

'Your talents, I see, are not only artistic but pedagogical: our own agit-prop man couldn't have put it better.'

'Thank you for your appreciation. To return to the matter at hand: it occurs to me that I might play a few Spanish themes from Bizet's *Carmen*, like the Habanera, for instance, or the Toreador's Song. Or maybe Ravel's *Boléro*, transcribed for the piano? Would that suit?'

'You're in an excellent mood, I see, despite appearing to be sunk in gloom.'

'I'm quite serious.'

'In that case you must have lost your mind. What you're proposing is close to sabotage.'

'Sabotage! Please. No offence, but your reaction reveals some serious deficiencies in your musical education – basic deficiencies. I suspect you don't realise what Bizet's *Carmen* is. Allow me to enlighten you. *Carmen* is a revolutionary opera. What was opera like before? It was all myths, legends and fairytales, full of gods, noblemen and aristocrats. And what is *Carmen* about? The proletariat! The lowest social classes. Ordinary people, the masses. Workers, soldiers, ethnic minorities – gypsies, I mean. And you're suggesting that using themes from such a politically correct musical classic would be an act of subversion! Really! Think what you're saying, comrade!'

'All right, all right, you can stop the playacting. You've had your little joke, and I trust you enjoyed it. But you won't make a fool out of me.'

'Come on, Bolly, let's be serious,' I said, switching suddenly to a familiar form of address and assuming a friendly, confidential tone. 'Who's going to know what it is? If I play the Smugglers' March, for example, no one's going to have a clue what it is: they'll just think, oh, it's some kind of march. Think about it! Don't you know what their level is? There's nothing to worry about: no one's going to catch on, not even your advisory council.'

He wouldn't be drawn. His only concession was to accept the switch to the familiar and address me by name. 'Is that your last word?' he asked.

Frustrated, determined to snare him, I tried again. 'Be kind enough to follow me,' I commanded, and started walking towards the music room.

Uncertainly, he obeyed.

I sat down at the piano and played a few bars from Joaquin Rodrigo's guitar concerto – haunting, melancholy tunes redolent of Spain, conjuring up images of barren spaces, scorched, rust-coloured earth and stark mountains.

'Well?' I asked. 'What do you think?'

'What is it?' he asked suspiciously.

'Just folk music,' I shrugged, taking my hands from the keys.

For a long time he was silent, sitting motionless with his head bowed and his hands on his knees. 'All right,' he said finally, 'it'll do. We'll take it. But,' he added, wagging a cautionary finger, 'we'll check it out, you can be sure of that.' And he rose to go.

'Just a moment,' I said. 'One more thing . . .'

'Yes, what is it?'

'If I'm going to take part in this, I'll have to miss some lessons. I'll need a note excusing me. Otherwise, nothing doing. I'm not going to use my spare time for practice.'

'It's community work!' he objected indignantly.

'Possibly. But I've told you what my conditions are.'

He turned on his heel and strode out of the room. But a few days later a boy unknown to me (his deputy, as it turned out) handed me the required note. It was stamped and signed by the Tapeworm.

When I first turned up at a rehearsal, preparations were well advanced, in fact almost complete: only a few small final touches remained – some last-minute cuts, some changes of tempo to make sure that the thing ran smoothly. Roach was directing. He sat at a small table with a lamp, the script and his watch (a Soviet-made Polyot) in front of him; from there, pen in hand, he surveyed the proceedings. When he saw me in the doorway he beckoned and indicated the chair next to him.

The participants in the celebration were of three kinds: orators, reciters of verse and the Exotic Trio. There was also an announcer-cum-narrator – Carl Broda, a tall boy from 10a (with English as the foreign language) – who was in a sense the most important person, combining the roles of master of ceremonies, Greek chorus and keeper of the eternal flame of memory.

The thing began with a famous poem by Wladyslaw Broniewski. Carl made a grand entrance, took his place at the microphone and, gazing ahead with great intensity, began to intone, slowly and stressing the *r*s, which vibrated like a sinister drumbeat, the following:

> *Republicans everywhere, as they lay dying,*
> *As into the gutters their scarlet blood ran,*
> *With bloodied forefinger, their final gasp sighing,*
> *Inscribed on the wall the words:* ¡No pasarán!

With each successive verse he was joined by three new performers, who at first stood silently beside him, heads bowed, and then, raising their heads in a dramatic gesture of defiance, came in as a chorus on the last line.

> *On barricades built out of blood, hearts and rubble,*

thundered Carl,

With fire and steel these words were engraved.
Madrid's glorious future was born of their struggle –

at which point the first trio joined in, in chorus:

More precious than life is the freedom they saved!

With six performers now on stage, the indefatigable Carl continued:

For two years oppressed by the fascist dictators,
Its freedom by fire and steel was forged;
A champion of liberty there was no greater –

whereupon he paused dramatically, and the sextet roared out:

Or more resolute foe of oppression and force.

With the last verse the procedure was slightly modified: the chorus of revolutionary fighters, now a grand total of nine, no longer chanted the entire last line, but only the last two words, the poem's main theme and title. As Carl reached the end, therefore, having waded his way through

Let freedom, equality, brotherhood conquer
The world as scarlet my poem's wounds run;

(regardless of how this was declaimed, it was unclear why or how the *poem* was bleeding, or who had wounded it) and

As bleeding it lies, let its death make us stronger,

(in Carl's rendering, the last word, perhaps because he was trying to make it rhyme with 'conquer', came out 'stonker'), he pronounced the words:

In death let its message be . . .

and ten throats roared out:

a semiquaver, two demisemiquavers and a quaver. On the last syllable each performer raised a clenched fist of defiance high into the air.

After a brief pause, Carl began his narrative marathon. The story he presented, richly encrusted with excerpts from speeches, resolutions, proclamations and appeals, was so teeming with contradictions that no ordinary mind, unfamiliar with the rules of dialectic, could wrap itself around it. Thus, although Spain's Republic was democratic, its government (albeit legitimate) was backward and 'bourgeois' – which circumstance in turn did not prevent the dark forces of Reaction from immediately instigating a treacherous conspiracy against the democratic state. This conspiracy was the work of a 'pathetic minority'; at the same time, however, almost all the forces of that 'still half-feudal state' took part in it. It should not be surprising, therefore, that this 'negligible and marginal group' nevertheless possessed a 'murderous and crushing advantage'. But the treachery of the forces of Reaction did not stop there: their 'crushing advantage', it turns out, was only ostensible. In fact, the 'bloody giant had feet of clay'; 'its time had passed', its 'cause was hopeless', and it could only be 'consigned to the rubbish-heap of history'. For this reason it was unable to foment rebellion by itself and had to seek outside aid from 'gangs of bandits'. The eager support it obtained from Germany and fascist Italy proved so strong and extensive that it would be misleading to speak of internal rebellion: it was, in fact, a case of foreign intervention. In other words, the Spanish civil war was not a civil war at all but an 'armed crusade of world fascism against the Spanish masses, which took the fate of their country into their own hands'.

Western policy toward the events in Spain was both profoundly hypocritical and short-sighted. Not that this was surprising for a society based on exploitation and ruled by filthy class interest. The United States and the countries of Western Europe perceived the struggle of the Spanish masses as a greater danger than the bloodthirsty conspiracies of world fascism! Hence, like Pontius Pilate, they not only washed their hands of the whole affair but also gave their tacit support to the intervention.

This is how the reactionary world, guided by self-interest, paved the way for criminal forces and at the same time exposed itself to the blow that was soon to fall. Everything might have ended in disaster had it not been for the Soviet Union, which immediately grasped what was afoot and rushed to the aid of the Spanish people.

It was not as a world power, however, that the Soviet Union rendered its greatest services to the Republican cause, but as the international homeland of the workers' movement. When voices cried out in protest in every corner of the globe, when the masses in every country expressed solidarity and declared their readiness to come to the aid of their Spanish brothers, the Soviet Union at once answered them and undertook to co-ordinate the action. Thus were born the now legendary International Brigades, composed of volunteers from scores of countries. Overnight, these men of principle abandoned their work, interrupted their studies, bade farewell to their families and rushed to the battlefields of Spain.

It was a historic moment, a new, unprecedented alliance. An alliance not between states, armies or governments, but among the masses, social classes and political parties of different countries. No one was interfering in anyone else's internal affairs (in the manner of imperialist states), for the *basic issue* was not an internal matter: the struggle of the Spanish masses for social liberty was not a local conflict but part of a broader process – a mortal class struggle being waged across the globe.

This apotheosis of internationalism was undoubtedly meant to be the main message of the programme. In force of expression, however, it could not compete with the national liturgy – the 'Polish Page'. This was also introduced by Carl, but soon the First Speaker appeared on the stage and took over, reciting the following passage from a PCP proclamation:

> The reactionary clique of generals in power made Poland notorious throughout the world as a place where workers

> and peasants were slaughtered on a mass scale, a country of lawlessness, oppression and corruption, where citizens were tortured to death in prisons. The reactionary clique of generals in power sullied and defamed Poland's name, making her, in the opinion of democratic Europe, a vassal of fascist Germany, an ally of the darkest forces of reaction, barbarity and backwardness.

The Second Speaker balanced this gloomy beginning with a more cheerful note:

> But today Poland's fame is quite different. It is the fame of People's Poland – a Poland fighting for liberty. Her fame has spread from the mountains and valleys and plains of Spain, where the best and the bravest of our sons, in battle units bearing the name of Dabrowski, are fighting to the death for the liberation of the people.

As the room resounded with the echo of these glad tidings, the Third Speaker appeared on stage, spokesman for the noble-spirited Dabrowski-ites.

> We followed in the footsteps of the men who fought 'for your Freedom and ours', for Poland's freedom and that of all other nations. In our Spanish struggle we were inspired by the heroes who fought first in Poland and then abroad, on the side of the Paris Commune.

Although this grand assertion gladdened the Polish heart, it was also somewhat surprising, especially when Carl announced, in a slightly different context,

> Today the Spanish nation sees Poles who are very different from those who fought in the Napoleonic campaigns, at Somosierra, Tudela and Saragossa, where old legionaries, naïve democrats foully deceived by the tyrant of Europe, waged war against the Spanish on behalf of a lost Poland.

A culminating moment of this part, indeed of the whole affair, was an excerpt from a speech by Dolores Ibarruri, the notorious La Pasionaria, in which she bade farewell to the Dabrowski-ites and thanked them for their generous aid. What raised it above the rest of the proceedings was not its form or its content but the figure of the orator. For it was declaimed by the school beauty: the tall, raven-haired Lucilla Rosenberg, the object of every schoolboy's attentions and sighs. And not only theirs: older representatives of the male sex, university students and playboys, were not immune to her charms, either. Lucilla (known as Lucy to an elect circle), in a tight black dress with a huge red carnation pinned over her left breast, black pumps with stiletto heels (apparently a present from relatives in England) and a scarlet band in her splendid, tousled black mane, made her way slowly on stage, paused for a long moment and then, in her low, throaty, sensuous voice, launched into the following speech:

> You have left behind your wives, your women and children, to fight your way here, through hardships and pitfalls, through treacherous traps and snares, through borders bristling with barbed wire and bayonets, so that you could say to Spain: We have come. You are not alone.

The effect of these words from Lucy's lips was indeed electrifying: you forgot whom she was supposed to be addressing and why. *She* was Spain, and the brave fighters were her admirers, ready to abandon their families, lovers and fiancées, to throw themselves at her feet and cure her loneliness.

> I was very moved by the letters I received from your wives and your mothers, your sisters and your fiancées. Even though you are here, risking your lives – and many of you have fallen on the field of glory – they are not angry; on the contrary, they are proud. Proud that their sons and their husbands, their brothers and their fiancés are fighting and dying for freedom; that they have not

> turned away from Spain as she lay bleeding, but have taken up arms to stand by her side even in these difficult times.

The grand finale approached.

Franco was stoking the battle with the last of his reserves; the German Condor Legion, mercilessly bombarding villages and towns, was being decimated by Soviet anti-aircraft guns; the Republicans and the *voluntarios internacionales,* the cry '*¡Venceremos!*' on their lips, were attacking where they could. The Palafox battalion and the Paris Commune hundreds were steadfast in their resistance to the barbarian invader; the communists, in their wisdom, were taking over the reins of government.

And yet, despite the victories, despite the steadfast resistance, the Republic was dying. One by one, cities and whole provinces fell: Andalusia and the fortress at Alcazar, Aragon, then Catalonia, finally Madrid.

Against the background of Picasso's *Guernica,* projected by the magic lantern, the First Speaker reappeared and began the epilogue:

> When the brave guardians of freedom fall under the brutal blows of the invading force, and die abandoned and alone, in unspeakable torment, when the chorus of jackals and hyenas howls with the invader the old slogan of the Roman soldier, 'Woe to the vanquished!' – then we, our ears to the tombs of martyrs to the same cause, more numerous in our country than in any other, reply with the slogan brought from the cemeteries of the 1863 Uprising: '*Gloria victis!*' – glory to the vanquished.

At these words the Second Speaker entered and dispelled the funereal mood with a message of faith and hope:

> No, no, a hundred times no! You are not vanquished! We have faith: the victory will be yours!

The last word fell to Carl Broda:

> The atmosphere of those days comes across better through literature than through even the best historical study. But that novel has not yet been written; we must wait, as Krzysztof Cedro waited for Zeromski. To think that it was a hundred years before those cavalrymen were immortalised in Zeromski's *Ashes*!

At this point the Exotic Trio began strumming 'La Cucaracha', and the performers favoured the audience with a collective rendition of another poem by Broniewski, this one entitled 'Gunpowder and Homage'. It goes as follows:

> *Battles behind us and battles before us.*
> *Friends, what a time! A historical age!*
> *Gunpowder and homage – the heart of a poet*
> *I'd send you across the great Pyrenees!*

Thus ended our school's celebration of the thirtieth anniversary of the Spanish civil war. In its category, it scaled the heights of awfulness, for it brought together, in concentrated form, the three worst elements typical of such affairs: communist zealotry, bombast and wooden speech. The only events to rival it in ghastliness were the ritual assemblies inflicted on us for hours on end at each anniversary of the October Revolution; the other burdens we were called upon to bear, such as the annual devotions performed on National Remembrance Month, Women's Day and, most important, May Day, were vaudeville acts by comparison.

And yet, curiously, the story of these remote events had an effect. Somehow it managed to survive its torture sessions on the rack of official celebration in its honour, and resisted its reduction to farce. It was the one item in the whole communist hagiography that eluded the effort to make it totally ridiculous and repugnant. But the reasons for this lay less in politics than in geography. Quite simply, the Spanish story took place in the West, and moreover in a part of the West where the language spoken was the same as that often heard in film westerns, just then at the height of popularity in Poland. How could even the most radically communist-flavoured story be repugnant when it took place on the banks of the Ebro, in Barcelona or in Madrid, in Catalonia or Guadalajara, in Bilbao, Granada or Las Palmas? Also, the Spanish civil war was the subject or background of several 'Western' novels by writers such as Hemingway, Sartre and Malraux, who at that time, and certainly in Poland, were more than just popular or admired – they were worshipped like gods, blindly and uncritically. Their books, which were still fairly recent, having been translated only in the late 1950s, were treated like holy writ: people read and reread them, sought truth and knowledge from them and liked to model themselves on the characters, dreaming secretly of their strong, virile lives. And one embodiment of such a life was to have fought in the Spanish civil war.

Our celebration naturally did not contain any such references. The myth of fighting Spain was made up exclusively of elements from the arsenal of Bolshevik history, propaganda and art. The only element that came from another order, another world, was Rodrigo's music. I'd sensed this when suggesting it to Roach and had dangled it before him for that very reason, but I hadn't foreseen how much it would influence the proceedings. It didn't even occur to me at the dress rehearsal. I didn't realise it until I was at the piano and had begun to play – and even then the effects were not immediately apparent.

When the celebration was beginning, and the reluctant audience, herded together from every class in the school, sent out the first waves of hostility, disgust and ridicule, I felt a twinge of uncertainty. Perhaps my act of subversion would go unrecognised; perhaps they would think I was just a sycophantic, collaborating creep, sucking up to the authorities by offering my services? My misgivings increased when an incident took place that reminded me of the antics of the rabble at the community centre's educational evening. One of the Speakers, droning on about the interests that bourgeois countries had in Spain, was launched on a long recital of Spain's resources in raw materials, listing such strategically valuable assets as lead, tungsten and pyrite as well as copper, mercury and sulphur, when someone (it may have been Butch) yelled from the back of the room:

'Especially the *copper* for *stunts*!'

Constructing impromptu Spoonerisms, the more obscene the better, was a popular game, and this example gave rise to indescribable hilarity, with much chortling and sniggering, shrill whistles and roars of appreciation.

'What savages!' muttered Roach with distaste in the darkness of the wings, where we were watching the proceedings.

'You're being too severe, comrade,' I said, coming to the defence of the audience, although I was weak with apprehension and worry. 'Though I can't help noticing that your assessment of student attitudes toward the anniversary we are honouring was perhaps not entirely accurate.'

'Don't you try to be clever with me,' he barked. 'You'd better concentrate on your own performance. You're on in a minute.'

When I made my way on stage, knees shaking, and sat down at the piano, it was in a silence eloquent with mockery and contempt. He's sold out, he's been bought, he's sucking up, I could almost hear them thinking, condemning me in advance. But when the first melancholy sounds of Rodrigo's theme flowed out from beneath my fingers, and especially when, swinging slightly, I incorporated the first jazz harmonies, adding a diminished tenth to the dominant chord to make a thrilling dissonance, the audience's severity began to melt. And when, after prolonging a sequence to the limits of human endurance, I finally resolved it on the tonic and finished up with a diabolical glissando, I knew I was forgiven. The whooping and shouting that greeted the end of my performance expressed not only full absolution but gratitude, support and encouragement.

This impression was confirmed as the programme went on. With each of my entrances on stage the sounds of enthusiasm were louder, the cries of disappointment and shouts of 'More flamenco!' at the end of each interlude more insistent. Again I was reminded of the prize-giving ceremony in the community centre at the end of the AST festival, and how it had been dominated by The Firecats. My role was not what theirs had been: I was the humble provider of background decoration who had unexpectedly become a treacherous fifth column for the event's main protagonists. My success with the restless rabble relegated them to a minor role, and the contrast between us further exacerbated the audience's aversion to them.

'We want to dance! We want fandango!' the excited audience yelled as I waited in the wings for my last entrance.

I glanced at Roach. 'The true voice of the people,' I observed. 'You just don't have a feeling for what the masses want, comrade. Your alienation is so far advanced that you have no idea of their real needs.'

'You're wrong, comrade,' he replied, in an ironic echo of my own mocking rejoinder to his baiting of me that day when he had come up to me in the upper corridor. 'On the contrary. If we didn't know what they really wanted, if, as you seem to think, we believed only what we knew to be established by theory, you wouldn't be here. We wouldn't have asked you to play. We asked you precisely because we *do* know – we know very well – what needs to be done to achieve the desired aim. When the elements you're dealing with are as backward and ignorant as this lot,' he went on, nodding contemptuously at the audience, 'you have to take it into account. You have to throw them a few sops, a bit of glitter, in order to attain your objective. Conditioned reflexes, Pavlov – I'm sure you know how it works. These days, comrade, you can't convert people by force. It's been tried, and it doesn't work. The carrot method is much more effective. You play them a few tunes, they have their bit of fun, they think they've had a good laugh – but they'll remember something. Something will have been drummed into those thick mutton skulls of theirs. Without your flamenco the effects would have been much less satisfactory.'

'Deceive yourself if you want,' I replied, although I felt much less confident than before. My self-satisfaction, and the conviction that I'd come out on top, had evaporated. 'You can't change the facts.'

'Don't imagine you've won,' he whispered coldly. 'It's a draw at best.'

For Whom the Bell Tolls (Constant's Story)

When my memory had obediently unearthed this material from its archives and I had begun a hasty reacquaintance with it as I followed the silent Constant downstairs, I suddenly realised I couldn't remember whether Madame had been at the ceremony or not. And this gave me pause. At events of that kind most of the teachers sat in the front row, and she, like a queen, always sat front row centre. When I made my entrances, and particularly my bows, I couldn't have failed to see her. And if I *had* seen her, I couldn't have failed to remember it – especially since I remembered the others, and quite clearly at that. The Tapeworm, for instance, as he reluctantly applauded or turned around to glare at the flamenco enthusiasts shrilly clamouring for more, or the Eunuch and the Viper, who sat next to each other and constantly exchanged whispered remarks and disapproving looks. But of Madame there was no trace, not even a blurred image, not so much as a fragment of an image – an expression, a gesture, the way she sat, some detail of her clothing. Nothing.

The more I tried to remember, the more I became convinced that there had been an empty chair in the middle of the front row, next to the Tapeworm, and the image of that empty chair became compelling. It also shed new light on the Tapeworm's behaviour; the abrupt way he kept twisting around to look behind him now made better sense. He wasn't just attempting to subdue the noisier elements of the rabble; he seemed, more and more clearly, to be waiting for someone. His twisting around was the restless, expectant fidgeting of a person impatient for someone's arrival. My impression that she hadn't been there, and that he was annoyed because of it, became stronger and stronger.

Now, in light of the story of which I had heard part and was about to hear more, Madame's absence from this particular event began to seem significant. But I had no time to reflect on its implications, for by now we were out on the street and Constant was talking.

'I don't know how much you know about the Spanish civil war, and I'd rather not know. What they teach you at school, if they teach it at all, is certainly a pack of lies, and you probably don't have access to literature – *honest* literature – on the subject, because it's forbidden. Anyway, there isn't much of it – of the honest kind, I mean. There can't be another episode in modern history that's been so distorted and lied about as this particular tragedy, and not just here, but in the West, in democratic Western countries, too.

'However, I mustn't lecture you about that now. I'll just tell you Max's story, and you can draw your own conclusions. But I repeat: everything I'm about to tell you is for your ears only. You're not to talk about it to anyone. Not anyone – not even your parents, let alone your school friends or, God forbid, in a lesson. You'd get into a great deal of trouble, and you'd get me into trouble, too. Promise?'

'I promise.'

'You give me your word?'

'Word of honour.'

'All right. Here we go. The Spanish civil war broke out in '36, on the seventeenth of July. It was a very strange time. A bad time, a time of sickness – like a plague. A certain world order was coming to an end. The infection that had been incubating for a good twenty years blossomed into a full-blown disease. The microbes multiplied and attacked. The fever grew and brought on delirium, madness and crime. In the Soviet Union the terror was beginning – purges and trials, deportations to Siberia, hunger and slave labour. And, at the same time, the "red virus" was being smuggled out and disseminated throughout the world; Soviet agents were sent out to spread the infection and prepare the ground for world revolution. Meanwhile, in the devil's other favourite playground, known as the Third Reich, the people were being spurred on to battle. On gigantic squares, among gigantic buildings, torches and blaring loudspeakers, inflamed crowds were succumbing to mass frenzy. *Lebensraum* for the *Herrenvolk*! The Third Reich would last for a thousand years! *Weg mit den Juden und Slawen!* The world belongs to us! And everywhere the scarlet banners, like a presage of spilled blood. Over there the yellow hammer and sickle, and here the black hooks of the swastika.

'And the world went on its merry, carefree way. Parades, parties and the band played on. No one seemed to notice. No one wanted to hear. People were too busy genuflecting before the temples of avant-garde art. There was something desperate about it – like some sort of death wish. When I look back on it now, and at myself as I was then, I realise that I, too, was affected. All those mountain expeditions, the summit-conquering, the thrill of the risk, the roof of Europe, Mont Blanc – nothing but a form of escape. Into thin, pure air, into sun and blue skies, to vast, faraway spaces.

'Max was also affected, and much more strongly. His constant travelling, his punctuality games, that extraordinary idea of his child being born on an Alpine peak – that whole mixture of extravagance and innocent mysticism – it was symptomatic of something rotten to the core. All very lofty and noble, of course, and carried off with great aplomb, but recognisable as whims typical of a decadent age.

'But this sweet madness and innocent folly, this *holder Wahnsinn*, didn't affect everyone in the same way. Some people rebelled. *L'homme révolté*, awaking suddenly and seeing that catastrophe was near, decided that a response was necessary, that something had to be done, attempted, at least, if only for the sake of rebellion. Have you read Conrad's *Victory*? It's all there, marvellously described. The protagonist, Heyst, is a man disillusioned with the world, full of contempt and loathing for it and the people in it, whom he sees either as locusts preying on each other or as dreamers chasing after rainbows. A Schopenhauer. A misanthrope. For him, the only solution is to withdraw from the game altogether. And he does precisely that. He decides to go and live on a tiny, isolated, almost uninhabited island somewhere in Indonesia. But on the way, as he's waiting in some port for the ship that will take him on the last leg of his journey, he sees something that shakes him profoundly. He witnesses a scene in which some unfortunate girl, playing in a musical band the hotel has hired to entertain the guests, is nastily humiliated by her vulgarian employer. There's nothing remarkable about it; he's witnessed hundreds of such scenes. But this time he cannot remain indifferent. Surprised at himself, he approaches the girl and offers his help.

'"I am not rich enough to buy you out," he says to her shyly, in one of the book's famous lines, "but I can always steal you."

'What happens after that is another story. You should read it some time if you don't already know it. The point is the sudden impulse, the kind of compulsion that sometimes makes you get up and leave or do things regardless of the consequences. I think it must have been something like that that seized Max. But why? Because of some atrocity in Spain? The bombing of Guernica? The mass executions? No. Something quite different and much nearer home, something that was happening here.

'Polish reactions to the war in Spain varied. The government procrastinated and shilly-shallied and secretly sympathised with Franco. Not a very laudable response, but then one must remember what kind of neighbours we had to the west. What I mean is that, compared to those other gentlemen of Europe who not only didn't stick their necks out, even though the danger to them wasn't nearly as great, but from time to time even agreed, for the sake of peace and quiet, to do the criminals a few favours, we weren't so bad, considering. At school they probably teach you that the main initiative in giving aid and support came from the communists; that's true, but there's more to it. For one thing, you have to ask yourself what the PCP really was, on whose behalf it was really acting. And then there's the question of whom it was really trying to help: the Republicans? the Spanish parliament? or the 'Jacobins', the radical left that was entirely under the control of Stalin's agents?

'It has to be said plainly: the Polish Communist Party was a gang of Soviet agents in Poland, and everything it did was done on orders from the comrades at central office – the Comintern. In other words, it acted in the interests of communist Russia, the interests of a mad criminal preparing his great assault on Europe. It was in his services, on his whims, that the PCP sent thousands of people to their deaths . . . But I'm straying from the subject.

'Max was basically an apolitical person. He lived in a different world. It was as if he never came down from his mountaintop. If I had to describe his political worldview, I'd say he was a slightly left-leaning liberal. He was sensitive to poverty and injustice, but he was as far as one can get from any kind of radicalism, especially of the Leninist sort. He feared Soviet Russia and he loathed the Bolsheviks – he used to call them the Asian plague. Yet when our government initiated proceedings to strip the Poles fighting in Spain of their citizenship, he took it very badly.

'"You just don't do things like that," he said. "It's hitting below the belt. And sooner or later it'll turn against everyone. Now it's them, and tomorrow it'll be someone else. It's a dangerous precedent. It must be opposed."

'He surprised me, as he often did. Why was he reacting so strongly? Why was he suddenly so concerned about people whose views were foreign, indeed loathsome, to him?

'I asked him about it. "Since when has the plight of 'microbes' worried you so much?" I said. "You must know what kind of people they are, and who they're connected with."

'"That doesn't mean they should be refused entry to their own country! Especially since most of them have been deceived. Don't you know by now what it means when they call something a spontaneous reaction? These people were recruited, they were pressured into going, they had no choice. They were too poor, or perhaps too marginal, to resist."

'I began to get impatient. "What a touching story! You surely don't expect me to be convinced by it. And anyway, even if it were true, what could you do about it?"

'"Very little, it's true. But one could always . . . go there, for example, and see for oneself."

'I was astonished. "What on earth for?!"

'"Well, you know," he said calmly, "to get an idea of what's really going on, and so as not to leave the field to them."

'I saw there was no point in discussing it further: his mind was already made up. He was merely informing me of his decision. "What about Claire and the child?" I asked.

'"Yes," he said quickly, as if this had been his main purpose all along in seeing me that day, "there's a favour I want to ask you. If you could stay in touch with her, and help her if necessary –"

'"*Why* might it be necessary?" I broke in.

'He shrugged. "Well, you know . . . all sorts of things could happen."

'I asked him whether he'd talked it over with Claire. He said yes, and that they were in complete agreement, as always. What could I say? I accepted the responsibility. Knowing him, I suspected he had everything worked out down to the smallest detail, and that the whole escapade was somehow connected with the people he knew abroad, especially in France. But I didn't press him for details.

'In any case, my suspicions were proved right soon enough: he got to Spain across the Pyrenees. For a few months he sent news of himself quite often, and fairly regularly. His contacts must have been in France, because his letters were sent from the Gard. And then, in '38, sometime at the end of May, they stopped. He disappeared without a trace. None of the people he'd been in touch with there was able to say what had happened to him. We assumed he was either dead or captured and imprisoned.

'She bore it all with incredible dignity. Her calm and composure, her unshaken conviction that he was alive and would return, were extraordinary. It was then, really, that I found out what kind of a person she was . . .'

Constant fell silent; the quiet was broken only by the sound of his footsteps. (His shoes, unlike mine, were leather-soled.) We continued walking down the dark street, along the wet pavement strewn with fallen maple leaves, Constant stooping slightly, his hands linked behind his back. I walked on his right, with my hands in my pockets. I glanced at him: he was looking down and muttering silently to himself. I realised this wasn't the first time he had broken off what he'd been saying and behaved strangely when Madame's mother was mentioned.

'You used the past tense,' I said finally, breaking the silence. 'You said "was". Does that mean she's no longer alive?'

'Of course she isn't alive,' he replied, with an edge of irritation in his voice.

'When did she die?' I couldn't help asking.

'Hold on! Just a minute! One thing at a time!' he snapped. 'I was wondering how to tell it: should I start with Spain, and what happened to him there (which I didn't find out about until many years later), or with what was happening here and what things looked like from my perspective?'

'Perhaps from your perspective . . .'

'No,' he said after a moment, 'it'll be better if I start with Spain. But remember: not a word to anyone!

'Max crossed the Pyrenees in December '37. First he was in Lerida, then near Saragossa, and finally in Madrid. He worked with a number of different groups, most of them French; he organised transport, and he got into a few scrapes. Gradually he came to know the country and its recent past – the history of the war. And he soon understood that there were two fronts, not one: that it wasn't just Franco and his supporters who were fighting against the Republic, but also Joseph Stalin, who was doing it more effectively and much more treacherously.

'The victory of the Left in Spain in '38 was both a success and a warning signal for the Soviet side. They'd been agitating there – as everywhere – for some time, but in a Catholic, agricultural country like Spain they hadn't really expected the experiment to succeed. When it did, however, they had to take immediate control: the revolution had to be carried out in accordance with theory. Moreover, and this was crucial, it must not be allowed to take its own course: it must depend on Bolshevik Russia. Remember, for that whole gang in the Kremlin – Lenin, Stalin, Trotsky – the worst enemy wasn't the "Right" or the "fascists" or "imperialists", but democracy. Always and invariably. Especially the true, decent Left, the kind of Left that fought legally, by political means, for the rights and interests of working people. That was what they hated most. Because it was a threat: it could dislodge them and take their place. And it hindered them in their own bloody methods and aims.

'So when the victory of the people's front failed to bring the expected results, the Reds rushed in to add fuel to the flames. The ritual burning, pillaging and slaughter began. Political murder and provocation, raids and assaults and unending strikes. The aim was to set off a spiral of anarchy and violence, let it escalate, and then, when the terror and general confusion were at their height, grab everyone by the throat and take control. And keep it. They might well have succeeded, too, had it not been for that other beast roaming around at the time, also intent on conquering the world. Seeing that a chunk of Europe was about to fall to its rival, it rushed into the fray to wrest the spoils for itself.

'That was the real reason for the war. That was how it really began. If it hadn't been for the Comintern, if the communists hadn't stirred up the rabble and unleashed them onto the streets, it probably wouldn't have started. But it did – and for the Soviets it was very convenient. Do you imagine they were really concerned about the "wretched of the earth", that they really wanted to help them "arise" and overthrow "tyrannies"? Oh, they wanted world revolution all right – but only if *they* controlled it, entirely, from beginning to end. They wanted to create colonies of the Soviet Union, states completely under the control of Moscow Central. Any other way of "liberating peoples from the yoke of poverty and exploitation" was out of the question – because it might reveal that Russia wasn't, after all, the undisputed leader in "building a better world", that she was indeed a leader, as always, but a leader in oppression.

'So what were their choices? They weren't strong enough just to take over Spain in a staged rebellion. On the other hand, if they fomented a real one, they couldn't let it spread freely, in unpredictable and possibly uncontrollable ways. That was far too risky. So Spain had to be slaughtered, like a sacrificial lamb. But before she was slaughtered she had to be milked for all she was worth. Which was why Franco's rebellion came as a blessing. Indeed the Soviets did all they could to provoke it. And when the war broke out, and Hitler and Mussolini joined in, all they had to do was manipulate things so that it went on as long as possible. For Russia, such a war was worth its weight in gold – quite literally, as you're about to discover. For one thing, the unwanted child was being murdered by "Herods", and not by its own mother, the "homeland of the proletariat". For another, the slaughter was invaluable for propaganda purposes: Russia could pretend to be helping the victim when in fact it was just prolonging its bloody and painful death throes. And finally, there was money to be made – huge amounts. Do you know how much Stalin managed to squeeze out of Spain during that war? Six hundred million dollars! In gold, not in slips of paper.

'You didn't really think he helped them for free? That he sent all those tanks and bombs out of solidarity with the masses? It was a fantastic business deal. All he had to do was send people – that cost nothing. Besides, they weren't even his own people: the only people from Russia were agents provocateurs and military advisers. The cannon fodder was recruited elsewhere, wherever there were Soviet agents: Austria, France, Italy, Czechoslovakia and the Balkans. In Poland the agency was the PCP. It was brilliantly planned! You provoked a war, you milked it for all the profit you could, and when your coffers were empty you precipitated the end: the eminently desirable fall of the Spanish Republic.

'How do you go about killing someone you're supposed to be trying to save? There's an old, tried-and-tested method. The Russians are masters at it, and the Soviets have perfected it to an art. What you do is attack the brain: you drive the victim mad. That was what "closing the ranks of the Left" was all about. Within a short time, on the Republican side, an atmosphere of such terror and suspicion had been created that everyone was at war with everyone else. The air was thick with conspiracies and denunciations, acts of provocation, intrigues and plots. While the situation at the front, in the trenches, grew worse and worse, the people at the top were busy slaughtering each other. All Franco had to do was sit and wait. Which, quite calmly, he did. And indeed, by the end of '38 they were so confounded and exhausted by all the purges that they could barely stand. Some time in December, the news came that Stalin was abandoning the Republic (having taken all the gold); that was when Franco launched his final offensive – the "Catalan" offensive. In January of '39 Barcelona fell, and the end of March saw the fall of Madrid.

'Franco wasn't much interested in the progress of the war he was waging. When they came to tell him it was over, he barely raised his head from his papers. What he did do, immediately and ruthlessly, was deal with the Republicans. Close to two hundred thousand people died, and more than twice that ended up in prison. Stalin breathed a sigh of relief.

'Max had disappeared from view because he was in hiding. He was a volunteer from Poland unconnected with the PCP, and as such he had begun to look, to the Reds, extremely suspicious. They decided he was a spy, a fascist agent. They pronounced a death sentence on him. He went into hiding with a Frenchman wanted for the same crime. The Frenchman, unlike Max, was a political type: an activist, an organiser, an ideological enthusiast. He'd gone to Spain to join the fight for a "better tomorrow for the world". It wasn't long, though, before he got caught up in the frenzied tangles of party intrigue and suspicion, and since then he'd come a long way across very slippery ground. In the end it was decided that he knew too much and would have to be got rid of. He escaped death by a miracle; in fact it was Max who, quite by accident, saved his life. From then on they stayed together and became good friends. It was from him that Max learnt the truth about Soviet "aid" and about the whole war, and it was also thanks to him that he managed to get out of Spain. He escaped at the very last moment, just before the fall of Madrid.

'I remember that day very clearly, the day when, after almost a year of total silence, the message came – a telegram from France. He was alive and well, it said, but he wasn't coming back; she was to pack her bags and come out to join him – with the child, naturally.'

At this point Constant again fell silent. He walked along, still stooped, gazing at the pavement.

'Why didn't he want to come back?' I asked softly.

'Because,' he replied, 'he was convinced that Poland would

be invaded at any moment. From two directions at once – from the east and from the west.'

'When was this exactly?'

'In April '39.'

'He could already foresee it then?'

'The day Madrid fell, Germany broke the treaty it had signed with Poland in '34 and a week later invaded Czechoslovakia and Lithuania. At more or less the same time, the chief Soviet diplomat told the French ambassador at an official meeting, without mincing his words, that the Soviet Union had no choice but to proceed with a fourth partition of Poland. This was well known; it was talked about in the press. But apart from that' – Constant halted and glanced in my direction – 'he had a nose for these things.'

We stood at the edge of a large puddle, in the dim circle of light from a streetlamp.

'Well? Did she go?' I said after a long silence, clenching my hands in my pockets.

'Yes. Almost overnight. I remember – it was evening, the central train station, the sleeping-carriage. That was where I saw her for the last time – through the open train window.'

Constant stood gazing at the puddle, on the surface of which our shadows moved and rippled. Then, skirting it carefully, he moved off again. Once more we walked in silence. I struggled with a confusion of thoughts. What should I say? What should I ask him? I decided to wait. Finally he spoke.

'She had a little less than thirteen years of life ahead of her then,' he said. I did a quick sum: she must have died in 1952. 'What happened?'

'A car accident. Except . . .' He let the sentence trail away.

'Except what?'

'Except it's unclear what caused it.'

'I'm sorry,' I broke in, 'where are we now? In France, or back in Poland?'

'In France, dear boy, in France.'

'So they didn't come back after the war –'

'No,' he replied shortly.

'What kind of accident? How did she die?'

'She was driving. She lost control of the car.'

'And what's unclear about it?'

'The essential thing: why it happened. On a straight, empty road.'

'Was she alone, or . . . with someone?'

'Alone. But Max saw it.'

'What did he see?'

'He saw that the car wasn't stopping. He saw it go off the road and hurtle down the side of the mountain.'

'And what did that mean?'

'It meant that the brakes or the steering mechanism wasn't working.'

'So?'

'So someone must have deliberately tampered with them.'

'Why? Or rather, who?'

'That's what's unclear. In any case, he believed – he was absolutely convinced – that it was a trap which had been set for him. That he was supposed to have been the victim.'

'And who was supposed to be behind it?'

Constant halted again, withdrew a silver cigarette case and a box of matches from his trouser pocket, extracted a Giewont cigarette and lit it with reverence. 'All I know is what Max told me,' he said, exhaling a cloud of smoke with relish. 'And frankly I don't know. I don't know what to think.'

'Why?'

'Listen.' In a swift, decisive movement he slid the cigarette case and the matches back into his pocket and moved off again. 'The Frenchman who had helped him get out of Spain was later involved in the Resistance. Their paths crossed again. He persuaded Max to join him. And that's when it all started again: the sick atmosphere, the acts of provocation, the murders. Under the pretext of bringing traitors and collaborators to justice, dozens of current scores and various old ones were settled. The circle began to close. One by one the people from the Frenchman's network were killed off, among them several other veterans of the Spanish war. Finally he was murdered, too. Max saw this as a sign that his own life was at risk; he was convinced he'd be next. So they fled, right there and then, all three of them. Into the mountains, somewhere near Mégève.

'Have you read Conrad's *Victory*? Oh, of course, I've already asked you that. You really must read it. This was something else that could have come straight out of it: you seek asylum, you take refuge somewhere, but the evil of the world, the world you've rejected with such contempt, appears personified on your doorstep and forces you to a duel. It comes in the form of Mr Jones, Ricardo and the terrible brute Pedro: the sinister threesome sent by Schomberg. Out of spite, meanness, resentment. Evil.

'That, at least, was how Max presented it to me.

'After a few years of peace and quiet, some time in '52, he again felt their breath on his neck. One day he saw a man he remembered seeing in Spain prowling near his house. He was a shady character who played a devious game with various sides – Max had been warned about him by the Frenchman. Now he got the impression the man was an agent sent to spy on him and find out where he lived. There were others who came after him – at least that's what Max claimed: I don't have evidence of it. I do, however, have reasons for thinking he'd gone mad.

'He was convinced they were following him, waiting to pounce. He was suspicious of everything that happened around him. He became pathologically distrustful; he smelt betrayal everywhere. On the other hand, it was a fact that the Russian Secret Police in those days were swanning about in France as if they owned the place. They seized people in the streets, abducted them in broad daylight, even in the centre of Paris. There were some notorious cases, much talked about. And then it finally happened: the car accident. For him it was an assassination attempt, and it confirmed all his fears: he was a marked man. He said they examined the car, went through everything with a fine-tooth comb. I don't know what they found. In any event, after that he cracked up for good. He became a different person: unstable, excitable – a nervous wreck. He indulged in torments of self-reproach; he was obsessively cautious and at the same time wildly rash. That was the state I found him in when he came back here with her soon after Stalin's death.'

'With her?' I asked, unable to stop myself.

'With his daughter. You didn't think I meant the coffin, did you?!' he snapped. 'With the person who is now your French teacher.'

'Oh, yes! Of course.' I feigned a delayed reflex.

'Do you understand what I'm saying?' He halted again, this time at the top of some steps that led to an underground passage beneath the viaduct. 'Do you realise the implications of what he did? He feels surrounded there, so what does he do? He comes *here*! He thinks he'll be safe *here*! He must have been mad! To come back *then*, knowing what it was like! Oh, he knew perfectly well; he was under no illusions. Yet he chose this as his place of escape.'

He took a deep, final drag on his cigarette, crushed the butt underfoot and began to make his way carefully down the slippery stairs ahead of us. 'It shows the state he was in,' he continued, in a slightly steadier voice, 'what his "duel with the world" had brought him to. It's a thing no sane person would have done.'

The dark tunnel smelt of dankness and urine. Water dripped from its low ceiling.

'He was a sick man,' Constant continued, 'and his sickness manifested itself as a kind of hunger, a hunger for fear and danger. It was a nervous disease. People who are afflicted by it *want* to be afraid; it's like a drug. And when nothing is happening they create situations that will confirm their vision of the world.

'He'd always had a tendency to challenge fate, but now, after everything he'd gone through, it was as if his best qualities had warped. His extraordinary courage, his sense of responsibility for others, his carefulness and discipline – they all dissolved into a kind of extreme recklessness and unpredictability. It was a way of seeking death. Although by the time he came back the worst of the terror was over, it still didn't take much to get yourself into trouble, and he seemed to go out of his way to stick his neck out. Instead of settling down in some quiet little corner and making himself inconspicuous, he immediately began blabbing his story to all and sundry. So in the end, of course, they locked him up. And not the ordinary Security Services, either, but Military Intelligence – the darkest circle of hell.

'He never came out. He died in prison. Heart-attack, they said. It could be true, I suppose, because they did release the body. But in those circumstances . . . they might just as well have murdered him; it amounted to the same thing. Plain, ordinary murder. So it finally happened: the thing he had so feared, and at the same time so desperately sought and done everything to provoke.'

A train rumbled above us. We quickened our pace and emerged at the other end of the tunnel. Slowly we climbed the stairs that led up to the other side of the tracks.

'And what about her?' I said, slightly out of breath, when we'd reached the top.

'Who?' he asked absently.

I almost said, 'His daughter; you didn't think I meant the coffin, did you?!' His reply still resounded in my ears. But I restrained myself and muttered, with only a hint of impatience in my voice, 'The child. The one he called Victory.'

'Oh, La belle Victoire! That's another sad story.'

At last! I thought, and crossed my fingers.

'After he came back and told me the whole tale, he often asked me, indeed he made me promise, not to abandon her, to look after her "if something should happen to him". Of course, I was ready to help in any way I could, but she wasn't an easy person to talk to – uncommunicative, shut up within herself, deliberately cold and unapproachable. Which wasn't so surprising. After all, Poland was like some foreign desert to her, especially then. Worse, like a penal colony. Poverty and terror everywhere, and isolation at home. No friends, no social circle, no one to talk to. Just the handful of her father's friends, most of them peculiar, embittered old men, crippled in one way or another by the war, apathetic and cowed. Imagine what it must have been like! Imagine yourself, at the same age, just as you're finishing school, suddenly being carted off to – oh, I don't know, to Lvov, let's say; it used to be a Polish city. It was where your father studied mathematics before the war. How would you feel? And for her the change must have been even greater. Imagine: the Alps, a French *lycée*, elegance and sophistication, and then suddenly rubble and political madness, and grey laundry soap instead of Chanel No. 5. It must have been terrible!

'She was like a bird in a cage. Desperate. Wouldn't leave the house. Max was very worried. I reproached him more than once. "Why on earth did you drag her here? If you decided you wanted to come back, fine, that was your affair, but to bring her into all this . . . I'm sorry, but it's just completely beyond the bounds of reason."

'"You don't understand," he'd say, "I *had to*. I had to get her away from there. I did it for *her*." Then he'd lower his voice: "She was *in danger* there. They wanted to prey on me by attacking my family. They were going to kill them both and leave me till last."

'I gave up.

'I got a better insight into the situation only when they locked him up and I wanted to help her, as I'd promised. At first I despaired of getting anywhere. She was so unforthcoming I felt like an intruder and a pest rather than a source of much-needed support. But I soon came to understand that her coldness wasn't directed at me personally. The problem was that I was a friend of her father's. And she wasn't just badly disposed to him but frankly hostile. I don't know if it had always been that way or if it was the result of recent events, of everything she'd been through. Whatever it was, she reacted very badly to anything connected with him.

'It was like something out of a Greek tragedy: father's best intentions harming his own daughter, injured daughter hostile to tormented father; the tragedy of a man who paid for his act of bravery with the loss of his wife, insanity, his daughter's hostility and a lonely death in prison. A horrendous price. And there was something tragic in my own role, because if I wanted to keep my promise to help her I was forced, in a sense, to turn against him. It was the prerequisite for getting through to her, taming her and persuading her to act in her own interests.

So when I saw that she'd been close to her mother, I tried to give the impression that I . . . too . . . had in fact been . . . closer to Claire than to Max. I told her about Claire's studies at the French Institute, and about the time when Max was in Spain . . . She didn't remember me – well, she was only three or four then.

'But mostly I tried to intimate, as best I could, that although Max was my friend, I disagreed with much of what he did. I'd been against the idea of the child being born on Mont Blanc, against his going to Spain and against their return to Poland. On the other hand, if it hadn't been for his love of the Alps she wouldn't have been born there – in France, in the West. And that one fact about her could turn out to be fundamental. For as the poem says, "stronger than hardship and education is the moment of birth": the *place* where "the ray of light greets the newborn". I tried to make her see that. And the same with Spain. If it hadn't been for that strange, inexplicable impulse which made Max decide to "pit himself against the evil of the world", she wouldn't have grown up in Western Europe. She wouldn't be bilingual – indeed, if she'd stayed in Poland under the occupation she mightn't be alive now. There's no evil that some good doesn't come of it. Perhaps this, too, would one day turn out to have been a kind of blessing. After all, she musn't forget her middle name! But if some good *was* to come of it, if Providence was to be kind to her once again, she couldn't turn away from it peevishly. She must help it along, give it a chance.

'Finally, after much persuasion, I managed to persuade her to go to university. To study French, of course – in the Department of Romance Languages. It gave her a goal in life, and she could meet people with whom she had something in common: a knowledge of French and of France. And her position among them would be strong, for she had a significant advantage: she'd been there. You have no idea what it meant then to have been to Paris – to have been to the West at all, let alone to have been born there and to speak the language without an accent.

'So she went. Naturally she had no difficulty with her

studies: top marks, prizes at the end of the year – I know all about it because she and Freddy were . . . in the same year. And even in those days, if you did well there were all sorts of opportunities, including trips to the West. Especially after October '56 and the "thaw" that followed. And sure enough, some time in '57, when *all sorts* of people started getting passports and going to the West, either "privately", to visit family, or to give lectures and attend conferences, she was one of two students to get a UNESCO grant for some sort of language course in Paris, at the Sorbonne. And then it all started.

'She was refused a passport. Even though she was the top student in her year and politically quite neutral; even though both the department and the rector's office intervened on her behalf. When I found out about it I decided to do something, though she hadn't asked me to. I got in touch with someone who had contacts in the Security Services and asked him to look into it. He came back looking troubled. There was nothing to be done; they wouldn't give their reasons. The thing didn't smell good. It probably had something to do with her father's death in prison. The reasons for his imprisonment. Whatever came out during the investigation. If he'd been rehabilitated, like so many others, things might have been different – but so far he hadn't been. And no one had even applied to have it done.

'"How can you apply to get him rehabilitated when he was never sentenced?! There wasn't even a trial!"

'My contact shrugged. "I'm sorry, there's nothing I can do. My arms aren't long enough."

'After this episode she became diffident again. Although she didn't know what this man had told me, she behaved like a person profoundly convinced of the ineluctability of her fate. She was caught in a trap. She would never get out. Coming back to Poland had been a curse of destiny. She was doomed to stay here forever.

'I wanted to fulfil my promise to Max. I tried to help her, to act in her best interests. But what *were* her best interests? What Max had wanted for her, or what she wanted for herself? Max had brought her here from France because he had feared for her life. Was he right or was he insane? How could one know for sure? I thought he'd made a great mistake, and made her unhappy. What was I to go on, whom was I to side with? In the end I said to her, "I'm told it was because of your father that they wouldn't let you out. Whatever happened to him, they're responsible, and they know that perfectly well. They're responsible for his death, and they'd like to conceal the fact. So I think it's time to put some pressure on them. The best defence is attack. It's time to act. You have to apply for his rehabilitation – even for damages. And you must do it now. If you want your freedom, you must fight for it. I'll help you in any way I can – I have some contacts here and there – but the first, decisive step must be yours. And I think you owe it to him. Whatever you think of him, however you judge him, he was a wonderful man. They don't make them like that anymore."

'She wouldn't even listen. She found it loathsome and repulsive and was highly mistrustful of everything. She thought any kind of contact with the realities of life here, especially with the authorities, could only harm her. She preferred a different strategy – concealment and disguise. The strategy of the sphinx. Behind her mask, by night, secretly, she would dig away patiently until, little by little, she got what she wanted. With no help from anyone. It was exactly what Max would have done! In that way she was just like him.'

Constant halted and straightened up. We were standing in front of my house.

'Well, here we are,' he said, in a lighter tone. 'You see, it wasn't so bad. Maybe just a bit cold.'

I looked around desperately for some handhold, something I could use to haul myself up. To have reached the summit without at least putting one's foot on it would be unforgivable – a defeat that was not to be borne. I had to think of some way to keep him talking. Unfortunately the props I had so carefully prepared now proved, as usual, quite useless. Once more I was forced to improvise.

'True,' I agreed cheerfully, 'even quite pleasant. Why don't we take one more turn? There's a very nice square just around the corner.'

'No, I don't think so. I still have to get home, remember.'

'Of course.' I hung my head. But I bounced back quickly and announced in a brisk, decisive tone, 'Well, in that case, now I'll walk *you* home a little way – at least back to the viaduct.' And to forestall any objections I moved off at once, saying as I did so, 'Well, it's been a good ten years since then. So did she get what she wanted?'

'If she had,' replied Constant, hurrying after me, 'she wouldn't be here. But, as you know, she is. It follows, therefore, that she didn't.'

'Do you mean that she didn't succeed or that she admitted defeat?'

'A person with a name like that never admits defeat,' he said, with a strange blend of sadness and irony.

'So what did she do? How did she try?'

'I told you. She tried all sorts of ways. First there was that woman, her supervisor, what's-her-name . . .'

'Surowa?'

'Yes, that's it – Surowa. She tried through her. Then, when that didn't work, she tried through the Centre, where she'd started to work – like her mother. And now . . . now I'm not quite sure. I can only guess. I lost touch with her.'

'Why? What happened?'

'Injured pride.'

'Yours or hers?'

'Hers, of course. You don't think I could take offence at anything she did?'

'What was she upset about?'

'She asked me a favour – it was the only time she ever asked me for anything – and it happened to be something I couldn't do.'

'What was it?'

'Oh, it's not very interesting.'

'Still . . . it's interesting to me.'

'Well, she asked me if Freddy, when he went to France, would meet a certain man, explain the situation to him and ask him, on her behalf, to marry her. To send her a so-called letter of intent, and if that didn't get her a passport, to come himself. And if that didn't work either, to marry her by proxy.'

'Was it love, or . . . a marriage of convenience?'

'What do you think! Of convenience, of course!'

'Then why couldn't you do what she asked?'

'Because,' he replied, 'Freddy absolutely refused.'

My heart skipped a beat. 'Why?' I asked, emanating unconcern. I even managed a slight smile.

'I don't really know. He never explained. I can only guess . . . she meant something to him.'

So it was true! I remembered Freddy's nervous laugh at the sound of Madame's name. 'But in that case,' I said, 'he should have been all the more eager to help her, surely? Why didn't he want to?'

'Think about it!' snapped Constant with some irritation.

I shrugged. 'I don't see anything wrong with it, if it was just a formality . . .'

'Oh, you're too young to understand these things.' He gave me a condescending pat and stopped again.

That's it, I thought. It's over. I was right.

'Well, run along home now, otherwise we'll be walking each other back and forth like this forever. And remember, not a word to anyone. If you talk, you'll get everyone into trouble: me and her and yourself.'

'You needn't worry,' I said, taking off my glove to shake his hand, seeing that he was doing the same. 'But there's just one more thing I'd like to ask, if I may . . .'

'Well?'

'When I mentioned that she was our headmistress, and that she was going to reform the school, Mr . . . Freddy, I mean, and you, too, you both looked surprised – taken aback. And Freddy said, "So she really did it . . ." as if she'd done something he'd expected. What did he mean?'

'You mean you still don't know? After hearing the whole story?' He shook his head in gentle remonstrance and looked at me pityingly. 'What kind of person can be the head of a high school in this country?' he asked. 'What is the one essential condition every candidate must fulfil?'

'There are exceptions.'

'You can't be serious!'

'You have no proof.'

'The end doesn't justify the means.' He extended his hand. I shook it. 'All the best! Good luck!'

His hand in mine was dry, cold, bony.

'Thank you for everything,' I said solemnly. 'Especially for your trust.'

'Trust isn't something you say thank you for,' he said, without releasing his grip on my hand. 'It's something you don't betray.' Then he let go of my hand and put on his glove.

We separated. I listened to the sound of his receding footsteps. Then there was silence.

My temples throbbed and I felt dizzy. I closed my eyes for a moment. In the darkness the image of an empty chair sprang out at me, as if the old electrician from the festival had turned a faint spotlight on it.

FOUR

The Logos-Cosmos Bookshop

In the dining-room the radio was on at full volume. Through its dreadful hissing, whistling and buzzing, like the howls of the damned from some infernal abyss, one could distinguish, faintly but clearly, the voice of a well-known announcer on Radio Free Europe. He was deploring, in the harshest terms, the latest iniquities of the 'Warsaw regime', just then indulging in a burst of vindictive repression after the perfectly innocent, as well as entirely sound and commendable, speech recently given at the university by a certain famous philosopher on the tenth anniversary of the 'Polish October' of 1956.

Deafened by the avalanche of information that had come down upon me in the past few hours, I longed only for complete solitude and quiet. But the screeching from the radio – 'subversive' waves, 'jamming' waves, and other less definable waves struggling for supremacy – had its benefits, for it gave me a chance to sneak in unnoticed by my parents and thus avoid questions about where I'd been and with whom – simple enough to answer, but inconvenient. Unfortunately, I had barely taken off my anorak and begun to creep stealthily toward my room when the din abruptly stopped, choked off by a twist of the volume dial, and I heard my mother's sharp voice.

'May I ask where you've been?'

I halted in mid-step, my hand on the knob of the door to my room.

'I was out for a walk with Constant,' I replied. I tried to make my tone convey the obviousness of this truth.

'Couldn't you have said so when you were going out?' she retorted, deftly returning the ball with a slight spin.

'Yes, I suppose so.' I tried to sound contrite, hoping that would be the end of it. 'I just didn't, somehow . . .'

'You just *didn't,* somehow . . .' she echoed, stressing the negative.

'Do you think I have something to hide?' I snarled, instead of swallowing the reproach and letting it go.

'I don't think anything. I'm merely making an observation,' she replied evenly. And the voice of Radio Free Europe sounded again as the screeching resumed.

After some hasty evening ablutions I got into bed and turned off the light. The house was quiet, the radio in the dining-room mute. I lay on my back in the dark with my eyes closed and inspected my spoils.

Just over two weeks had passed since the moment when, sitting on the park bench after my mauling at the hands of the Viper, I had made the bold decision to investigate Madame and taken my first uncertain steps in that direction. In that short time I had, contrary to my own expectations, progressed a very long way. When I started out I'd known next to nothing; now my knowledge was simply immense. How many other people (apart from the Security Services, of course) knew as much as I did? The saga of her birth, the wartime peregrinations, the escapes, the French *lycée*, the catastrophic return, the death of her parents; the harassment, the feeling of being besieged and the struggle to get out at any price, even through a pact with the devil. I knew her life, even her motives, as if I were a member of her family: a brother, a close friend, a confidant.

I thought back to the moment when, excited and pleased with myself, gloating over the fruits of my reconnaissance mission, I had seen where she lived. This paltry achievement had then seemed stupendous. The distance separating me from the star that was the subject of my observations seemed to have shrunk by light-years, transforming what had been a flickering point of light into a huge solar disc. I looked back on this now with a pitying smile. If that was such a huge step forward, the events of this evening, by comparison, were like landing on the surface of a planet.

Indeed I was standing on solid ground. Before me was a landscape of varying hues and shapes, light and shadows. But could I understand what I was seeing? Or, rather, did the things I saw represent the ultimate reality? After all, what we see is merely appearance, one of the many forms or masks that reality assumes; beneath it lie other, perhaps infinite layers. The blue of the sea and sky, the green of mountains and forests look different at each stage of our approach; our view changes as we go from magnifying glass to microscope to the physics of elementary particles. Where, then, does seeing end? Does it have a limit?

Madame was not quite thirty-two years old. That, I calculated, was exactly 11,613 days. Which came to sixteen million minutes, or just over a billion seconds. If you subtracted half of that for sleep, and then another hundred million or so for the years of her early childhood, that left a conscious life of roughly four hundred million seconds, or seven million minutes. How much of that had elapsed since I had known her – before my eyes, as it were? What percentage of her life overlapped with mine? Three hundredths? Four? And even in that small fraction I had seen no more than the surface, the appearance – what philosophers call the phenomena. I had no access to the reality beneath, to the thing-in-itself. Every single one of those seconds was filled with something. But what did I know about them? Nothing, absolutely nothing. Not to speak of the time she spent elsewhere, out of my presence.

I thought about the various moments of her life, important and less important, trivial and unnoticed. The year 1939: the central train station in Warsaw. Evening, the sleeping-car, Constant on the platform. She's looking at him through the train window – in her compartment or in the corridor? Does she remember the moment? Does she remember there *was* such a moment? Is she aware of the nature of Constant's feelings for her mother? And then France: home, school, lessons; her teachers, her friends. Long days, mornings, afternoons; her first sleepless night. Holidays: the Alps? the Atlantic? the Mediterranean? Her hours of solitude, her dreams. Maturity: discovering her own body. And then the accident: the death of her mother; the day of the funeral. How much had she known about her father's life, his Spanish adventures, the whole tangled story that led to his death? How much had she understood, and how much did she understand now? Why hadn't she come to the celebration? Who was the man she'd wanted to marry, and what did he mean to her? And what was the story with Freddy? Had there been anything between them?

As the questions succeeded one another, I realised that my newly acquired knowledge was affecting me in ways I hadn't anticipated. Instead of inducing a pleasant excitement and a feeling of curiosity satisfied, inspiring me to invent further verbal games with which to assail her, it was making me nervous and confused. The more I knew, the more I wanted to know; at the same time, the knowledge that this 'Alpine flower', this proud and unbowed 'victory', had been deeply hurt and touched by tragedy gave my insouciant longings a darker shade and made them, paradoxically, all the harder to bear.

As the proud, distant Ice Queen she had inspired dreams of savagery and violence, making one want to rip off her disguise and strip her naked, catch her off balance, uncover her weaknesses – find out, in short, if there was another side to her nature, and if so what it was like. But when she appeared as a person of flesh and blood, when the concrete details of her life, in all its harshness and bitterness, struck her down from her Olympian heights and returned her to earth, the dark, feral lusts and perverse longings gave way to awe and mute fascination, with a solid base of respect and sincere sympathy. And that was hell; that was the intolerable thing. Because there was no hope of remedy. The choking excitement, the injured pride and sense of insignificance I had felt before could be dealt with or at least assuaged. In my plan to learn as much as I could about her and then taunt her with my knowledge, play with her, pester her, draw attention to myself, there had been at least a chance of consolation, if not fulfilment. But a fascination full of respect and pity left me helpless. What could I do with such a combination of feelings? How was I to seek consolation? Through words, through speech? Go on playing with risky allusions and deliberate ambiguities? Make it clear that I knew everything about her? There was no point any more; it might even be harmful. Besides, I had promised Constant silence; I had given my word. I could still feel his iron grasp on my hand.

What now? What next? I had no idea what to do, how to find a way out that wouldn't harm anyone or betray Constant's trust but would still give me something, some profit, some gain. Something that might at least allay my humiliating torments. Nothing came to mind. In the meantime, my overheated imagination had dissipated all desire for sleep. I was trapped. I reached out for the light switch and turned on the lamp. I took a volume down from the shelf, settled myself on my side, and began reading Conrad's *Victory.*

I was woken by my mother's voice.

'It's twenty past seven. Do you want to be late for school?'

I hauled myself, with some effort, into consciousness. 'I'll be up in a minute,' I mumbled blearily.

'What's the matter? Don't you feel well?' she asked, with grave concern. 'Why is the light on?'

I opened my eyes and closed them again quickly. I wondered what time I'd fallen asleep. 'I was reading,' I said sleepily. 'I must have fallen asleep over my book. I feel fine.' I sat up slowly.

'In that case you'd better hurry up,' she remarked drily, eyeing the slowness of my movements, and vanished behind the door.

Accustoming my eyes slowly to the light, I looked down at Conrad's novel, lying open, spine upwards, on the floor beside my bed. I bent down lazily to pick it up and looked at the page I'd got to. 'I'll drift,' was the first sentence that caught my eye – Heyst's announcement of his decision. I looked at the preceding paragraph, something about reflection as a destructive process that instilled mistrust in life. 'It is not the clear-sighted who lead the world,' writes the narrator; great achievements, he claims, are born of impulse, 'accomplished in a blessed, warm mental fog', not in cold calculation.

I got dressed, threw my school things together and, skipping breakfast, left the house. On Mondays, French was in the fourth period: the first period after morning break, at ten forty-five. I had done a lot of thinking by ten forty-five.

At first I was lighthearted and optimistic. What a fuss, I thought; nothing to get so worked up about. True, my hands were tied: I knew all about her and I couldn't reveal my knowledge. But that wasn't the end of the world. It made things difficult, certainly, but not impossibly so. There were always other cards to play. Simone de Beauvoir, for instance. There – just the thing! Even better, in fact. Especially when I had an ace up my sleeve: I'd heard Freddy's arguments and opinions on the matter. The perfect handle. If I managed it well, it might prove more effective than anything else. Opening that door would give me an insight into practically every aspect of her character that was important to me: literary taste, personality, ideals, emotions, intellect, political views. A conversation about Beauvoir, initiated and conducted with appropriate subtlety, would be an infallible test. It wasn't a subject one could talk about without revealing something of oneself in the process. If my questions were well thought out, her replies would speak volumes about her.

After a while, however, my optimism began to flag. Literary debate as a way of plumbing another's soul, snatching those 'illusory moments of closeness', was a lovely idea, but what did it mean in practice? For one thing, it would take a vast amount of preparation. I'd have to plough through those dreadful novels and dreary memoirs all over again, and reading them wouldn't be enough: I'd have to study them in detail – learn them by heart, almost! A hellish prospect. And then, of course, I'd have to think out my strategy for the conversation itself: how to steer it in the direction I wanted, how to phrase my questions so that they would subtly elicit the desired *confessions*. The backbreaking effort this would require was beyond me. And even supposing that I managed it all, how was this conversation supposed to arise, and where? In a classroom? In her office? Unlikely, to say the least. As if I hadn't witnessed enough efforts, with aims far more innocent than mine, nipped in the bud!

By the end of the third period I had lost the remnants of any faith I'd had in my various schemes. I no longer believed there was any action I could take to ease my Werther-like sufferings. And then a new fear took hold of me. I became convinced I was completely transparent, that my pathetic and humiliating torments, as well as the fact that I was harbouring some secret knowledge, must be plainly visible. And the thought that in half an hour I would be face to face with her made me panic. No, I couldn't let her see me in this state. I would have to abandon the field until I was in better shape.

During the first break, without a word to anyone of my intentions, I quietly slipped out of school.

At first I wandered the streets for a while, trying to imagine what was happening in the French class, and especially how it had begun. She would take attendance; when I didn't answer she would check the register: no 'ab' for 'absent' in the first three spaces of the column next to my name. That meant I had been present earlier. '*Qu'est-ce qu'il y a?* Where is he? He was here before? And then what? *Disparu?* Did he have permission to leave? No one knows? Curious habits the boy has.' What would happen? Would she lower my mark for the term? Would she ask me about it? Demand an explanation? And what would I say? My notebook! That's it. 'I haven't got my notebook. *Vous le gardez toujours.* Besides, I thought you'd had enough of me and my clever ways. So I didn't want to impose . . .' That wasn't bad. What would she say to that?

The thought of my notebook inspired me to action. In Paris Commune Square, not far from the spot where the unhappy Ruhla had met its fate, I boarded a bus that took me down to Aleje Ujazdowskie, where there was a bookshop called Logos-Cosmos. It stocked mostly foreign-language books imported from the West; the Soviet and East German art books prominently displayed in the window were exceptions. You could order books there (the wait was four months if conditions were favourable, a year if they were not, and an eternity if they were frankly inclement), and they specialised in antiquarian volumes, of which they had an excellent selection. I liked going there and did so often, although my visits tended to be painful: the astronomical prices, especially for new books from 'bourgeois countries', meant that I usually couldn't afford anything. But I continued my visits undeterred, even when I wasn't looking for anything in particular. For besides its wide range of stock and its services, the Logos-Cosmos had other attractive features: its interior, the attitude of its staff and the process of effecting a transaction were all much more pleasant than in other bookshops, and, most important, you could *browse*. The bookshelves and counters were set against the walls, and the customers were actually allowed to approach them and take down the books they wanted *by themselves*. They were even permitted to *shuffle randomly* through the stacks piled up on the counters and shelves. But if you were in a hurry or couldn't find the book you wanted, an eager and polite assistant was always on hand to help you; you might even be invited to 'please be so kind as to follow him' into the mysterious back regions of the shop.

I pushed open the heavy door and with pounding heart headed straight for the French section. Would it be there? Yes, there it was! Or, strictly speaking, there *she* was – for 'Victory' in French is a feminine noun. The eight red letters of the title stood out strikingly on the cream-coloured cover:

Joseph Conrad
VICTOIRE
Du monde entier
Gallimard

I looked at the back, where the price was marked. Eighty-two zlotys! A fortune! For that amount of money I could buy at least three chess books in the bookshop known as 'Soviet' or a decent LP in the music shop, not to mention other *desiderata* and pleasures such as the cinema (seven tickets), the theatre (at least three) or taxis (five rides from home to school). But I didn't hesitate. Setting my teeth and clasping my find firmly to my breast, I went on to the German section.

Schopenhauer, Joanna. *Jugendleben* something something. I couldn't find it. But I did find Friedrich Hölderlin's *Gedichte*, an old hardcover edition in Gothic script. On the flyleaf was a circular black stamp with a swastika and an eagle and the words: *Stolp – Garnisonsbibliothek*. I looked at the table of contents to see if the *Rhine* hymn was there. It was: *Der Rhein*. The price was six zlotys. Excellent. Sold.

At the cash desk I asked nonchalantly, with the air of a world-travelled scholar, whether they ever had Joanna Schopenhauer's *Jugendleben und . . . Wander*. 'You know,' I added, 'the mother of the philosopher.'

The assistant paused in the wrapping of my precious acquisitions, looked at me keenly and disappeared into the back regions. A moment later he returned bearing a book with a yellowish-cream cover and a title in black Gothic-style letters:

Joanna Schopenhauer
MEMORIES OF A GDANSK YOUTH

'Is this what you had in mind?' he inquired with a hint of amusement.

'Well, well! A Polish edition!' I exclaimed in the confident tones of an expert, trying to conceal my surprise. 'When was it published?'

'Oh, a good seven years ago,' he replied politely. 'In '59. It's catalogued as antiquarian.'

Slowly, unconcernedly, I began to turn the pages, looking for chapter thirty-nine. 'Is the translation any good?' I asked offhandedly.

'It's Ossolineum – best publisher in the country!' he said with feigned indignation. 'Do you have doubts about their competence?'

My eye, in the meantime, had alighted on some of the French phrases, printed in italics, that I'd seen in the Gdansk edition of Joanna's memoirs at Constant's. '*Ah, quel chien de pays!*' Yes, this was it. Here was the description of the journey back to Gdansk through Westphalia. I looked hastily for some stylistic infelicity, found it, and proceeded to read aloud:

> We were reluctant, however, to stray from the main roads through which we had to crawl for days on end, called highroads, which were bestrewn with huge stones from the fields, for the smaller roads which ran alongside, which were called summer roads, in which our carriage sank in the mud up to its axles.

Raising my eyes from the page, I said with a grimace of distaste, 'You think this is good? It's hardly what I'd call a balanced sentence. All those subordinate clauses, for a start, flung in any old how, with no order or rhythm, and then those whiches all over the place – through which we had to crawl . . . which were bestrewn . . . which ran alongside . . . which were called – you must admit it doesn't exactly bowl one over with its syntactical beauty. And that peculiar choice of verb: bestrewn?! Please!' I rolled my eyes. 'It's all so clumsy and stilted. I'm sure this isn't how Joanna Schopenhauer expressed herself. Now if *I* were writing this,' I went on, 'and had to stick with this unfortunate choice of vocabulary, at least I'd arrange it better. For instance, oh, I don't know – like this: 'The main highroads were littered with huge stones from the fields, so that we had to crawl along for days on end. We were nevertheless reluctant to abandon them for the smaller roads that ran alongside, known as summer roads, for there our carriage sank to its axles in mud.' Isn't that better? Clearer? And it gets rid of all those whiches. And the phrasing . . . the rhythm . . . the balance.' I closed my eyes in blissful contemplation. 'I trust you appreciate the difference.'

The assistant laughed as if I were a monkey which had just performed a clever trick, but there was respect in his amusement. (It was in just this way that S. had laughed when I'd suddenly begun to recite Shakespeare and then improvise.)

'Oh, indeed I do,' he said, chuckling, 'indeed I do.'

'How, then,' I pursued, adopting a mock-serious tone, 'do you propose to express your appreciation in your attitude to me as a party in the transaction between us?'

He chuckled again and took up the game. 'In what way, if I may ask, do you imagine that it might be expressed?'

'In what way? Obviously,' I replied, 'by reducing the price.' I widened my eyes in surprise that this simple solution had not occurred to him. 'By a magnanimous rebate. Let's see.' I closed the book and placed it on the counter, back cover up. 'The original price was . . . twenty-eight zlotys. And what is it now?' I glanced inside the dust jacket. 'Ten zlotys more! How do you justify such a drastic increase? Surely not by the quality of the translation.'

'It's not the translation that determines the price. It's demand.'

'Do you mean to suggest that Joanna Schopenhauer's memoirs of her Gdansk youth are in demand in this country as an article of the most urgent necessity?'

'Perhaps not the *most* urgent,' he conceded with a straight face, 'but urgent enough to justify thirty-eight zlotys. Hardly excessive, I would have thought – indeed, it's something of a bargain. Many people,' he continued, picking up the book and stroking its cover as if he were brushing away dust, 'would *happily* pay *double* that amount for it, and be grateful.'

'Possibly, but where are they?' I looked about me. 'They don't appear to be exactly crowding around. I'm not sure it would be wise to bet on them. Here, on the other hand, you have a sure thing: a customer eager to part with his cash. Wouldn't it be more prudent to meet him halfway than to wait God knows how long for that fabulous beast, the buyer who'll allegedly be happy to pay even more?'

'What exactly do you mean by meeting him *halfway*?'

'Oh, very little, really. Annul that draconian increase and revert to the original price printed on the cover.'

'Twenty-eight zlotys?!' He laughed with derision. 'You must be joking!'

'All right, then, thirty-two. That's all I can pay. One hundred and twenty zlotys is the sum of my assets.' I extracted two crumpled bills from my pocket and displayed them: a brick-coloured hundred-zloty note bearing a portrait of the Worker and a dark-blue twenty with the Peasant Woman. 'For these two,' I said, nodding at *Gedichte* and *Victoire,* 'I owe you the horrendous sum of eighty-eight zlotys. That leaves thirty-two. Which is all I have.'

'In other words, you're demanding a reduction of six zlotys.'

'Not demanding – suggesting. As the natural conclusion.'

'Do you realise what it would mean if I yielded to your pressure?'

'I'm not pressuring you, I'm merely making an observation.' My mother's rhetoric had its uses.

'If I agreed to it, then.'

'It would mean a good sale: three books in one go.'

'Not at all. On the contrary. It would mean I'd be giving you one book – the German one – for free.'

'A commendable deed on your part.'

'Why commendable?'

'Have you seen what's inside?' I lowered my voice. 'A swastika! Would you want to make a profit on something like that?' I shuddered with horror and indignation. 'And that's not all! Look at this,' I hissed, opening the book at the flyleaf. '*Garnisonsbibliothek!* A military library! Do you realise what that means?'

He gave me a smile of resignation and shook his head. 'All right, all right.' He closed the book and placed it on top of the memoirs. 'You've missed your vocation. You should be in a cabaret.'

'Actually, I am sometimes,' I said coyly.

'Shall I wrap them?' He was amused.

'No, thank you, you needn't bother.'

He pushed the little pile over to me and put the banknotes away in the till.

I put my spoils in my satchel, said goodbye politely and left the bookshop.

Queen's Gambit

The rest of that day and the next were spent reading. I finished *Victory,* skimmed through the French version, acquainted myself with Joanna Schopenhauer's memoirs and learnt to decipher Gothic script. I also started a new notebook. But instead of furnishing it with the usual identifying signs (name, class, subject), I wrote on the cover only the enigmatic title '*Cahier des citations*' and copied into it various passages and phrases from the books I'd been reading.

The first to go in were three stanzas from the *Rhine* hymn: the one Constant had quoted, 'But now, from within / The mountains' hidden depths . . .'; the one that began, 'It was the voice of the noblest of rivers . . .'; and the one with the sentence I had seen in the dedication, which began, 'A mystery is the pure of source . . .' I carefully underlined the lines 'C.' had quoted, and next to them wrote out Constant's translation ('For as you were born, so will you remain . . .'), too.

On the following pages (of recycled paper, as a notice on the cover informed me) I copied out extracts from the memoirs, mainly from chapter thirty-nine, which was devoted to the journey back from England. Among them were the following:

> Moreover, I had set out, quite unconsciously [this underlining was also mine], in a state in which women ought not to travel unless they are obliged to do so by the most urgent necessity . . .

> My fluency in the language and the ease with which I adapted to the local customs and ways made me a welcome guest.

> For a long time I was thought to be much older than I was. [I had altered this sentence in what one might call a fairly fundamental way: the author had in fact written that she had been thought *younger* than she was.]

> And I constantly sighed to myself: *Ah, quel chien de pays!* [This, too, I had altered, although only slightly: she had merely written 'again', not 'constantly'.]

After that came a series of passages from *Victoire*. These were the most numerous, partly because of the language, since of my three books – collected, after all, with rather singular criteria in mind – this was the only one in French, but mostly because of the content, although my interest in it was not quite the same as Constant's. For him the main interest lay in the character of Heyst: Heyst was Max, and in Heyst he sought the explanation for Max's responses, for his impulse to rebel, and later for his mortal struggle with the evil of the world. For me, on the other hand, the most important and, in a way, most familiar character in the book was Alma – or Lena, as Heyst came to call her: the young English musician, beautiful, proud and brave, quite alone, thrown back on her own resources, ensnared by the owners of the band and struggling to escape the yoke of slavery. I felt that her plight was in many ways similar to Madame's. And then, of course, there was that title: that one word printed on the cover, standing alone, without the feminine article. It read like a name – the name of the book's protagonist, like Lord Jim or Phaedra. To me it seemed a sign that the whole novel was about a character called Victory.

And indeed, might not sentences such as these – 'And I am here, with no one to care if I make a hole in the water the next chance I get or not . . . There's nothing so lonely in the world as a girl who has got to look after herself' – have issued from Madame's lips at some stage in her past, in a moment of desperation, perhaps in the course of a conversation with Constant? Or that time she came to him asking for help (for that one special favour), might she not have said, '*You* do something! You are a gentleman. It wasn't I who spoke to you first, was it? I didn't begin, did I? It was you who came along and spoke to me . . .'? And might he then not have replied, like Heyst, 'I am not rich enough to buy you out, even if it were to be done,' and added, after a moment, 'It will be all right'?

The book was full of things that could be taken as applying, in one way or another, to Madame's life. Another passage, near the end of my selection, contained the following words, spoken by Heyst: 'I only know that he who forms a tie is lost. The germ of corruption has entered into his soul.'

The final chords of my peculiar anthology sounded like a postscript added by the scribe: I heard my own voice coming through them. They were, of course, Heyst's famous words: '. . . can I do anything? What would you wish me to do? Pray command me' ('*Je suis à vos ordres*').

In the course of this labour – reading, choosing the quotations and weaving them into a net of my own singular design – I was hindered by an uncomfortable awareness that I was sinking to the level of the *Ashes* worshippers. It made no difference what the book was and whether its heroine was the passionate Helena de With or the musician Lena. The effect, or rather the intention, was the same: to imagine you were experiencing something modelled on the story. Pretending that a character in the book was someone you knew, you seized on phrases that sounded suggestive or ambiguous and then fetishised them and excited yourself by imagining them uttered in a different context. Take, for instance, the following sentence I copied out: 'But you do it most charmingly – in a perfectly fascinating way', which in *Victory* referred to Lena's charming smile; taken out of context, it could be made to refer to whatever one liked. Wasn't it exactly the same sort of thing as that exhortation in *Ashes* which everyone had underlined, 'Well, take off your clothes!'?

Yes and no. For while the practice may have been similar, the fetishised objects were very different. It was hard to believe that the two books had been written at almost the same time by men of the same generation (the author of *Ashes* was only seven years younger than Conrad) and nationality. One was fascinating and immensely readable: its plot was intriguing, its prose simple and elegant, its characters convincingly drawn; and it posed the philosophical problem of the human attitude to evil. The other was either tedious and turgid or, in the romantic bits, sentimental and grotesque – mostly all four at once. In short, it was kitsch, and you cringed as you waded through its pomposities and laboured prose.

Could Roz Goltz have been right when he said that if Conrad hadn't gone to England and changed his language, he would have written like 'that precious little wonder of ours, Zeromski'?

* * *

On the day of the next French lesson, I came to school equipped with my new 'aids': *Victoire,* my *Cahier des citations*, and Joanna Schopenhauer's memoirs. But before deciding to put them to use I checked the register to see whether I had been put down as absent the last time. I hadn't. Odd. Attendance had certainly been taken, for others who had been absent (from the first period) did have an 'ab' in the fourth space next to their names, clearly in Madame's writing. Then why didn't I? Had some kind soul covered up for me and somehow managed to explain away my absence? Or had Madame filled in the sheet after the lesson, mechanically, guided only by the entries that were already there? The latter was more likely; if it had been the former, someone would certainly have told me about it. In any event, whatever the reasons, I made my decision.

Before the class began, just before she walked in, I took out my 'aids' and put them next to me on the edge of the bench (*Victoire* on top and the *Cahier* on the bottom). During the first quarter of an hour (questions and conversation) I sat motionless, without taking my eyes off her, and thought about how all the things I had found out about her accorded with my own impressions – with the person I knew. I was no longer afraid. Perfectly calm and certain of my position, I waited for her first move.

But she made no move. She paid attention to the others and none at all to me. This was not unprecedented behaviour on her part. She had resorted to it several times in the past, and since the confiscation of my notebook it had become almost the rule.

I launched my offensive – Operation Queen's Gambit. I picked up *Victoire,* took the *Cahier des citations* from the bottom of the pile and put it on top, opened the novel on the page with the words 'Pray command me', and ostentatiously set about pretending to read. I slid down on the bench, sprawling comfortably, stretched out my legs, crossed at the ankles, and propped up the book on the edge of the desk so that the red title was visible from the teacher's table at the front of the room.

I'm waiting, I'm all ears, I thought to myself, mentally

parodying one of her favourite provocative little sayings. Will you take my offering? This cream-coloured piece is quite unprotected, entirely exposed. Those two pawns over there, on the edge of the bench, can also be taken with impunity. Well? Do you accept? I must remind you that time is on my side. I've used up far less than you. The time on your clock has almost run out. You'd better hurry up!

This telepathic bluster provoked no reaction whatsoever, which was perhaps to be expected, but my ostentatious behaviour was equally ineffectual. Madame not only failed to initiate any of the proceedings so dear to the eternally lurking Viper (invasion, confiscation, pillory, record of iniquities committed entered in the register) but did nothing to call me to order. She couldn't have failed to notice that I was boycotting her lesson; of that I was certain. I had made myself conspicuous enough. Besides, I had occasion to observe, when I periodically glanced up from the book to check her reactions, that she knew perfectly well what I was doing. Yet she said nothing. No hint of remonstrance showed on her face; she appeared determined to ignore me. If you think you can provoke me this way, her eyes seemed to be saying as they wandered in my vicinity, you are deeply mistaken. After all, *I* don't care whether you learn this language or not, or what kind of mark you get. If you think you already know it all and have nothing to gain from participating in this class, fine – that's your choice. It's no concern of mine. On the contrary, it makes my life easier: one thing less to worry about.

Yes: she might well think that way; it would be just like her. She knew that my French was much better than the others', indeed that it went far beyond school level; to this she was completely indifferent. When she had first discovered that I spoke more or less fluently and with a good accent, she hadn't commented on it – hadn't said, for instance, '*Mais tu parles bien! Tiens, tiens!* Where did you learn to speak like that?' – but had passed over it in silence. Later, when I began to indulge in conspicuous displays of my fluency, forever interrupting with some remark and flashing my good accent around, she seemed to cool off even more.

But she can't be entirely indifferent to everything I do, I

thought, looking down at my book, it's just not possible. Here I am, reading a book that has as its title the word that is her name, a word, moreover, which has already been mentioned in a significant context – in the message woven into my essay. Could she have failed to notice? Could it all be *still* not provocative enough?

In order to exclude this possibility I went a step further. I laid the memoirs on the bench (open at the page where I had underlined *Ah, quel chien de pays!*); in front of me I placed the *Cahier des citations* (open to the last of my selected quotations, with the phrase '*Je suis à vos ordres*'); finally, I put the open novel *vertically* on the right-hand corner of the desk, its cover to the front of the room, so that the title was visible. Thus entrenched, shielded by *Victoire* and dug in behind the memoirs, I huddled low over the '*Cahier*' and set about pretending to make notes.

This manoeuvre, too, failed to provoke a reaction from the opposition: she disregarded it as she had disregarded the others. Not only did she not retaliate by shooting, she didn't even send out a reconnaissance squad to determine the extent of my resources and nature of my weapons. As she passed me on her way to the door at the end of the class she deliberately, ostentatiously looked the other way. The more you try to draw attention to yourself, she seemed to be saying, the less attention I shall pay to you. *Tu ne m'intéresses pas!*

I refused to admit defeat. Patience, young man, patience! said Freddy's voice in my head. A siege takes nerve and endurance. We'll take this citadel yet; if we can't shoot our way in, we'll starve the enemy out. I resolved, therefore, to stick with it. From then on, at every French lesson I went through the same routine: I'd spread my three baiting aids around me on the bench and pretend to be absorbed in my work, waiting tensely for the longed-for attack.

For several days nothing happened. She continued to behave as if I weren't there. I began to lose hope. Still I persevered. And this turned out, quite soon, to be the right tactic after all.

One day at the end of the lesson, when I had been particularly assiduous in my 'note-taking', she told the boy on classroom duty to collect everyone's notebooks, since she wanted, she claimed, 'to get an idea *de quoi ils ont l'air* before handing out our final marks at the end of term'. My head spun. It had worked after all! She had taken the bait, hadn't been able to resist! She wanted to get an idea, did she? How interesting. I meekly handed over my *Cahier des citations*, after furnishing it with my initials.

During break, and over the next few days, I tried by various methods to discover whether she had ordered a similar inspection in her other classes. No one had ever come across this particular form of 'pressure'. 'She took away your notebooks?' people asked incredulously. 'To go over them? And it's going to affect the results for the term? *Adieu,* then, *"suffisant"! Bonjour, "insuffisant"!*'

But the bells in my own head were pealing in triumph, not alarm. For the evidence clearly indicated that the inspection had as it sole purpose to settle accounts with me.

Future events neither contradicted my suspicions nor confirmed them. The *Cahier des citations* was returned to me as it had been collected: by the duty boy. It bore no marks or annotations of any kind – it might not have been examined at all. This conspicuous absence of any indications that it had been scrutinised or even read might of course be construed as significant in itself; it was, after all, a reaction of a sort. But it could be so construed only on the supposition that it was unique, and this was not the case: the absence of comments or marks was general. Everyone's notebook came back in pristine condition Nor was there any verbal summing-up of the results of the inspection. She just took them and then gave them back, without a word – as if the whole procedure had been merely an exercise in the enforcement of discipline, or a whim whose purpose was best known to herself.

The one clear, unquestionable act of retaliation on her part did not come until later, when I discovered that I was the only person in the whole school, not just in the class, to get an A for the term.

The Knight's Way, the Courtier's Way and the Scientific Way

What did it mean?

Was it supposed to show that Madame knew how advanced I was in French and was prepared, despite my far from exemplary behaviour, indeed my frank impertinence, to give credit where credit was due? Utopian surmise, about as plausible as the heartwarming but trite story of the undisciplined young genius and the patient, devoted teacher. Experience taught a different lesson: that one's marks depended not just on one's competence but also, in large measure, on one's 'attitude' – in other words, on good behaviour. You could soar above everyone else and still not get an A; if you were late, or didn't pay attention, or seemed too cocksure, or failed to be organised enough in your note-taking, the coveted mark was lowered or withdrawn. This case contradicted experience. That had to mean something. But what?

The only answer that came to mind was that it was a trick, a deceitful ploy intended to disarm me. My advancement was nothing but an attempt at a manoeuvre known in the language of politics as 'kicking someone upstairs'. In other words, she wanted to defang me; she was promoting me to be rid of me. I hope he enjoys it, she must have been thinking, I hope he's satisfied with his triumph. So long as he stops pestering me. Here's your A, and now leave me alone! That's what this meant. You've got what you wanted; now for God's sake go!

How was I to react? And what were my options?

There seemed to be three. The first and simplest was to admit defeat. To say to myself, Well, it didn't work. Too bad. That's how it goes. You can't force these things, and it's self-defeating to try. They either work or they don't. If this is her way of showing that she can see through my manoeuvres and refuses to play the game, or, at best, of giving me fair warning that I musn't count on anything, well, I'll just have to respect and accept that.

This was the chivalrous way; the way of submission, the

way of the gallant medieval knight. The response of Schiller's knight Toggenburg.

The opposite of submission was refusal. This was the second way: to refuse to submit at any price and, instead, to attack. To launch a resolute, vigorous and undisguised offensive. Perhaps in something like the following style: I throw off all scruples and restraints, I cast away all sense of shame. I walk up to her, fearlessly, unhesitatingly – right after class would be best – and ask her straight out to what I owe the honour of such a high mark. To my charm? My eloquence, perhaps? The *Cahier des citations*? Or was it, after all, mainly my essay about the stars? I admit I put considerable effort into that *confession.* But it was worth it. No, I don't mean my mark; I mean the results, the high standard of work. Since I haven't heard any criticism from her, I conclude that it *was* high, which, of course, pleases me greatly. But then, what's grammar, after all! We have language in order to communicate, to share our thoughts. So I'm wondering what she thought of what I wrote. Does she share my views about astrology? Would she agree that people born under certain signs were meant for each other? And she herself . . . yes, what sign is she? Oh, please, surely she won't refuse to answer this time? It's a perfectly innocuous question. Well, all right, if for some reason she'd rather not, I won't insist. 'But whatever it is . . . *vous êtes . . . ma victoire.*' – 'Victoire?' – '*Mais oui*: my victory over myself.'

This was the Renaissance way; the way of Elizabethan courtship, the way of the bold Shakespearean lover.

The third and last way lay somewhere between the two: not to submit and yet not to attack. To wait, but not idly. To try to transfer the game to a different court, outside school, to throw the ball onto neutral ground. Somewhere where school rules no longer applied, where, instead of mistress and servant, headmistress and pupil, there would be just two people.

This was the most ambitious way, a way worthy of the enlightened rationalism of Voltaire and Rousseau. It was also the most tempting of the three.

Mute submission, although the simplest, I couldn't accept. It would leave too bitter a taste, too many regrets. The

'Renaissance' lover's onslaught, on the other hand, with all its outspoken boldness and dashing repartee, I felt was beyond me. That kind of thing required a lightness of heart I didn't have; one couldn't pull it off when consumed by passion. Which, unfortunately, I was. For passion renders one helpless, or at least it weakens one's control – over one's face, one's voice, one's gestures and especially one's language. Passion is always gloomy and devoid of lightness . . . I'd read that somewhere (could it have been in *The Magic Mountain*?); now I was discovering for myself how true it was.

I chose the third way.

Unarmed and unequipped, I set off for new territories.

Centre de Civilisation

The inspiringly named Centre de Civilisation Française no longer inhabited its old quarters in the massive, stately old Staszic House on the Royal Way, in that delta of the New World Boulevard which forms the gates of the Krakowskie Przedmiescie, the street that leads to the Old City. It had moved out almost a quarter of a century ago to take up residence in a dilapidated university building on Obozna Street. The same building was also home to the Department of Romance Languages and, ironically enough, to the equally dilapidated Biology Department, poverty-stricken and stinking permanently of mice and experiment rats. The interior aspect of its quarters was no doubt also far removed from the grandeur and spaciousness of the room known, before the war, as the Gold Room. Three cramped little cells where desks, shelves and filing cabinets with a card catalogue jostled for space acted simultaneously as archives, records room, lending library and, according to a notice tacked onto one of the doors, *salle de lecture*. This was the face that French Civilisation, in other words French Culture – that embodiment of Rationalism, Progress, Modernity and Freedom – presented to the world.

And yet, despite it all – despite the pokiness and shabbiness and poverty, the flimsy doors, the disgusting floors, the seedy office furniture, the windows unwashed since the Flood and the general air of decline – one felt this place was different from other places, even from others in the same building, places like, for instance, the office or reading room of the department I had recently visited.

The first thing that struck one as different was the smell. It was a pleasant, delicate and somehow invigorating mixture of subtle (not sweet) lily of the valley and good tobacco (Gitanes and Gauloises, as it turned out). Then there were all those ingenious, well-designed, attractive little items of office paraphernalia that you never saw anywhere else: different-coloured drawing-pins and rubber bands; shiny paper-clips in an oval dish with a magnetic 'crater' at the bottom; rolls of Sellotape (both clear and opaque) in those clever round little plastic gadgets with a serrated edge to tear it off neatly; and, finally, a huge collection of non-refillable Bic pens. They were mainly of the straight, polygonal kind, made of some sort of translucent material, with different-coloured caps (blue, red or black) and metal tips, slender and tapering like the nose cone of a missile, with ink to match; but also some of the rounded kind with long, straight, transparent tips and a small vertical slit at the side where you clicked a triangular sort of tooth in and out.

To this rich panoply was added the equally unusual appearance of the books on the shelves and the newspapers and magazines neatly arranged on a long, sloping stand. For the books were not covered in the grey cardboard or coarse brown wrapping paper familiar from other libraries; here, bright bindings and colourful jackets (and quite a few of them had jackets) gleamed through smooth layers of laminated plastic or stiff Cellophane, materials not employed in the manufacture of book bindings in any of the Warsaw Pact countries, not even in the eastern part of the homeland of Gutenberg, technically the most advanced. The magazines, even the daily newspapers such as *Le Figaro* and *Le Monde*, looked quite different from ours; even the print was different. Polish newspapers were printed on coarse, fibrous paper that tore at the slightest provocation; the print was ugly, uneven, badly-aligned and easily smudged.

Here the paper was thin and smooth and yet quite resistant to tearing; the magazines were glossy; the print was clear and graceful and pleasing to the eye.

Finally, behind a massive desk covered with green baize, which also served as the reception desk, sat a woman of distinguished and elegant aspect, as unlike the personnel one met in Polish secretariats, reading rooms and administration offices as it was possible to imagine. Around sixty, slim and sharp-featured, with short, well-cut hair touched with silver-grey, she wore an attractive pair of rimless spectacles with a delicate gold bridge and equally thin gold legs, a beautifully cut suit of grey wool, and at her neck a wine-coloured scarf. She sat perfectly straight and typed with energy and competence. There were silver rings on her long, bony fingers and a silver bracelet on her right wrist. On the baize, near the hand with the braceleted wrist, lay a packet of Gitanes, a red cylindrical lighter of transparent plastic, and a white ashtray that said 'Courvoisier'. In the ashtray was the crushed stub of a Gitane with a trace of red lipstick.

On the way in I had assumed, in my ignorance and possibly also under the influence of the vision or, less grandiosely, *l'imaginaire* evoked by the name of this shopwindow of French *esprit,* that the place would be buzzing with activity, perhaps even crowded, so that my quiet entry would go unremarked. The unexpected calm that reigned inside was disconcerting. My self-assurance deserted me, and I fell into a state of confused indecision. Instead of crossing immediately to the empty reading room and there thinking through the details of my plan in peace and quiet, I lingered foolishly at the newspaper stand and began to leaf uncertainly through *Le Figaro*. The results of this slip, or rather this schoolboy error, were no more than thirty seconds in coming.

'May I help you?' asked the silver lady, interrupting her typing. Her voice was deep and low, and strikingly like the voice of one of the women newsreaders on Radio Free Europe.

Once again I had to improvise. My only compass was the rule book of chess, and the rules of chess said: don't attack too early, especially not with your queen – reserve her for later;

choose, if you can, one of the less popular openings; develop your strategy steadily and wait for your opponent to make a mistake; don't launch your offensive until your position is well secured. In the present case this boiled down to gaining the favour of the silver-haired Marianne, or even winning her heart.

'Well, I'm looking for something a bit out of the ordinary,' I said, approaching the desk, 'and that's why I was hesitating whether to ask you at all. I saw you were busy, so I didn't want to interrupt you.'

'What is it? Ask away.' She measured me with a careful glance. 'There's nothing that can't be managed. It's only a question of determination. At worst, of time.'

'That's a rare attitude; it's very nice of you. But I wonder if it really can be managed in this case. You see, what I'm looking for has a connection with French culture that's . . . well, rather special, unusual, not immediately obvious.'

'As long as there's *some* connection,' she replied, smiling.

'It's a translation. Specifically, a French translation of the *Rhine* hymn by Hölderlin. You know – that amazing German poet who crossed the Alps to Bordeaux, alone, and then, on his way back, still alone, and on foot, experienced a vision and went mad. Apparently, while he was up on some peak, he saw Dionysus and talked to him. And in Paris . . . but anyway, that's not the point. The point is, I'm writing an essay on romantic journeys – the Marquis de Custine's, Joanna Schopenhauer's – and I need a quotation from Hölderlin's *Rhine* hymn. And the reason I need it in French, and not in Polish or German, is that I'm writing it for a competition in the journal . . . *Perspective de Genève,* and they want all the quotations in French. I've got the same problem with Joanna Schopenhauer, but at least that's prose, so at a pinch I can do the translation myself. But poetry – and a poem like this!' I shrugged and raised my eyes heavenwards. 'Anyway, I've been everywhere. All the libraries: the main library, the departmental libraries, even the national library. None of them has it. No one could help me. Finally someone told me I should come here; they said it's the kind of thing you'd be able to help with. The Centre, they said, wouldn't let me down. So here I am. You're my last hope. And I ought to mention that the first prize in the competition is a month's stay in Switzerland – not something to be sneezed at. With trips to the Alps, and not just anywhere in the Alps: to the sources of the Rhine, in the St Gotthard Pass and the Adula range, where *trembling forests* –'

I galloped on with a shameless imitation of Constant, my eyes half-closed, my head thrown slightly back, reciting in German, with a dreadful accent and some inaccuracy,

> *. . . and crags high above*
> *Look down, every day,*
> *There, in that icy abyss . . .*

and stopped, unable to remember the rest. To cover up the lacuna I quickly added, as if it were the final chord of the melody, the beginning of the third stanza, the one I knew best:

> *. . . the voice of the noblest of rivers,*
> *The freeborn Rhine . . .*

The silver-haired Marianne was regarding me with a smile worthy of the author of the *Treatise on Toleration.*

'To the Adula range, you say,' she remarked finally, as if the name stirred some memory, and added elegiacally, in German, 'There, into that icy abyss,' with a perfect accent and an appropriate change of case.

I froze. She knows German . . . she knows everything! She's seen through me! I'm done for! But my fears proved groundless. Her tone and expression had been no more than a game, a playful form of irony.

'Make sure you don't fall in.' She raised her eyebrows in mock caution.

'I can assure you I intend to follow your advice,' I replied, returning her smile and lowering my eyes. 'However, first I have to win the competition.'

'Well, if that's the goal' – she rose energetically and strode to the card catalogue – 'to work! Hölderlin's *Rhine,* you say . . . German Romanticism, then.'

She stood at the catalogue with her back to me: elegant, dignified, statuesque. There was something regal in her demeanour. Even in such ordinary and trifling movements as those involved in the pulling out of drawers and shuffling through index cards she displayed harmony and grace, moving as though picking delicately through jewels or playing the harp. And suddenly it struck me that her way of carrying herself, her whole way of being, was in many ways similar to Madame's. Of course! The *pas,* the gestures, the 'choreography' of the whole – it was all there. The elegance, the precision, the always slightly excessive haughtiness; the same sharp, nimble tongue; the same irony and playful contrariness. Only with her it was friendly and appealing, not icy; it didn't, as with Madame, freeze the blood in your veins.

What would it hurt her, I thought wistfully of my queen, to play an 'open', not a 'closed' variation of this 'French *partie*'; to play it in a major, not a minor key. She would gain so much! We would both gain so much by it!

The silver-haired Marianne, meanwhile, had hauled down from the stacks a tome of imposing dimensions and was now engaged, balancing it against the edge of a conveniently situated shelf, in turning its pages.

I wondered where Constant had taught this poem to Claire, and how he went about it. Had he recited it to her, as he had to me? Or had he given it to her to read? Whatever he did, if it was in the Centre (wherever it was quartered at that time) it was being repeated now – like a musical theme. Once again someone was singing this song to someone who works here. As if it were an echo coming back, years later. The 'holy fire' still burns, then! The old times *are* returning!

'*C'est ensuite seulement que les impies . . .*' Marianne's deep alto resounded suddenly in the silence. She was reading from the book open in front of her, pointing with the tips of two fingers to a place roughly in the middle of the page. The fingers proceeded downwards as she read out the rest of the text:

. . . flouting their own laws, in sure
Defiance of heavenly fire,

Chose to scorn the ways of mortals; then it was
That in their arrogant contempt they strove
To be the equals of the gods.

She raised her eyes from the page and turned to me.

I understood the words, but I wasn't sure where they came from. The poem whose translation into the language of Clovis and his descendants I allegedly wanted was not a poem I knew well, to say the least. In fact, I knew (from the German edition) only that it had been written in 1801 and dedicated to someone called Sinclaire; that it consisted of unrhymed stanzas; that there were fifteen of these, and that they were long, most of them fifteen lines. This was all I knew about its form. My knowledge of its content boiled down to the one fragment pencilled faintly on the title page of Joanna Schopenhauer's memoirs and a few of the lines above and below it, which Constant had translated for me during our conversation and which I had later copied out into my *Cahier.* About the rest of it, how it went on and what other themes it contained, I had not the slightest idea. So the 'impious' who flouted their own laws and defied the heavenly fire, although they sounded just as grand as 'the noblest of rivers', didn't quite seem to fit. It was prudent, therefore, to proceed with caution.

'*C'est une allusion à moi?*' I asked lightly, hoping above all to conceal my uncertainty and make it clear that I had understood the lines, but also to give the impression that an appropriate response, in a foreign language, presented no difficulty for me.

'*Pardon, mais pourquoi?*' She frowned and tilted her head to one side.

'*Voilà que moi . . . ,*' I hunted about feverishly for a suitably pithy phrase, and finally found refuge in: '. . . *je voudrais chasser un tigre avec un filet à papillons.*'

'You want to do what?'

'An old Polish expression: hunting a tiger with a butterfly net. *Un filet à papillons.*'

'*En français,*' she informed me in an amused tone (again, rather as Madame might have done, but in a friendly way), *'on dit plûtot "vouloir prendre la lune avec les dents"*: one wants to seize the moon with one's teeth.'

'Of course,' I agreed quickly, as if I'd known it all along and merely forgotten. Amused by the French expression as well as by the fact that the word *lune* was a feminine noun, I added with a smile, 'In fact, that's much more apposite in this case.'

'Apposite? Why?'

'If my moon is language – the art of speech,' I explained, deftly camouflaging the real cause of my merriment, 'then teeth are a more appropriate instrument than a butterfly net.'

'*Tiens.* Perhaps.' She shrugged. 'In any case, that wasn't my point. Your poet, according to what it says here,' she continued, glancing back at the book, 'was referring to people who foment revolution in the name of some noble idea but instead of creating a better world create hell on earth. Historically it's a reference to the leaders of the French Revolution, but morally it can be taken as applying to despots of any kind, especially usurpers in the clutches of *hubris* – overweening pride.' She looked up again.

'Well, if it wasn't an allusion to me, then why did you read that particular fragment? It's a very long poem – there are fifteen stanzas.'

'It's the one that caught my eye,' she explained. 'There are only excerpts here, not the whole poem. It's not an anthology of *poetry*' – she raised the book slightly – 'but a collection of essays on the poetry of the Romantic period by French scholars of German literature. And that's what's quoted here from the poem you're looking for – at least, it's the first excerpt I happened across; perhaps there are others.' She took the book back to the desk, laid it down on the dark-green cloth and began to leaf through it methodically.

Home at last! I thought. 'What I really need are the first three or four stanzas. Mainly the one that talks about how "the ray of light that greets the newborn" is stronger than adversity or education.'

'*Car tel tu es né, tel tu resteras*,' she read out with a questioning smile. 'Is that the one you mean? *Rien n'est plus puissant que la naissance, et le premier rayon du jour qui touche le nouveau-né*?'

'You've found it?!' I cried.

'*Mais qui, mieux que le Rhin,*' she continued in reply, '*naquit pour être libre?* Yes, it *is* rather good, isn't it,' she observed approvingly. 'Where is there another so happily born to be free? How did you come across it?'

I made a deprecating grimace, intended to imply that I was endowed with remarkable intuition. I also decided the time had come to launch my offensive.

'In fact,' I said, adopting a serious expression, 'it was because of a woman . . . a pianist . . . a rather extraordinary person that Providence sent my way. She taught me music and piano. And she had a rare and enchanting eloquence of expression. I could listen to her forever. (My own way of talking, which I think has struck you and has even, I notice, evoked a rather sardonic smile of long-suffering indulgence, is undoubtedly a remote . . . lame echo of the graceful, fascinating artificiality of her speech.) She adored literature, especially German poetry, and she often read me parts of poems to emphasise something she wanted to convey. And the *Rhine* hymn had a special place in her golden treasury of verse. She knew it by heart – all of it, in its entirety; she would recite it like a prayer . . .'

The smile spreading across the face of the silver Marianne was now a smile worthy only of the author of the *Discourse on Method.*

'It's partly as a tribute to her,' I continued, 'that I want to quote from that poem, but I also believe it has a magical power that will bring me victory.'

I took up the book of essays that lay on the baize in front of Marianne, found the excerpt on the page to which it was open and read it aloud (the version I give here is a translation from the French):

For as you are born, so will you remain;
Whatever the constraints
And the education,
Nothing is stronger
Than the moment of birth,
And the first ray of light that touches the newborn.

I raised my eyes and looked at Marianne with an expression intended to convey mingled wonder and gratitude. She, meanwhile, had seated herself on the right edge of the desk and lit a Gitane.

'So is that supposed to refer to you,' she asked, inhaling deeply and expelling the smoke through her nose, 'or your extraordinary piano teacher?' The ghost of a smile lingered at the corners of her lips.

'Both,' I replied pleasantly, 'but in different ways.'

'Well, there you are,' she said with finality, 'you've got what you came for.' But although her tone seemed to indicate the discussion was at an end, she made no move to rise. She continued to observe me with a playful, faintly questioning smile. Are you sure that's really all? it seemed to be asking.

'Thank you so much,' I said firmly, as if I, too, wished to wrap things up. 'I'll go and copy it out now.' I turned quickly and crossed over to the reading room.

I sat there somewhat longer than was necessary to copy out eleven lines of text. This was partly because, having discovered that the footnotes contained other excerpts of the poem in French translation, I copied them out as well, but I was also glad of the chance to rest a little after my latest bit of play-acting. Moreover, tactically it was a good idea to wait a while before going on with the game, which would shortly enter its last, decisive stage. So it was about half an hour later that I returned to the chessboard.

'Thank you once again,' I said quietly, but instead of putting the book down on the desk or anywhere else, I continued to hold it in my outstretched hand.

'Put it there,' she said, indicating a little table next to the desk and once again interrupting her labours at the huge Remington typewriter. 'And it was no trouble, really. That's what we're here for, after all.'

'We?'

'This institution. The Centre. That's our job.'

I decided there was no point in delaying. 'Actually, since you mention it, there's something else I'd like to ask, if I may.'

'Go ahead. Ask and ye shall receive.'

'Well, is it true that the Centre is helping to set up schools with French as the language of instruction?'

She looked surprised. 'It's the first I've heard of it. Who told you that?'

Pulling down my visor, I rushed to the attack. 'I couldn't really say where I heard it. These things get around. That's why I'm asking.' I tried to sound as casual as possible. 'I even heard that one such school is already in existence in Warsaw. Apparently the headmistress is a Frenchwoman; at least, she's supposed to be connected with the Centre.'

A glint of amusement twinkled in the eyes of the silver Marianne. She knows her, I thought, it's obvious! What will she say?

'Did you happen to hear her name, by any chance?' she asked, deadpan.

'Unfortunately not.' I spread my arms in a gesture of helpless ignorance and remained in that position, waiting for her next move.

'Well,' she said presently, 'I'm afraid I can't confirm it.'

'I'm sorry – what, exactly, can't you confirm?'

'To tell the truth, none of it. The Centre isn't setting up these schools, it doesn't have anything to do with it, and the headmistress in question – if I'm thinking of the same person – certainly isn't French.'

'I take it, then, that some bells *are* ringing, but not in the same church.'

'What do you mean?'

'Well, it sounds as if there might be a grain of truth in what I've been hearing.'

'I expect the project you've been hearing about is the Ministry of Education's. It's something they worked out in the context of an agreement between Poland and France about joint educational projects – co-operation, and so forth. But the French side of that is being looked after by the Service Culturel –'

'The Service Culturel?' I broke in.

'The cultural division of the French Embassy.'

So we've come as far as that, have we? A wave of heat went

through me, and my heart began to thump. 'And France appointed a school head who isn't French?' I affected astonishment. 'At least, they agreed to the appointment?'

'Don't you know where we are?' she said impatiently.

'Yes, I suppose you're right.'

'So are you, though,' she conceded. 'There were difficulties.'

'They couldn't come to an understanding, I suppose.'

'Despite everything agreed on during the talks, the Ministry of Education wouldn't hear of a French head. So the French side declared that in that case, if the head was to be Polish, at least they reserved for themselves the right to choose who it would be. The Ministry accepted this but in practice did its best to be obstructive. They found something wrong with every candidate who was proposed.'

'But they did accept . . . this woman . . . in the end?'

'Don't you believe it! Not at all.'

'How was she appointed?'

'The French dug in their heels. They decided that their prestige was being undermined, and they made it a condition: either she was appointed or the whole agreement was off and the project would be shelved.' She paused and added, with a derisive smile, 'The Poles agreed immediately.'

I remembered what Freddy had told me about 'exchanges abroad', the procurement of invitations and 'trade in human livestock'.

'There must be something in it for them,' I said in the tones of an expert.

'For whom?'

'For the Ministry of Education.'

'I doubt it,' she replied sceptically. 'It's more like a kind of tribute they have to pay: like serfs to the landed gentry. These agreements are imposed in the name of international co-operation, and they have to follow up.'

'I'm afraid you've lost me.'

'Well, what on earth do you think they want? Do you imagine anyone here cares about learning foreign languages? Especially French – that symbol of the culture of landed gentry and "bourgeois intelligentsia", that "relic of a past now consigned to the rubbish-heap of history"? *They* only want the material profits that can be squeezed out of this kind of deal; that's why they make concessions on education. Which don't usually come to much, in any case.'

'You mean they're doing it –?'

'Yes!' she broke in, 'they're doing it for show. Believe me, nothing will come of it.'

'But something already has, surely.'

'What?' She raised her eyebrows and stared at me.

'Well, this school . . . this headmistress, at least.'

'That's a trial thing, an experiment they call it. In a year, or perhaps two or three, they'll say it was a nonstarter, and that'll be that.'

'Yes, but in a year, or two, or three, it probably won't matter to me. It interests me now – in connection with my plans, with which you are acquainted. I'd like to know if there's any way I could get in touch with the school in question . . . or rather, with the headmistress . . . since I gather you know her?'

'How do you gather that?'

'You asked me whether I knew her name, which clearly implied you were thinking of someone in particular. Is that not a logically sufficient basis for my supposition?'

'You have a Cartesian mind!' she smiled, laughing at me.

'*You* said it,' I replied, returning her smile.

'So what is it, exactly, that you expect me to do? Give you her address?' (I have that already, thank you.) 'Her phone number?' (And that as well; I got that first.) 'Her number at home, perhaps? Or just at school?'

'No, no! Let's not exaggerate!' I raised my hands in a gesture of surrender. 'I wouldn't dream of pestering someone I don't know like that – especially besieging them at home!'

'Well, then?'

'I was thinking of something else. The Centre is a kind of forum: from what I've heard, you have film showings, lectures and literary discussions that draw the cream of Warsaw's Romance language scholars and a wide circle of local Francophiles as well. I imagine that the head of a French-language school, even if it is only at the trial stage, must be part of all that – of the life of the Centre – a person in such a position couldn't *not* be. So if that's the case, and assuming, of course, that admission to these symposia is open to everyone, I might come to some of them and look for an opportunity to meet him and talk to him there.'

'Meet whom? Now I'm lost.'

'The head of this school, of course!'

'It's not a he, it's a she.'

'A head is a head. "He" in this case is an unmarked term. A function has no sex.'

'But a person does.'

'Surely that's irrelevant?' I snapped, perhaps too impatiently.

'Not always, *mon ami* – not always,' she replied with a mysterious smile, making a little *moue* with her lips and gazing at me wide-eyed.

I was unable to prevent a blush from spreading over my face.

'So you think, do you,' she continued, having achieved her aim, 'that you'd like to participate in the symposia at the Centre.' She picked up a stray paper-clip from the floor and threw it into the magnetic crater of the oval paper-clip dish. 'There's nothing to prevent you. Admission is open. *Tu es le bienvenu.* But I'm very much afraid you'll be disappointed. You overestimate the Centre; your ideas about our activities are highly exaggerated. It's true that we screen French films and organise lectures and discussions with French academics, but you don't know what kind of films or what kind of discussions and what sort of people come to them! I'll tell you: the films are third-rate, years old; they're screened in a room on the third floor of the Geography Building; the film quality is dreadful. The lectures are aimed at a narrow group of specialists. The audience consists of a few students – not many – and a few lecturers.

'Why should this be, you ask? Why does the reality fail to live up to the appearance – the grand-sounding name Centre de Civilisation?' She shrugged. 'No funding.' She raised a finger. 'And no permission for anything else. Nevertheless,' she continued, 'you're quite right in supposing that there *are* events that draw *le beau monde* – the cream of French-speaking, "European" Warsaw society – including the . . . *head* you're so eager to meet. But getting yourself admitted to those isn't so easy. You have to be in with the right crowd or you have to be invited. And sending or giving out invitations is the prerogative of the Service Culturel.

'Have you any other questions?' She picked up a Bic (one of the rounded kind) and began to play with it idly, clicking the mechanism repeatedly, in and out, watching the tip extrude and retract.

'Certainly,' I replied. 'And I'm sure you know what they are.'

She stopped her clicking and gave me a keen, penetrating glance. Then she reached for a thin black plastic box with an array of buttons on top. Each button had a letter, or several letters, underneath it. She pressed the first one (marked A), and the smooth part of the cover snapped open and sprang erect to reveal a card with a set of preprinted spaces into which telephone numbers had been written by hand. She picked up the phone and dialled six numbers. After a moment her deep alto burst into a chatter of throaty *r*s.

C'est elle, de la part du Centre, oui, oui, de la rue Obozna. She's ringing about the following matter: there's a young man here with her, *gentil et résolu,* sophisticated, well read, with decent French, and he'd very much like some direct contact with the living language and Western culture. Can she put him down on the list of permanent guests of the Service Culturel? . . . In principle not really? . . . Limited space? . . . Controls? . . . Still, perhaps an exception could be made? Personally she thinks he deserves it. He's a young man with a future . . . *D'accord,* then? . . . Send him round? . . . She'd send him round at once. *Merci.*

She put down the phone and turned to me.

'You heard,' she said. 'And I trust you understood. You're to take the 117 bus, which stops in the Aleje Jerozolimskie, right in front of the Party headquarters. It'll take you across the river into the Saska Kepa district. You get off at Alliance

Square, opposite the Sawa Cinema, and from there you walk down Victors' Street until you come to a narrow little cross street called Zakopianska. You walk down it until you come to number eighteen, which is the French Embassy, and you go in. If anyone stops you and asks what your business is, you're to give them my name (Zamoyska) and say you have an appointment with Mademoiselle Legris. She's the person who will see you and put your name on the list; she may even give you an invitation there and then – I know that any day now an exhibition of some much talked-about Picasso drawings is opening. Mademoiselle Legris will certainly want to talk to you, get to know you a bit, so please don't disappoint me. In any case it's in your own interests, as I'm sure you realise. Good luck. *Au revoir, jeune homme.*'

The Discovery of America

And the young man set off . . .

Whenever the swift pace of life relented a little and gave me some respite from my various roles, one of those brief intermissions – between the acts, as it were – when I had no part to play, I used to imagine myself as a character in a narrative, as if everything that happened to me and around me were part of a story told in the third person and in the past tense. Now, as the number 117 bus moved off from the stop in front of the Party headquarters, I instinctively fell back into this pattern.

Since the bus wasn't crowded, indeed was almost empty, he didn't go astern to stand in his usual position by the rear door, but instead took a seat by the window, on the starboard side. Outside, beyond the thick safety glass and its layer of old grime, a procession of depressing sights unrolled backwards before his eyes: massive museum buildings – the National Museum and the Polish Arms Museum; cheerless grey tenement blocks along the viaduct; the wide swathe of river, with its murky, sluggish water. On the bridge he realised suddenly that he was travelling east.

And yet, he thought, amused, I'm going to an island of the West. Like Columbus, only in the opposite direction. I wonder what I'll discover?

At the Washington Roundabout some people got on: a very old woman and an elderly gentleman with a package. They were followed by two middle-aged men who jumped on at the last minute and, instead of punching their tickets like everyone else and sitting down (there were still plenty of free seats), took up nonchalant poses by the ticket-punching machines, one at the front, the other at the rear, and gazed stonily out of the windows.

Ticket inspectors, he thought. And although he had no reason to be afraid, for a valid monthly pass for all forms and routes of urban transport snuggled safely in his anorak pocket (despite himself he patted the place nervously to make sure it was still there), he tensed and his heartbeat quickened.

What are you so afraid of? he said to himself. *You* have nothing to worry about. And supposing you did, what would happen that would be so terrible? All right, so you'd have to pay a fine? But you wouldn't have to pay on the spot; you could ask for a form that lets you pay in two weeks, and then put it off for years – that's what most people do. What else? The shame. What's there to be ashamed of? Defrauding the state, since it's a state-owned company? But what does 'state-owned' mean? Isn't it tantamount to saying it's yours? And if it's yours, how can you defraud it? It would be like defrauding yourself. Besides, is the party with which you have entered into a contract (assuming it to be a separate entity and not identical with you), namely the Urban Transport Authority, pure as the driven snow? Does *it* honour all *its* obligations? And do *we* have the same rights regarding it as *it* has regarding us? How about *our* right to inspect *it*, for example? Does it keep to its schedules? What are the conditions of travel it provides – especially in rush hour? Are its drivers polite? Why shouldn't *we* be able to exact fines from *it* when it fails to meet its promises? Fines for its chronic unpunctuality, for instance, and for the constant interruptions in service, or damages for every time our health has suffered as a result of being crushed by the crowd or caught in the doors. But can we? Of course not – *it* doesn't pay *us* a penny, doesn't even feel guilty. It's only we who have to pay. Then what's the problem? Where's the foul crime, the hideous offence? Inequality before the law relieves us of the obligation to stick to the rules of fair play: isn't that what the history books and most of our schoolbooks teach us? The struggle against the exploiter is a noble and progressive one. Breaking the laws of bloodsuckers is a virtuous act, not a sin. In a world of violence and oppression it's permissible to seek justice in any way one can . . .

Constructing this imaginary defence of a passenger trying to hitch a free ride brought him no relief, however. On the contrary, it exacerbated his nervousness. Instead of forgetting about the bus company and concentrating on matters of much greater and more pressing concern (how to win the favour of Mademoiselle Legris, what questions to ask, in what direction to steer the conversation), he stared intently at the back of one of the supposed guardians of the Urban Transport Vehicle, waiting in suspense for his suspicions to be confirmed.

They were. For presently the two men, without looking at each other, reached under the lapels of their coats and displayed the gold-coloured round tin badge that each wore on a short ribbon pinned to his breast, like some sort of mountaineering decoration. Placing themselves solidly, feet apart, in front of the passengers sitting closest to them, they simultaneously intoned the sacred formula: 'Tick-ets-please.'

You'd think after this he could have relaxed: the tension had been released; he had sniffed them out, he had guessed correctly, his intuition was good. But for some reason he couldn't. He was still filled with nervous excitement and continued, in spite of himself, to give free rein to his anger and irritation.

Look at him, the rotten creep – look at that shifty mug! All the nasty deeds you could imagine written on it in great big letters. And yet he goes around blithely *demanding* things of people! Inspecting their tickets! Expecting *me* – me, a free monad, proud and untamed like the Rhine, on my way to pay a visit to the French Embassy – to submit to his insolent will, to sacrifice my time for him, to make a move because *he* wants it! Outrageous! Unacceptable! It's beneath my dignity! An intolerable constraint on my freedom. Insufferable! I *will not* submit to it! But how can I not? Refuse to show him my ticket? Ignore him? Then he'd only assault me physically, poke me, shove me around, shake me and finally grab me under the armpits and haul me off the bus at the next stop. No question that's what he'd do. And that would be worse – far worse. Is there nothing to be done? But . . . that's force! oppression! terror! Help, Rousseau!

The spirit of the author of the *Discourse on the Sources and Principles of Inequality Among Men* (a work regrettably not distinguished by the Academy in Dijon) and of the better-known *Social Contract* must have heard his plea, for the yoke of oppression which had seemed imminent was spared him. The manner of his deliverance was morally somewhat dubious, however, for it was accomplished at the expense of another. What happened was that the ticket inspector working the front of the bus, after checking the elderly gentleman with the package, did not move on but instead eyed the package and observed, 'Big, that.'

'Space heater,' the passenger explained. 'Electric. Just back from the repair shop.'

'I don't care where it's from,' snapped the inspector. 'It's luggage. No different from other luggage. And luggage you pay for.'

'What are you talking about? This isn't luggage!' the traveller objected. 'Luggage is a suitcase. Or a pram. Or a bicycle.'

'It takes up space just the same,' insisted the inspector.

'What space? Whose space? It's on my knees! And anyway, the bus is empty!'

'So what if it's empty?' replied the inspector, unmoved, and added, looking aside, 'another ticket for the luggage, please.'

'All right, all right, I'll punch one,' said the elderly gentleman, rising and reaching into his pocket.

'Now?' snorted the inspector. 'Too late for that now!' he said, barring the man's way.

'What are you doing?' The man with the package was visibly losing patience. 'Let me punch the damn ticket!'

'Should've done it before. I gave you a whole minute. You didn't take it.'

This cold observation set off an avalanche. The exchange, which until then had been fairly calm, became heated. Insults and *ad hominem* remarks flew back and forth. The argument degenerated into a slanging match, and it wasn't long before the other passengers, who until then had been silent observers, leapt into the fray, united in staunch defence of the owner of the heater. At the head of this chorus of outraged citizens was an invalid – a stocky, elderly man with a stiff leg who occupied a seat reserved for war veterans. His ticket had already been inspected, and he had been forced, despite his manifest disability, to show the certificate that entitled him to a half-price fare. This had probably rankled, and it may have been why he now took upon himself the role of chorus leader.

'You lazy slob,' he thundered in a stentorian voice, 'why don't you do some real work, instead of making people's lives miserable! Like herding cattle – or cleaning pigsties! You'd look better with a pitchfork in your hand. You think we don't know why you're doing this? You think we don't know you get a commission on fines?'

'Hey, hey!' snarled the inspector. 'Don't you talk to me like that!'

'You were crapping in your pants when I was fighting for Poland, you little shit!' The worthy Veteran, having delivered himself of this opinion, drew himself up and raised his walking-stick as if it were a sword.

'What did you say, you pathetic legless gelding?' growled the inspector through his teeth, approaching the Veteran.

'You heard me, you prick,' declared the Battle-Scarred Hero. Then he rose and began to make his way to the front door of the bus.

'You'll regret this,' promised the inspector, and muttered something to the driver.

'You know where you can shove it!' announced the Righteous Patriot and Defender of His Land with a grimace of scorn for this threat of vengeance, and positioned himself by the fore gangway.

The inspector, meanwhile, returned and demanded an identity card of the passenger with the heater, who laughed in his face (actually he said, 'You can whistle for it, you fat hog!') and, clutching his box, made his way to the door to stand beside the General, whom he thanked for his support –

At this climactic moment my narrative unfortunately came to an abrupt end, for events swept me up and sucked me into their whirlpool. (You can't write an epic when you're fighting for your life.)

What happened was this: the stop at Alliance Square, my own destination as well as that of several others of my *socii malorum,* had now been happily reached. But the captain – that is, the driver – did not lower the ladder; that is, he did not open the front doors, before which those of us who were intending to disembark stood expectantly in an orderly file, with our Commander-in-Chief proudly at the head. He opened only the rear doors, which in principle were reserved for embarking passengers.

The initial reaction to this was purely verbal: several voices, among which that of the General was prominent, shouted, 'Well, get on with it! Open the doors!'

There was an ominous silence as the driver continued to sit there, motionless. When it dawned on the owners of the voices that his action, or rather lack of action, was not the result of sluggishness but a deliberate refusal, tumult and confusion erupted. A panicked stampede for the rear exit ensued, with much cursing and swearing, as everyone tried to shove his way to the back door, through which the last of the embarking passengers were coming.

'Close the door!' yelled the inspector guarding the fore gangway to the captain at the helm.

The pneumatic mechanism of the doors hissed as they swung into action. But their compressive force was blocked by the figure of a large, aggressive-looking youth who was just clambering on board – having managed, in one elaborately determined movement, to place his huge foot firmly on the first step, wedging it in the door and keeping it from closing.

'Move!' commanded the inspector at the aft door.

Time to jump overboard, I thought. Hoping that the youth would catch on and display his solidarity by continuing to hold the door open, I shouted, 'Insects!'

He didn't disappoint me. Wedging his great bulk firmly in the door (the foot having been followed by the rest of the body) and leaning his back against it, he made a narrow passage for me to squeeze through. By then, though, the bus was already moving.

'Jump!' urged the youth with kindly insistence, and, observing the chaotic desperation of my efforts to do so, added helpfully, 'Sideways, you oaf, not head on!'

The advice came too late: I was already in mid-air. Having blindly jumped as I did, perpendicular to the pavement, I not only fell flat on my face as soon as I hit the ground but rolled for some distance from the force of the impact, with unfortunate results for my clothes.

'Poor fool, why did you run?' The phrase (where had I read it? heard it, perhaps?) flashed through my mind as I picked myself up and with mounting dismay surveyed the extent of the devastation. The sleeves and front of my anorak were scuffed and smeared with mud, a seam under the arm had ripped, and there was a huge and conspicuous tear in my right trouser leg, just above the knee, where a triangular shred of cloth hung limply down, exposing the flesh beneath.

I can't see Mademoiselle Legris like this, I thought desperately. How can I even show up at the embassy in this condition? They'll probably refuse to let me in; I must look like some sort of homeless lunatic. And would it be right to bandy about references to the silver-haired Marianne in this wretched state? I'd damage her reputation, sully her aristocratic name! No, I can't do it. If I still mean to go there, I'll have to get cleaned up first.

Ignoring the stares of passers-by, who stopped to gaze at me in outrage or fascinated horror, I began to plod slowly in the direction of the Sawa Cinema, which had a bathroom where

I could effect the necessary adjustments to my toilet. As I crossed the street I glanced back at the bus, now disappearing in the distance and bearing with it into the unknown my companions-in-arms: the General, the ancient woman and the owner of the heater, foully and treacherously kidnapped in revenge for their refusal to submit to the will of the oppressor.

Saved from the Transport! was the title I gave to my abandoned epic.

The challenge of returning my clothes to a state of approximate decency in the conditions that obtained in the Sawa Cinema's lavatories proved considerable but not insurmountable. In one of its three cubicles I found deliverance in the form of shreds of newspaper (clearly recognisable as the *People's Tribune*), which hung, in lieu of toilet paper, from a nail stuck into the wall like a bit of barbed wire. With these, and some of the rust-coloured water that roared in an icy torrent from the broken tap, I scrubbed most of the mud off my anorak. Next I took a grey rag that lay on the ribs of the broken radiator and used it to wipe off my Czech shoes, even managing to give them a bit of a shine – not a dazzling shine, perhaps, but better than nothing. Finally, with the aid of two small safety pins which I always carried with me (a scout's habit picked up from Constant) I closed the gash in my right trouser leg. As I did so I practised in my head, just in case Miss Legris noticed this new seam and was horrified by it, the explanatory phrase, '*J'ai eu un accident.*'

Having done all I could with my clothes, I turned my attention to my body – specifically, my hands and face. Here the need for repairs was equally urgent. But soap was evidently an extravagance to which the munificence of the management did not extend. Undeterred, I made my way to a nearby kiosk, purchased a bar of the most expensive kind they had – Lilac Flower, manufactured by the firm Beauty – and, returning with it to the cinema, completed my ablutions.

Clean, fresh and smelling of *fleur de lilas,* I set off slowly in the direction of Zakopianska Street.

The young man who loved Conrad's *Victory* strode along Victors' Street to the conquest of Victoire.

The glass militia booth in front of the embassy was manned by a moustachioed sergeant, deeply absorbed in an issue of *Sports Weekly.* I bid him a silent *adieu* as I passed. Then I crossed the frontier of the state and entered foreign territory.

And indeed, as soon as I crossed the threshold I felt I had stepped into another world. The building that housed the French Embassy was a massive, two-storey villa with a tiled roof, probably dating from the 1930s; its interior stood out from even the grandest and most splendid interiors I had had occasion to see anywhere in the People's Republic of Poland. It was no longer merely a question of the smell or some other detail of the kind that had struck me at the Centre; here everything was radically different. From the hallway floors carpeted with crimson-and-pale-blue runners, through the snow-white walls and the pictures (reproductions of paintings, photographs of Paris and posters) ingeniously lit with little spotlights, to the modern furniture in pleasant colours and graceful shapes – on and on, wherever the eye rested, it met beauty and richness of a kind it had never encountered. It was as if these things were made of stuff that came from a different planet.

Awed by the sight of these surroundings, and acutely conscious of the presence of the safety-pins in my trousers, like a thorn (albeit one that pricked the mind rather than the flesh), I approached the reception desk and presented myself. The receptionist (a Pole, and superficially not unlike the silver-haired Marianne, but without the breeding) had clearly been warned to expect me. She took up the phone to inform someone, no doubt Mademoiselle Legris, of my arrival, and then, smiling pleasantly, entertained me with conversation. She knew my French was fluent, but was I sure it was fluent enough? If not, she was at my disposal for any help she could give me. She wouldn't want me to be nervous. I thanked her politely; it wouldn't be necessary. She was pleased to hear it, but if at any time I did find myself in difficulties, I mustn't hesitate . . . she'd be right there. I nodded regally: thank you, I can manage.

In the meantime, quite noiselessly (those carpets!), Mademoiselle Legris had appeared at my side. She was the model of the office divinity (Western variety, of course): slim and shapely in a tight-fitting suit, very *soignée*, with chestnut-brown hair and greenish eyes. A secretary straight from the glossy pages of a French fashion magazine. We exchanged greetings (without shaking hands) and she invited me to follow her upstairs to the offices of the Service Culturel.

Her voice was gentle, pleasant and melodious, and she spoke calmly, in simple clear sentences. As she spoke she also gazed into my eyes in a slightly inquiring way, as if to make sure I understood. She was probably just doing her best to make things easier for me, but taken together, these elements of her behaviour – the careful enunciation, the velvety tones, her expression and in particular her way of gazing deep into my eyes – made it seem as if she was . . . exerting her charms on me. Someone who didn't know the language or the subject of our conversation, seeing us together and hearing only the tone of her voice and the sounds issuing from her lips, might have been forgiven for thinking she was trying to entice me, to draw me into her net, to woo me with the sweet magic of her words.

A siren, I thought, gazing entranced as the cooing chatter of French flew from her lips. Why hadn't the silver Marianne warned me to tie myself to the mast?

In reality the song of this green-eyed temptress was perfectly innocent and matter-of-fact, indeed rather official-sounding. Its gist was more or less as follows:

France, represented here by the ambassador, the director of the Service Culturel and finally herself, the humble *secrétaire*, was of course gratified that the programme devised to present modern French culture in Poland, which the Service Culturel had the honour of directing, the fruit of a happy collaboration with a number of important institutions, the Ministries of Culture and Foreign Affairs chief among them, should have met with such lively interest and ready acceptance on the part of the Polish people. They were pleased that so many Poles were drawn to French culture and art, and that *tout le monde* seemed eager to participate in the events they organised – especially, it appeared, gallery openings with cocktail receptions. But everything, alas, had its limits; even the largest auditorium or reception hall had a fixed number of seats and couldn't hold more than a given number of people. And the embassy had many obligations, to various people – matters of protocol, in most cases. Places at the openings, *spectacles* and other events to which admission was restricted were reserved first of all for members of the government and holders of various high offices, and for the diplomatic corps. Next on the list were prominent figures in the arts and sciences. The *milieu* connected with Romance studies, alas, came at the very bottom of the list, and by then – she would like to make this quite clear – there were very few places left, and they were all taken. So *elle regrette, elle est désolée*, but there could be no question of putting me down on the list of permanent guests. But please, I was not to worry, because she had already thought of a way around this. People on the so-called A-list (government representatives and members of the diplomatic corps) were often unable to honour these events with their presence; there were always a few people who failed to confirm or who just didn't turn up *tout court*. And that's where there was hope for me. I could fill in the gaps: take the place of a no-show. I'd be given a special pass, a sort of admission ticket, that would allow me to get in; after that I'd have to find myself a place wherever I could. *Compris? Eh bien, c'est parfait.*

Well, then, a few words about upcoming events. I must have either extraordinary luck or remarkable powers of intuition (or perhaps someone had mentioned something to me?) to have approached them just now, at this particular moment, because the programme of events the Service Culturel had scheduled for the near future was truly stunning – they would be real *événements*, productions of the highest quality, of which France was justly proud. First of all there was an exhibition of Picasso drawings; the opening was a week hence at the Zacheta Gallery – Zashetà, as she charmingly pronounced it. It was, *tout simplement*, spectacular; and – here her carmine-red lips paused for an instant in an enticing, mysterious smile – *très scandalisant* – for the *bourgeoisie*, she meant, not for her, of course. Then, after the New Year, the Comédie Française was coming to Warsaw with their much talked-about production of Racine's

Phèdre. There would be only two performances – at the National Theatre. Finally, on the twenty-seventh of January – this was probably the biggest sensation of all – there would be a screening of this year's Grand Prix at Cannes: the internationally acclaimed *A Man and a Woman*, by the brilliant Claude Lelouch. Just one screening, for a restricted audience – by invitation only! At the Skarb Cinema on Traugutt Street. That was it for the time being. *Pas mal*, I had to admit. And here was her card. *Que je m'amuse bien. Voilà!* Any questions?

As she seemed eager, after this crisp conclusion, to bring the meeting to an end, there was no time for shilly-shallying. I replied that yes, actually I did have a few questions, but about something else. They concerned the joint Franco-Polish project in education: I'd heard there was already a French-language school somewhere in Warsaw, set up under the auspices of the Service Culturel. Was there any truth to this? So many contradictory rumours were flying around. And if it *was* true, which school was it? And how exactly was the French side involved? Was it true that the . . . the head of this school was someone sent over from France? My curiosity about this was fuelled not by any personal interest – my own school days were behind me – but by concern about my . . . about my younger brother, who, seeing how much I owe to my knowledge of French, was eager to follow in my footsteps and become as fluent as possible as quickly as possible. Unfortunately this was not feasible at his own school. So, in short, he wanted to move – if there was somewhere to move to, and if it could be managed.

The green-eyed Ondine listened to all this with a sweet smile and nodded at the end of each sentence, as if to embolden me. ('*Oui, oui, je te comprends*; you're doing very well. Go on, dear boy, go on!') When I'd made it to the end and stopped, she straightened herself in her chair, placed her hands demurely together in her lap and launched into her reply: *C'est vrai*, there *was* a plan to create a network of French-language schools in Poland, but organising it was a lengthy, complicated process, not yet past the initial so-called experimental phase. The problem was that the Polish Ministry of Education wanted it run exclusively by its own people – entrusted to local manpower, as it were; all it wanted from the French side was teacher training and textbooks. France, on the other hand, felt, on the basis of its experience in other countries, that such a project made sense, and could be expected to bring results, only if at least some of the teachers were French, not Polish. A compromise was sought and found: the teachers would be Polish but trained in France. Those selected – or, rather, *accepted* – by the French side, on the basis of language tests and proven qualifications, backed up with documents attesting to their pedagogical achievements, would be sent to France for a special training course, and after that for six months' classroom experience in schools for foreigners. Only after that, when the proper people had been trained in the proper way, could the project go ahead. *Malheureusement* the aspirations of my *frère cadet* could not be fulfilled, for the school in question did not, as yet, exist. Only the *people* existed – the candidates for the posts, who were now undergoing preliminary trials in selected schools.

When the sentence that laid bare the heart of this blessed compromise ('the teachers would be Polish, *but trained in France*') fluttered from the lips of the Green-Eyed One, my pulse quickened and a wave of heat flooded over me. It was as if, after a long sea voyage, full of doubts and fears and despair of ever reaching shore, I had finally sighted land – far away on the horizon but clear and unmistakable. As it turned out, this was merely a prelude to far more powerful emotions. For what happened when I went a step further exceeded all my expectations.

But I musn't anticipate. Slowly. One thing at a time.

Still emanating concern for my fictitious *frère cadet*, I asked shyly whether any deadlines had been set, at least for the results of the preliminary trials and the selection of the first batch of future teachers.

Yes, they certainly had. The training course in France was being planned for the summer, so the selection – or, rather, *acceptance* – of candidates would be taking place quite soon, at the end of the first quarter of the coming year. Time was needed for them to put their affairs in order and go through the lengthy procedure of obtaining passports.

One other question: 'language tests' I could understand, of course, but what exactly did she mean by 'proven qualifications, backed up by documents attesting to their pedagogical achievements'? What form were these documents supposed to take? Teaching practice? A certificate from a school governing board? A university degree? A PhD in education?

Oh, no, nothing like that! Mainly the opinion of *French* experts, based on visits to the classroom during lessons, and whatever information the candidates themselves supplied about their teaching methods and results – supported, of course, with documentary evidence. She could show me the sort of thing she meant, if I was that interested.

Swivelling gracefully in her chair, she reached up to a white shelf just above her and took down a fat, shiny file. After another 180-degree turn, she laid it open on her desk and began shuffling through its contents, a number of clear plastic folders holding papers of some kind. Here, she said, was the documentation I wanted to see: descriptions of lessons, tests, examples of *compositions* . . .

It was then, when she pronounced that word, that I discovered America: for there, imprisoned in the plastic sleeve she was holding, like an insect or a dried flower pinned under glass, was my blue notebook with the essay about the stars. Attached to it with a shiny silver paper-clip was a note in Madame's handwriting: 'Essay by a pupil in his final year. A year and a half's study by the intensive method.'

I was thunderstruck. So that's what she'd done! And on top of that it was a lie! 'A year and a half' of study?! It was barely three months! By an 'intensive' method?! It was a perfectly ordinary, common or garden method; in my case one might even call it a rather restrained method. The worst lie, however, was implicit, since my proficiency in French in fact had nothing to do with what I did at school: I'd had private lessons since I was very young, and from my childhood my parents had constantly nagged me to read French books and practise speaking the language at home. They pestered me with comments about how being less than fluent in French was a 'shameful handicap', 'a sign of uncouthness', even a 'disgrace'. 'In the old days,' they'd intone, 'every young man from a self-respecting home knew *at least* one language, and that was French. The fact that times have changed and that this is no longer the case is no excuse. It's just proof of your stupidity if you try to use it as one.'

My father would open a volume of Zygmunt Krasinski's *Collected Writings* and show me a letter Krasinski had written in French to a childhood friend, a young Englishman called Henry Reeve. It was over a dozen pages long, and amounted to a lecture on Polish literature. 'He was seventeen when he wrote that,' my father said. 'Would you be able to write even an ordinary letter in French?'

Thus goaded, I would grit my teeth and return to my books. I slogged my way through dozens of rules, phrases and idioms until I had attained something approaching fluency. I also devised other strategies: for instance, I tried to write in Polish as if I were writing in French. This consisted of simplifying my thoughts and expressing them so that they could be easily translated into a foreign language. I committed to memory entire sentences in French, even whole passages of prose, whatever struck me as useful or effective-sounding, so that I might slip them airily into conversations at appropriate moments.

This was how I had become fluent in French: through years of effort and practice. Madame's contribution was less than negligible. And yet she *could* have contributed, even in the short time she had been teaching us. She *could* have improved my proficiency if she had wanted to. If she had paid me a little more attention, if she had been a little less cold towards me, a little less forbidding, a little less determined to be unapproachable. If she'd just talked to me – as the silver-haired Marianne, for instance, had talked to me: in a friendly, playful way, with that teasing but graceful irony. Even that would have helped. If I'd sensed that she liked me, felt even the slightest sympathy on her part, I would certainly (knowing me) have spared no pains to impress her; that in itself would have been good training and I would have made progress.

Why didn't she care whether I did or not? Why did she make no effort to get more – anything – out of me? After all, the 'document attesting to pedagogical achievements' that I had unwittingly provided was a heaven-sent opportunity for her. And she had used it. And yet she'd made no effort to obtain it, let alone to improve my French to the point where she might hope for it. On the contrary, she had done her best to put me off. Was it calculated? Might she have decided that in my case this was the right approach, and would have the desired effect? Unlikely. Then why? What were her motives?

In a fever of speculation I tried to imagine what might have happened if she had acted differently. I went through all the possible variations, as if working out the consequences of a hypothetical move my opponent might make. What if, having discovered my abilities, she had concentrated on me, taken me under her wing, perhaps even given me special 'individual' coaching, as the physics teacher had done for the 'genius' Roz Goltz? If, in short, she had singled me out as her special concern, her favourite pupil? Set above and apart from the rest in this way, the only one to be admitted into her favour, I would have given freer rein to my feelings for her; they would have been much stronger. It wasn't hard to imagine how her attentions would have affected me: to be praised by her in public, held up as an example, and especially to be given extra work . . . in the form of conversation lessons, after school, in her office . . . I would have lost my heart to her completely. I would have done anything for her. I would have written her a dozen *compositions* that could attest to her 'pedagogical achievements'. Yes – but then? How would I have felt then, discovering what I had just discovered now, but on a much greater scale? Like a deceived suitor. Betrayed, ridiculed, made a fool of – in my own eyes as well.

Could it be that she realised this? That her coolness to me, her distance, her stand-offishness, the behaviour I interpreted as hostility – that eternal Alpine winter which prevented the coming of spring, ruthlessly killing off every defiant bud, every green thing struggling to come up through the earth, freezing them over so that they withered and died – was in fact her attempt at fair play? The result not of excessive pride but of a sense of fairness and decency – and sensitivity? Perhaps, knowing her own strength, she was reluctant to abuse it, to manipulate my feelings? And that was why, when I unexpectedly gave her something she could use to further her own ends and she used it accordingly, she limited herself, in settling the account, to a businesslike A and distanced herself even more? Perhaps what seemed like rank ingratitude was in fact a sign of honesty and responsibility?

I tried to reconstruct the thoughts behind her actions. 'I didn't ask for anything,' she might say. 'I did nothing to exploit you. But since you offered me this tribute of your own accord, and since it happened to be something I could use, I used it. I had the right to. Were your efforts not rewarded with an A? If I bestowed it in silence, with no comment, in an atmosphere of distaste and suspicion, it was to stress that it should not be seen as a return favour, much less as encouragement to more efforts and offerings on your part . . . And another thing. You know my middle name, which not many do. *And* my date of birth. I wonder how – certainly not from me. I'm forced to conclude that you've been sniffing around, secretly gathering information. Do you deny it? No – you can't. So don't hold it against me if I repay you in kind.'

'Is everything clear now?' The melodious rhythm of the French question broke through my confused imaginings and returned me to my surroundings. For a moment I was bewildered, but as soon as I saw those two green eyes, studying me inquiringly, I shook myself awake and recovered my wits.

Yes, indeed, quite clear, and I was very grateful. It was really most kind of her to have gone to this trouble. I slipped the admission card into the sleeve of my diary and rose to take my leave.

Oh, no trouble at all. The Green-Eyed One also rose, and emerged from behind the fortress of her desk. It had been a pleasure, she assured me. She would see me out.

For a moment I wasn't sure whether to broach the subject, but as we descended the stairs in silence (the Green-Eyed One in front, with me half a step behind), I threw caution to the winds: in a confidential, off-the-record tone I asked, smiling, what she thought of the essays produced by these pupils subjected to the 'intensive' method – assuming, of course, that she had read them . . . or at least one of them.

Well, she replied, *en principe* it wasn't part of her job to read them, so officially she had no opinion. Unofficially, however, she could say that she had come across essays that were quite astounding – in their originality, their style and the richness of their vocabulary. That *essai* about Nostradamus, for instance, was a masterpiece. Her boss, the director of the Service, was so impressed when he read it that he couldn't contain himself. He kept bursting into spontaneous cries of amazement and hoots of laughter, and interrupted her work every few minutes to read out selected passages. And, as she recalled, the essay was indeed *très amusant et parfaitement bien écrit.* One thing had stuck in her memory – that strikingly original, wonderfully perverse and funny interpretation of Aquarius – *le Verseau.* But then that wasn't surprising, since Aquarius was her sign . . .

My memory unfailingly called up the relevant passage from my *composition*: '. . . although embodied in the form of a man, Aquarius actually represents all that is female. By giving water he gives life; he watches over life's creation. And at the same time, with the sound of splashing water, he beckons; he tempts.'

'So, did it fit?' I asked with a smile.

'*Peut-être . . .*' she replied mysteriously.

'It could just as well have been Pisces,' I muttered in an amused undertone, half to myself.

She caught the remark, though. '*Poissons? Pourquoi?*' she asked as we neared the reception desk.

I looked into the green eyes. Are you not a siren? I thought. And aloud I said, 'They're next to Aquarius.'

She laughed gracefully and shook my hand. Goodbye, charming boy, her eyes seemed to say, don't forget me!

On my way out I noticed the receptionist watching the scene with attention. She was smiling.

I nodded to her politely and left.

* * *

Calm down, I said to myself as I went down the path through the courtyard to the main gate, trying to control the confusion of my thoughts. Not now. Get home first. Pull down the blinds, lie down, cover yourself with your old wool blanket, and then you can start examining your spoils and digesting all that's happened. But not before. Not now. Now just take a deep breath and relax.

I closed the gate behind me, obediently took a deep breath and turned in the direction of Alliance Square.

'Just a moment, citizen!' a stentorian male voice sounded from somewhere behind me.

I turned.

The moustachioed reader of *Sports Weekly* was emerging from his glass booth. He came towards me and halted, saluting. 'Your documents, please.'

I was completely taken aback. For a moment I just stood there and stared, dumbstruck. This was something I hadn't foreseen.

'I'm sorry – what's the problem?' I finally managed to ask.

'Your documents, please,' he repeated, as if that were explanation enough.

'I'm sorry, but why? Why do you need to see them?'

'I don't have to explain myself to you. I have my reasons.'

'I'd like to know what they are.'

'You will. In good time. Right now your ID, please.'

I didn't yet have a proper ID, although I was old enough for one. I'd begrudged the time I'd have to waste on the lengthy and laborious formalities at the Militia Headquarters (the agency in charge of this administrative procedure), and I simply hadn't bothered. So my 'identity papers' still consisted only of my school ID. This I had on me, but I decided that producing it in these circumstances would be unwise: it identified my school and thus opened the way to possible intervention there, which would have been fatal – especially since the school badge, a bit of red felt that bore the identifying number of my school in Roman numerals and should have been sewn on my sleeve, was patently not there, and its absence was regarded as a serious infringement of the school code. I preferred not to provide firepower for my enemies.

In order to gain time and sniff out the sergeant's intentions, I made a show of searching for it: at first calmly (inner pockets, outer pockets), then more and more frantically (back trouser pockets), and finally with the resignation of one who knows he searches in vain. 'Unfortunately I don't seem to have it on me,' I conceded in a pained voice. This didn't seem to help matters, so I added, 'I was wearing different clothes yesterday, and must have forgotten to transfer it.'

'No excuse,' said the sergeant phlegmatically. 'It is the *duty* of *each and every* citizen to have his papers on him *at all times*.'

'Oh, I quite agree,' I said to mollify him, 'but how can I help it if I forgot? Man is a fallible creature.'

'If you have no papers or refuse to produce them when asked, you could be arrested,' announced the sergeant, unmoved.

'What for?!'

'That remains to be established.'

'But I haven't done anything!'

'How do I know that?'

'You expect my ID to tell you?'

'You won't talk your way out of it, citizen. Do you intend to produce your documents or not?'

'I'm telling you, I haven't got them!'

'You want me to call the police car?'

'Jesus, what do you want from me?! You want my *name*? My *address*?' I reached into my pocket and took out my monthly bus pass. Salvation. 'Here you are: first name, surname, address and photo with the stamp of the Urban Transport Authority, so that you don't have the *slightest* doubt that I really am who I claim to be.'

He took the pass and gazed at it with absorption, turning it this way and that, as if he had found something suspicious.

'It's valid, I assure you,' I broke in, unable to bear the suspense. 'The stamp is *glued* on, and it has the number written on it.'

'I'm not a ticket inspector,' he reminded me curtly. 'For me this does not constitute a proper document.' Switching suddenly to an official and businesslike tone, he asked, 'What was the purpose of your presence within these grounds?'

So that's what he's after! I was disconcerted. How on earth could I explain? I tried the naïve approach: 'Is entry forbidden?'

'Did I say entry was forbidden? I asked about the purpose of your visit. There's no consulate here.'

'So what if there's no consulate?'

'It means you didn't come here for a visa. What *did* you come for, then?'

'Am I required to explain?'

'Since I'm asking you . . .'

It was clear that further discussion boded ill. If I wanted to come out of it intact, I'd have to offer him some sort of *quid pro quo*: get him to agree to an 'exchange', at least.

'It's to do with a chess match between Poland and France,' I said, deadpan. 'We're working out the final dates and things. And just so you don't think I'm making it up,' I continued, reaching into my inside jacket pocket and taking out my club card, 'here's the proof. Go ahead. Take a look.'

He took the pass and began to inspect it. I went on, getting into the flow: 'If I'm not mistaken, you read *Sports Weekly*. You might have seen me mentioned there: junior vice-champion, Marymont Workers' Club.'

There was a moment of silence.

'You're free,' he growled finally, handing me back the bus pass and the club card.

'I certainly am . . .' I muttered ambiguously.

He saluted and turned back to his booth.

As I was putting away my credentials I happened to glance at the façade of the embassy. In a ground-floor window I clearly glimpsed the face of the receptionist.

I raised my head and gazed upwards with the concentrated air of one who has just had a brilliant idea, or perhaps is looking to heaven for inspiration.

Above him, on its tall white mast, the flag of the French

Republic fluttered proudly in the wind. Victory! he thought, with renewed hope.

Onward! Westward Ho!

A victory, yes, but a Pyrrhic one. Not because of the price I had paid for this 'voyage across the seas' (the row with the ticket inspectors, Lord Jim's jump overboard, the damage to my clothes, the run-in with the policeman), but because of its psychological effects.

These could be summed up very simply. On the one hand, I had gained the longed-for opportunity to shift the game beyond the wasteland of school. On the other hand, upon discovering Madame's strategy, and especially her true motives and aims, I had once again, this time perhaps definitively, lost faith in my 'wooing' and, consequently, my desire to continue it.

What could I hope for, knowing what I knew? That I might succeed in striking up a conversation with her at the Zacheta Gallery or in the theatre, and that things would be different there? That *she* would be different – towards me? That she would talk to me freely, playfully, informally – like the silver-haired Marianne or at least the Green-Eyed One?

No. Not really. *Not any more.* At least, I couldn't imagine it.

How was this conversation supposed to happen in the first place? And more to the point, why should it be any different? What did 'there' have that would make the ice melt and break – what actions, what words unavailable elsewhere?

Of course, I had one move open to me: pretended blackmail. I could exploit my knowledge about her, notably about her plans, make it clear to her that I knew where my notebook was, and why . . .

'*A propos*, you've only been teaching me three, three and a half months, not *a year and a half*. Your modesty is excessive. You shouldn't disparage your astonishing results in this way. But then, a year and a half is good time, too. As long as no one finds out . . . you're leaving in the summer, is that right?'

She didn't know much about me: what kind of people I knew, what 'contacts' I might have – 'who I was,' in short, or 'where I came from'. So a sudden attack of this kind might frighten her into a response. After all, maybe I knew someone from the Service Culturel? Since I seemed to be able to get into the exclusive events it organised and knew French so well? Or maybe I had contacts in the secret police? Since I went about so confident and self-assured, as if I could do whatever I felt like? And even if I didn't and wasn't up to anything, how could she trust me to hold my tongue, a young fool in love like me? I might blab, my sort were unpredictable, no telling what I might do. It would be better to tame me, defang me by granting me favours.

With all her suspicions (for which she had grounds) and the wariness that Constant had mentioned, she might well reason this way.

But was that what I wanted? Would the longed-for response have any value for me if that was how it was obtained? No – none whatsoever. The very thought revolted me. To achieve my aim this way would be pathetic – and loathsome. I'd feel degraded. It would be a defeat, not a victory.

I recalled Freddy's story about Dr Dolowy – the smuggled caviar and the ballpoints, how Freddy had discovered these lucrative little deals, and how it had then occurred to him that he could exploit his knowledge. 'Revolting, wasn't it?' I could hear his voice, and the bitterness in it. He'd added: 'When everything around you is despicable and corrupt, you, too, become despicable and corrupt. Remember that!'

The memory was a warning signal. This is it, I thought, the fun and games are over. The air is stifling, and the ground below my feet more and more slippery. One false step and I'll be in the bog up to my neck – and then I could get sucked under. Perhaps I should turn around? There's still time.

Turn around? Retreat? said another voice in my head. Now that you've come so far? No, unthinkable! You *must* go on – you *must*! You can't give up! You must follow the current:

drift, like Heyst. Remember, reflection and excessive caution are not the best counsels. Blessed fog: *that's* what you should put your trust in if you want to get anywhere. You'll get nothing without risk; there's no life without sin. Besides, where's the sin? Where's the risk? That you'll succumb to the temptation to play dirty or do something foolish? That's always a risk, even if you don't go on. But what did God give you a mind for, if not to control yourself? This is no time to hesitate. Be resolute! Onwards!

'Onwards' meant attending the opening of the Picasso exhibition, and perhaps seeing her there. But there was still a week to go until then – and in that week I had three French classes to get through.

At these I abandoned my recent behaviour. I stopped my ostentatious pretence of reading and annotating Conrad's *Victory* and Joanna Schopenhauer's memoirs and emerged from my provocative passivity. No longer sullen and moody, I became industrious, eager and attentive – a model pupil. The aim of this strategy was to lull her vigilance, and the message I wanted to get across went something like this:

'I was angry at you, it's true – I don't deny it. I was angry because you didn't answer my serenade, and because of your cruel and incomprehensible treatment of me, as if you were punishing me for something . . . in short, for your unfairness, your harshness, your insensitivity. But that's all over and done with. Love forgives all. I'm back to my old self, as you see – more submissive than ever, in fact.'

Strangely enough, she accepted this quite readily, even, it seemed, with a kind of relief. When I made my first conciliatory gesture (answering a question about the pluperfect tense that no one else seemed eager to attempt), she didn't respond with ostentatious distaste – a possibility I had envisaged and even expected – but heard me out with well-inclined attention, as if there had been no Cold War, no tension, no sulking, as if I were the ever-polite, ever-submissive Agnes Wanko. And after that she was neutral: not hostile but not visibly well disposed, either. Although, on the other hand . . .

In the third class something unusual happened – something quite astonishing, in fact. We were learning about the sequence of tenses in sentences with subordinate clauses. She dictated an exercise for us to work out on paper and then strolled slowly among the rows of desks, surveying our work. When she came to mine she halted, paused for a moment, and then, in an undertone, so as not to disturb the others in their work, said to me, *in Polish* (which she almost never used in class), 'Go and bring me the exercise book with the *concordance des temps.* It's on my desk. In the middle.'

Stupefied, astounded, unable to believe my ears, I rose and without a word began to make for the door.

'*La clé*,' her voice recalled me. I turned.

Her right arm was stretched towards me. Between two fingers of her hand she held out a round tin tag from which dangled the key to her office.

As I took it, my glance went involuntarily to her face and met her eyes. They seemed to have been waiting for it. She was studying me carefully, and with something like inquiry; her pupils held an obscure question. I gave the slightest of nods, as if in confirmation or apology, and quickly left the classroom.

What is this? I thought excitedly as I hurried along the silent corridors and ran down the stairs, what is it supposed to mean? Does it mean anything at all? Is it just an ordinary, insignificant errand? Or is it something more? Is this her first move in a new game? A response to my show of reconciliation? Before I could begin to unravel my tangled thoughts I was in front of her office door.

I wasn't entering this room for the first time, but the last occasion had been a very long time ago – something like two years, at any rate long before Madame came on the scene. I had a vague memory of dark, highly polished glass-fronted bookcases holding mostly crystal vases, sports cups and an elaborate tea service. I also remembered an enormous desk with two telephones and a flexilamp, and a huge palm in a wooden tub like a bucket.

The sight that met my eyes this time when I opened the

door was radically different in both style and content. The palm, the crystal and the high polish had gone, replaced by an elegant simplicity: plain 'rustic-style' chairs of natural, light, gold-coloured wood, a trestle table for a desk, a graceful standing lamp with a straw shade. There was a dark-green carpet on the floor, and dark-green curtains at the window. Ordinary bookshelves held books. Against one wall stood a sort of couch or upholstered bench that could seat about three people, and in front of it a low coffee-table covered with an embroidered linen cloth. There were also two small armchairs with low backs and wooden arms.

I looked at the bookshelves. The overwhelming majority of the books were French. On the lower shelves stood dictionaries and reference books, anthologies, dozens of textbooks and the Grand Larousse; above them was a literary medley, with a good number of paperbacks. A small bookcase next to the couch held albums and illustrated magazines; on top of it, between two decorative wooden bookends, gleamed a row of gold-embossed Pléiade editions: Apollinaire, Baudelaire, Corneille, Molière, Racine – almost all the classics, arranged in alphabetical order.

Where did she get all this, I wondered, amazed. Does she buy it? Import it from France? Through the Service Culturel? And why does she keep it here? What does she need it for? Not for lessons. For show, then? But for whose benefit? For the legendary commission on its visits of inspection?

Tearing my gaze away from the books, I approached the table to look for the exercise book she had asked for. And that was when I saw something that took my breath away.

A handbag. *Her* handbag. Hanging from the chair behind the table. Not closed, open. Gaping open, in fact.

My immediate impulse was to look inside.

Her ID! Her photo! I thought excitedly. Her marital status! Will it be single or something different? Her description, her distinguishing marks – did she have any? . . . What were they? . . . And her place of birth! What would that say? France? Where exactly? . . . There might be photos: of her parents? Of a man, perhaps! . . . And all her other documents – her

Party membership card! And all the rest. All of it, everything!

I flung myself at the door and turned the key in the lock. But when I had run back to the table, my hand already stretched out for the treasure chest that dangled in front of me on the back of the chair, I froze. I saw that inquiring look she'd given me when she had held out the key, and then I saw the scene in the hotel room that Freddy had described, when he had rifled through Dr Dolowy's luggage.

I almost did it, I thought, I almost succumbed. That's how the Tempter works – you don't even notice when you fall into his clutches.

I grabbed the exercise book and ran from the office as if I were fleeing demons.

It's obvious, I thought, pounding up the stairs several steps at a time: it was a test – of my honesty. She wanted to see if I could be trusted. She probably had everything meticulously arranged in that bag so that she could see at a glance if anything had been shifted even the slightest bit. Thank God I didn't touch it, thank God something stopped me at the last minute! Something . . . Freddy's story, or that inquiring look when she handed me the key? Which?

Not wanting to draw attention to myself, I slipped into the classroom as calmly and quietly as I could.

She was standing between the rows of desks, her back to me, bent over a book she was holding in her hands. I went up to her and in silence handed her the exercise book.

'Ah, yes, thank you,' she muttered mechanically, and took it without interrupting her reading.

I waited a second, possibly longer. Then I held out my right hand, on the open palm of which the key reposed as if on a salver, and said in an undertone, '*Et voilà la clé.*' And locked my gaze at the level of her eyes, so that when she turned around she would have to encounter it.

Which is indeed what happened.

'*Ah, oui,*' she muttered again, but this time she seemed disconcerted, almost flustered. One possible sign of this was that as she took the key she accidentally, lightly brushed against my hand.

FIVE

Here is My Space!

The opening of the exhibition at the Zacheta Gallery was on Sunday at noon. I got there at least twenty minutes early, but even so there was already a crush, at the entrance as well as in the vestibule, and much loud and animated chatter. French seemed to predominate – at least it stood out, perhaps because of its melodiousness and distinctive coloratura – but several other languages could be distinguished in the hubbub: Italian, Spanish, English and occasionally, rarest and faintest of all, the familiar sounds of Polish.

On a wide landing at the top of the first staircase two microphones had been placed in front of an enormous photograph of Picasso, with his hugely magnified signature scrawled across it. Below this, on a small plinth, stood a sapphire-blue vase with several dozen red and white carnations, and slightly above, on either side of the sweep of marble banisters leading to the first floor, bristled an array of cameras and lights on tripods.

The cloakroom was manned by a uniformed porter and a tall, French-speaking woman with a badge that said 'Service – CBAE' pinned to the lapel of her suit. (This, for those who may have forgotten, stood for 'Central Bureau of Artists' Exhibitions'.) As each guest's outer garment was entrusted into their care, one or other of them would politely ask to see the owner's invitation, then acknowledge it with an obsequious 'thank you' or '*merci beaucoup*'.

As I waited my turn I felt a stirring of anxiety. How would they react to my *carte d'entrée*? Would they give it the same 'thank you' everyone else got, or would they be surprised, perhaps even express reservations? It bore the stamp of the embassy and, above it, the sprawling signature of the director of the Service, but there was no name on it. What would I do if they asked me who I was and how I had come by it? Should I tell the truth or try to pass for someone else? But who? A Frenchman? Too risky. Someone connected with the diplomatic corps? I couldn't make up my mind.

Finally I had an idea. My invaluable safety-pins were in their usual place in my wallet. I extracted one, stuck it through the card, and pinned the latter in a prominent position on my chest. Thus embellished I inched forward with the rest of the queue. Once I had reached the front, and heard the porter's respectful 'Your invitation, please,' addressed to me, I assumed the distracted air of one who is in a great hurry and, affecting bafflement, as if I didn't quite understand what he wanted, I pointed discreetly at my chest.

'*Oh, excusez-moi!*' intervened the woman from the CBAE, chagrined, and, as if to compensate, handed me the catalogue.

'*Merci, merci, Madame*,' I said with the best accent and rolling French *r* I could manage, and, smiling inwardly, handed over my coat.

This trial behind me, I proceeded at once to a methodical inspection of the assembled guests, trying to spot Madame among them. Not seeing her, I looked about for a strategic position, found it (on the steps to the right of the door, behind an easel bearing a board with the exhibition poster), stationed myself at it, and from this excellent vantage-point, hidden from view, observed the crowds streaming through the entrance.

It occurred to me that I had yet to work out a plan of campaign for when she did arrive, and in particular to decide when best to make my move. Exhaustive consideration of the pros and cons led me to conclude that it would be wisest to bump into her later rather than sooner: not at the very start, and not even during the exhibition, but afterwards, when she had seen everything there was to see and was thinking of leaving. Her attention would by then no longer be concentrated exclusively or even mainly on the drawings; she would have had her fill and would be ready to return to the world around her, which earlier she would surely have ignored or even treated as a hindrance, an irritating distraction in her contemplation of the works of art before her. And it would give me a better pretext for striking up a conversation: what more natural beginning than a casual question about how she had liked the exhibition? Even the briefest of replies would serve as a basis for continuing and developing the exchange. Lastly, there would be a real chance of leaving the gallery in her company – together!

Given these premises, the conclusion was clear: most of the time I'd have to follow her movements while remaining unobserved myself, to watch without being seen, to control the situation so as to pick the most propitious moment for the attack.

An exciting task. But it required her presence – and of this there was still no sign.

The vestibule, meanwhile, was becoming more and more crowded. People were literally squeezed against one another, arms pinned to their sides, waiting impatiently. My eye roamed slowly over the faces of the assembled guests, trying to omit no one. Alas, none of them was identical with Madame.

At last the thing began. There was a glare of camera lights and a rasp from the microphones, the cameramen took up their positions behind their tripods and three men, attired in suits that were clearly their Sunday best, descended the stairs to the wide landing and halted in front of the microphones.

The first to speak (or, rather, to read, from a slip of paper he took from his pocket) turned out to be a representative of the Ministry of Culture.

After the first few sentences I stopped listening, for he was droning on in the best wooden officialese, and resumed my surveillance. Presently, however, my attention was drawn back to him: I heard the words 'Guernica' and 'fascism', then 'Franco' and 'Spanish civil war'. That was when I discovered that Picasso 'stands – as he has always stood – firmly with the forces of progress, and his membership of the Communist Party is eloquent and indisputable proof of this. For twenty years now,' thundered the representative of the Ministry of Culture, 'he has marched in its front ranks, and the Party is proud of him. Just as it is proud of Louis Aragon and Paul Eluard, France's greatest living writers.'

Having thus concluded his speech, the Ministry man recited (this time from memory) the conventional formula about being honoured and delighted, etc., and handed over the floor to the director of the cultural section of the French Embassy, M. François Janvier.

Instinctively my hand went up to the card pinned on my breast. Bending it up and sideways, I peered at the signature scrawled over the name on the stamp. Yes, that was it.

So the person standing before me was the Green-Eyed One's boss – the man who had read my essay and who, reading it, had been 'unable to contain himself'.

I hastily unpinned the card and slid it, together with the safety-pin, into my pocket.

M. Janvier was a good-looking man of forty-odd with raven-black hair and a tanned face, looking as if he had just come back from the Côte d'Azur. He was clad in an impeccably tailored cream-coloured suit, a pale-blue button-down shirt and a dark-blue tie with diagonal scarlet stripes. Over the shirt he wore a thin olive-green sweater, and on his feet well-made shoes of nut-coloured suede.

He spoke without notes, fluently and with confidence, gesticulating lightly. The gist of his speech was more or less as follows:

Modern civilisation, despite its constant appeals to the idea of progress, reason and freedom, despite its claims to be guided by high ideals and its alleged desire to liberate man and raise him up, in fact enslaves, fetters and confuses him. Despite extraordinary advances in technology, science and education, despite a higher standard of living, man is not happy in these new conditions. He is alienated, he is frustrated. He feels inferior, constrained and artificial. He feels deeply *false*.

Picasso, the genius ever in advance of his time, perceives this more clearly than anyone else. And he appeals to us to abandon this path.

For what? you may ask. And he answers as Rousseau did two hundred years ago: for Nature!

'Your promises are false!' he says to modern civilisation. 'Instead of a better life you have brought genocide, instead of greater freedom we have constraint and shame. I no longer believe your claims! I cannot trust you!'

The master turns away from modern civilisation towards what is real and true, innocent and unsullied, towards our root and our source: *le corps. Le corps humain*. Here is man's true paradise; here, only here, can man be himself, truly himself. This is where his happiness, his true happiness, lies. *L'amour. L'amour physique.*

'Yes, *mesdames et messieurs*,' said the director, winding up, 'Pablo Picasso's message in these masterpieces from his latest period makes me think of Shakespeare's Antony and his seditious reply to the news that an envoy has come from Rome. Let me quote it to you. This is what he says:

> *Let Rome in Tiber melt, and the wide arch*
> *Of the ranged empire fall! Here is my space.*
> *Kingdoms are clay. Our dungy earth alike*
> *Feeds beast as man. The nobleness of life*
> *Is to do thus: when such a mutual pair –*

at this point the director paused suddenly and peered upwards, as if looking for someone, or perhaps merely trying to remember the next lines; but this turned out to be only for effect, for, momentarily casting off his role, he went on to explain that upon these words Antony draws Cleopatra to him and they embrace (he used the word '*étreinte*'). Then he finished:

> *– when such a mutual pair*
> *And such a twain can do't, in which I bind,*
> *On pain of punishment, the world to weet*
> *We stand up peerless.*

The director's words were greeted with enthusiasm. There was much clapping, accompanied by cries of '*Bravo!*' (with the rolled *r* and the last syllable accented), as if he were some great operatic tenor. He, for his part, acknowledged this reception like a professional actor, bowed, and then once again peered upwards, somewhere in the direction of the first floor, as if it were the balcony of a theatre and part of his audience were seated there.

The end of the opening ceremony was brief and purely formal. A representative of the Zacheta Gallery and the CBAE, a weedy, frightened-looking individual in a grey suit from the Polish Fashion collection, came forward to thank 'all those wonderful people who have made this exhibition possible', especially Messrs Daniel Henri Kahnweiler and Maurice Jardot of the Louise Leiris Gallery in Paris, who had so graciously decided to lend this collection without a fee and had even taken care of the insurance, which would have had to be paid in foreign currency.

'Polish artists and art lovers will be eternally grateful for their extraordinary generosity.' As he uttered these words the wretched man bent his scraggy body almost double in a painfully servile bow towards the director, who acknowledged the homage with a hand-on-heart gesture and a modest inclination of his head.

The Ministry man, meanwhile, immobile as a rock, observed this 'Polish tribute' with an expression of ill-concealed distaste.

'This exhibition of Picasso's drawings,' squeaked the weedy man in a voice trembling with emotion, 'is hereby declared open!'

The crowd in the vestibule surged upstairs. I remained where I was as it rolled by, scanning the faces of the guests. I followed only when the last of them had passed.

On the landing, as I turned to the second flight, I glanced instinctively up to the white balustrade that went the length of the first-floor passage, and observed that it did actually form a sort of gallery. There might well have been people (members of the diplomatic corps? A-list guests?) up there during the opening ceremony; most likely it was indeed at them that the director had been gazing when he had recited the Shakespeare, and again at the end of his speech.

I finally made it upstairs, entered the first room – and froze, thunderstruck by the sight that met my eyes. No, it wasn't Madame. It was the pictures on the walls – the drawings.

It wasn't as if I'd had no idea of what to expect. I was familiar with Picasso's work from his various periods, including the post-war ones, and I hadn't forgotten the Green-Eyed One's remark about how it would be '*très scandalisant*' for the bourgeoisie, or the director's public allusion, in his speech, to the cult *du corps humain* and *de l'amour physique*. So I was prepared for the sight of things that were daring and provocative, perhaps titillating, possibly even obscene. And yet, faced with the graphic – in both senses – expression of that cult, immortalised in these drawings, I was stunned. I felt embarrassed and ill at ease, as if I were the one being exposed, as if I were being stripped naked and ridiculed.

The walls were covered with naked bodies. Wherever the eye alighted, it met representations of the naked human form, in varying sizes, more often female than male, and always grotesque, monstrous and hideously deformed. Most shocking was not the nakedness itself or even the deformity, but the way the primary sexual characteristics – the reproductive organs, in other words – were brought into relief. Crotches and genitalia were prominent in the foreground, the centre of gravity of each drawing, as it were. And although they were roughly, almost symbolically sketched, barely suggested by the dots, dashes, circles and occasional black splotches of which they were composed, in their deliberate crudeness they were tremendously, powerfully expressive. At times they made one think of the kind of thing children might draw in their early 'genital' phase – the iconography by which they express their first anatomical discoveries, particularly the fascinating and mysterious anatomical differences between little boys and little girls; at others they reminded one insistently of the art of primitive peoples, in which sex also tended to play a considerable role.

Of course, Picasso's drawings were less naïve than either of these. They exuded a pointed, almost vicious irony. The brushstrokes and ink lines seemed to echo with the sound of his laughter – at once ribald and sardonic.

What was the Master laughing at?

Put simply, he was laughing at man's unconvincing and silly pretence of maturity; at the deathly seriousness with which he took himself, at his risible pride in being the creator of Culture, his feeling of superiority to the flora and fauna and his mistaken conviction that he had surpassed them.

So, the paintings drawled at me in a mocking voice, you think you know everything, do you? You think you've become gods? Or at least, with the kingdom you've built on earth, with its morality and spirituality and pious ceremonies, far outdistanced your four-legged relatives? Well, let me show you something, let me remind you of what you really are. You are still, irredeemably, ineluctably, subjects of Nature: slaves to blind instincts and animal drives, biological forces over which you have no control. Whatever you may quaintly imagine, your only purpose on this earth, and that goes for each and every one of you, is to reproduce, to procreate, to propagate the species. That's it, there's nothing else. All the rest is meaningless – a pretence, an illusion. Whistling in the wind.

Look at him, *Homo sapiens*, puffing himself up! Look at his airs and graces and his posturing! And yet below the waist he's still a savage – wild, incalculable, ridiculous. All those fissures and protuberances, those holes and concavities where the act of procreation takes place – how ludicrous they are, how absurd, when you look at them like this!

I forged my way through the crowd, trying to avoid the front rows of spectators and barely pausing before the drawings. I gave each of them a lightning glance, trying to take in as much as I could, and then moved on, affecting indifference. I was tense and wary, and tried hard to be inconspicuous. I would have preferred to disappear altogether. At some point I realised I was paying more attention to the spectators than to the exhibits, and no longer because I was looking for Madame but for an entirely different reason.

The people around me were mostly embodiments of maturity, in terms of both age and social status. They were an élite in every respect: professional, financial, artistic, physical. Their bodies were sleek and well fed, confident and well cared for; their clothes were expensive; the experience of life etched on their faces was rich and varied. One glance was enough to see that their schooling in the realm of emotion and sex had been extensive and thorough. They had learnt their lessons well, mastered the material, passed their share of exams in the subject; their knowledge of human passion was solid and well tested.

I had been assuming, not altogether consciously, that if I observed them well, especially when they were absorbed by the nudes, some of their knowledge would be passed on to me; that the expression on their faces, caught, as it were, *in flagrante*, in the act of perception, would disclose their secrets, allow me to glimpse the traces of some other act, committed by them in the murky and distant past and now remembered.

A deluded hope, of course, but exciting nonetheless. And it grew in a tangle of unanswered questions: what do they feel when they look at these drawings? Or rather, what goes on inside them? What echoes, what shadowy memories return, prompted by the shapes before them, what feelings, what sensations come flooding back? And what form do they take? Do they return as a memory of some past experience? As a shiver of fascination, a sudden stirring of desire – or revulsion?

These questions became more urgent when I passed into a room with a cycle of drawings entitled *L'étreinte*, the word the director of the Service had used in referring to Antony and Cleopatra's embrace; the Zacheta Gallery had translated it as *Embracing*.

The drawings depicted couples *in coitu* in various positions and from a variety of perspectives. In most of them a hairy man resembling a satyr was thrusting, in a half-lying, half-kneeling posture, into the body of a woman; she, legs bent and drawn well up, urged him on, either gripping his buttocks, beneath which a huge, pendulous bulb of testicles swelled, or propped up on her arms, back arched, straining to meet him and pushing out her spreading, liquid breasts. In some of the drawings this coupling was presented from several perspectives at once, including impossible ones. Picasso seemed to be taking apart his subject – the *actus copulationis* – into its primary elements and then reconstituting it as an abstract sort of synthesis. This, the drawings seemed to be saying, is how man mates; this is what it looks like. Here are the various angles, viewpoints and cross-sections that make up the complete picture.

This room was the most crowded of all; you had to push your way through a crush of bodies to get from one picture to another. I couldn't decide whether I wanted to look at the drawings or the people. My thoughts raced wildly. I felt feverish.

The questions gathered and spilled over one another. What did all this mean? Why were these people so mesmerised by these drawings, why did they stare at them so greedily? And why the heavy atmosphere in the room? After all, this was simply Nature as Picasso depicted it – ordinary, basic nature, perfectly familiar to them all. Then why the excitement? Why the flushed cheeks and nervous glances? Why didn't they respond like this when they looked at other manifestations of Nature in art, such as motherhood, beauty, suffering or even death?

But perhaps this was the wrong question to ask; perhaps it should be turned around and directed at the creators, not the spectators, of art: why did the *artists*, portrayers of Nature, omit this subject when they painted everything else? Why did they not portray conception and birth? I couldn't think of a single example of a classical painting that showed either of these two crucial acts. Why should they be taboo? They were human, after all. Why did no one ever mention them? Why were they never depicted – or, if they were, labelled pornography? The Greek *porne* meant 'debauchery'; was the sexual act, then, debauched?

I struggled with the chaos of these questions, giddy with speculation, unable to impose order on my thoughts. I couldn't understand what was happening to me. What was I asking? What did I want to know? Why this confusion in my brain? Why was I worked up to such a pitch of nervous excitement – I, the rationalist, the champion of Reason?

Finally I began to understand the causes of my disquiet. They were connected with Madame – in several ways. For one thing, the exhibition, which was supposed to have been a useful springboard for striking up a conversation with her (circumstances permitting), had turned out to be more of an obstacle:

talking to her here would be problematic. What would I say? How did you like it? What did you think of it? How true to life do you think it is? It would feel awkward, somehow. Embarrassing. She might think I was mocking her. On the other hand, if I said nothing and began to talk of something different without even mentioning the drawings, that would seem odd, too. After all, the drawings were the main reason we were there.

But this, however inconvenient, wasn't the main thing that was troubling me; it was quite possible that I might not see Madame here at all. The true source of my consternation lay deeper – in the realisation, awakened in me by Picasso, that my whole world of feelings, desires and dreams was a pretence, the result of profound self-delusion. And the effects of my disillusionment were devastating.

I was a sensible, clear-thinking kind of person; indeed, I sometimes suspected myself of excessive rationalism. And yet until this moment I had thought of my feelings for Madame as a spiritual passion, separate and distinct and belonging only to the soul. I had genuinely believed this. I had trusted my feelings and acted accordingly, seeking fulfilment in the sphere of language, of words. And now Picasso, the pagan, the follower of Dionysus, had brought me down to earth with a thud. I could hear his gleeful sniggering, his obscene chortles of delighted mockery. It was a rude and painful awakening, like a bucketful of cold water sloshed over my head.

So, *jeune homme*, you say you're in love? With *Madame le professeur*? And you long for a 'victory'? What form do you imagine it would take, if I may ask? What is it you're hoping for? A glance? A kind word? A friendly atmosphere for your elegant *dialogues*, oops, sorry, I mean *conversations*? Well, let me tell you, my high-minded young fellow, that's pure delusion, Nature's way of tempting you to do what she wants you to do. The real, the only, point of it all is for you to couple with her and give her your seed. And that looks just like what you see here on these walls. Look at it: *this* is the true object of your longing, whatever you may think, however you may imagine it. *This* is the real purpose of your sweet wanderings.

And remember, little one, these are only pictures: art, representation, irony. In real life it's all much more powerful and far less civilised. Violent, savage, uncontrolled. Delirious, abandoned.

I stared in a paralysed sort of daze at the lasciviously writhing, copulating bodies, finally asking myself the question I had for so long suppressed: was this what I wanted with her? In the hypothetical, extremely unlikely event that such a thing were possible, of course, and assuming on her part a measure of desire, initiative and boldness.

But the magnetic needle of the compass that was my 'I' – what I thought of as myself, what I identified with – behaved strangely. It didn't point unequivocally to *no* ('north', in the blue field), but neither did it point to *yes* ('south', in the red field). It oscillated wildly between the two and then came to rest in the middle, at the dead point, as if I were standing at one of the poles.

Why, I insisted, backing myself against the wall with the last of my strength, why don't you answer? And why not *yes*?

Because it can't bring the satisfaction you seek, said a voice from somewhere within me, a voice that was chilly and strange. It can only soothe. It can deaden the delusion, but it can't satisfy.

It can't?

No. In the realm of sweet delusion there can be no fulfilment.

Why not?

Because there is no form in which it can be realised.

I lowered my eyes and bent my head. Then I moved on, to the next room. But its entrance was roped off: a red velvet cord, attached on either side to two low metal posts, hung across it, forming a sort of smile. And indeed the interior thus guarded seemed far from sad. It wasn't empty or dark. It was bathed in bright light, full of *haute société* and buzzing with animated talk.

Tables draped in white cloths that fell nearly to the floor held batteries of glasses, silver-plated buckets with champagne bottles and crystal dishes with pretzels, crackers and olives. In the middle, on a round *plateau* of golden wood, was a circle of cheeses with little knives stuck into them.

People stood around in small groups, talking animatedly, drinking and smoking. From time to time they idly sauntered over to a table to refill their glasses with champagne, nibble on an olive or a cracker or both, and take a bite of cheese; then they returned to their group and chattered on. Here, in contrast to the vestibule before the opening, where the sound of Polish did occasionally break through, the language spoken was exclusively French.

Pretending to be absorbed in the catalogue, I scanned the room with my eyes.

The silver-haired Marianne . . . the Green-Eyed One . . . the director . . . Professor Levittoux (whom I recognised from photographs). They were all there. And – yes! There she was. Madame.

She wore a tight black polo-neck sweater and black, sharply creased trousers. Her shoes were elegant and narrow, with high, gracefully shaped heels; at her neck a single pearl on a silver chain gleamed against the blackness. She held herself very straight, her head slightly tilted, her left hand on a small bag (quite different from the one I'd seen at school) hanging from her shoulder, her right holding a glass of champagne. She was talking to a dignified-looking elderly couple, a tall, grey-haired man with a bow tie (like Constant) and a woman in a hat and a georgette dress. This, it shortly turned out, was the French ambassador and his wife.

I was stunned by the sight of her. Her presence alone had a powerful effect – there, at last, she was, and my predictions had been proved right. But I was also struck by the way she looked, the confidence with which she moved and held herself. I knew that situations like this – grand parties and other special social occasions where self-assurance, a certain smoothness of manner, a measure of wit and charm, or at least quick repartee, were called for – could diminish people. Even the normally bold, self-confident and socially adept can become suddenly awkward and gauche; their self-assurance deserts them, the right words won't come and they flounder uncertainly, stumbling and stuttering. They come off looking pathetic. But not she. In this exclusive *milieu*, full of *esprit* and *brillant*, not only was she not diminished – she was spectacular. Conversing easily, doubtless with a wit and *élan* worthy of Simone de Beauvoir herself, she stood in her sleek black clothes, the pearl glistening at her neck, one leg a little forward and bent slightly at the knee, the other straight and firm on the ground on its high heel – she was dazzling!

But I paid dearly for the sight of this apotheosis. It struck the final blow to my already fading hopes of engaging her in conversation (let alone leaving with her), but it also brought home, painfully, the absurdity of my ideas about her status. To have assumed that she'd be an ordinary visitor here, like me, anonymous and solitary, and that after wandering around the exhibition with the rest of the common herd she'd fall into the net I had spread for her – how ridiculously, pathetically naïve!

And not only that. In the figure now before me, so striking in black, so proud and imposing, I saw an oddly disquieting response, a sort of challenge, to the nakedness and raw biology of Picasso's drawings. There was a conflict, obscure and strangely hard to define, between what I had seen as ink on paper and what I was now seeing in the flesh in this brightly lit room. Art, representing illusion, was on the side of 'truth'; Nature, embodied in the figure of Madame, representing reality, was on the side of 'illusion'. Picasso ripped off the clothes, stripped us down to our naked, biological selves and said, '*Ecce homo*. This is what you really are.' *Mais non!* the human figure in black and high heels replied, *C'est moi qui suis l'Homme!* This figure then picked me out of the crowd as its star witness and launched into its examination:

Well, my lad, which do you prefer? it seemed to ask. Nakedness? The animal laid bare, shameless and uncivilised? *Le corps sauvage et nu?* Or dress? This is what the clothed human being can look like – *voilà!* You see? Of course you do. Naked, the human being is a thing without dignity; at any rate, of lesser worth than a human being dressed. The naked body can never win in an argument with a clothed one. It will always lose, however attractive it is. That old joker Picasso wants us to believe that the True Human is Naked, or that Nakedness is Truth – whatever. Very well, let's suppose for the moment he's right. But what sort of truth is it that everyone is so ashamed of? It can only be something disgraceful. I prefer another kind of truth, thank you. The truth of clothes, not nakedness. The true human is the clothed human; clothes are a human characteristic as essential as two-leggedness or speech. And the better the clothes, the more human the person – the closer to being divine! Now, which is it to be – would you have me as you see me now, elegantly dressed, upright, graceful, charming you with my look, my wit, my words? Or stripped naked, supine, wallowing in some obscene position, howling like an animal in heat? Choose! Would you *climb* with me? To the Alps? Ascend Mont Blanc, attain the human summit? Or *fall* into the Marianas trench? *Crawl* into the depths of some primeval, murky pit, some dark protozoan lair?

With these beautifully phrased but deeply disturbing questions the figure in black abruptly fell silent: my receiver had stopped transmitting its words. This was because a change had occurred in the scene before me.

The director of the Service Culturel, wielding a champagne bottle with a white napkin wrapped around its neck like a scarf, bore down upon the constellation of three people I had been observing. He refilled their glasses and said something to them, presumably inviting them to follow him into another room, for that is what they did.

They know each other, I thought. Then they disappeared from view.

About an hour later, on my solitary way across the square in front of the Zacheta Gallery, I saw the elderly man in the bow tie and the woman in the hat again. They were getting into a limousine – a black Citroën ds21. It had a thin, silvery sort of aerial attached to its front bumper on the right-hand side and on it fluttered a small red, white and blue flag.

Almost overnight the Picasso exhibition became the most exciting subject of discussion in Warsaw. Newspapers and magazines, radio and television were full of reports, debates, articles and analyses. Most of them were wildly enthusiastic, full of praise and admiration, more eulogies than reports. 'Tremendous Vitality' screamed the headings of the reviews, 'Resounding Paean to Life', 'Ecstatic Expression of Optimism Drawn from Nature'. Reporters wrote of violent and frenzied scenes at the gallery entrance just before opening time. People came close to rioting. 'Never in the history of the gallery have there been such crowds,' announced the newspapers, especially the afternoon tabloids, 'the senior members of the staff can't recall seeing anything like it.' 'Three teams of goalkeepers unable to hold off charge of frenzied Picasso-worshipping crowd.'

But there was criticism as well. Some reviewers expressed distaste, even disapproval, of Picasso's 'sex mania', his 'revolting obsession with sexual organs', the 'pathetic exhibitionism of a senile artist'. The critics also made fun of the public's enthusiasm – and of the government's policies. 'What is it that draws these crowds?' fulminated one guardian of morality in an accusatory tirade. 'What is it that they're so greedy to see? Is it painting? Is it art? Is it beauty? Hardly. The answer becomes obvious when we take a cross-section of the visitors and look at their ages: the majority of them are schoolchildren and soldiers on leave! After that come university students, and then a section of the urban populace which (as studies show) is not in the habit of frequenting museums; indeed the overwhelming majority (according to polls) was entering one for (good God!) the first time in their lives!

'Since when, I wonder, are Joe Bloggs, our young people and members of our armed forces so enamoured of avant-garde art?

'Dear reader, I shall tell you since when: since the main efforts of avant-garde artists turned to representing scenes that resemble illustrations from the favourite sex manual of our youth, *The Ideal Marriage*, and in ways that show these scenes from all possible angles at once: above, below, in profile, full-frontally and even inside.

'Who benefits from this? *Cui bono?* Who is quietly encouraging it?

'Unfortunately, to our collective shame, it is the agencies and institutions which are the heirs of the great Polish tradition of learning and education, the National Educational Commission foremost among them. Impotent for years in the face of the urgent need to prepare our youth for mature sexual life, it has received this exhibition with relief and grateful enthusiasm.'

This and other similar articles gave me an idea. At first I intended to carry out my plan alone, but as it took shape in my mind I thought it prudent to enlist someone's aid. As my assistant, therefore, I selected a boy from my class who was quite proficient in French and also had the unmistakable makings of an actor (he had been in school plays, and in my memorable show had played Mephistopheles).

I showed him a few of the tastiest reviews and then tried to cajole him into bringing up the subject at the next French lesson, during the conversation period, asking Madame with a straight face whether a school trip to the exhibition might not be arranged.

'Why don't you do it yourself?' Mephisto asked suspiciously.

'You know what she's like with me,' I said, shrugging. 'She doesn't like me. In fact, she hates me! She's so suspicious – whatever I do or say, she always thinks it's some kind of trick, that I'm trying to make a fool of her. I'd never manage it.'

'And you think *I* can?' He was still sceptical.

'I'll be there,' I assured him. 'I'll cover for you. I'll tell you what to say, if need be.'

After some resistance he let himself be persuaded. We worked out a plan: a step-by-step script and a question-and-answer list that anticipated a number of possible exchanges. On the chosen day, when the time came for the French class, we sat at the same desk.

'*Depuis plus d'une semaine*,' Mephisto began boldly when Madame gave him permission to speak, 'for more than a week Warsaw has lived and breathed Picasso. His drawings are on everyone's lips; thousands of people have been streaming to see them. They've been discussed on the radio and written about in the newspapers. The exhibition is an *événement*; it has to be seen. Unfortunately it's almost impossible to get a ticket. The Zacheta Gallery is under siege, and queues start forming at dawn. In effect, this means that people like us, who have school in the mornings, don't have a chance. Not individually. But the school could organise a trip – other schools have. The whole class could go. And we'd have a very good chance of getting tickets, because the Ministry of Education has said that schools will have priority –'

'*Je ne suis pas au courant*,' Madame broke in. A faint smile hovered on her lips.

'The papers have been full of it,' I prompted in a whisper, bending low and putting my finger on the appropriate place in the question-and-answer list.

'*La presse en a parlé*,' he repeated convincingly, deftly taking the baton I had handed him. 'Besides, seeing the exhibition in *your* company, Madame, would be an additional privilege. You must be familiar with this art; you could *commenter . . . expliquer* . . . for us.'

'*Moi?*' she broke in again. 'Why should I know anything about Picasso's work?'

'It's part of French culture,' said Mephisto automatically. (This was not in the script.)

She shrugged. 'I don't see the relevance.'

I hastened to Mephisto's aid. 'For us you are not only . . .' I whispered in French.

'*Vous êtes pour nous non seulement* . . .' repeated Mephisto carefully.

'. . . our French teacher . . .'

'. . . *la lectrice de français* . . .'

'. . . but also our instructor . . .'

'. . . *mais aussi notre maîtresse* . . .'

'. . . in culture and in life.'

'. . . *de culture et de vie*.'

She gave a brief snort of laughter. '*J'ai grand plaisir à l'entendre*,' she declared, in elaborate (and quite graceful) late-rococo style. 'I'm delighted to hear it. But I'd be happier if the sentiment weren't expressed so ridiculously.'

'What's ridiculous about it?' asked Mephisto, abashed.

She shook her head. '*Passons.*'

'Wait . . . about this exhibition,' I prompted.

'Yes, well, can we count on your taking us to the exhibition?' Mephisto persisted, translating deftly.

'*Allez-y dimanche*,' she advised matter-of-factly.

'On Sunday?' asked Mephisto, taken aback.

'Did *she* get in on Sunday?' I hissed in his ear.

'Did *you* get in on Sunday?'

'*Cela n'a pas d'importance.*'

'Well, what day *did* she go?' I whispered again.

'Well, what day *did* you go?' Mephisto inquired politely.

'*Je n'y suis pas allée*,' she replied calmly.

She hadn't been? I was astonished by her answer.

'*Pas allée?*' repeated Mephisto obediently.

'*Non. Pas encore.*' Then she quickly changed the subject.

The Hand of Hippolytus

I had no doubt Madame would reject this request; I hadn't even expected her to take it seriously. I had no illusions on that score. But it hadn't occurred to me that she would deny having been at the exhibition. Now that she had, I was struck by how obvious her solution was: outright denial was much the simplest way to deal with inconvenient questions. And I derived a certain satisfaction from her lie: it gave me an advantage, and it also provided a basis for further games of the imagination.

She had lied, lied blatantly. As if she wanted to conceal something, to cover up a betrayal; as if she had gone not to see the drawings but for some other, private purpose. To satisfy some obscure, secret passion? To meet a lover? Was the exhibition a cover for some clandestine tryst? It was like something out of Proust! Indeed, was there not something intimate in the act of looking at those drawings, however openly, however publicly? Something shameless, almost treacherous? In looking at those scenes, in admitting them into her sight, into herself, was she not betraying the Veil of Clothes? And in betraying it, betraying me as well – for was it not with the Veil of Clothes that she had tempted me? After all, wasn't the perception of the act a substitute for the act itself? She had good reason, then, for lying!

This game of pretending to be Marcel to her Albertine or Swann to her Odette – someone in the sway of a jealous passion and desperate to find out the truth about his deceitful lover – was so exciting and absorbing that it began to take over. Gradually, imperceptibly, what had been a fantasy became real. I was no longer seriously considering the possibility of continuing my game on neutral territory, indeed no longer cared whether or not I won. In truth, at this point I would much rather I didn't. I was seized by an urgent, overwhelming desire to spy on her, follow her movements, observe her surreptitiously. It was an intense, consuming need, and it obsessed me like a craving for a drug.

So it was with mounting impatience and an obscure, unhealthy excitement that I awaited the performance of the Comédie Française at the National Theatre. There was to be one on Saturday and another on Sunday. Naturally, I decided to go to the opening night; if Madame failed to turn up, I would return the following day.

I had my admission card, so I had no trouble getting a ticket. The only question was where to sit, and answering it was rather like solving a chess problem: deciding how best to position one's king in an endgame. I had to find, by a process of elimination, the point in the auditorium best suited to my purposes, regardless of where my opponent placed, or rather *seated,* his king. Logically, the best place was one with the widest and most natural view of both audience and stage, so that I wouldn't have to strain or peer. Here this condition was fulfilled by the boxes at either end of the first balcony, a narrow U-shaped strip running around the back of the auditorium. They gave a good view not only of the stalls and the other boxes but also of part of the second balcony, which was low-hung and steep. But these boxes had the significant disadvantage of being reserved for the privileged few – the *haute société.* Judging by what I had seen at the Zacheta Gallery, it was possible, indeed probable, that this was where Madame would sit. And that would not be a happy coincidence. On the contrary, it would seriously upset my plans. I wanted only to observe, to watch from the shadows, unseen. After a moment's reflection, therefore, I chose the middle of the first row on the second balcony. It meant giving up the view of the back of the stalls and the centre boxes, but it gave me a perfect view of most of the other places where Madame was likely to sit.

When I arrived at the theatre that evening – again, as at the gallery, with a good deal of time to spare, and equipped with a pair of opera glasses – I did not go straight to my seat. I stopped in the lobby, stationed myself behind a poster and once again scanned, as I had at the Zacheta Gallery, the faces of the arriving guests.

Tonight the Fates were kinder to me, although they took their time. She arrived at the last minute, after the second bell. But there was nothing hurried about her behaviour. Other latecomers dashed in madly, flustered and wild-haired, and rushed to the cloakroom, struggling out of their coats as they ran; she, cool and composed in a well-cut sheepskin, high-heeled, knee-length boots and a colourful scarf at her neck, sailed in quite calm and dignified, almost majestic, and didn't take her ticket out of her bag (the same one she'd had at the gallery) until she was at the entrance to the foyer, where the ushers stood. She exuded an air of unshakeable confidence that the performance would not start without her.

I followed her at a suitable distance. She handed her coat to the cloakroom attendant, checked her make-up in the mirror, smoothed down her hair, and then, having procured a programme, made her way to the stalls. My heart began to beat more confidently. All's well, I thought, as long as she doesn't go to the back. Before taking off my coat I peeked through another door into the stalls. She was going into the fifth row, making her way past the people already seated there, who stood up to allow her to pass. I rushed upstairs to the balcony (and the cloakroom there).

My seat gave me a perfect view. A very slight movement of my eyes was enough to shift my gaze from the stage to her.

She was sitting in the middle of the row, reading the programme with concentration. On her right two elderly ladies were chatting. The place on her left was empty.

The sight of that empty place naturally prompted a flood of speculation. Who was it meant for? No one in particular – a stranger? Or was she expecting someone? And if so, who? Who was the person she was supposed to have come with, or to meet? And was that person now definitely not coming, or would he turn up later, at least for the second half? Her composure seemed to argue that she wasn't waiting for anyone. Which meant that she could, indeed, be alone – as she had come.

Alone! Unaccompanied! And with a free place next to her to boot! Could anything more propitious be imagined? Was this not precisely the kind of assumption, the kind of *imaginaire*, that had formed the basis of my plans to transfer the game to neutral ground? It was exactly the opportunity I'd dreamt of. Well, then? Confronted with the reality, I was paralysed: incapable of acting, unable even to imagine it. I fled from the thought of what would have happened if I had ended up taking that place by accident – especially if I had got there first and sat down not knowing who my neighbour would be.

I was paralysed because I was afraid. Afraid of her reaction at the sight of me, afraid of rejection, humiliation, her expression of distaste. The consciousness that my presence was annoying and unwanted, that I was nothing but a pest, would be too much for me to bear. And this feeling was so strong that I preferred to gain nothing, attempt nothing, to running the risk of defeat. Even if victory lay ahead. I clung to the guarantee of safety that lay in inaction.

I took the tortoiseshell opera glasses out of their case and focused them on Madame, then swept them over the stalls, row by row, looking for familiar faces. There were quite a few actors (among them Prospero and the beautiful Helena de With), a sprinkling of film people (among them the director of *Ashes*) and several well-known writers of the older generation. I shifted my gaze to the boxes – and froze. For there, in the last box on the right (the one that had first caught my attention), was Freddy. He sat slightly stooped, his elbows on the railing, and was engaged in the same activity as I: sweeping his opera glasses over the audience. I followed the line of his sight, and Madame reappeared in my field of vision. She was still reading the programme. I shifted back to Freddy. He hadn't moved; his black opera glasses were still glued to his eyes. He did not interrupt his observation even when the gong sounded and the lights dimmed.

I had seen *Phèdre* once before, two or three years ago – in Polish, on television. Although it had been played by some of our leading actors, I hadn't liked it much. I was disappointed; I'd turned off the television disillusioned with Racine. *This* was supposed to be the *chef-d'oeuvre* of French drama – the 'continental Shakespeare' as the television presenter had been at tedious pains to insist (apparently the tag was Stendhal's)? I'd been incredulous. It had been off-puttingly, toe-curlingly bad. Stiff, bloodless, tediously rhetorical – dead. I could feel no sympathy for these pompous heroes and their bombastic passions, so larger-than-life that they lacked all verisimilitude. Their tragedy left me cold.

This time I was entranced – from the very first words. The text sounded so different: incomparably purer than in Polish, clear and modern, without a trace of archaism, and above all beautifully rhythmic and melodic. The classical alexandrines, foreign to Polish prosody, rolled out like the soothing clickety-clack of a train: da-da-DUM, da-da-DUM, or, faster more urgently, da-DUM, da-DUM, da-DUM, lulling one into a trance. Yet nothing sounded false or artificial; the rigour of the form, far from being constraining, enhanced the meaning. The melody, the rhythm, the intonation were in perfect conformity with the spoken language; indeed, they were the ideal of French. No operatic stiffness, no trace of pathos or grandiloquence. Everything was real and credible and at the same time crystalline, wonderfully pure.

Then the actors! One was struck not just by their discreet, subtle, perfectly controlled performances but also by their appearance, their stage presence. Handsome, distinguished-looking, eloquent, graceful, expressive – there was something godlike about them. They had what used to be called breeding. Especially the ones who played the four main roles: Hippolytus and Phaedra, Aricia and Theseus. Tall, slim, with long, elegant necks and regular features, they moved with harmony and grace and exuded a kind of magnetic power. They were ideal-types: the proud and severe youth; the mature *Grande Dame*; the charming young beauty; the strong and virile master. They evoked admiration and awe close to worship, and also an obscure longing mingled with a profound sadness – a sadness born of the knowledge that they were from another world, and that world was unattainable. *They* were unattainable. One didn't know them and would never know them. And even if one could meet them, privately, outside the theatre, they'd probably be quite different from how they seemed on stage.

One might say they fulfilled the highest ideal of art: they had the power to move, to stir our emotions, to evoke our sympathy for something that didn't actually exist – fictional characters in an imaginary world. And they made us want, childishly, ridiculously, to be part of that world. They made us dream. For it is only in illusion that there is a chance of fulfilment – just a chance, nothing more. And in the vicarious experience granted to us by the passionate dramas enacted on stage that chance is invariably, irredeemably lost. The fate of those beautiful creatures is ineluctably tragic: they are doomed to defeat – to death without fulfilment.

Theseus, king of Athens – legendary hero and lover, slayer of Sciro, Procrustes and the Minotaur; beloved of Ariadne, whom he perfidiously abandoned; conqueror of Antiope, queen of the Amazons and mother of his son Hippolytus; and, finally, stately husband of Ariadne's younger sister, the fiery, hot-blooded Phaedra – set sail more than six months ago for distant Epirus to help a friend in need, and has not been heard of since.

Meanwhile, at his palace, in his native city of Troezen, major changes have taken place. Hippolytus, his son, left behind to guard the palace hearth, a pure, proud youth who until now has scorned love, succumbs to a passion for Aricia, an Athenian princess, the last descendant of a house hostile to his father, being held under strict guard at the palace. At the same time, Phaedra, Theseus's wife, who has long adored her stepson in secret, begins to burn with uncontrollable desire: her love is transformed into a passion that bursts into flames.

Both of them, haughty and proud, shocked by the disgraceful nature of their feelings, struggle as well as they can with love's poisoned arrows: he seeks oblivion in desperate chariot races and hunting expeditions; she plays the cruel, forbidding stepmother. In vain. Aphrodite is stronger. Finally they reach the limits of their endurance. He decides to go away and she to depart from this world.

It is here that the action of the tragedy begins. And this is what happens:

They have barely made these decisions – it remains for them only to take their leave of each other – when news arrives of Theseus's death. It is sad news, but it brings a certain relief, even a spark of hope. For with Theseus gone, the shame and disgrace of their illicit feelings is at least lessened; perhaps now there is even a chance of fulfilment. After all, no blood tie links Phaedra to Hippolytus; their union would now violate no taboo. Indeed, it would further the interests of the state, for it would eliminate dispute over the succession. More natural still would be a marriage between Hippolytus and Aricia, for the only thing preventing their union was his dead father's enmity towards her house. Did not Theseus himself take as his wife the queen of a house with which he was at war?

Thus does Aphrodite add fuel to the fire. The dreams, lusts and desires that were to have been extinguished for good burst forth again, raging with a new and even stronger flame.

Two meetings take place: between Hippolytus and Aricia, and between Phaedra and Hippolytus. These last two seem intent on sticking to their decisions, despite the changed circumstances after Theseus's death; they both want to cut through the knot that fetters their will and painfully constricts their hearts. But they also wish to depart reconciled, by atoning for past wrongs.

Thus Hippolytus repeals his father's cruel sentence condemning Aricia to perpetual slavery and returns Athens to her, for Athens is hers by right. Phaedra, for her part, regrets her past hostility and cruelties to Hippolytus, and appeals to his generosity. But creeping through these gestures of reconciliation and words of contrition an entirely different tone and content can be discerned; all at once, the settling of accounts and the pleas for forgiveness become open declarations of love. The walls of shame crumble; the reins of pride are loosened and fall. Words lose their ambiguity and meanings become clear. *Puisque j'ai commencé de rompre le silence* – Hippolytus swerves suddenly from the path of his speech and plunges into a confession (I give his words in translation):

> *Now the silence is broken and I have begun,*
> *I'll go on, for I must. My lady, I'll speak.*
> *My heart is too swollen, my will is too weak.*

And in a long, passionate speech he spills out the whole truth: how he was wounded by love, how he suffered and struggled, how in the end he succumbed to the power of *un amour si sauvage.*

The effect of this confession on Aricia is not at all what Hippolytus feared: she is filled with astonished joy. It's like a miracle, a dream, a glimpse of heaven. It's the last thing she expected. For years enslaved, sentenced, she thought, to eternal chastity, by now reconciled to her unhappy fate, here she is suddenly being granted her freedom, love and a kingdom – all at once, and from the hands of a man who captivates her. She blossoms like a flower in the sun:

> *I accept all the gifts that you wish to bestow.*
> *But your empire, so glorious, so great and so wide*
> *Is not the most dear of your gifts in my eyes.*

She accepts his confession! She returns his love! It is a happy moment; a respite, at last, from his lonely sufferings. Is there anything more worthy, more desirable than this?

The scene was played with charming subtlety and finesse: Hippolytus, emboldened by Aricia's acceptance, slowly extended his arm to her, with open hand, as if asking her to dance; she responded by raising her hand to meet his. But they did not touch. When their fingers were no more than an inch apart they froze, immobile, and held the pose – like God and Adam in Michelangelo's Sistine fresco.

There was a moment's silence, and then applause. Immediately I looked down, to the fifth row of the stalls.

She wasn't applauding. She sat still and unmoved.

Meanwhile, the drama was approaching its climax. Phaedra had appeared on stage for her great 'aria'.

Yes – she knows Hippolytus is repelled by the sight of her; she has done everything to inspire his loathing. Nevertheless, circumstances being what they are, she appeals to him to stay his revenge for the wrongs she has done him, and in particular not to take vengeance on her young son, his half-brother. More: she wants Hippolytus to accept him as his own and watch over his safety. He alone can defend the child against its enemies:

Only you have the strength to defend him for me.

This is already a somewhat suggestive-sounding request (*defend him* – in other words, become his father – and thus her husband?). But there is more; this is just the beginning. Phaedra is carried away and loses control over her words. She begins to identify her stepson with his father:

But no – not dead, my lord! For he lives on in you.
When I see you before me, it's his face I view.

And she begins to recall the events of long ago, in Crete, when Theseus slew the Minotaur with the help of her sister, Ariadne. In those days he was the image of Hippolytus: young, splendid, beautiful. That was when he first inspired her love. But she was too late; Ariadne had got there first. And when she did marry him, years later, he was a different man, and that other, younger self had gone. She did not understand this fully until she saw Hippolytus for the first time, in Athens: a replica of his father in the days of his glory. Those features, that body, that enchanting figure – it was her destiny, whoever it belonged to, father or son.

That is the terrible, unendurable thing: it is not we who choose. We are merely playthings in the hands of the gods. We suffer, we burn with passion, we writhe about in a frenzy, and the gods, vastly entertained, laugh with delight. An echo of their sardonic laughter can sometimes be heard in the moans and sobs of their victims.

So if mortal man has any dignity, he should refuse to tolerate this sorry spectacle, this unequal game. He should do away with himself. End it all, and put a stop to his humiliation. And Phaedra, having confessed her love and thus sunk, in her own eyes, as low as it is possible to sink, entreats Hippolytus to kill her. Since there is nothing else he can give her, let him at least give her this – her death:

Here's my heart. Take your sword. This is where you must strike.
It leaps forth in my breast to atone for past harm.
Impatient it waits for the blow from your arm.
Strike. Or if such a blow is beneath your estate,
If your hatred denies me so gentle a fate,
If my blood is too vile to sully your hand,
Then lend me your sword. Have pity. Unbend.
Let me have it.

As Phaedra pronounced these words there was another bit of silent choreography, corresponding to the last but negative where that had been positive – in a minor key, as it were. It was beautifully and very precisely done. On those final words, that short, suggestive 'Let me have it', Phaedra, standing on Hippolytus's left (from the point of view of the audience), reached across with her right hand for the short sword strapped to his left side. At this Hippolytus's right hand went to the hilt of his sword, in an attempt to prevent her. Then she, with her left hand, grasped that arm at the wrist and pulled it towards her, while with her right she slowly drew out the sword and raised it aloft. And in this position, turned in three-quarters profile to the audience, they froze, immobile, for several long seconds.

It was a magnificent *tableau,* and pregnant with layers of meaning. Hippolytus's hand hung limp, like the head of a dead bird, in Phaedra's grasp, while the blade of the upraised sword in her other hand, in striking contrast, was rigid and straight. As they held this position they looked defiantly into each other's eyes. There was a hint of perversion and masochism in the scene: violence trying to provoke violence. Kill me, or I'll cut you down! cried Phaedra's arm, extended by the sword. Take the sword and strike! Or, if you won't take it, use your bare hands, and strangle me! Let me die in that sweet embrace! Or at least . . . at least do *something* with that limp, helpless hand, unworthy of a man and so insulting, so humiliating to me! Turn it outwards, at least, and take . . . take me . . . by the hand . . . just for a moment!

If Hippolytus had done this – if he had freed his wrist from Phaedra's grasp and taken her hand – he would have transformed their position into the classic marriage pose. They would have stood, facing the audience, like a couple at the altar. But he did not do this – perhaps for that very reason. He stood motionless and withdrawn, a grimace of revulsion on his face.

It was an allegory of rejection and contempt. It said that unrequited love was something irrevocable: nothing could kindle it if it did not burn with its own flame, not curses or entreaties, not threats or violence. These two human elements cannot come together; nothing can bring them together. The more one attracts, the more the other repels. Unfulfilment. Unhappiness. The tragedy of loneliness.

After a moment of tense silence there was another burst of applause. I looked down. This time she did applaud, but not as enthusiastically as the rest of the audience. I shifted my gaze towards the box where Freddy, opera glasses to his eyes, was observing the actors.

When the applause finally died away, Phaedra, in a fury of injured pride, violently pushed Hippolytus away and left the stage, taking his sword with her. Shortly afterwards, like a bolt from the blue, came the news that Theseus was alive and just sailing into the harbour. Here the first half of the play ended.

People began to get up and go out for the interval.

My chin propped on my hands, I observed the stalls. She made no move. I thought at first she was only waiting for the crowd in the aisles and at the doors to thin out, but when the auditorium was almost empty and everyone (including Freddy) was gone, she remained where she was. What's more, she resumed her study of the programme. It seemed clear that she intended to stay put for the whole interval.

The opportunity was ideal; it was hard to imagine a better one. An almost empty auditorium, with her in it, alone, and almost fifteen minutes at my disposal. An utter reversal of the situation at the Zacheta Gallery. I felt another wave of apprehension and the rapid beating of my heart. A voice in my head, a voice that was becoming familiar, said, *Now!* Go down to her, quickly! What are you afraid of? If you can't get up the courage in these conditions, you'll never do it. And if you don't, that means you're not worthy of her. Follow the current! Drift! Blessed fog . . . Go on, what are you waiting for? There's no time to lose; every second is precious! And approach her from the left, where the empty place is. Perhaps you'll be watching the second half from there . . .

I rose and made for the stairs.

Although I thought I was walking with a firm step, the way down took longer than the way up had done. And when at last I looked through a door into the stalls, this was the sight that met my eyes: in the middle of the fourth row, in front of Madame and facing her, stood the director of the Service Culturel. They were talking. Or, rather, *he* was talking, animatedly and with much gesticulating, leaning slightly towards her, while she sat unmoved, gazing up at him and occasionally interjecting a word or two. When the bell rang for the end of the interval and the audience flowed back into the auditorium, the director straightened up and, with a glance at the central box, made gestures signifying that he had to go. Mouthing an '*à bientôt!*' he backed out of the fourth row and disappeared.

Shortly thereafter he duly reappeared in the central box, along with the ambassador and his wife.

I ran back upstairs. On the way I encountered an usher and hurriedly bought a programme. I got back to my place just before the curtain rose. The place next to Madame was still empty. Freddy was leafing through his programme. I took a look as well. Just before the lights dimmed I glimpsed his name, somewhere at the top of a page.

The second half of the play lacked the power and beauty of the first, although the acting was just as good, and executed at the same pace and rhythm. The reason probably lay in the nature of the play itself; for after Theseus's return, as the course of events slowly rolls on towards the inevitable tragic end, the temperature drops and the suspense abates. The outcome is settled, preordained from the very first scene – the dialogue between Theseus and Phaedra. There is nothing, now, that can be repaired or undone. The catastrophe can only be delayed – by a game of pretence, by lying and concealment. But these no longer move one in the same way: the conspiracy of silence and the false accusations lack the power, the passion and the drama of the conflict between spirit and flesh, between duty and the heart. That, despite the costumes and the artificiality of form, had been powerful and true; the intrigues, ambiguities and insinuations which come later, however plausible, were too theatrical, too conventional, too predictable.

Only two brief episodes flamed with the fire of the first half: Phaedra's scene of jealousy, and the scene in which Hippolytus tries to convince Aricia to flee Troezen with him.

Phaedra's cry of incredulous horror when she hears Theseus say, during his tirade, that Hippolytus loves Aricia, her terrified 'It can't be!' as her knees give way and she clutches at a pillar for support, sent a shiver up one's spine. Hippolytus's scorn, as long as it seemed to arise from pride or a refusal to sully his purity, could be borne, like hunger or terrible thirst; but when it turns out that its cause is his love for another woman, it becomes a catastrophe of cosmic proportions. Phaedra feels swallowed up by a hopeless despair, as if she has been flung into some infernal pit; she literally feels the ground give way under her feet. The pain of being rejected for another is unendurable.

Her second attack of hysteria takes place when Oenone, her nurse, tries to comfort her, saying,

What fruit will they reap from their love? It's all vain.
They'll not meet any more.

Whereupon Phaedra breaks in with a terrible, savage scream, entirely out of keeping with her position and breeding:

But they'll love just the same!

These sudden changes of tone, from high to low, from regal to common, superbly rendered by the actress, brought home how fragile is the shell of man's dignity and nobility. There, look, they seemed to say: goad the unsatiated will, throw a pinch of salt and wormwood into the boiling blood, and at once the backbone of sublimation gives way. All the forms and customs developed over generations to clothe our animal nature crumble to dust, and a great lady is transformed into a slut; a proud queen becomes a bitch in heat.

The atmosphere of the meeting between Hippolytus and Aricia is quite different. It is here that the last spark of hope in the tragedy is briefly kindled. For although events take a turn for the worse and the circle of conflicting claims begins to close in, all is not yet lost; something can still be rescued from the ravages of passion, the fire that rages through the house: *their* happiness. They can escape together, flee Troezen, now, at once.

Hippolytus musters all his eloquence to plead with the virtuous Aricia to throw away her hesitation and put her trust in him. It is a beautiful speech:

Cast off the sad yoke that this house makes you bear.
Escape with me. Be with me. Follow me. Dare.
Abandon this putrid and poisonous place
Where Virtue must breathe an air foul with disgrace.

Ah, if Madame were to turn to me with such an appeal!

It dawned on me then that I was seeing this performance, just as I had seen Picasso's drawings and read *Victory* and the verses from the *Rhine,* through the prism of 'my misery', as Chopin called a certain love of his. But it was not a matter of deriving emotional thrills from the faint resemblance of the two protagonists to real people: I didn't try to pretend that I was Hippolytus and Phaedra was Madame or anything like that. Their story was quite different. My fantasies were not grounded in any specific correlation; the drama being enacted on stage merely provided elements for the drama unfolding in my head, and my imagination played with them freely. The result was a sort of projection of my unexpressed daydreams:

Madame's father, a bold and restless spirit, an idealist who likes to challenge fate, commits a catastrophic mistake, like Theseus Tartarus-bound. In the throes of madness or persecution mania, flying in the face of common sense and ignoring the warnings of friends, he returns from the wars to his native land, now enslaved by a regime of barbarians from Moscow and governed by their local chums. More horrifying still, he drags along his only daughter, beautiful and proud, born in the heart of the Alps – the daughter whom, as a sign of his trust that Fortune would always smile upon him, he has named Victory.

The blunder is fatal: the wretched Max-Theseus dies in the dungeons of military intelligence, swallowed up in the pit of Tartarus, while the beautiful Victoire, thrown upon her own resources, is cut off from the world by an impregnable Iron Curtain. At first she is desperate. Then, gradually, like the free-born Rhine, she tunnels her way to open spaces, in the direction of the setting sun: to the plains of France. After numerous setbacks and failed attempts, she finds an opportunity more promising than any she has encountered so far, for it is singularly connected to the interests of her oppressors: their success in snatching some of those mouthwatering Western morsels for which they are so greedy depends in some measure on whether they restore her freedom to her. That, in short, is how the situation now presents itself. All she has to do is prove her worth as a teacher – in the eyes of a foreign body of judges.

It is here that the main action of the drama begins.

The school to which she is sent and which it is her task to reform is – like everything else in this debased, lawless country where Bolshevik tyranny rules – rotten and backward. The teachers are dull, embittered and cynical, the pupils slothful, fractious and of limited intelligence. Working in these conditions is like ploughing ground that has lain fallow for too long. Her life is one of lonely drudgery. No one to talk to, no common language. She is totally isolated.

In these dark, gloomy, foul backwoods, in the herd of crude, thick-headed youths who are her pupils, she encounters, shortly before she is due to regain her freedom, a young man of rare talent – sophisticated, articulate, charming. He is intelligent, polished and well bred. He is witty – his conversation can be scintillating. Yet at the same time he is curiously shy – sad and withdrawn. He intrigues her. With time he inspires her sympathy and affection. But she conceals these feelings and – like Phaedra – plays the cruel mistress. She avoids all forms of unofficial contact with him, even the most innocent. Sooner or later, she thinks, it would turn against her. Besides, what do her feelings matter! Sentiment is the last thing she needs. And she is leaving soon, never to return; she can't permit herself such extravagance. 'He who forms a tie is lost.' It would be folly.

But there is more to this unusual pupil of hers. Not only is he a charming young man, but he seems secretly to worship her. He never takes his eyes off her, covertly tries to dig up information about her, smuggles sweet confessions into the essays he is set. And how charmingly, with what skill and ingenuity! It's quite endearing. Is there anyone else in the world who would set her apart like this? Well, perhaps *le petit Frédéric* – the son of the man who had been her father's friend and her mother's suitor. But what a comparison! Freddy's lugubrious passion for her is tedious and dreary. It repels and embarrasses her; it leaves her cold. It's neurotic, hysterical, pathetic. And quite apart from that, how pale is the love of a Man, how unstable and irresolute, how tainted by doubt and uncertainty, compared to the first stirrings of love in a Boy, so passionate and uncritical! At any rate, for someone already past the flush of youth, a mature woman in her thirties.

He adores her. Worships her! He has built an altar to her! And yet he has so many girls his own age to choose from. It's flattering and strangely exciting. It makes you want to reach out, acknowledge his love, become an omnipotent goddess for him. It is tempting.

But it's out of the question to succumb. It would be far too risky, apart from being dishonest and mean. On the other hand, doing nothing and continuing to play the cold and heartless Ice Queen is no solution either.

An inner struggle ensues between vanity and responsibility, between the instincts of the heart and the promptings of reason, common sense and discipline. She should do something for him, offer something, but not so as to inspire great hopes. Yes, she could give him some friendly attention, even make him happy – as Hippolytus makes Aricia happy – for an instant, a brief, fleeting moment, inconsequentially.

She gives him an A. The only one in the whole school. And she passes on his essay to the commission of foreign judges with a suitable note. Who knows – perhaps it will lead to something? Perhaps the chief, Monsieur le Directeur, will notice him – as Professor Billot once noticed the articles of *le petit Frédéric* – and do something to help him? Offer him a grant, invite him to Paris? But all that lies in the future, and it's by no means certain. What about now? What can she do for immediate effect? She could single him out on some minor matter, set him apart, show him that she thinks him deserving of her trust. She could send him to her office, with its treasure chest of personal belongings, open and unguarded. Give him the key – as a gesture, a symbolic way of giving him access to her. Say to him, '*La clé!*' and then, looking him in the eye, hand it to him – with a gesture like that of the Creator in Michelangelo's fresco.

And that is indeed what happens. But it doesn't work; it misses its mark. The play of allusions and metaphors doesn't satisfy him. No radiant flush of happiness suffuses his face. He is still as he was: downcast, dejected, pained. It will have to be done differently. Take him to the theatre! To see the Comédie Française, which has just arrived with *Phèdre*. She has an invitation from the embassy; it says *valable pour deux personnes*. It's the perfect solution.

But the hand of Providence, for good or for ill, prevents it. It puts a spoke in the wheels, it muddles things, and in the end her plans are thwarted. She goes to the theatre alone, wasting the other ticket. The place next to her is empty. It must be the only one, at least in the stalls. She watches the performance, regretting that things turned out this way. And when she hears Hippolytus say, 'Cast off the sad yoke that this house makes you bear,' and then, a moment later, 'Abandon this putrid and poisonous place,' she realises, in a sudden flash, that this is precisely what she should say to him.

If only he were here, sitting beside her! If only he could hear those words! (She would have made sure to draw his attention to them somehow.)

But he *is* there! And he *has* heard them. He is sitting at the front of the balcony. And when the curtain falls and the applause has faded away, in just a few minutes, they will meet at the cloakroom or at the door of the theatre. All is not yet lost! *This* play has a happy ending . . .

This idly spun tale, unfolding somewhere in the recesses of my consciousness, was so enchanting and suggestive that when the play was over, mindless of what I had seen and deaf to the voice of reason, I set off with a firm step to write an ending for it – a real one.

I retrieved my coat, ran downstairs and, sighting my Phaedra in the crowd besieging the cloakroom, went outside to wait for her there – at the foot of the front steps.

Suddenly, in the entrance, I saw a radiant Prospero, surrounded by the usual crowd of young admirers. He was evidently discoursing on the performance, for he talked uninterruptedly, stopping every few seconds to re-enact some gesture or pose. I put a few more steps' distance between us, so that he wouldn't see me. But he gave me an inspiration. Of course!

I should approach her as I had approached him – in verse! This time in alexandrines. Since the ploy had worked so well before, perhaps it would work now, too. Besides, since the scene was supposed to resemble one from a real drama, how else should I speak to her?

I put my right hand up to my brow (as Constant had a habit of doing), squeezed my eyes shut and tried to concentrate my mind.

Madame! Est-ce bien vous-même?

I composed my speech.

Mais quelle coïncidence!
Quelle étrange et curieux concours de circonstances!

The first rhyme released the flow. The words began to come more easily; each reminded me of another with a similar ending, and finally they began to come not in pairs but in threes, even fours. By this mechanism I arrived at the rhyme '*question-conversation*'. It reminded me of something. Of course! That lesson! Just before I'd begun my surreptitious investigation. It cried out to be worked in somehow.

I tautened the bow of *l'art poétique*:

Profitons-en pour faire une conversation;
Pour nous poser enfin quelques bonnes questions.

Pleased with my efforts, I released my hand's grip on my brow and opened my eyes. And this was the sight that met them:

At the kerb, in front of the entrance, was a blue Peugeot, its engine purring, its lights yellow. Its front passenger door was wide open; in the seat beside the driver sat a woman whom after a few seconds I recognised as Mademoiselle Legris. She was gesturing to someone. That someone was Madame, just at that moment coming down the steps. She went up to the car, opened the back door and with a quick, graceful movement slid inside. Two sets of locks clicked, and the car moved off in the direction of Obozna Street. I tried to get a glimpse of the driver, but failed. Probably the director. But I saw the registration plate quite clearly: wz 1807 (the year of Napoleon's victory over Russia and his creation of a new Polish state called the Duchy of Warsaw). Slightly below and to the left was an oval plate with the letters CD.

I put my hands in the pockets of my grey coat (one of which also held the programme) and set off slowly, with bowed head, towards New World Boulevard and the nearest bus stop, next to a travel agent's called Wagons-Lits–Cook.

Taking Stock

I was well aware that this latest brief scene in my own live drama (more film-like than theatrical), however painful, had left me relatively unscathed. It could have been worse. What if, in a surge of recklessness, a moment of mad audacity, I had been impelled to act? Waylaid her in the queue for the cloak-room, for example, or (worse) in the foyer? The consequences of such a step did not bear thinking about. And yet, though I knew I had been let off lightly, I could not rejoice in my luck. Something gnawed at me – a sense of disappointment, of something unfulfilled. And an awareness that I was a person – a *creature* – of a lower category, a lesser breed.

For two hours I had watched as a drama woven from Greek myth unfolded before me on stage. Its protagonists, although mortal, were like Titans; one felt that here were the fairest specimens of the human race. Their fate, the passions that enflamed them, all that they felt and endured, seemed on a different scale: majestic, noble, grand. And the actors who played them also seemed, here in the bleak reality of a 'People's republic', to belong to a world apart. Here were men and women of untold beauty and charismatic power, dazzling charm and crystal-clear voices. And they came from the West! From 'bourgeois' France, the Olympus of life and art! From the legendary Comédie Française! How talented they must be, how sensitive, how experienced, how rich in their inner life, how open to the world! And the lives of such people, their everyday, personal lives – what must they be like, over there, under the Eiffel Tower and the Arc de Triomphe?

And here, watching these godlike mythic characters played by people who themselves seemed partly divine, was this rare creature, this woman who to me was like a goddess. Born of mysterious, exceptional parents, like the Rhine in the 'holy Alps', where 'only the pure is forged'; handsome, quick-witted and strong-willed; sorely tried by Fate's adversities; caught and imprisoned by the Bolshevik pygmies occupying Poland and now exerting all her cunning to find a way out of the trap. Who else in this wasteland had such strength, such beauty, such intelligence? Where was there another 'so happily born, to remain free'?

As befitted a proud *femme emancipée*, she had arrived alone and at the last minute. When she left, a car with diplomatic plates was waiting, like a chariot for a goddess, to whisk her off to the dinner or banquet – at the embassy perhaps, or maybe the Hotel Bristol – for the French actors; she'd be drinking champagne, holding her own, conversing with *esprit* and *brillant*. An equal among equals. In a different dimension.

And who was I compared to this? Compared to them, compared to her? Was I not a lesser being, a 'baser nature'? Baser even than those that come between 'the pass and fell incensed points of mighty opposites', for not even that small comfort had been granted me. What was my own life? A childhood in the ruins of Warsaw; the macabre world of Stalinism; a sad, poor world, crude and boorish and bleak. A pathetic round of daily rituals in a wretched conquered province, a dump in the middle of nowhere, a wasteland. A world of used goods and hand-me-downs, old, ugly, crippled. A world where you relied on 'drops' and parcels of frumpy cast-offs from the West and listened to Radio Free Europe. And where you constantly heard the same refrain: one day, somewhere . . . not here . . . finished, it's finished . . . My life's prose was indeed, as a certain poet said, lacking in syntactical beauty.

Fate is not everything, however. After all, Madame herself – although the course of her own life was rare, indeed unique

– had spent many years plodding through the same wasteland. But she had something that counts just as much, perhaps more: spirit, an inner fire, a flame that burned hot and bright and strong. And I – what did I have? Where was *my* fire? How bright was its flame? Here again, I paled in comparison. I was stunted, a cripple. I was a good student, certainly; I could hold my own in a conversation, speak French and play the piano; I had been initiated into the *arcana* of chess, game of kings; I was blessed with a prodigious memory. I was good with words and could juggle them in all sorts of subtle ways. I could even speak in verse. So what? Where did any of this get me? It was all so conventional, so civilised and 'cultured', so polite – a game of manners, abstract and cold. It wasn't *real*. There was no madness in it, no divine folly, no ecstasy. No faith except in reason, no sensibility, only sense. The mind was all, the body nothing. I preferred dress to nakedness. I would rather have semblance than truth. Enclosed within myself, inaccessible, locked in the impregnable armour of my brain, I was nothing but irony and superficial wit, the eternal court jester, the buffoon. I paled at the sight of blood. I was ashamed of my own nature. I had no access to deep feeling, for there was no form in which I could assimilate it. I could not be transported by passion, for I could not make it part of me. I could not express love.

Could a figure like this be the protagonist of a drama? Perhaps, but never a Hippolytus, never a Phaedra, never . . . an Antony. At most perhaps someone like Shakespeare's Jaques, like Molière's Misanthrope, like Beckett's Hamm. A caricature or anti-hero, a negative figure embodying sickness, doubt and exile from the world.

And Madame, whoever she really was – the Ice Queen, the Rhine, Lena or a *femme fatale* – must have sensed this. And since she did, she could never be drawn to me; she could only be repelled. If like me she was cold, overly proud, caught in the coils of her own reason and shame, someone like me could only intimidate, even paralyse her, as might an image in a distorting mirror. If underneath that icy mask was a young woman of courage and determination, fighting to escape from her cage, then someone like me was of no use to her: she needed a Heyst, a Captain – a man, not a confused, insecure boy, with an inferiority complex and chasing after will-o'-the-wisps. And if, finally, she was a Helen or a Cleopatra, a *contessa*, a lioness of the *salons,* then someone like me simply did not exist for her: I was like an irritating, buzzing insect, or at best an unnoticed extra in a crowd.

This conclusion, in all its layered complexity, was an oppressive burden. In an effort to dispel the cloud of apathy threatening to envelop me, I took up the programme and looked inside.

The back cover was taken up by a picture of Racine, a black-and-white reproduction of a portrait attributed to François de Troy. It showed him as a fairly young man, still in his thirties. His gaze is fixed longingly on something off to the side; his almond eyes seem to be looking at someone sitting next to me, on my right, and he has a sad, almost imperceptible smile.

He's looking at her, not at me, I thought bitterly – at the figure, not the background. For him I am merely . . . an empty place.

I turned over a page, looking for Freddy's name. I soon found it, above a title – 'A Genius' – and a dense column of text. It was a profile of Racine, written with great gusto and enthusiasm, interwoven with biographical details, and depicting an artist full of inner contradictions.

In this pious, solid, worthy citizen, his spiritual upbringing shaped by a reclusive life at the Port Royal, by the Jansenists' rigorous asceticism and firm belief in the doctrine of divine Grace, breathed the spirit of genius. His talent, under his burgher's cloak, was diabolical. This much by way of introduction. But there was more: in this poor orphan from the provinces, kindly, well meaning and shy, smouldered a dark hunger, a lust for fame and success, a greed for worldly things; within the iceberg of logic steamed a volcano of passion. In the cool follower of Apollo, Dionysus ran riot, performing acts of unbridled debauchery; within this bright, open Christian soul, full of hope and serenity, lurked the gloomy depths of an unbounded pessimism.

The fruit is according to the seed; as is the soil, so is the harvest. In every aspect of the writer's life and work the contradictions of his nature were glaringly evident. It was a strangely torn life, full of deep conflicts and sharp, jarring dissonances. The first nineteen years were a model of propriety: an angelic childhood and exemplary youth devoted to prayer and study (albeit sometimes betrayed in favour of titillating romances read furtively under the school desk). Then came the age of manhood, and with it sin and lust, illicit love, the fever of desire, the passions of the flesh; flights of genius, royal favours, a spectacular career and not a few *diableries*. Within ten years he produced seven tragedies, each one better than the last; he shone in high society and dazzled at court. He sought and won the hearts of beautiful actresses. He was scaling great – and lucrative – heights: fame, riches and prestige lay before him. He was in sight of the summit. And then it stopped. Suddenly, when he was barely thirty-seven, he broke with the theatre and the life of the libertine, that 'gross illusion and marketplace of vanity'. Like the prodigal son he returned to the bosom of the Port Royal; in an act of contrition, he burned all his notes for further plays, and proceeded to wed a dull and worthy townswoman, the quiet, pious daughter of a prosperous notary. She never read a single line of any of his plays. They had seven children, five daughters and two sons, in whom he did his best to inculcate a loathing of literature. Twenty-three years of this upright life turned him into an adept courtier with a tendency to bigotry.

And yet even then his extraordinary genius would out. This is what happened. Mme de Maintenon, the pious and no longer youthful morganatic wife of King Louis XIV, had under her patronage a well-known boarding school for the daughters of the less wealthy nobility. Here the dramatic arts, for the girls' elocution and the perfection of elegant manners, were among those encouraged. Plays were carefully chosen; a high standard of suitability was required. It was decided that the 'golden syllables' of the author of *Bérénice* would do very well.

No one could have foreseen the consequences of this decision. The girls acted too well, awesomely well – with such fire and passion that their God-fearing patron stopped the rehearsals. Loath to squander an opportunity, however, and eager to put this extraordinary pen to some use of her own, she commissioned Racine to produce a new play just for her – for the school in Saint-Cyr. But it must be a 'moral' play, 'with songs', and no hidden 'dangers for the soul'. The poet at first refused: for twelve years now he had kept unswervingly to the path of virtue, and he saw all theatre as the work of the devil. But then he wavered. Finally, tempted by the prospect of labouring for the greater glory of God, he agreed.

Esther was duly written. Its effects were astonishing. The tragedy was based on Holy Scripture, but despite its lofty themes and utter lack of anything impure to which blame might be attached, it awakened an unhealthy excitement among the girls. The atmosphere became heated: intrigues and rivalries flourished, ambitions collided and a fever of agitation broke out. Then, when society began to gather to see the play, the school, that strict bastion of chastity and propriety, became a veritable *salon*. The temple of the Vestal Virgins was transformed into a den of depravity. Emotions burst through, passions were aroused, coquetry and undesirable intimacies were indulged in. The poet, too, felt the old spirit stirring within him. As in the days when he had lived and breathed the theatre, attending scrupulously to every line, every accent and word uttered by his actress-mistresses, he began to scrutinise the interpretation of his text in minute detail. This so absorbed him that when the girl playing Eliza stumbled in her soliloquy he was moved to cry out in anguish, 'Girl, you are killing my play!' and stop the performance. She, frightened and abashed, disintegrated into loud sobs; he was at once contrite and rushed to wipe away her tears. One thing led to another: begging her forgiveness, he tried to calm her – and himself. His lips sought hers. Thus were they reconciled.

And thus again – yet again! and in what circumstances! – did frenzied Dionysus triumph over cool Apollo; again, quite unintentionally, indeed despite the efforts of everyone concerned, art had kindled fire. The power of its godless beauty was infinite. Which was why, when the poet wrote *Athalie*, another biblical play (to be hailed years later as one of the great masterpieces of French theatre), for Mme de Maintenon, her wards at Saint-Cyr were permitted to perform it only once, before the King, and attired in everyday dress.

On the bottom of the page where this sketch ended was a reproduction of another portrait of Racine, this one by Charon, painted from the imagination almost a century after the poet's death. It depicted him in the act of reading his *Britannicus* to the Roi Soleil. The poet (foreground, left) sits in an armchair, holding before him a book, open somewhere roughly in the middle, at which he gazes with an expression of bliss. The King (a touch deeper in the background, right), stretched out on a sofa, his head on one hand, is watching him pensively and approvingly, as if to say, How nicely you write, Racine, and you read quite nicely, too.

This little scene gave me pause, and caused me to resume my interrupted analysis of my own life.

If one is not a king, I thought wistfully, but with a tiny, flickering flame of hope, if one is not even cut out to be a hero, and yet is not content with mere daily bread, 'the common round, the simple task', if one dreams and longs for inexpressible things, and constantly plays the clown because one cannot express emotion in a normal way – then the only form of fulfilment, the one consolation, is to become an artist – a pupil of the world, a magus.

I saw myself then through the eyes of my imagination, saw myself sitting all day long at a desk in a room, writing, with a pen or a typewriter, filling page after page with characters, gradually turning each from white to black. I saw myself weaving fascinating tales, drawn from reality but so much better, so much more attractive and enticing than reality itself, composing them like music, extracting their rhythm, making my words, read aloud, sound like a poem. Choosing a word, selecting a phrase, constructing a sentence, until there, at last, was a paragraph, pure and clear and perfectly formed. And then I would go for a walk, to think about the next.

This, I whispered to myself, this will be my life. And I put away the programme.

On Monday, after school, I went to the library and took out Racine's tragedies in French. Then, trying them out, as it were, I carefully copied out Hippolytus's monologue and Phaedra's 'aria' into my *Cahier.* After reading them through several times I knew them both by heart.

A Man and a Woman

Since the day she had sent me to fetch the exercise book from her office, Madame seemed to have warmed to me; indeed she was more gracious with every lesson. She not only acknowledged my presence but paid me more attention than she ever had before. The harsh, mocking tone was gone; she spoke to me politely, and more often than to any of the others, usually when someone didn't know the answer to something or had made a mistake. She would look at me and ask, 'Well, what do you think?' or 'Was that correct?' as if I were the ultimate arbiter; then, 'Well, then, what *is* the right answer?' When I gave it she uttered an appreciative '*Voilà!*' and resumed the exercise where she had interrupted it.

She treated me like a teacher's pet: the infallible, exemplary pupil. I can't say that the role appealed to me much, but I bore it with good grace for the sake of the special and quite unexpected favours that came with it.

She began to use me as her assistant at the blackboard. She would catch my eye and say (in Polish), 'Come here; you can help me,' and hand me the chalk. Or she would have me read some passage from a newspaper, with a 'would you be so kind' or a 'would you, please?'. And during dictations or written verb exercises, when she was in the habit of strolling among the desks, she would come up and say to me in an undertone, 'You don't have to bother with that.' Once – but only once – she even spoke my name, and she used the familiar, abbreviated form.

I was at a loss to understand this change. What had caused it? What was behind it? Had she met up with Freddy, had *he* said something to her? Had she been warned that a visit from the French inspection committee was imminent, and was she merely trying to smooth my feathers in preparation for it? Or perhaps there *was* no special reason? Perhaps it was just a whim, a desire to play games with me? Whatever her motives, I decided that the best response to this 'opening' was to stay calm and wait. Or, in the language of chess, to 'refuse her gambit', just as she had refused mine.

Let her develop her game, I thought to myself; I'll hold off until her strategy becomes clear. Before I make my move I should know what she's aiming for, and why. That's what theory tells you to do, if you don't want to be slaughtered. The Caro-Kann defence. Keep quiet and go with the game. She wants me to play the teacher's pet? Fine. To be her errand-boy? No discussion, just do it. Am I to sit there, then, listening to her wheedling, almost wooing tones, executing her errands and her suggestive-sounding wishes, hearing her call me – amazingly! – by the familiar version of my own name, and not react at all? Not the least bit? Yes. Too bad. I'll just have to grit my teeth and wait, wait for the hour to strike. Who knows, perhaps it will be soon . . . at the Skarb Cinema on Traugutt Street, at an invitation-only screening . . .

The twenty-seventh of January. A Friday. Eight o'clock in the evening.

It was her birthday, a fact I remembered only when I was leaving the house and a fragment of Mozart's *Requiem* (the *Dies Irae*) came on the radio. And in the bus another thought occurred to me. Just as I had been travelling in the wrong direction, like Columbus, when going 'west' to the French Embassy, so now, in terms of time as measured by the order of the days of the week, I seemed to be going backwards. The Picasso opening had been on a Sunday. I had seen *Phèdre* on a Saturday. And here I was, going to see *A Man and a Woman* on a Friday . . .

I wonder where I'll get if I keep going in reverse like this? he thought, amused. Perhaps this way I'll be able to make up some of my fatal tardiness in coming into this world, and the holy moment will finally be granted me?

This time his secret investigator's equipment consisted, in addition to the opera glasses (which since the evening at the theatre he was never without), of a pair of sunglasses and an old issue of *L'Humanité* to serve as cover if necessary. He also had in his possession a complete set of documents – his *carte d'entrée*, his school and Marymont chess club IDs, the monthly bus pass. In the left pocket of his trousers was a serious amount of money: seventy-five zlotys (three twenties and a further fifteen in change); the right contained a clean handkerchief and the two invaluable, ever-present safety-pins.

He got off at the corner of Traugutt and the Krakowskie Przedmiescie, in front of the building which now housed the university's Philosophy Department but which, before the war, had been the Zygmunt Wielopolski high school (numbering among its pupils the writer Gombrowicz and also the prototype of Tadzio in *Death in Venice*). He passed the church of the Holy Cross and turned into a gate next to the Classics Department. The gate led into a wide courtyard, through which the approach to the Skarb Cinema was more pleasant than from the street side.

The evening was cold and crisp, with a full moon. Here and there a dark windowpane gleamed with its ghostly reflected light.

He stopped, raised his hand and looked at his watch. A quarter to eight. Perfect, he thought. He put on his dark glasses, took the newspaper out of his pocket and began walking slowly towards his destiny . . .

In front of the cinema, as well as inside the doors and in the lobby, an animated crowd was already gathering. As before, at the Zacheta Gallery and at the theatre, there was much excited gesturing and chattering. The sound of French, interspersed with peals of pearly laughter, mingled with the smell of Gauloises and Gitanes, cigars and Western perfume; there was some eccentric dress, and quite a bit of posturing and showing off. And, again, a few familiar faces: people from the theatre and film world, the diplomatic corps, the Academy of Fine Arts, the Department of Romance Languages.

She was already in the audience when I went inside. She sat more or less in the middle, in the company of . . . Freddy.

Well, well, this is something new, I thought with an inward smile, and sat down two rows behind them.

She was wearing a chic jacket of deep scarlet, with a blue-and-white scarf around her neck. Her dark-brown sheepskin was thrown loosely from her back, its collar and shoulders hanging, inside out, over the back of her seat. Freddy was wearing a suit and held his coat over his knees.

They were talking. But it was an odd sort of conversation. They didn't look at each other, and she fidgeted nervously all the time, twisting and turning in her seat to look around the auditorium (rather as the Tapeworm had at the celebration of the anniversary of the Spanish civil war).

I raised a folded-over sheet of *L'Humanité* in front of my face and, sheltered by this splendid organ of the French Communist Party, continued to observe them.

There was tension between them, evident in their voices and body movements. They were unnatural. He was stiff and gloomy, she nervously on edge. But I couldn't discover the reasons for this inner turmoil, for the chattering around me was so noisy that I couldn't make out a word of what they were saying.

Bother this din, I thought crossly, and allowed myself to drift – on a sea of speculation. Why were they here together? What did it mean? Had they been reconciled at the theatre? Did they meet at *Phèdre* and decide to renew their acquaintance? Or somewhere else? Or maybe they didn't come here together at all – maybe Freddy simply came and joined her, seeing the free place? (I didn't even consider a different sequence of events.) And now they were having a hard time of it. Were they bringing up past quarrels? Flinging accusations back and forth? Was he pestering her with amorous advances?

The auditorium, meanwhile, was filling up. Every seat was taken, and people were still flowing in, standing at the back or sitting on the floor in the front. Finally the doors were closed and the director of the Service Culturel, straightening his bow tie, mounted the low stage. There was a round of applause.

He raised his hand, pointed to his watch (it was a quarter past eight) and jokingly reassured the audience they had nothing to fear: no speeches. (This was greeted with laughter and more applause.) Only a few sentences, by way of introduction. In a moment we would see a film that had taken the world by storm. He didn't mean the Palme d'Or at Cannes or other, lesser awards; he meant its success with the public. Since its release over a year earlier, hundreds of thousands of people had flocked to see it. Film critics, sociologists, even philosophers were all asking themselves why. What was the reason for its astounding popular success? And they concluded that it was simply because this film expresses the longings of man in the modern world: his disenchantment with the philosophy of negation, doubt and absurdity, with nihilism, alienation and frustration, and his desire to return to a faith in love and simplicity of feeling. 'Man wants to be ordinary,' says Claude Lelouch. 'He wants to love, to rediscover his joy in life. He's had enough of Kierkegaard!' (More laughter and applause.) 'After years of pretending to be what he is not, years of posturing and hiding under a false façade, he wants to be himself again: to be . . . a man and a woman!'

I looked at Freddy. The expression on his face – at least its right profile, all that was visible to me from where I sat – was an eloquent mixture of pity and contempt, as if he were thinking, My God, what a moron!

'*Attention, s'il vous plaît!*' the director shouted over the hubbub after the last round of applause. 'After the film, the Cultural Section of the French Embassy invites you all to a modest reception and a glass of wine. I look forward to seeing you there. *À bientôt!*' He disappeared behind the screen.

After a few seconds the lights dimmed.

Modern man's longings and dreams about an 'ordinary' existence were embodied in the figures of a script girl and a rally driver. He spends his days putting racing cars through their paces at the track and after work rides around in a white Mustang; she parades around a film set with a script, constantly fiddling with her hair. Their naturalness and lack of pretension are expressed in their behaviour and dress. She, for example, on location in the tropics (her film is set in Africa: camels in the desert), is clad in a sheepskin coat with a wide collar and knee-length boots; he is seen behind the wheel of his Mustang, amusing himself by executing controlled skids on a sandy stretch of shore while smoking a fat cigar and reading *Time*, all this in dark glasses.

The lives of these two perfectly ordinary thirty-somethings, Anne and Jean-Louis, are equally straightforward. Each has been through a typical, mundane marriage, and both have lost their spouses. Jean-Louis's wife, when she heard that he'd had a serious track accident and might never regain his former vigour (sportswise? physically? as a man?), succumbed to depression and committed suicide. Anne's husband, an actor and a fearless stuntman rolled into one, fell 'in the line of duty' during a film stunt. Until then, however, the couple's life was simple and happy. They spent a lot of time in their country house (horses, bulls, sheep and hunting dogs), sitting companionably together on a huge unmade bed and cultivating the arts of music and poetry: the agile, multitalented stuntsman, his wife by his side, would compose a song, strumming his guitar and singing with a cigar stuck in his mouth, squinting as he blew smoke into his eyes; then he'd write down the lyrics he had lightly tossed off on a typewriter that lay casually among the cream-coloured folds of the bedclothes. They also liked to roll around in the snow in the Alps, clad in large white sheepskins, or to kiss in the jagged ruins of a medieval castle.

Widow and widower are brought together in the most natural way: through their children, who are at a boarding school in Deauville, a picturesque resort on the Normandy coast also frequented by Marcel Proust. They meet at the school one Sunday while visiting their children, and strike up an acquaintance: since it is raining, the thoughtful Jean-Louis offers to take Anne back to Paris in his Mustang. And that's how it all begins.

A week later they meet again in the same circumstances. This time they spend the whole day together as a family. They eat together at a local restaurant, take a boat trip and go for a walk along the beach, revealing their familiarity with the work of . . . Giacometti. Several times Jean-Louis is a hair's-breadth away from touching Anne, but each time he restrains himself – doubtless because of the children. He overcomes his restraint only when they have drawn up in front of her house (number 14, in Montmartre) and Anne is about to get out of the car. She doesn't pull back her hand, but nor does she abandon herself to his tender caresses, and Jean-Louis, regretful but not too bitter, sets off for Monte Carlo to compete in the Grand Prix.

In Paris, Anne leads the life of a working woman. She can be seen bravely clearing a path for herself through the crowds on the Champs-Elysées, weaving her way among the cars in the road (she never crosses at the lights) and hailing taxis; for psychological balance she contemplates a swan gliding across a lake and an empty bench in a park; finally, to relax after the breathless pace and turmoil of her day, she goes to the hairdresser's.

Meanwhile, Jean-Louis just happens, in the most ordinary, natural way in the world, and without really trying, to win the Grand Prix. Anne's spontaneous reaction when she hears this news on television is to send him a telegram with this simple message: 'Well done! I love you! Anne.' Although the address she gives ('Monte Carlo Racetrack') is perhaps not as precise as it might be, the telegram happily finds its way into the hands of its intended recipient: it is delivered to him – again, in the most natural way – at a formal banquet, on a silver-plated salver, by a waiter in full livery.

At this Jean-Louis – hero of the day and guest of honour at the banquet – instantly casts away the world of luxury and decadence, fashion and pretence, and races (clearly above the speed limit) in his old Mustang towards an ordinary but real love. He drives with one hand, while with the other he shaves himself carefully with an electric razor.

Anne, however, is not in Paris. He races back to Deauville. Yes! His intuition was right: there she is, walking along the beach with her children.

There is a joyful reunion. They are ecstatically, drunkenly happy. They have dinner at a hotel restaurant, and then take a room.

But then – what's this? In the arms of her lover, who spares no efforts to make her swoon with rapture, Anne is suddenly tense and constrained; instead of co-operating, she frowns tragically and starts to fiddle with her hair again. It clearly isn't going to work; there will be no conjugation of these two bodies.

'Why?' the Man whispers, bewildered.

'*A cause de mon mari*,' replies the Woman.

'*Mais il est mort!*' objects the Man, refusing to give up.

This makes no difference. There is nothing to be done. Clearly it's still too soon.

She is torn. They suffer. There is much inner turmoil. A 'grain of bitterness' in the humdrum lives of Ordinary People . . .

Since they accept it meekly, however, they deserve a reward. It duly comes – not in heaven but here on earth, and quite soon, too. After a gloomy morning in the hotel and a painful parting on the platform at Deauville, the Man tears off in his Mustang to race the train speeding away with the Woman. He catches up with it; he overtakes it. He waits for her in Paris.

The outcome is certain: 'love is stronger than both of them'.

That, at any rate, was the claim made by Francis Lai's song.

I watched this at first with a scornful smile, then with mounting irritation and incredulity.

I couldn't believe my eyes. It was pure kitsch! Corny trash, sentimental rubbish in the worst petit-bourgeois taste! Its success with the masses was one thing, but its popularity with the élite, the *haute société*, the *beau monde*, was beyond me. *This* had won the Palme d'Or at Cannes? *This* had been nominated for an Oscar? Why? For what reason? *Pourquoi?* They must be mad!

As I was thinking this, a creeping anxiety mingled with my disappointment and shock. What was Madame's reaction to the film? Could she have liked it? Was it possible that she, too, saw merit in it? No – that would be dreadful. That would be catastrophic!

I concentrated with all my strength and tried to send her

desperate telepathic entreaties and pleas for confirmation: Don't you think it's awful? Aren't you repelled by it? You *can't* like it! You can't *possibly* feel anything but contempt for it. Can you? Please tell me that you don't; give me some sign – something, anything. A shrug of the shoulders, a grimace of distaste . . . I know you can.

But her behaviour was inscrutable. She sat quite motionless, gazing at the screen, and her face (again, I had a profile view) expressed nothing whatsoever, neither approval nor revulsion. This was all the more striking because of the contrast with Freddy, who not only made no effort to conceal his disgust but displayed it openly, indeed ostentatiously, to the great annoyance of his neighbours. He shook his head pityingly, he snorted and clucked with disgust, he writhed in his seat and covered his face with his hands.

This led me to think that if they were, as I suspected, quarrelling, and especially if *she* had a bone to pick with *him,* then that could be the reason for her behaviour. In other words, it might be sheer contrariness on her part; his unrestrained and unconcealed aversion to the film might be driving her to take the opposite view out of spite, just to get at him. This possibility frightened me so much that I sent silent entreaties to him as well: Dr Monten – Freddy – please! For God's sake, stop! Calm down! Consider what you're doing! Restrain your commendable disapproval! If there is some disagreement between you, your behaviour, instead of turning her away from evil, will only push her further and further towards it. Your high-mindedness will lead her into error and bring about her downfall!

Alas, my appeals had no effect. Freddy continued his furious hissing and writhing and exasperated clucking. And who knows, perhaps it really was his relentlessness that finally provoked what happened.

But I shouldn't run ahead of the story. All in good time.

When the film ended and the lights came on, the most difficult moment of my mission had arrived. I had to manoeuvre so as not to lose sight of them while remaining unseen myself. This wasn't easy. The Skarb Cinema was small. After a protracted series of about-turns, sudden surges of speed and abrupt decreases of pace, a lot of dodging about under cover of the crowd and some stealthy skulking along the walls, I managed, when everyone had gone through to the lobby and congregated into well-defined groups, to find a safe and fairly convenient spot from which to observe them further.

Madame and Freddy were standing together near the 'buffet' – three tables draped in black plush – on which stood an array of glasses with white wine.

My mentor couldn't stop talking. He went on and on, like a machine, laughing and gesticulating. There was no doubt he was making fun of the film. Madame was listening to him with visibly increasing *ennui.* She stared in front of her or watched the people around her, and on the rare occasions when she spoke it was curtly and with an edge of irritation, as if she were sick and tired of his carping. My God, her lips seemed to be saying, how much longer are you going to go on about it? What are you so worked up about? But he wouldn't stop. And when two caustic Frenchmen (his friends, not hers, for he introduced her) joined them and the defender of Racine's poetry launched into an even more fervent denunciation of the foul betrayer of Great French Culture, his beloved – la belle Victoire, Madame – made her excuses and took her leave.

Only then did I see the bottom half of her outfit. Below the jacket of deep scarlet she had on a pleated black skirt, slightly longer than knee-length, and her legs were encased in a pair of tight-fitting, dark-brown zip-up boots.

It was evident, as she walked across the room, that she had no particular aim in mind, for at the tinkle of knife tapping on wineglass and the sound of the director's sonorous voice she halted immediately and changed direction.

Silence fell.

The director thanked everyone for being there and giving the film such a warm reception and added a few snippets of information about it, interspersing his *dossier* with quotations from an interview with Lelouch that had appeared in the review *Arts.* The gist of the 'brilliant Lelouch's' comments was roughly as follows:

'I have told a story about a man and a woman: the story of their love. In a way it's a sort of answer to the fiasco that was my first film, which was also about love, but between much younger people, barely past the age of twenty. This film is about mature people, in their *thirties*: the best age, the age of flourishing; the age when one really soars, when one is already experienced but still fresh, when anything is possible: a brilliant career, money, love . . . the prime of life! The *prime*! I even thought about calling this film *La Mi-temps*. And I think that thirty-two' – here the director paused, raised his eyes from the text and surveyed the audience with a smile, as if trying to catch someone's eye, then bent back over the open page – 'that thirty-two is the best, the most wonderful, the perfect age for a woman. That's when she's at her most beautiful and most intelligent.'

He put down the magazine, took up a wineglass and, once again scanning the assembled guests, proposed a toast: to the *force de l'âge*.

I was dumbfounded.

You're mad! I upbraided myself, trying to rationalise my way out of the shock. You're completely out of your mind! It's an obsession! It's ridiculous to interpret everything as an allusion to her.

On the other hand, I thought, the coincidence *was* significant. She was exactly thirty-two today. And then that '*force de l'âge*', straight out of Beauvoir – could that be coincidence, too? And what, or rather *whom*, had he been seeking when his eyes had roved about the room like that? Was he merely playing to the audience? It strained credulity. On the other hand, if he *was* looking for her, he certainly hadn't found her or caught her eye; I'd been watching her all the time, and I would have noticed.

The thought of that coincidence would not leave me. With the utmost caution, my face shielded by *L'Humanité*, I strolled over to the buffet, ostensibly in search of a drink, and in picking up my glass cast a casual-seeming glance at the magazine lying there, open to the interview. The comments the director had quoted weren't hard to find, since they were underlined. It was all there, just as he'd said. Except for one thing: the age. The wunderkind of the cinema had said '*trente*'. The director had added two years.

I was right after all. It had been a deliberate performance, put on for her. He could easily have found out her date of birth and the title of her thesis by looking at the documents she'd handed in with her course application.

And then I remembered that moment during the opening at the Zacheta Gallery when the director had broken off in the middle of Antony's speech and looked up in that curious way. At what point had it been? I concentrated, trying to remember. Surely just after the words, 'When such a mutual pair . . .'

This memory precipitated others: his approach with the bottle of champagne during the cocktail reception at the gallery; their conversation in the theatre during the intermission; her departure in the blue Peugeot; the Green-Eyed One's remark about his reaction to my essay. (Had he read every one of them with such attention, I wondered; had he read any of the others at all?) And the silver-haired Marianne's coy remark, with reference to Madame, that sometimes sex *was* relevant, and the enigmatic, teasing look on her face when she had made it.

No doubt of it: the director was making advances to Madame or was already having an affair with her. Moreover, he favoured an approach similar to my own: wordplay and allusion, quotations, secret signals woven into public utterances. (What had he thought of my essay, I wondered; had he understood its message? Had he noticed the allusions? Did he, too, like Constant and Freddy, know Madame's other name? Did he know about 'Victoire'?)

On the other hand, the events that followed this toast did nothing to confirm my conclusion. On the contrary, they seemed evidence against it. For the director paid her not the slightest attention; he didn't even go up to her. To everyone else, Poles and Frenchmen alike, he was attentive and charming, discoursing affably and wittily, but he didn't even glance at Madame, although he had several occasions to do so. This was all the odder because after quitting Freddy's company she was alone and seemed unsure of what to do with herself. She was smoking, which I had never seen her do before, and she looked disconcerted and lost – in striking contrast to my memory of her at the gallery, talking to the ambassador. I had never seen her like this. It was as if some flame inside her had been extinguished, taking her strength with it. Her poise and confident expression did not give her wings; the cigarette, the elegant clothes – sumptuous jacket and stylishly narrow boots – did nothing for her. She looked small and wretched, downcast, unsure of herself.

I felt sorry for her.

Thirty-two years ago, I thought, watching her from behind the curtain at the entrance to the auditorium, somewhere in the Alps – in France? Switzerland? – she had seen her first ray of light. A cry, a breath, beating heart, misty images. Outside cold and snow. White. Blue sky, strong sun. Mountains. Savage, menacing peaks from an era before man. Inside warm and cosy. Happiness, innocence. Hope. The starting point. Infinity of time. The first day, on and on, as if it would never end. And then, suddenly, it takes off. Accelerates. Dizzying speed. Days, weeks, months. Millions of seconds. Impressions, experiences. Thoughts. Thousands of sensations. Flying. Racing. Faster and faster. Turmoil. A whirl. And suddenly far from home. No home at all, no friends. A room with a kitchen in the hallway in a wretched, debased country. A foreign homeland, rotten, putrid, foul. Counting the days. Like prison, counting the days to the amnesty. Until now; until this 'here now', this moment in this space, this glance at this Swiss watch (inherited from her mother?) and another drag on this cigarette. Thirty . . . thirty-two years! Hard to believe so few.

Once again I was tempted to go up to her, especially since the director had departed, throwing effusive farewells right and left as he went.

You've never had a chance like this! I thought excitedly. You *have* to do it now. And for God's sake act normal. Don't fawn or preen or posture, don't pretend, stop playing a role. Just relax. Be yourself for once!

Myself? And who might that be? said the now familiar voice, cold and off-putting.

What do you mean, who? Someone ordinary. Natural, real.

There is no such person. Everything is pretence and disguise.

Everything?

Everything except pain. And death. And pleasure . . .

Madame cast another nervous glance at her watch, stubbed out her cigarette and made for the door. I emerged cautiously from behind the velvet folds of the curtain and followed.

Like Aschenbach following Tadzio, he thought, amused. Only now it's the younger who is the pursuer, and the older who is being pursued.

When she pushed open the glass doors and went outside, Freddy suddenly shot out of the crowd of chatting people and raced after her, struggling into his grey coat as he ran. I hesitated. Then I, too, stepped outside and with pounding heart started after them.

Madame made her solitary way down the same path I had taken three hours before: the 'inner route' through the wide courtyard to the gate by the Classics Department. Freddy caught up with her after about twenty yards. For a few moments they walked along side by side; he was turned towards her, speaking intensely. Then she came to a sudden halt, pronounced a few curt words in a decisive tone, made an abrupt about-face and set off with an energetic step in the opposite direction, towards Traugutt Street. Freddy stood there for a moment, drooping; he looked stunned. Then, head hanging, he shuffled dejectedly away into the darkness of the courtyard.

Keeping a safe distance behind, I followed her.

When she came out of the gate she turned right, toward the Krakowskie Przedmiescie. The street was deserted. The sound of her heels on the pavement echoed in the cold, crisp night air. She vanished around the side of the Philosophy Building. I quickened my pace, stopped at the corner and peered around it. She was walking towards the pedestrian crossing, in the direction of Obozna Street. I passed the Philosophy Building and ran up the flight of steps leading to the church; from there, hidden behind the plinth supporting the figure of Our Saviour bent under the weight of his cross, I could observe her without all this skulking and rushing about. She crossed to the other side of the Krakowskie Przedmiescie, cut across Obozna Street and went on in the direction of Staszic House – towards the statue of Copernicus.

Where are you going, woman?! he cried to her silently. To the old quarters of the Centre? The Gold Room on the first floor? To the ghost of your mother, who brought you into this world thirty-two years ago today? A worthy and commendable act of piety, indeed, but at this hour the place is closed. The day is over. It's night.

The woman, instead of replying, vanished behind the statue. A moment later the entrance of Staszic House was lit with a golden glow. This was no miracle, however, but the headlights of the blue Peugeot, nosing slowly out from behind Copernicus. A car door slammed. Then the car shot forward like Jean-Louis's Mustang and raced, in defiance of the speed limit and several other rules of the road, towards the New World Boulevard.

In order to see where it was headed – straight on along the boulevard or right or left on Swietokrzyska Street – I had to lean quite far out over the balustrade. It certainly hadn't turned left (east, to the Saska Kepa and Praga districts) or gone straight (south, to Mokotow), because I would have seen it. So it must have turned right – west, to Ochota and Wola. I hung there, the whole upper part of my body suspended precariously in space, wondering where they could be going. And then I saw Freddy, who had emerged from the gate by the Classics Building and was plodding with a heavy, weary step in the direction of New World Boulevard.

Poor fool, why did you let her get away? he thought regretfully.

I caught my balance and slid down from the balustrade. As I stood up I glanced involuntarily at the statue of Copernicus. With a compass and a model of the solar system in his hands, he was looking up at the sky, clear and lit by the full moon. I followed his example and looked up, trying to find Virgo and Aquarius and locate Venus. Instead, my eye met the eye and face of Our Saviour, towering over me. His bent head seemed from my perspective to be turned slightly towards Copernicus, as if he wanted to say, Stop your stargazing and come with me. The index finger of his right hand pointed north.

Is Golgotha north? he wondered, trying to picture the map of Jerusalem. North-west, I believe.

And that was when it hit me. Of course! How could I have missed it! It was the only place they could have gone!

At this hour of the night, in the capital of this '*privislansky krai*' – 'province-on-the-Vistula', as the tsars used to call Poland – governed by the enlightened system of people's democracy, almost all the bars, restaurants and nightspots were long closed. Hotels and diplomatic residences were under strict and permanent surveillance. None but the ridiculously naïve or the completely desperate, or those who actively sought contact with counter-intelligence, would go to a hotel with a diplomat. The diplomat's residence, assigned to him by the Polish Housing Office, was an even worse idea. (The situation was the same for all foreigners posted here who had unofficial contacts with the natives.) The only place that might be relatively safe and discreet (and not always) was a Polish citizen's private residence. In this case the residence was located, as I knew, in a four-storey building on a small housing estate that did indeed lie in north-west Warsaw.

Trusting to the 'faith and sensibility' inspired in me by the figure of Our Saviour, I descended the steps of the church and set off, like Madame, in the direction of Obozna Street. I did not, however (feeling hostile, just then, to 'reason and sense'), turn towards Copernicus but went past him to a parking area where there was a stand for 'automobile-type hackney carriages', as taxis were officially known then.

The first car in line was an old Warsaw model, already quite rare, with its humped back and heavy, bulging front adorned by an equally heavy, clumsy-looking oval-shaped missile. The idea of riding in it was distasteful. I didn't like Warsaws; they crawled along, jolting and juddering, and they reeked of petrol. But I had no choice: the Warsaw had priority. I tugged at the doorhandle, slid inside and gave the address.

The ancient driver in his dark leather cap yanked twice on the handle of the meter.

'Night rate,' he announced.

'Yes, I know; I'm prepared for that,' I said, discreetly touching the left-hand pocket of my trousers, where I kept my money. Having assured myself that it was still there, I asked chattily and with a note of insincere concern, in revenge for his low assessment of my means, 'So, this antique Warsaw is still holding up, is it?'

'Warsaw! This ain't no Warsaw, mate!' he snorted, amused. 'This is your original Pobyeda! Vintage 1953. She still remembers Stalin – well, his funeral, at least.'

'A Pobyeda?!' I exclaimed, with inward delight – for *pobyeda*, I should perhaps explain for the benefit of those who have forgotten their obligatory school Russian, means 'victory' in that language.

'What d'you think it was? Didn't you see the Russky letters?' He tapped on the glass of the instrument panel, pointing to the letters 'TAHK' next to the fuel gauge.

I looked at the dashboard and saw that, sure enough, everything was in Russian. There was even something faintly Cyrillic about the shape of the Arabic numerals on the speedometer. To the right, the middle of the dashboard had been designed to look like a radio, with chrome slats of the kind used to conceal speakers and, in the centre, the long, thin metal silhouette of a skyscraper topped by a spire (like our Palace of Culture) with a red star on it, evidently meant to resemble a vertical frequency scale with the dial at the top.

The sight of this Soviet emblem, together with the expressive outward form of the made-in-the-USSR instruments and the details of design that recalled the period of the 'cult of the individual', affected me like the taste of a Proustian *madeleine*.

I was transported to a time I remembered from my earliest childhood. But now I was no longer an innocent tot who saw only the surface of people and things and had no idea of what went on beneath; I was who I was: a young man in his final year of school, raised in a Radio Free Europe atmosphere, brought up by people with an outlook similar to Constant's. I knew what the hammer and sickle really meant and what kind of world was symbolised by the red star. And this was probably why the contraption in which I was riding through the city's dark and deserted streets was transformed in my mind, for a brief moment, from an 'automobile-type hackney carriage' into a menacing security-police car racing to a night raid – a raid in which someone would be arrested. It must have been in a car like this that Max had been taken away. Who knows, perhaps it was this very one, before its reincarnation as a taxi?

And now they're going after his daughter, he thought with a shiver of dread. Ricardo is behind the wheel; Mr Jones is in the back. Only Pedro is missing . . . The holy fire still burns! The old times are returning! They're pursuing Victoire, imprisoned in the Duchy of Warsaw in a blue Peugeot and fleeing to Golgotha in January with Mr Janvier; they're driving a Russian Pobyeda.

The needle of the speedometer was creeping up to ninety.

'Well, what d'you say to that?' said Ricardo. 'None of your old Warsaws could get up to this speed.'

'Is the gauge really reliable?' I asked sceptically, pointing to the speedometer.

'What d'you mean, reliable?!' he snarled, offended.

'Well, the radio looks as if it's real, too,' I explained placatingly, 'but it's not.'

'Oh, that.' He was mollified. 'That's something else – that's Russian-style crap. *My vpyeryod!* "Forward, comrades!" and all that. They have to be leaders in design as well. But it's the engine that counts, and I'm telling you, mate, this one's tough as old boots. And you know why, son?'

'Well, why?'

'Because it's German!' He chortled delightedly. 'A Pobyeda!' he guffawed, mimicking the Russian pronunciation of the name. 'It's an Opel!' He changed gear. 'They took home the whole factory, lock, stock and barrel! War spoils, see?'

We entered the housing estate where Madame lived. I didn't want to drive too near, so I told him to let me out just past the bus stop where I had alighted several months back on my reconnaissance trip. The meter said forty zlotys and fifty cents. I took the money out of my pocket and handed over two bills with the Peasant Woman, and then, when he was putting them away, added another five in coins.

'Keep the change,' I muttered.

'Thanks a lot,' he said. (A 10 per cent tip was considered very respectable indeed.) 'Cheers, mate!'

He drove off, leaving me in the darkness. I set off down a path I had cleared once already, carefully noting every parked car. Would it be there? Yes, there it was! Or, strictly speaking, there *he* was – for Peugeot was clearly a masculine name.

It stood directly in front of the building, on the right, dark, empty and silent. WZ 1807.

That's rather careless, he thought. Not very prudent, leaving a trail like that. Downright reckless, in fact. Don't they care? Aren't they afraid of the ever-vigilant, ever-curious building superintendent, who'd spill everything he knows at the slightest prodding even if he's not in the pay of the security services? Love of comfort will be their downfall – even Lenin said so. Are their brains so addled by the film that they've forgotten where they are? Do they imagine they're in Montmartre or Deauville, instead of a city where, in May '55, 'in response to the aggressive policies of the West and the Cold War scheming of German revisionists', the Warsaw Pact was created? He should really have taken the trouble to park somewhere else.

I looked up at the windows. Her light was on, and though the shutters were closed, in the big, four-paned window a fairly wide crack was clearly visible between them.

My heart pounding, I made energetically for the familiar entrance of the building opposite. Here, without turning on the light in the stairwell, I went up to the third floor, took the tortoiseshell opera glasses from their case and with trembling hands raised them to my eyes.

For less than this Acteon was turned into a stag and torn apart by dogs, he thought, amused; but it was a grim kind of humour. He didn't feel in the least like laughing – although what he saw wasn't 'that most terrible of all things to be seen on this earth', as Zeromski put it in a memorable scene in *Ashes*.

When I had adjusted the focus and could see the crack of

light and beyond it the room, a fragment of picture on the opposite wall presented itself to my eyes: the thin grey spire of a church. I knew that shape and that brushwork. It was a print of one of Buffet's better-known Parisian scenes: the steel-grey corner of the Boulevard St-Germain with the spire of the church of St-Germain-des-Prés shooting up into the sky, and opposite it the legendary café Aux Deux Magots, mecca of bohemian Paris and existentialism, favourite roosting place of Simone de Beauvoir.

So for her it *was* something of a cult after all! The atmosphere, at least – that rather melancholy Left Bank atmosphere in the reign of Sartre.

But I did not have time to dwell on this, for something quite different now claimed my attention. A light went on in the kitchen, where, as it turned out, the window was not shuttered, and Madame appeared, with the director behind her. She still had on the deep scarlet jacket and the scarf; M. Janvier, on the other hand, had discarded his jacket and bow tie and unbuttoned his shirt collar. Madame took a bottle of champagne from the fridge, handed it to M. Janvier and took two flutes from a wall cupboard while the director busied himself with the champagne. But before she had time to hold out the glasses the cork shot out, sending an arc of foam straight onto the lapel of her jacket. She jumped back, flapping her hands about and laughing, and he at once rushed up, all apologies, and set about blotting the stain with his handkerchief, talking all the while. These measures must have been ineffectual, however, for after a moment she persuaded him to desist and began to undo the gold buttons. Then she took off the jacket and disappeared somewhere with it (presumably to the bathroom). During her absence the director poured the champagne. When she came back, jacketless, he presented a glass to her with a courtly gesture and, raising his own, said a few words.

A birthday toast, he thought, staring at the scene in a daze. I wonder what he said? They stood immobile for a moment, looking at each other. They're going to kiss now, he thought, and froze in a horror of anticipation.

But they didn't. They merely clinked glasses, took a small

sip and left the kitchen, turning off the light. A moment later I glimpsed their silhouettes through the lighted crack in the shuttered window of the other room.

What happens now? he thought. What are they doing . . . and what am I supposed to do? Go on standing here like a martyr, waiting . . . for what? For something else to happen? Do you expect them to throw open the shutters, he asked himself, like the curtain in a theatre? And even if they did – would you really want to see it? To see 'that most terrible of all things to be seen on this earth'?! He gave a scornful laugh. My God, what kitsch! he thought. Look at you: how low you've sunk! Much lower than the readers of soppy romances: you've become the hero of one! You reached the summits of knowledge, and now you've sunk right back down to the bottom. Come back to your senses! Run! Run away from here!

But he didn't move. He continued to stand as if hypnotised, the opera glasses glued to his eyes, even though all he could see was a fragment of picture with a grey church spire.

Then he heard a familiar voice. There's no art without kitsch, it said. Just as there's no life without sin. What did Racine read under the school desk? And what do you think his love affairs with the stars of the stage, du Parc and Champmeslé, looked like?

That's something no one knows, he said defiantly.

Ah, but they do, they do, the voice replied calmly. You just have to read a little. I'll tell you what they looked like: they were pure kitsch. In the worst of taste.

That's a risky argument, he said, unconvinced. With that kind of reasoning you could end up in hell.

You could, but not necessarily. It's only a question of coming down to earth. And if you try to avoid that lest, God forbid, you dirty your nice clean little shoes, you'll never get to heaven.

I know that tune. It's Mickiewicz.

'Too winged by far is your thought. It runs after a light breeze.'

Possibly, but who said that the earth was all dung, or at least kitsch?

You ought to know; you're the Shakespeare scholar.

You can't identify Antony with Shakespeare. It might have been meant ironically. Shakespeare could have made him say it to make him look ridiculous.

'Use your head, can't you, use your head, you're on earth; there's no cure for that.'

He could think of nothing to reply. Instead, his thoughts, as if to counteract the lofty tone of this Platonic dialogue he was holding with himself, swerved and ran off in a different direction, like an unruly child.

Her boots! Those tight boots! Did she still have them on, or had she changed into something else? He could not determine this by recalling the champagne scene in the kitchen, still fresh in his mind. If she *had* taken them off, what had she changed into? A pair of old house shoes? Slippers? Pink fluffy mules? A pair of ordinary shoes? Pumps? Court shoes? Such a small detail, but so suggestive, so significant! And it would involve taking off the boots, the *act* of taking off the boots – a perfectly ordinary act, one would have thought, and yet so different from taking off a hat, or gloves, or a coat: more eloquent, more intimate, even, than taking off the jacket of a suit! Had she done it in front of François? In his presence? Or more discreetly, on the side somewhere, in the bathroom or the hall? But perhaps she hadn't taken them off at all . . . which would mean –

Suddenly the room went dark. They had turned off the light.

Well, it's all clear now, he said to himself. The show's over. Have you any more questions?

Indeed I have. Several, in fact.

For instance?

Who turned off the light? And is this the first time? And how did they pass . . . from culture . . . to nature?

You want to know too much. The reply echoed Madame's words to him in that lesson when, in trying to determine her age, he had overstepped the bounds. But it could not hold off the next swollen, tormented wave of questions that burst from him.

How is it possible, he thought, looking up at the stars, what is it that makes two grown-up people suddenly cast off all outward forms and agree to an act that degrades them? (If it didn't degrade them, would they turn off the light?) How does it come about? How can it be explained; how can it be expressed in words?

Words are unnecessary, said the voice. You stop speaking . . . reading –

Reading?! he cried. He couldn't understand himself.

Whatever that means in your life. And whatever the text. Like Paolo and Francesca, reading the book about Lancelot. Don't you remember that scene from the second circle of Hell?

He remembered it very well. Constant had read it to him one day in the mountains. It had been raining, and they'd stayed in the shelter. He'd wondered then why Constant had picked that particular passage, why he had taken such pains to comment on various details. (It turned out later to have something to do with Claire.)

You have to betray the Word, then . . . He almost said it aloud.

Why *betray?* You have to make it Flesh.

But that *is* betraying it. It's a *betrayal*!

That's how the world begins. It can't begin any other way.

Not in glory, but in disgrace.

In silence and in darkness.

Then he wept, and he wept for himself.

And when, after a long time, the dying-and-beginning was at last over, and a light appeared once more in the room, fainter this time, and from somewhere to the side (a bedside lamp, perhaps?), and soon another, in the stairwell, showing the lover running downstairs, he took hold of himself, straightened himself up and, like Heyst on the bridge of the ship, again raised the opera glasses to his eyes.

The director, his head bent and his coat unbuttoned, a cigarette in his mouth, was walking slowly and wearily towards the Peugeot.

Like Antek after a hard day's work, he thought exhaustedly, in a forlorn attempt to cheer himself up.

I turned the key in the lock of the front door as quietly as I could, and once inside I didn't turn on the hall light. With precise, careful movements, like a mime's, I took off my coat and started off on tiptoe for my room. But just as I felt for and found the doorknob, a light came on in my mother's room, and a moment later she appeared in the doorway.

'Do you know what time it is?'

'I'm sorry . . . I didn't realise . . .' I tried to sound contrite.

'What? What didn't you realise?'

'That it would go on so late.'

'That what would go on so late? What are you talking about?'

'The discussion . . . and the cocktails. At the Skarb Cinema, on Traugutt Street. There was an invitation-only screening. You know, that Lelouch film . . .'

'A discussion? After a film by Lelouch? And that's why you needed the opera glasses, I suppose?' She pointed to my hand, in which I was still holding the case.

'Oh, those.' Involuntarily I raised my hand. 'No, no, they weren't for that. A friend just gave them back to me.'

'A friend just gave them back to you. A pair of opera glasses. At the screening of the Lelouch film.' She enunciated the words slowly through her teeth. 'And you expect me to believe that?'

'It would be best,' I said sadly and shut my door. Then I locked it.

The Dream

I couldn't sleep. I lay there, bewildered by what I was feeling, my head whirling with a confusion of images and fantasies, like a badly edited film, my thoughts circling obsessively, out of control. Finally, around dawn, I fell into an exhausted sleep. But my dreams were neither sweet nor consoling – although they began pleasantly enough. Blissfully, in fact.

I'm in an aeroplane. Jagged peaks outside, snowy and glittering in bright sunlight, and here, beside me, Madame. We're flying to Geneva. I've won first prize in the competition for the best essay about romantic journeys; they've invited both of us, me and my teacher, to the prize-giving ceremony. I'm ecstatic, bursting with happiness and pride. I've won! I'm going to the West! And not just anywhere in the West: to Switzerland, the land of the legendary Alps! With *her*! And not just as her pupil: as her liberator! Her Heyst! I'm the one who has finally freed her from the Bolshevik yoke of slavery. I can feel the warmth of her admiration and gratitude. And I can sense the direction of her thoughts:

Language, literature, her eyes seem to be saying, he knows all that. He's a talented boy; he doesn't need my help there. But life – passion, feeling, pleasure, the world of the senses . . . She smiles pityingly. He knows nothing of that. *There's* something I could help him with. I could teach him about love, bring him down to earth. Become for him a goddess more powerful than a mother! Make him be born anew, make him reborn! Be his first victory!

Cut to another scene:

We're going up Mont Blanc, or perhaps up the St Gotthard Pass, where the sources of the Rhine are. We reach the summit. I can see the Vallot refuge, which I recognise from the photograph. She is walking in front of me. Suddenly she stops to gaze at something in the distance. Then she turns, points upwards and says, 'Look . . . There! Can you see? That,' she says with a strange smile, 'is where I was supposed to be born. But it didn't work out that way. My father's dream didn't come true. So let his wish be fulfilled now, in a different way: let his grandchild, my first-born son, be conceived there. You will beget him. Tonight. I shall name him Arthur. He will be beautiful like me, and sad like the sadness of your soul. And he will write like . . . Simone de Beauvoir. Come to me!' she says in a voice that brooks no denial and stretches out her hand like Michelangelo's God to Adam.

Hand in hand we climb, higher and higher.

The sun sets blood-red, and with it ends my last day of innocence.

But what's this? Where are we now? These aren't the Alps – these are the Tatra mountains! I know those crests. I can see red-and-white poles and a sign that says: 'Warning! National Frontier.'

'Just a moment, citizen!' booms a stentorian male voice, and the stocky, moustachioed sergeant looms up before me. 'Your documents, please.'

I search nervously through my anorak pockets and hand him my monthly bus pass.

'I'm not a ticket inspector,' he growls at me. At this moment two men in plastic raincoats with little round tin badges pinned under their lapels appear beside him. One of them takes the ticket.

'You want to cross the border with a monthly pass?' he sneers in disbelief.

'*Sneak across* the border,' puts in the other one, with emphasis.

'ID or passport, please!' demands the sergeant menacingly.

I look through my pockets again and, not finding these documents, hand him my trusty chess club ID.

'What's this?' he asks.

'It's my chess club card. Marymont Workers' Club. I'm supposed to play in a tournament in Slovakia. I'm a junior champion.'

'First of all, he's not any kind of champion,' Kugler's voice floats up from somewhere. 'Maybe a vice-champion at most. And secondly, even that's a title he won by sheer luck.' Then Roach appears from a cave in the rock face, with a contingent of 'rabble', strangely dressed, in grimy black trousers and red shirts. Are they Spanish fighters? Splendid Dabrowski-ites? No! They're the men of marble, dressed as brigands: the miners, steelworkers and peasants from the statues in front of the Palace of Culture and the Young People's Housing District, with hard, brutal faces and enormous paws.

In his right hand Roach is clutching a huge hammer, like one of the miners' pickaxes; in his left he wields a huge hook.

'So, comrade, you say you're going to a tournament in Slovakia,' he says with mock gravity. 'And that's what you need these field binoculars for, I suppose?' He gestures at my torso, where, sure enough, a pair of field glasses dangles from a cord around my neck. 'And you expect someone to believe that?' He grins contemptuously. 'Your mummy, perhaps. But not me. You can't lie your way out of it this time.'

'*¡No pasarán! No more!*' shouts the band of activists.

'There you are,' says Roach, pointing with his hook to the rabble, 'the voice of the people. It demands your unmasking, comrade.'

'Expose him! Punish him!' cries the rabble chorus.

'I have no choice. The people have spoken,' says Roach, spreading his hands in insincere apology, and launches into an accusatory tirade in the style of Vyshynsky (Andrei, that is, the prosecutor): 'You wish to know, honoured comrades, who this chess master, this virtuoso and mountaineer, this multitalented stage artist and lover of truth who walks the path of virtue really is? I'll tell you. Let the facts speak for themselves. Let us start from his childhood.

'When the working people and the youth of our villages and towns were trying to encourage mass tourism, organising trips and hikes along Lenin's trail, *he* preferred to go his own way, privately, with a certain Mr Constant of bourgeois stock (he wore breeches!) as his guide, lolling around in a double in a hostel near Morskie Oko.

'When the pioneers of the Service for Poland work brigades were sweating to strengthen their muscles by rebuilding cities and working in the fields, *he* preferred to take music lessons, privately, from a certain "piano lady" of landed gentry (she wore a velvet ribbon!), not wishing to sully his lily-white hands.

'When the juniors in the chess club, to which I also belonged, were studying the games of Botvinnik and Tal, *he* preferred to go his own way and, besotted with an instructor from the intelligentsia (he went around with a flask of vodka in his pocket!), studied Reti and Capablanca.

'Let us continue, as Comrade Stalin says (and writes!):

'What kind of thing does this noble spirit learn at home? Marxism, biology, the history of the All-Russian (Bolshevik) Communist Party, perhaps? Does he at least study the language of our Great Brother? Or Soviet literature? Oh no, my friends. That would be a miracle, and we, comrades, don't believe in miracles. He spends his time studying *French*! That symbol of intellectual bourgeois culture, of aristocracy and landed gentry, that relic of a past rotting on the rubbish-heap of history! And the rest of the time he listens to Radio Free Europe! Breathing the miasma of the West!

'The fruit is according to the seed; as is the soil, so is the harvest, comrades! An individual brought up in this way cannot but turn out rotten and warped. He sows anarchy wherever he goes. He conspires, he foments plots, he stirs up rebellion.

'You want evidence? There's plenty of it. Let us take three examples.

'How does this artist begin his career in his collective? To what use does he put those lily-white hands of his, those delicate, coddled little fingers with which he has learnt to tickle the ivories? Perhaps he helps out the singing teacher? Or the choral society? Does he support and encourage the Exotic Trio in their noble attempt to compete for the Golden Nightingale? No, my friends – not he! *He* prefers jazz. *He* wants his own jazz band. The model he worships is Tyrmand, renegade and slanderer who fled to the West.

'Isn't that how it was? First witness! Comrade Eunuch!'

'If not worse,' confirms the Eunuch's voice.

'Hardly had we ripped off the ugly head of that foul Hydra,' continues Roach, 'than another sprang up in its place. He takes over the dramatic society. And what kind of play does he put on? And by whom? Soviet playwrights, or at least Russian ones? Or at worst by his own native Polish ones? Oh no, my friends – not at all! *He* wants only Western plays. Shakespeare! Aeschylus! That vindictive barbarian Goethe! His activities are cut short at once and their resumption is strictly forbidden.

'Second witness! Comrade Tapeworm! Isn't that how it was?'

'It was far, far worse,' replies the Tapeworm's voice.

'There you are! But this subversive element makes light of the decree forbidding his hostile activities. He goes on with them, pulls the wool over the jury's eyes and hoodwinks them into awarding him the first prize. He is presented with a watch, manufactured in the GDR, our ally and friend in the Soviet bloc. And what does he do with this precious gift, when he decides that it's of no use to him? Does he give it to the poor?

Does he exchange it for something else? Does he at least pawn it? Oh no, my friends! He does none of these things. He savagely, barbarically destroys it, giving vent to his deep contempt for the light industry of a socialist country and endangering our neighbourly relations with it.

'And here is the third of our examples.

'In spite of his unconcealed hostility towards our political system and his acts of what can only be called terrorism, we, in our magnanimity and our belief in man's goodness, still refuse to cast him off. We give him another chance; we hold out a hand to him. We ask him to participate in the celebrations of the thirtieth anniversary of the outbreak of the Spanish civil war. Let him be of some use for once. Let him play us some of those revolutionary songs so dear to us. And how does he respond to this generous gesture, this honour we have deigned, in our munificence, to bestow upon him? First he makes fun of it; he mocks and he jeers. Then, greedy for more selfish gratification, he cynically bamboozles the school into giving him a note excusing him from lessons. And finally he hatches his plot and performs an act of sabotage!

'Naturally, we checked out his proposed programme – as we said we would. And what did we discover? That this Rodrigo of his was a fanatical reactionary and a loyal follower of Franco! It was a blatant attempt to subvert the masses! What did they shout, those primitive, backward, ignorant peasants, when he had deliberately inflamed them by his treacherous musical interludes? Revolutionary slogans? "*Arriba parias*"? "Down with Franco"? I call the next witnesses! Fighting comrades, how do you testify?'

'They shouted, "More flamenco!"' the band of socialist brigands replies in chorus.

'Honoured comrades!' Kugler continues indefatigably. 'The time has now come to pose the fundamental question: was he acting alone? Or was it a conspiracy?'

'A conspiracy! The coward wouldn't have done it alone!'

'Yes! You're quite right, comrades! And do you know who he plotted with? Who his co-conspirator was? You won't believe your ears when I tell you. It was she! She who stands before you now: the beautiful headmistress! Oh, his betrayal is rank, it stinks to heaven!

'Recall the second witness! Comrade Tapeworm, please tell us: was your superior present at the celebrations in honour of the Spanish civil war?'

'She was not. The chair was empty.'

'Exactly! And why? Because this foul progeny of reaction, this warped monster whose hatred of working people was imbibed along with her mother's milk, this child of a flunkey of that bloodthirsty fiend Franco nurtures so violent a loathing of peace and the forces of progress that the very sight and sound of the symbols and slogans which represent the struggle for the liberation of the oppressed masses of the world makes her foam at the mouth with fury like a rabid bitch. So she was afraid lest her unrestrainable reactions betray her.

'That's all very well, you might say, but in that case how did she get where she is? How could she have been entrusted with the responsibility of educating our youth? And how did she come by such a high position? You are right, my friends: this is the key question.

'The answer is that she was imposed upon us by a hostile power: bourgeois France. And it was done by blackmail. It was made abundantly clear to us that if we cared at all about Dr Dolowy and his future development, we must accept her appointment.

'I call the fourth witness! Comrade Gromek, is that not what happened? Do you confirm it?'

'I do. Every detail,' says the voice of Gabriel Gromek, MA.

'Fifth witness! What about you, Dr Dolowy?'

'I can't deny it, although I wouldn't be quite so harsh . . . because of the interests involved: foreign trade and light industry (ballpoints for pens!).'

'You are magnanimous, comrade. But one can't cry over a rose when whole forests are ablaze.

'We come now to the last, fundamental question, namely: *why* is this so important to *la douce France*? What exactly is the French interest in this matter? Or perhaps the question should be phrased differently: what did Madame la Directrice do for France to deserve such fervent support?

'It was the foulest of her betrayals. It was so vile, comrades, that it is best passed over in silence. Let us not sully our lips by naming her crimes.

'But does any of this bother our virtuoso? Is he at all shocked or revolted by that act of corrupt love? Not in the slightest! On the contrary: it excites him! It makes him rub his hands with glee. For here is the possibility of further gain: he might turn what he has seen to his advantage. He could make himself useful and get something in return. Or, if that doesn't work, he could resort to blackmail and extortion. For this talented artist, comrades, has the morals of a pimp.

'Moreover, he knows perfectly well that this whole "experiment" with French as the language of instruction is a complete sham. Its true and only purpose is to send a fifth column to the West for training in subversion.

'Accordingly, he tries to signal to her that he can be trusted: he does not hide his hostility to our people's democracy. And then, like a faithful dog, he exerts himself in her service, writes her elaborate essays so that she can have something to show her masters, practises his eloquence for the benefit of foreign experts on their visit of inspection, memorises poems to impress with his erudition.

'He doesn't have to wait long for his thirty pieces of silver.

'As the first sign of her trust she gives him the key to her office! Then she gets him an admission card to snobbish events where bourgeois art is celebrated. And *then* . . . then, comrades, comes the crowning moment: he is invited, on her recommendation, to a training course for spies in Tours. And they go there together – sneaking across the border.

'There, comrades, you have it: the real truth about this romantic couple, this pair of turncoats, these wolves in sheep's clothing, seething with vicious hatred and venom for our party and our government.'

At this point Carl Broda emerges from the band of brigands and, like a choirmaster, begins to intone:

How best shall we deal with them? Spare them or
seize them?
Show mercy or favour oppression and force?

Then, like Wladyslaw Broniewski at a rally, he turns to the assembled crowd and says:

The people alone have the right to release them.
Their will must decide it.
– OPPRESSION AND FORCE!

The 'red-and-black' rabble roar out in chorus, raising their fists into the air. And Carl Broda pronounces sentence:

The people see through your fine airs; they'll no longer
Permit your vile plotting to make their wounds run;
Your crimes deserve death, and your death will make
stonker
Our will to go on saying: '¡No pasarán!'

'And what about her?' Kugler asks, pointing to Madame, as if wondering how the action of this scene should be resolved.

The question is hardly out of his mouth when Lucilla Rosenberg, or Lucy, wafts slowly down from the clear blue sky, made up and dressed as Dolores Ibarruri, and in her sensuous voice pronounces the verdict:

Let these youths, so strong and virile,

(pointing at the band of brigands)

Seize her in their manly arms.
They can play with her awhile;
Let them *taste some of her charms.*
Let them throw her to the ground,
Spread her there and pin her down!

At this Kugler slowly raises his huge hammer, crosses it with the sickle and pronounces the following words (profaning one of the nation's most sacred texts):

Listen well, folk, and heed our behest,
For such is our will and command:
Those who never put out in this land
Can forget about trips to the West!

I can feel that this is it: in a moment I shall see 'that most terrible of all things to be seen on this earth'. And so I decide to act.

'You can eliminate me,' I say to him, 'but you'll never win. I'm better than you.' My challenge seems effective, for Kugler turns purple with rage.

'We'll see about that!' he screams, swallowing the bait. 'Mephisto, the chessboard!'

And there is Mephisto, obligingly setting out the chess pieces.

'Just a moment!' I say. 'First let's agree on the stakes. If you expect me to give you a chance to get even just because of your pretty face, forget it!'

'What do you want to play for, then?' asks Kugler.

'For Victoire,' I reply.

'For what?!' he grimaces uncomprehendingly.

'For her,' I explain calmly, nodding at Madame. 'If I win, she's mine.'

'Fine. Have it your way, you pathetic little clown.' He laughs contemptuously and then snarls, 'Not on your life, you bastard,' and with the hand holding the sickle makes a gesture expressive of what he thinks of my chances.

We begin to play. I gain an advantage over him and exploit it. Soon only the kings and two of my white pawns are left on the board. I let out a sigh of relief. Victory! Now it's just a matter of time; a few moves, and it'll be over. I calmly promote my pawn and transform it into a queen.

'Check,' I say, beginning the attack.

'And mate!' cries Kugler, taking my king with his.

'That's an illegal move,' I assert in a superior tone. 'This isn't a lightning game.'

'You should have said so at the beginning,' replies Kugler, and spreads his hands (i.e., the hammer and sickle) with insincere regret.

I fling myself at him, screaming, 'You bastard! You filthy swine!' But my voice is drowned out by a piercing, shrill noise which fills my ears. The whistles of the red-shirted rabble? A phone call for Kugler?

No – the alarm clock, which I had set for seven.

I woke up drenched in sweat.

The Day After

When I emerged into consciousness I found it not much better than the nightmare. At first I wasn't even sure whether I was awake or asleep, for the events of the previous evening, between the film and the phantasmagorical visions of my slumbers, seemed so otherworldly and unbelievable I felt I might have dreamt them as well. And when I had shaken myself entirely awake and could no longer doubt they had really taken place, I can't say I felt wildly cheerful. In fact, I felt dreadful.

If the information I had acquired with Constant's help could be compared to the experience of landing on the surface of a planet, the knowledge I possessed now was that of a miner and a geologist rolled into one. I had gone deep down under the surface, through the crater and into the volcano.

And what had I gained from it? Divine omnipotence? An advantage, at least? Not even that. On the contrary: I had only the bitter taste of defeat, torments of suffering, a sense of hopelessness. The path to knowledge had turned out to be the way to my doom. Instead of discovering the water of life I had stepped into some infernal fire.

My suffering came in several stages and degrees of intensity. The humiliation, mingled with burning shame, was the least of it. Far worse was the consciousness that all hope of fulfilment had vanished: all the things she could conceivably give me – conversation, language games, friendliness, signs of favour – had lost their value. None of them could now bring consolation, and the only thing that might was inconceivable. But most painful was the injured pride. Not my 'manly' pride (because she preferred the director) or anything like that, but the pride I'd always had in the power of my mind, my reason, over the heart and the flesh. Now, like Hippolytus, I had weakened and broken. I had allowed myself to 'drift'. I had betrayed Reason and succumbed to passion. I had not thought I could sink so low.

I felt like a torture victim who had been on the rack. My immediate future, my plans, the rest of my life meant nothing to me now. Final exams, university, an artistic career were as sounding brass. Even the thought that my Young-Werther-like sorrows could be put to literary use was no consolation.

My only consolation could take the form of poor Tonio Kröger's wistful dream after his unhappy dance with the carefree Ingeborg, and again after his encounter with her, years later, at a ball in Denmark. I knew (not only from the narrator of that wonderful novella) that such things seldom happen on this earth; nevertheless I got up, dressed and, inspired by the hope of an unprecedented miracle, dragged myself to school.

Just to see her, to address her, to be the recipient of even the most trifling favour, I thought as I walked along in the grey morning light. A look, a kind word, the smallest gesture . . . perhaps to hear my name in the familiar, shortened form? At any rate, to see her, to look at her. To see . . . to see what people look like the day after.

On Saturdays French was in the fourth period. The time that separated me from it was not idly spent: at every break, burning with impatience, I ran downstairs and loitered around near her office in the hope of catching a longed-for first glimpse. Fruitlessly: there was no sign of Madame. In desperation, I armed myself with the first pretext that came into my head ('Is there a lesson today? Someone told me there wasn't'), went to the door of her office and depressed the handle. It was locked. I repeated the operation with the door of the staff room. She wasn't there, either. Disconcerted, I returned to the classroom and waited in suspense for the end of the long break. At last the bell rang, but Madame did not appear. Instead the Viper strode into the classroom and announced that she would be substituting.

So she really wasn't there. My heart raced and I felt a hot flush spread over me. What had happened? What did it mean? Had she arranged her absence in advance? Or had she called in sick that morning? Both these intriguing possibilities offered rich soil for speculation and surmise. If she had arranged her absence with the school, it could mean that the events of the previous evening had also been planned in advance – and that she'd known she would need a day off after her birthday night of heated passion. But if she had called in sick that morning . . . that could mean anything!

My fever of speculation gave way to depression. To die, to sleep, a voice in my head suggested; no more . . . The Prince of Denmark's whispers were tempting: just then it was indeed a consummation devoutly to be wished. The worst nightmares would be better than this reality. All I wanted was to sink into oblivion.

I was rudely snatched from the sweet embrace of Melancholy and Death by the voice of the fearless Viper, who, guided by her infallible naturalist's instinct, had approached my desk and now loomed over me. 'Oh, dear,' she said, 'what *can* the matter be? Why so pale and wan? Why the sunken cheeks, the glassy gaze? It must be all those feverish late nights . . . reading romantic novels. Or could it be because there's no French today? Because instead of nourishing your soul with sparkling *esprit* you'll have to chew on the dry bread of biological fact?'

'I'm at a loss to understand the reason for your remarks,' I said coldly. 'Am I in your way?'

'Oh, not at all!' she replied with heavy sarcasm. 'Not in the least. I merely wanted to bring you down to earth, to make you abandon your lofty perch for a moment and see if you'll deign to flutter down into the valley to join in the lesson. A little of your attention would be gratifying. And seeing you sitting there so gloomy, I thought I'd put your mind at rest. There's nothing to fear: I'm not going to test you on the rabbit.'

The class burst out laughing, and I was seized by a cold fury.

That's it, I thought, I've had enough. There's no reason I should have to sit here and listen to this.

'In that case,' I said, in a tone of false disappointment, 'there's nothing to keep me here.' Whereupon I rose and started for the door.

A hush fell on the room.

'Think what you're doing!' hissed the Viper.

'I have,' I replied calmly, and left the classroom.

My composure was purely external, however. Inside I was trembling. In the corridor my control abandoned me entirely. Not wanting anyone to see me in this state, and fearing the Viper might give the command to launch a pursuit, I fled to the lavatories, locked myself in and waited there until I had calmed down. When I had regained some measure of control over myself, I slipped through to the cloakroom, and by the time the bell rang for the end of the fourth period I was well outside the school grounds.

To recover completely and think things through in peace, I went to my traditional place of retreat: Zeromski Park. It looked quite different from the last time I'd been there, pondering the consequences of my first run-in with the Viper and planning the campaign from which everything had begun. Now, instead of an array of pastel colours shining in bright sunlight under a blue sky, I saw a bleak, steel-grey landscape cut through with the occasional slash of black or white: bare branches and tree trunks, sad piles of dirty snow and splotches of yellowish-grey grass. Like a Bernard Buffet, I thought with a bitter smile as I passed my usual bench.

Three months had passed, and in that time I had more than fulfilled the task I had set myself. I had not only learnt a great deal about the course of Madame's life but discovered her secret goals and the subtle ways in which she proposed to achieve them. If someone had told me I would come to know all this,

I would have laughed incredulously. Even if I *had* believed it, I'd probably have been thrilled at the prospect of such an advantage, for I thought then that I could win any game I wanted if only I had the right cards. It hadn't occurred to me that knowledge would change me – that once the means of achieving my goals were within my grasp, the goals themselves would no longer interest me; that once equipped for the game of allusion, suggestion and mild provocation I had longed for, I would no longer see any point in it and would lose the desire to play it.

There were many things I could do with what I knew. I could indulge in the coy, innocent wordplay of my initial dreams, or I could engage in more perverse and menacing games, games with a whiff of blackmail about them. But the power I wielded gave me no satisfaction, and the thought of exploiting it filled me with disgust, as Freddy had been filled with disgust at the thought of how he could humiliate and terrorise Dr Dolowy. My reasons for self-revulsion were even stronger, for while Freddy had felt only contempt for his colleague, I adored Madame. More than that: emotions, as we know, can lead people to commit the basest acts, and to say I adored her was to omit something much more important. Despite my reservations about some aspects of her personality and her literary tastes (Simone de Beauvoir), reservations for which my grounds were in any case quite inadequate, I respected her. She was proud and strong and undaunted, and somehow beyond the influence of the drab, dismal, perverse reality of our People's democracy. With every atom of her being she said no to it; everything about her – her appearance, her behaviour, her language, her intelligence – was a resounding, defiant refusal to accept this reality. She was mute testimony to the ugliness and absurdity of our lives, an eloquent reminder that it *was* possible to live differently.

I knew she was right. She was my North Star.

Hence the conflict that was tearing me apart. If I was for her, I could not be for myself; our interests conflicted – indeed, they were mutually exclusive. If I wanted to act in *her* interests, I should give up the game. Surrender and retire from the field. Like Schiller's knight Toggenburg.

I realised, to my astonishment, that this would be easier if I could be certain she had no serious feelings for the director. I'd rather she went to bed with him from vanity or snobbery, even sheer opportunism, than from a sincere engagement of the heart. I preferred cold, self-interested calculation to genuine passion. Cynicism I might deplore, but could forgive; love was harder to bear. Love, paradoxically, was unforgivable.

It was only now that I really began to understand Phaedra's scene of jealousy.

I was seized by an irrational desire to find out. That's all I want, I thought feverishly, just that, no more. If I could only establish that, I would be satisfied; I would seek nothing more. But how? After all, it wasn't something you could see; to establish it you needed language, conversations, confidences . . . *des confessions* . . . And it was unrealistic to hope for that.

But that isn't the only way! I thought excitedly. A truly Machiavellian scheme had occurred to me. There *are* other ways of finding out. By trial of fire: news that someone close to us is dead or in mortal danger. That's an infallible test, a true trial of the heart. The reaction to such news, especially the first reaction, is always revealing.

Yes, I went on, as details of this insane plan tumbled about in my mind, I could go back there and call her from the phone box downstairs; I could alter my voice and pretend to be a doctor from the casualty department or a paramedic calling from an ambulance . . . ask her if she knows a dark-haired man . . . 'looks like a foreigner . . . probably French . . . Unfortunately he has no documents on him, so that's all we know . . . the only clue is a scrap of paper with this telephone number . . . But perhaps it's a mistake? A misleading clue? A coincidence?' And then, when the inevitable question comes – 'But what is all this about?' or, more likely, '*But what's happened?*' (how would she ask it? calmly? or hysterically? that would already tell me something) – I could inform her with regret that 'he's had a serious accident . . . he's in intensive care . . .' and then, in a more official tone, 'Could you give us some information? His name, his address? Who to contact? . . . Or perhaps it *is* you? Are you the person we're looking for?' And then wait and see what she does. Would she run out of the house, get a taxi, rush to the hospital? Or . . . not?

Such an exercise was not beyond my skills, dramatic and vocal. I had played hundreds of practical jokes like this on the telephone, with great success: even close friends had been taken in. So I wasn't afraid that my voice would betray me or that I might lose my nerve or inspiration. And even if it didn't work and she realised it was a hoax, it was still unlikely that she'd think of me. She had no idea how much I knew about her and didn't know what my voice sounded like over the phone. Sooner or later her suspicions would turn in a different direction: not to any one person but to an institution – the security services. Something like this was just in their line; it could only be them. In which case . . . in which case I would be playing their part. Involuntarily, I would have taken on the role of her persecutors. That would be the price of the exercise.

This held me back. The thought that I would be inscribing myself in her life as the instrument or agent of the dark forces of the world, as 'Mr Jones' or 'Ricardo' or 'the terrible brute Pedro', was unbearable – even if I knew it wasn't true, even if I had a guarantee I'd never be found out. I couldn't do it. Her life, for me, represented Myth – that 'one day', that 'somewhere', that world of heroic greatness of which I dreamt and to which I aspired, which I had yet to encounter but hoped one day to touch, at least to brush against. She was both the 'there' and the 'then', the Past made present and Distance made closer, the dimension of Legend, the stuff of Tales. To appear in that tale, that life, playing so base and vile a role would be an ignominious, ultimate defeat.

I went home. Mercifully no one was in. I threw myself down on the bed and tried to sleep, but in vain. A witches' sabbath was going on in my head. Exhausted, unable to take any more, I rummaged in my father's desk for sleeping pills (he used Phanodorm). I couldn't find them. I did, however, find an opened bottle of Danish eggnog. Heedless of the consequences (which would be manifold), I finished it off in less than half an hour. For a while I felt better. Everything started to seem funny: my own state of nerves, my longings, the whole 'affair' with Madame. Then I began to feel sick, and soon brought up what I had drunk and returned it to Nature by way of the drains. After that I finally fell asleep. A deep sleep, and quite dreamless.

The next day, a Sunday, wasn't much better. Nothing happened to inspire any hope of improvement.

SIX

Handicrafts

On Monday things did improve, although none of the celestial signs augured well: the day began miserably. (The last drop, perhaps, in the cup of bitterness I had to drain in order to propitiate Fate.)

The first echoes of my run-in with the Viper reached my ears almost as soon as I got to school, and they boded very ill indeed. According to the reports, my ostentatiously defiant exit had driven her to an attack of unprecedented fury ('she foamed at the mouth' was the succinct description): she had raged and fumed and threatened, pronounced with venom that I was out-of-this-school, at least could certainly-forget-about-graduating-this-year, and sworn to make-sure-that-my-behaviour-was- properly-dealt-with by the school board. True to her word, she must have started a song-and-dance about it at once, for soon thereafter our history teacher (known as Old Livy, less because of the way he taught history than because of his venerable-old-historian look) had burst in and ordered a search party to be sent out. When this brought no results, he had launched an investigation. Some people said he gave the impression of being on my side, for he seemed to do his best to find extenuating circumstances that might mitigate or at least explain my crime. It was also common knowledge that he disliked the Viper and often found himself at loggerheads with her, whereas he quite liked or at least respected me. Others maintained that this impression was deceptive and that he was impartial at best: while he wouldn't fan the flames, he'd not go out of his way to help me, either.

Whatever the truth of the matter, there was no doubt that thunderclouds were gathering, and lightning was not far off.

The view taken by my classmates seemed to be that I was an admirably bold and reckless spirit caught through a stroke of bad luck and now forced to sit and await sentencing like a condemned man. They treated me kindly and offered sympathy, cigarettes and chewing gum (also frowned upon at school). 'Don't worry,' Prometheus said encouragingly, 'have a smoke. There's nothing to be afraid of; they won't do anything, and even if they did, so what? At worst you'd just have an extra year to wait. What's a year? You can hibernate. You'll have some peace and quiet.'

Despite the fuss and the dire forecasts, no lightning struck. No one summoned me anywhere, no one demanded to see my parents and no one officially informed me of anything. Lessons crept on in their usual somnolent way. The last class of the day was woodwork.

Woodwork was not a subject in which I had a consuming interest, to put it mildly. I had neither liking nor talent for 'crafts', and the results of my efforts were always hopeless. I also couldn't stand the so-called workshop where the classes took place, a dark, fetid hole in the basement, next to the boiler room, stinking of glue and grease. Just being there was depressing, and the poisonous fumes and the din gave me terrible headaches that lasted for hours. Fortunately, the teacher, an affable character known as the Workman, was not (unlike the Viper or the Eunuch, say) prone to excessive ambition; in his class the less-than-enthusiastic and the less-than-talented – those who were 'all thumbs' – were treated with tolerance. He would give them a C ('your basic no-frills mark') and demanded only that they turn up.

It was my bad luck that today of all days, owing to a special burden that had been imposed on him, things were rather different. He was required, namely, to prepare the school for the ball that was held a hundred days before graduation. This involved a serious amount of work, for it meant doing up the whole gym where the ball took place, as well as constructing the centrepiece of the decorations, and naturally he wanted to impress the school with what he could do. So discipline was tightened and we were all put to work.

I was entrusted with the task of sawing branches for an imitation fire, and was making my usual ham-fisted job of it. Every few minutes the Workman would come by, survey with horror the results of my efforts, throw up his hands in despair and exclaim, 'Good heavens, boy, what on earth is that supposed to be? Can't you even handle a saw? What a feeble specimen! You'll never find a woman if you can't even do the simplest things around the house! Now, watch me.' He would take the saw from me, place it at the appropriate angle on the branch and cut through it in a couple of smooth and effortless movements. 'There, that's how it's done. Lightly and evenly. No need to thrash around. There's no strength involved; you can cut through any thickness of wood just as easily if you go about it the right way.'

I would take back the saw and try to imitate what he had done, but already on the second or third pull the thing would get stuck or come out of its groove and slide dangerously about. In the end it slid straight into the hand with which I was holding the branch, cutting the base of my index finger. It was a deep gash and soon it was bleeding profusely.

'He's cut himself!' cried Mephisto, immediately scenting a possible excuse for getting out of the lesson.

'I knew it,' said the Workman with gloomy resignation, and then fired off a round of orders: 'Take him away, someone! Get him to the sick bay. Put some iodine or spirits on it, and he'll need a tetanus injection. Go on, get on with it! Get a move on! Quickly!'

The second volunteer for the job of stretcher-bearer, in addition to Mephisto, turned out to be Prometheus. Eagerly abandoning his lathe, he leapt to my side and at once offered his services. The two of them, with expressions of concern proper to the gravity of the situation, faces arranged into what they evidently hoped was a convincing I-am-completely-to-be-trusted look, seized me under the armpits and hauled me out of the room as if they were bearing a wounded comrade-in-arms off the field of battle.

'Arm up! Keep his arm up!' the Workman cried after them. 'Up, up, up! Or he'll lose all his blood, and then God knows what we'll do . . .'

The sick bay, as always when it was needed, turned out to be locked. We sat down on the bench that served as the waiting-room and Prometheus ran off to the office to make inquiries. He reappeared with the news that the doctor and nurse had both gone off that morning to buy medical supplies and had not yet returned, but added that the secretary (an old-fashioned woman in horn-rimmed spectacles), in proffering this piece of information, had made strange faces and rolled her eyes, signifying her utter lack of faith in its veracity. That was what *they* had said, the two who weren't here, that is, but she didn't believe a word of it. Did they really expect her to fall for a story like that when it was perfectly plain to everyone that the two of them had a thing going? It wasn't any of *her* business, of course; she didn't care *what* they did, as long as they didn't do it at the expense of our schoolchildren's health. But there it was, times had changed, that was how people behaved nowadays, doing that kind of thing right under her nose – not to speak of the way this school has been run ever since . . . at this point she had trailed off into eloquent silence, accompanied by a meaningful look in the direction of Madame's office.

Prometheus's account stung me like a spur. I knew Madame wasn't popular among the staff, but it hadn't occurred to me that she was surrounded by overt hostility. If her secretary – a low-ranking subordinate – permitted herself remarks of that kind (to a pupil!), she clearly thought she had nothing to fear. Worse, it meant she was sowing rebellion; it was part of a premeditated plan of subversion. If so, Madame might be in danger – in which case the present situation could well be the final nail in her coffin. It would be enough for one of her enemies – the Tapeworm, for instance – to send a 'note' (in other words, a denunciation) to the school board about the dangerous chaos that reigned in the school ('severely wounded pupil fruitlessly seeks aid in sick bay; doctor doesn't care; basic discipline falling apart'): that was just what the board members – and others higher up who knew the political background of her appointment – were waiting for, a perfect excuse to get rid of her. They'd probably been told to kill off the whole 'experiment' at the first opportunity, before it had a chance to get off the ground. All they needed was a good pretext to show the French: 'We've been flexible, we've agreed to everything, but our good will has been abused; your candidate, however distinguished in her field, simply does not have the qualifications for the post. She's a disaster! Under no circumstances can we allow this experiment to wreak havoc with our schools; you will understand that we cannot permit it to go on any longer.' A note from the Tapeworm would be their call to arms. A special inspection would be organised, and every single defect and omission would be put down to Madame's account. She would be dismissed immediately.

It was hard for me to judge if these gloomy visions were really justified or merely the result of my weakened state; the loss of blood might have affected my brain. Justified or not, they spurred me to action. Pretending to be rapidly fading and about to faint, I turned to Mephisto and, like the dying Hamlet to Horatio, gasped weakly, 'Go . . . go and fetch Madame. Tell her . . . she ought to know what's going on here . . . It smells like a case for the prosecutor's office . . . Let's see what she has to say.'

This time he didn't need much persuading. Whatever he thought of my swooning act, he shot off at once.

As I waited for the resolution, I thought with a bitter smile that perhaps this was Fate's mocking riposte to my idea of submitting Madame to a 'trial by fire of the heart'. You concocted vile, treacherous schemes against the director, Fate seemed to be whispering somewhere in the dim reaches of my weakened consciousness; you wanted to kill him off verbally or at least hurt him in order to see whether she really cares about him – if her heart is really engaged. But why such a shy, roundabout approach? Wouldn't a direct way be better? Why not find out whether she has any room in her heart for *you*? The heart is an ample thing, with space enough for more than one. Did not Mademoiselle Champsmeslé, with all her lovers, still find room in her heart for Racine? Then what do Madame's feelings for the director matter? They're neither here nor there; what matters is whether she has any feelings for you. And that's why this accident has been ordained: so that you can find out . . .

Then I heard a familiar click of heels.

Now I've got delusions, I thought weakly, feeling my strength fading. I'm hearing things. It's the loss of blood.

But it was no delusion. For all of a sudden Prometheus, who had been watching over me during Mephisto's absence, jumped up and bent almost double in a subservient bow; then Mephisto ran up, panting excitedly. And finally, there, unquestionably, she was – Madame, standing before me.

She was wearing a suit of light-coloured checked tweed, a white silk blouse with a silver brooch pinned at the neck and low-heeled brown shoes, long, narrow and pointed, with a thin strap that clasped the foot gracefully just below the ankle. Her lips, eyelids and lashes were discreetly made up, and her hair was impeccable.

'Well, now, what have we here?' she began ironically, but her voice held a discernible note of concern. 'Weary of life already?'

'Frankly, yes,' I replied quietly.

'Far too soon,' she pronounced. 'Well, get up, what are you waiting for?'

'For help. For a doctor,' I said provocatively, not quite sure where she was headed. 'In vain, it seems.'

She ignored this. 'Help him up, you two,' she commanded, 'since he seems unable to get up by himself. And bring him to my office,' she added, leading the way.

The two good Samaritans hastened to do her bidding, one grabbing me by the waist and putting my arm around his shoulders while the other took tight hold of my wrist and held up the wounded hand. Thus entwined, like something out of a Delacroix painting, the three of us hobbled into the different world of Madame's office.

'Sit him down here,' she ordered, leading the way to the sofa. Then she went round to the other side of the desk and took her handbag from the back of the chair, where it hung as it had hung before, slightly open.

Mephisto and Prometheus, having executed her orders, stood there like two statues, their eyes avidly following her every movement.

'What do you two think you're doing? Providing the audience?' Her hand, which had been rummaging in the handbag and had seemed to be about to extract something from its depths, stopped in mid-movement. 'Back to class with you! At once! Your mission is over.'

'B-but,' Mephisto stammered desperately, trying to find some way of maintaining his position, 'the woodwork teacher told us to help.'

'Thank you, I can manage,' she replied with a sarcastic smile, and waited until they had gone before resuming her rummaging.

Her hand emerged from the bag holding a small bottle with a square label that said 'Chanel No. 5' (not the *parfum*, as it shortly turned out, but the *eau de toilette*, in a spray). Then she delved back into the handbag, this time with both hands, and withdrew a large wad of cotton wool. It looked as if she had torn it off a larger piece, which presumably was why she had needed both hands.

She carries cotton wool in her handbag. The sentence formed itself suddenly in my mind, as if it described a fact worthy of note. And then a vague question: *three days after . . .*? But I had no time to consider its significance, for suddenly she was beside me or rather, strictly speaking, sitting opposite me.

'Well, now, let's see what you've managed to do to that poor little finger of yours,' she said lightly. 'Can it be saved, do you think, or will we have to amputate?'

Uncertain whether I might not be dreaming again, whether all that had happened since I had entered her office was really happening to me, I obediently stretched out my wounded left hand. Madame grasped it firmly from below (also with her left), just under the wrist, pulled it towards her and surveyed it critically.

'*Oh là là!* It looks bad,' she observed with mock concern. 'You've really done a good job this time.'

I didn't recognise her. She was a different person. Like – oh, I don't know . . . an Amazon? Hercules in a skirt? An energetic, no-nonsense nurse with a masculine disposition? I would never have suspected that in such a situation she would behave like this. I would have thought she'd go pale, lose her nerve, panic – or assume a remote and contemptuous air, approaching my bloody problem with disgust and annoyance. But instead it appeared, curiously, to stimulate her; it was as if she drew some kind of strength from it, as if it had tapped into some hidden reserves. It also seemed to have set off a kind of 'thaw' in her demeanour: she was freer, warmer, less stiff and constrained. I had never seen her so relaxed; she was almost . . . mellow! And at the same time confident, efficient and fully in control – the perfect soldier.

'Now we'll see if you're a real man or not,' she said, reaching for the bottle. 'This is going to sting, I'm warning you!' With which words she set about alternately spraying the cut and rubbing it with the cotton wool.

Indeed, it was not a *partie de plaisir*; it stung dreadfully. But I gritted my teeth and bore the pain in silence. I had a harder time controlling the chaos in my head.

For here it was at last, the thing I hadn't even dared to dream of, a situation that even in my wildest fantasies I hadn't envisaged as possible. I was actually alone with her, here in the quiet of her office, and she, with her own hands, was dressing my wound with Chanel No. 5, holding my hand and uttering remarks full (albeit unintentionally) of suggestion and ambiguity. And in a sense she was dependent on me: it was now in her interests to help me.

To me, corrupted as I was by literature and with my propensity to fantasise, the situation bordered on the perverse. The blood, the cotton wool, the tight grip on my hand, the inflicting of pain (for my own good) – all with no expression of sympathy or concern, yet with a strange excitement and curiosity – it felt like some perverse sexual encounter. She was humiliating me, eagerly and violently; hurting me, testing my powers of self-control to the limits, and seeming to derive pleasure, or at least excitement, from doing so.

You're not reacting, I imagined her thinking wildly. Why? Not a quiver, not even a gasp of pain . . . very well: I'll intensify the torture. Let's see how much you can take . . . I want to break you, force you to yield . . . hear you groan, just once!

I won't stop until you do. You can't win with me; no one ever wins with Victoire! Go on, scream! Cry out! I can't bear it any longer!

But I didn't cry out. I didn't even flinch. I only closed my eyes, the more intensely to feel her touch and more distinctly to hear my own thoughts. They came in a breathless jumble, teeming with a rich variety of words, phrases and whole sentences I could now use to fulfil my dream of the Great Game – the game of words through which I could experience what was happening as something quite different. Through the magic of language I could change the water of first-aid to the wine of ecstasy. I could create by naming; through the Word I could transform reality.

But I didn't want to. I saw no point in it; the game had come to seem empty and futile. I wanted something else: the real thing, the truth. I wanted to make the Word flesh or the Word made flesh. Yet I feared it.

'Why have you gone so quiet?' she said suddenly. 'Cat got your tongue? You, who are always so eloquent . . . you're not going to faint on me, are you?' She raised her voice slightly. 'Open your eyes! Look at me! Don't leave me alone.'

'You can't talk to me like that,' I replied sleepily, paraphrasing Aschenbach's memorable unspoken remark in response to Tadzio's Narcissus-like smile.

'Like what?' she asked. 'What do you mean? And why?' She gave me another squirt of Chanel. 'Did I say something unsuitable?'

'To talk to me like that,' I began, my voice full of suffering, 'you'd have to . . . you'd have to have some . . . you'd have to have the *right*,' I trailed off, unable to articulate my thoughts more precisely.

'The right? What are you talking about? I can't understand a word of what you're saying. You're clearer when you speak in French.'

'It's easier in a foreign language. Hans Castorp did it, too, when he wanted to –'

'Who?' she broke in, frowning.

She hadn't read it! How awful!

'This character in a novel. *Un boche*. In the Alps.'

'*Ah,* La Montagne magique*! Oui, oui, bien sûr que je l'ai lu*.'

I breathed a silent sigh of relief.

'Well, when he wanted to . . . what?'

'When he wanted to say something important. He used a foreign language.'

'You want to speak French? *Vas-y! Ça me ferait plaisir!*'

'I'm not sure. Unless –'

'Unless what?'

'Unless you liked my essay about the stars. *A propos,* I've been meaning to ask you what you did with my notebook. Why didn't you return it to me?'

'Was I supposed to?' She smiled. 'I thought it was a gift. You don't return gifts.'

I was speechless. 'That's true,' I stammered finally, 'but you're supposed to do *something* in acknowledgement. To *say* something, at least . . . make some allusion to it . . . *some* sort of comment.'

'Didn't you get an A?' she asked, with feigned outrage. 'The only A in the whole school! Doesn't that count? Isn't that enough?'

'Of course it's not enough,' I replied, sounding offended, like a hurt lover. 'Not nearly enough! Not for someone who dreams and writes. Someone like that doesn't care about marks.'

'Then what *do* you care about?' she asked with a little pout, and began delicately blowing on the wound. 'What does he dream about, this writer? Fame and recognition, I suppose?'

'Not only that, and not mainly. Certainly not at the stage *I'm* at.'

'*C'est à dire?*'

'The educational stage. I'm just taking my first steps. At this stage one needs something quite different.'

'*Quoi?* What does one need? *J'aimerais le savoir*.'

'Guidance. A helping hand.'

'Am I not guiding you? Teaching you? Helping you?' She applied a larger piece of cotton wool to the cut and pressed it firmly to staunch the flow of blood.

'Not in the way that a lover of language and *belles-lettres* would like. The way the physics teacher does with Roz Goltz, for instance.'

'And *what* exactly is it that he does with him, and how does he do it?' she asked with mock horror in her voice.

'You know perfectly well!' I shot back. 'He does the second-year university course with him. Quantum mechanics and relativity theory. He stays behind with him after school. They meet at home, too. And they go to conferences together, and national competitions, and things like that.'

'I'm afraid there are no national competitions in Romance languages. I can't help that.'

'But there *is* quite a bit of literature one could talk about. And read together . . . like Paolo and Francesca,' I added in a low voice.

'Like who?' She made a movement with her head.

'These two characters. *Un couple*. Centuries ago, in Italy.'

'I don't know who you mean.'

'Dante talks about them.'

'Ah, *La Divine Comédie*! I've never read it all the way through, only the *Inferno* and *Purgatorio*. These two sound as if they're in *Paradiso*.'

'Unfortunately not. They're in the second circle . . . *la Cité dolante*.'

'So that's what you're proposing?!' she laughed teasingly, taking a folded white handkerchief from her bag. 'That I should find myself in hell?'

'*On dit que "l'enfer, c'est les autres"* . . . there's no escaping it.'

She gave a brief snort of laughter. 'You see: you know everything!' She spread out the handkerchief, folded it into a triangle and rolled it up carefully to form a narrow strip with pointed ends. 'What more could I teach you? What could I . . . read with you?' She took my hand and began to bandage it with the handkerchief.

'Oh, there's no lack of books,' I said, smiling sadly. '*Lancelot*, for instance.'

'*Ah, Lancelot! Oui, oui: le Chevalier à la charrette. Chrétien de Troyes.*'

'Correct,' I said, and realised with horror that I was beginning to talk like Freddy.

'Why that in particular? A medieval legend? Do you know how difficult it is?'

'Yes, I do. That's precisely why –'

'You want my help.'

'*Vous l'avez dit, Madame.*'

'Assuredly you overestimate me.' She tied the ends of the handkerchief together and made the knot secure. 'I only teach language. I am, as your friend so amusingly put it, *seulement une lectrice de français*. By the way, I had the distinct impression you were prompting him.' She gave me a provocative look.

'So did you go to that Picasso exhibition in the end?' I shot back, unruffled.

'Why in the end? I went at the very beginning.'

'But you said –'

'What did I say?'

'You said, *Je n'y suis pas allée.*'

'And that was the truth.'

'I don't understand. What do you mean?'

'I mean that I went to the opening but didn't see the drawings. That's what you're really interested in, isn't it?'

'Me?'

'Your friend, then,' she corrected, in mock concession.

'Forgive me, but there's something here I still don't quite understand.'

'Yes? What is it?' The ironic little smile hovering on her lips made her look even more enchanting.

'How could you go to the opening and not look at the drawings?'

'What's so extraordinary about it?' She shrugged. 'It's perfectly normal. When you've lived a bit longer you'll understand.'

'But then why go?'

'There can be all sorts of reasons.'

I felt a cold shiver go through me. I had it on the tip of my tongue to say, 'The happy fate of Cleopatra, perhaps?' but I restrained myself.

'Besides,' she added, after a pause, 'I don't really like Picasso.'

That was a relief, at least. 'To tell you the truth, neither do I,' I admitted, seeking common ground.

'There, you see? That's one thing we agree on!'

'And who *do* you like?' I asked. Then, succumbing to temptation, I decided on a riskier move and added, '*I* like Bernard Buffet.'

She didn't even blink.

'Especially those still, steel-grey views of Paris,' I went on calmly. 'Do you know his work?'

'Of course! It's very well known.'

'And?' I looked into her eyes. 'Do you share my taste?'

She shook her head. 'It's not great art,' she said, 'but I admit it has a certain charm.'

I was tempted to go a step further ('and what about that view of the church of St-Germain-des-Prés? Is that just *charming*, too?') but didn't, for a better idea occurred to me. 'You know who else I especially like?' I said.

'We're still talking about artists, I take it.'

'Yes.' I smiled.

'Well? Tell me.'

'Alberto Giacometti,' I announced, letting my smile fade. 'What do you think of *him*?'

'Interesting,' she conceded with a nod. 'Mysterious . . . subtle.'

'I'm told he's enormously popular now. Everyone's talking about him.'

She shrugged. '*Je ne suis pas au courant.*'

'I read about it in the papers,' I lied smoothly. 'And I also heard that there's some mention of him in some . . . melodrama.'

'In a melodrama?'

'Yes, a film by that director, what's his name . . .' I pretended to be suffering from a temporary memory block, 'you know . . . the one they call *l'enfant prodige du cinéma français*,' I added, quoting the subtitle of the interview in *Arts*.

'You mean Lelouch?'

'*Voilà!* Exactly,' I said, and looked into her eyes again.

She tilted back her head slightly and narrowed her eyes. Then she gave a snort of laughter and said with a pitying smile, 'Possibly . . . but how ridiculous!' She shook her head in disbelief.

'I'm sorry, what's ridiculous?' I asked, feigning incomprehension.

'To see his films as expressing a current trend.'

'Have you seen it, then?' I asked, incredulous.

'Yes, I have, as a matter of fact,' she replied indifferently.

'But where? When? How? It hasn't been released here yet!'

'No, it hasn't. But I've seen it.'

'And?!' This time my curiosity was genuine.

'What is it, exactly, that you're asking?'

'Well, just your general impression.'

'A melodrama – as you just said.'

'But do you agree with that view?'

'What view? About which genre it belongs to?'

'Opinions differ,' I said more confidently, regaining some of my aplomb. 'Some people seem to think it's a reply to the philosophy of negation – an answer to existentialism: to *all that nihilism, alienation and frustration* . . .'

She laughed her pearly laugh.

'So, you *don't* agree with that!' I couldn't prevent a note of hope from creeping into my voice.

'I don't know what you mean.'

'I mean . . . what is *your* opinion of the film?'

She shrugged. 'Light entertainment. Silly. Harmless.'

'*Harmless*?' I burst out.

'I don't see anything to condemn in it. It's just a bit of fluff. *Des belles images*. A bit of social flirting. A fairytale.'

Blood was seeping through the handkerchief wrapped around my hand. I lifted my arm slightly and held it out to her in a 'look-at-that' gesture.

'What shall we do now?' I asked with exaggerated concern. 'Such a pretty handkerchief.'

'You can keep it,' she replied with a smile. 'Tit-for-tat. In exchange for your notebook.'

'That's nice of you.' I drew back my hand and added, again looking into her eyes, 'I trust it's not from some Othello.'

'And not from an Antony, either,' she said coyly. Then she rose, approached the small table with the telephone, picked up the receiver and pressed the red button that connected her to the office.

She told the secretary to get a taxi. Someone was to go to the taxi stand and bring one round. To the main entrance. Quickly.

Again I felt my heart pound. Who is it for? I thought with trepidation. For me? For her? For both of us? Does she intend to take me home in it? To the hospital casualty department, perhaps?

Whatever her intentions, one thing was certain: my time was running out. The small red flag on the face of the watch that had ticked on silently throughout this office game was almost at its zenith, and would soon begin its descent. I applied myself hastily to working out a strategy for the endgame.

Everything that had happened during this encounter – the dressing of my hand, the verbal sparring, the conversation which provided answers to so many vital questions – far exceeded the scope of my dreams, not to speak of my actual plans. Even the exquisite dialogues I had composed that day when, lying on my bed, I had fantasised about her reactions to my essay ('What then, my lad? What then?'), those subtle, impossibly splendid *conversations*, which at the time had seemed doomed to remain forever confined to the sphere of my imagination, paled by comparison to the one now taking place in reality.

And yet, although I had soared higher than I had imagined possible, I still felt unsatisfied. This new side to her nature which my predicament had somehow disclosed – cheerful and natural, at once tender and masculine, full of playfulness, wit, charm – awoke a raging thirst for . . . well, for what? What did I really want? How could my longings be satisfied? Where could I find fulfilment?

Then it came to me.

I should take her king with mine! Move her . . . touch her . . . use the familiar form of address. And then stop speaking;

then . . . 'read no more.' That was the consolation I sought. It would be a kind of fulfilment.

I launched myself.

'Have you seen *Phèdre*?' I asked. 'The Comédie Française?' (First move.)

'Of course I have.' (I breathed another silent sigh of relief.) 'I wouldn't have missed something like that!'

'Which performance did you go to, the first or the second?'

'The first. Opening night.'

'Unfortunately I went to the second,' I lied, in order not to frighten her off.

'Why *unfortunately*?'

'Well, an opening night is always special.'

'I don't think it can have made any difference in this case.'

I advanced my king. 'It was fantastic, wasn't it?'

'Yes, it *was* well done,' she agreed, rummaging in her handbag again.

'Those people! The way they looked . . . the way they spoke . . . the rhythm!' I gushed. 'Those frozen *tableaux*! I couldn't sleep afterwards. I still can't stop thinking about it.'

'Your susceptibility to the charms of art is excessive,' she remarked without looking up. 'A bit of moderation would not go amiss. A little distance.'

'Yes, I suppose you're right,' I conceded, crestfallen. 'Still, can you think of anything else so worthy of it?'

'Of what?'

'Heartfelt admiration. Wonder. Love.'

She looked up from her rummaging. 'Yes. The theatre of life. *Life,*' she repeated, sliding her right hand, closed in a fist as if she were hiding something in it, into her pocket. Then she perched herself on the table like the silver-haired Marianne.

'Yes, all right,' I replied and, riding a wave of inspiration, went on, 'that's true, but on condition that some sort of form is imposed upon it. And only art – *l'art* – can do that. What would the theatre of life be without its masks and costumes, without the charm of words and song, without the magic that only the artist can give it? Just a bleak, flat, desert landscape, boring and grey. Or kitsch.'

'You exaggerate. Highly,' she replied, looking down at me with friendly condescension.

'Exaggerate? Then think, just think of what we would be – no, forget us, that's too easy – think of what *they*, the characters in *Phèdre*, would be reduced to, what their tragedy would look like, if you took away all that their creators, the artists, from the ancients to Racine, endowed them with! Without culture, custom or taboo, and especially without *language*, without the subtle art of speech, Hippolytus would be nothing but a male animal raging with lust, and Phaedra . . . Phaedra just a bitch in heat. But this way, this way you have Michelangelo's Adam and his Creator, and a subtle allegory about human unfulfilment . . . and since we're on the subject,' I rushed on, time running out, 'which scene made the greatest impression on you? Hippolytus's confession or Phaedra's?'

Please, please tell the truth, I begged silently, half-shutting my eyes and calling up in my mind the memory of her at the theatre as she applauded Phaedra's harassment of her stepson, when she throws herself on Hippolytus and wrests his sword from him.

'The second,' I heard her say. 'And you?'

'The first,' I replied, returning to the present.

'That's what I thought.'

'Why?'

'Because I see you like sweetness . . . despite your claims to the contrary.'

'And you prefer bitterness?' I asked, involuntarily echoing Freddy's memorable remark to me.

'In art – yes. In life – no.' She withdrew her hand from her pocket and straightened her skirt.

I decided there was no time to delay.

I rose, approached the bookshelf with the Pléiade editions and picked out Racine. I quickly found *Phèdre*, and then Hippolytus's first conversation with Aricia.

'Would you do something for me?' I asked, approaching the table. 'To sweeten my life?' I added, gesturing to my bandaged hand.

'It depends what it is,' she replied.

'Oh, nothing extraordinary . . . just read this to me.' I handed her the open book and went back to the sofa.

She looked at it and began to read (I give the text in translation):

My lady, before I can start
I must give you some news that will gladden your heart.

'A bit further on,' I directed in a whisper.

She stopped, went down the page and resumed at Aricia's second reply:

Confused and bewildered by all that you've said,
I'm afraid it's a dream – just a voice in my head.
Can it be? Can I . . .

'I'm sorry – a little further down.'

'Well, where exactly *do* you want me to start?' she asked, with an edge of impatience.

'From "*I, my lady, hate you?*" If you would.'

She found the place and began for the third time:

Though my pride may elicit dislike and offence,
I'm no monster devoid of all feeling and sense.
There's no fury so savage, no hatred so base
Would not soften and melt at the sight of your face.
How could I be unmoved by your delicate charm?

'"*What, my lord?*"' I interposed, supplying, from memory, Aricia's exclamation, which came at this point.

She looked at me with a smile, and went on:

How my tongue has defeated my calm!
Reason yields to compulsion; restraint is undone.
Now the silence is broken and I have begun,
I'll go on, for I must. My lady, I'll speak.
My heart is too swollen, my will is too weak.
It's an unhappy prince that stands here at your side,

An instructive example of arrogant pride.
I, who prized only Dignity, scorning Love's pains,
Who so mocked the poor mortals enslaved by her chains,
Who deplored the sad shipwrecks her galley-slaves bore
And resolved to stay safe from the storms on the shore,
Am now shackled like them, and borne off, struggling still,
On her tide. I am forced to submit. I, too, bend to her will.

She raised her eyes from the page. 'Is that enough, or should I go on?'

'Just the last lines.'

She held my gaze for a moment, looking deep into my eyes, shook her head, as if to say, It's a risky game you're playing, and resumed:

But my gift should be dearer by this fact alone,
That I speak to you now in a tongue not my own.

She stopped again, and said teasingly, 'That's not right: *I'm* the one reading this, after all.'

'All right. I'll read now,' I said, stretching out my hand for the book.

She slid off the table to give it to me, then sat down in the little armchair opposite.

'I'm sorry, but I think we have to switch: that's where I should be sitting, and you should be here.' I needed to get her on my right.

'Why?' she asked, surprised.

'To conform to Charon's picture. Who is the king here? You are. So you have to be on the sofa. Please,' I said, indicating that she should sit. 'While I, as Racine, will sit in the armchair.'

'The things you think of! How green you are still!' She rose and sat where I had indicated. 'Well, what are you going to read me?' She assumed the pose of Louis XIV. 'And be sure to read nicely, rhythmically,' she added, raising an admonishing finger. 'You remember that in alexandrines you have to put in syllables that are never sounded in ordinary speech.'

'*Mais Votre Altesse!* How could I forget?'

'*Allez-y donc, Seigneur.*'

I turned over the page to Phaedra's great aria, and began to read:

No, my lord! I have been clear enough
You have heard me too well; you can have no more doubt.
So be it. It's done; the true Phaedra will out.
Yes, I love you. And yet, though I love, I'm not blind;
Don't imagine my feelings have clouded my mind.
I condemn my own weakness; my guilt gives me pain.
It's no innocent passion that poisons my brain.
And the vengeance of heaven has not left me free:
I loathe myself more than you, sire, could hate me.
The gods can bear witness: it's they who inspire
The corruption that burns in my heart with such fire . . .

I knew the passage by heart. More than that: I had practised reciting it until every detail – every stress, every cadence – was perfect, and brought out the rhythm and logic of each phrase. The words flowed by themselves; I didn't need to concentrate on them. And as they flowed, I suddenly heard myself from outside, as if it were not I speaking but someone else in my voice; and I felt a familiar shiver run through me. It was a shiver of ambition and the will to conquer; that thrilling shiver I had felt whenever I had determined that by art – by poetry or music – I should triumph over life: win over Prospero in the ASTB offices; subjugate the rabble during the prize-giving at the municipal community centre; captivate the audience at the Spanish civil war celebration. I wondered if Racine felt the same sort of shiver when he was writing his tragedies, especially when he was reading them – to the actresses and to the king. He was shy and unsure of himself; no blue blood ran in his veins; women, the court, the world around him, life in general seemed like some Goliath, some rampant giant towering awesomely over him. His one weapon against it, against the world, was his divine spark: the gift of words. If he was to win, he had to subdue that giant and render him helpless by his magic.

My hour had come. This was it; now or never. I wanted to do it; I *could* do it! I could break through the magic circle – reach her, touch her. Penetrate the myth and taste it, know it, at last.

Conscious of the effect this always had on my audience, I raised my eyes from the page and, still speaking, slowly closed the book and put it down on the table. Then, gazing into her eyes, I continued from memory:

Here's my heart. Take your sword. This is where you must strike.
It leaps forth in my breast to atone for past harm.
Impatient it waits for the blow from your arm.

She was observing me carefully, still smiling that slightly condescending, slightly provocative smile, but her eyes gleamed. I could see, at last, a spark of wonder and respect. How nicely you write, Racine, they seemed to say, and you read quite nicely, too. Go on . . . don't stop . . . more . . . more . . .

I went on:

Strike. Or if such a blow is beneath your estate,
If your hatred denies me so gentle a fate,
If my blood is too vile to sully your hand,
Then lend me your sword. Have pity. Unbend.
Let me have it.

On these words, as if I were imitating Phaedra's gesture at the Comédie Française, I reached out and with my right hand grasped Madame's left wrist.

And then it happened. Perhaps it was an instinctive reaction, or perhaps she only meant to indicate that she knew it was a game and was willing to indulge me. Whatever her reasons, she did something astonishing. Turning her slim, cool hand in my hot grasp, she withdrew it a little so that it met mine; then she pressed, hard, from below. It was precisely the gesture that the despairing Phaedra had seemed to want from Hippolytus when she held his wrist in her hand: the gesture of human solidarity that he, in his pride, had refused her.

But Madame meant something quite different by the manoeuvre. She intended not an expression of sympathy, pity or mercy, but a demonstrative correction, a kind of taming of my own action – which, for all its trappings and the forest of imagined quotation marks surrounding it, had been crude and savage. It was a lesson, not unlike the lesson the Workman had given me when he had tried (fruitlessly, thank God) to show me how to hold the saw.

No, not like that, silly boy, her gesture seemed to say, that's not it at all. If you're going to commit the sacrilege of reaching for my hand, for the hand of any woman, at least learn how to do it right. And do it openly and unashamedly, with your head held high, not slyly and half-heartedly and in disguise. Admit what you're doing; don't pretend it's something else. Look: *this* is how it's done. Your right hand on top, my left underneath. The hands touch and the fingers intertwine. The ritual of marriage.

'*C'est extraordinaire!*' I exclaimed, trying to mask my emotion. Then, still pretending that my enthusiasm was purely aesthetic, I made my final move. I pronounced the word, and took my king with hers. '*Tu as fait justement ce qu'Hippolyte n'avait pas fait*,' I said. You did exactly what Hippolytus failed to do.

She seized on it at once. '*Tu?* Either you're carried away by your part, or . . . I'll have to take back that A, since you seem unable to distinguish person and number.'

'*Mais la concordance des temps était irréprochable*,' I replied with a smile, and wanted to go on, to say that perhaps more than the sequence of tenses had been correct, to say anything, just to prolong this communion with her, make it last a moment longer – but then the door to the office burst open and there, panting and out of breath, in their coats, were Mephisto and Prometheus.

'The taxi –' one of them began, then stopped as if petrified by the sight before him.

I released Madame's hand.

'Go and fetch his coat, please,' she said to them, as if nothing out of the ordinary had occurred. 'Why do you always have to be reminded of everything?'

They crept away, discountenanced. Madame rose, closed the door behind them and took fifty zlotys out of the right-hand pocket of her tweed jacket.

'Where do you live?' she asked.

I gave the name of the street.

'That should be enough,' she said, and gave me the note with the Fisherman.

'It's far too much,' I said, taken aback.

'How are you so familiar with the fares? Do you ruin yourself gallivanting about in taxis?'

'A taxi doesn't have to mean immediate ruin –'

'Stop it, please, and take it!' she interrupted, and, since I still made no move to take the money, took a step forward and slid the bill into my shirt pocket. 'And now,' she said, '*adieu, mon prince.*'

And she opened the door.

Endgame

For a long time afterwards I was in a daze. I went on digesting and redigesting everything in my memory, like a snake that has swallowed too much. Lying on my back on my bed, my eyes closed, I ran and re-ran my mental tape of everything that had happened in the office, trying to extract its essential significance – to understand what had happened and what it meant.

How was I to interpret the extraordinary, astonishing change in Madame's behaviour? Was it merely a part she'd been playing, from anxiety or fear – for her position and the plans that depended on it? An attempt to make the best of a bad situation, to put a good face on things? A conscious and deliberate act of sacrifice, intended to disarm me and prevent me from raising the alarm? Or a genuine unveiling? Had she cast off her mask and shown me her true face? And if it *was* genuine, what did it mean? What had made her do it, what mechanism had prompted her to enter into a game that went far beyond the bounds of what was necessary or proper in the provision of first-aid? Whim? Vanity? Curiosity? Or perhaps . . . perhaps affection, after all? An affection she had concealed and stifled?

One moment I saw it as a cold and cynical female ploy, calculated to overwhelm me and beguile me into holding my tongue; the next I thought it was a sincere expression of affection – that she had a weakness for me which until now she hadn't wanted or hadn't permitted herself to reveal, and that my predicament had somehow, at last, allowed her to express it.

I so badly wanted this second interpretation to be correct that I gradually came to believe it. And this soon gave rise to a need to have it confirmed: I wanted proof, which in this case, by the very nature of things, would have to be a repetition of the theme – the sweet melody of our duet in her office. The means of getting it that occurred to me shone with a simplicity proper to a work of genius. I would simply fail to turn up at school the next day. My absence would give rise to anxiety about my fate; steps would be taken to determine it; an inquiry would be made by telephone. If someone else rang up, whether or not on her behalf, I would paint as bleak a picture as possible of my condition and ask that this report be passed on to Madame. And if I heard her voice, I wouldn't overdo it, but nor would I put her mind completely at rest; I would manoeuvre so as to entangle her in another discussion and extract something else from her – a tone sweet to the ear and heart.

Thus determined, I turned my attention to working out possible opening moves and compiling question-and-answer lists anticipating every conceivable turn the conversation might take.

I needn't have bothered. No one rang all day, either to find out how I was feeling or for any other reason. I swallowed the bitter taste of hopes unfulfilled, and on Wednesday, clinging despite everything to the belief that there would be some sort of sequel, with my hand bandaged and supported by an entirely superfluous splint, I set off for school.

I had assumed my classmates would treat me with the same sympathy they'd extended after the incident with the Viper, albeit doubtless tinged with an element of sarcasm and prurient inquisitiveness that I would have to repel. But I was greeted by indifference, even a certain coldness. Not only did no one ask about my hand, let alone about what had occurred in Madame's office, they gave the impression of avoiding me. I felt surrounded by a conspiracy of silence; I'd been sent to Coventry. Conversations ceased in my presence and resumed as soon as I had gone; I sensed that I was the subject of whispers and covert glances. It was behaviour characteristic of people who feel betrayed or let down. They acted as if they had been somehow deceived, or made fools of.

We thought he was one of us, their eyes and expressions seemed to say, a companion in suffering and humiliation; now it turns out that all the time he's been leading a double life, furtively insinuating himself into the good graces of his French Princess, being rewarded with favours none of us would dream of! *Now* we know why he struts around so blithely and confidently and takes such liberties: he knows he can do anything he likes and get away with it! Look at him, teacher's pet!

Under these circumstances, my hunger for a second course with Madame, or even just some pudding, in the form of a question from her (on the side, of course) about the state of my health, gave way to a much more modest need: now all I wanted to know was what the next French lesson would bring. How would she behave towards me after what had happened? How would she behave in general? And how would the rest of the class see it?

The answer, when it came, was not encouraging. Madame not only failed to express the slightest interest in me but reverted to her old habit of ignoring me entirely. No more asking me to correct other people's mistakes or provide the right answers; she behaved as if I weren't there, just as she had after the annexation of my notebook. My classmates remained suspicious, smelling pretence and deceit everywhere. Convinced that her refusal to speak to me was a sham, intended to mislead, they not so much disregarded it as placed no credence in it;

the 'radical wing' even saw it as a sign, indeed as proof, that relations between us were intimate. 'She won't speak to him,' I overheard a snatch of whispered conversation in the cloak-room, 'because she knows her voice would give her away. You can always tell when people are living together; you can hear it in their speech.'

The atmosphere of malicious gossip, suspicion and mockery wasn't too worrying. I didn't much care what people said. What did bother me, indeed disquieted me profoundly, was the turn-about in Madame's attitude.

Why is she doing this? What is it all about? Every day I went through the same litany of questions. Has she taken fright after all? Is she offended? What's behind it – this sudden change, this silence? Or maybe, I thought, seeking consolation in mythical truths, maybe that's just the way it always is; maybe that's the price you have to pay for casting away shame . . . for pleasure . . . for fulfilment? You've gone too far, said the voice, my old familiar friend; you have tasted the fruit of the gods . . . you've touched her . . . you've known her. The price of that is a cloud on the face of God. Expulsion from Paradise. The Fall. Into the vale of tears.

I tried to think of explanations, solutions, ways of reversing or undoing what had happened. But time was rapidly running out. The hundred-days-before-graduation ball came and went; already the end was in sight. Normal classes were almost over and we were into the revision period. There was all the material in the main subjects to be gone through, there was extra coaching, there were preparations for university. I no longer saw Madame.

But I heard about her from time to time: she had been given permission to put through the reforms; she had received a visit from a delegation from France; she had embarked on negotiations with school authorities about replacing the teachers with French-speaking staff. Other, lesser titbits, to me much more important, also reached my ears. One of them in particular meant a great deal to me. The kindly Old Livy disclosed one day, in confidence, that if I was being allowed to graduate at all it was owing principally, if not exclusively, to the intervention of 'our dear headmistress', who had preferred to accept the resignation of the Viper rather than bow to the latter's demands concerning my fate. Apparently there had been a real storm at the board meeting at which my case had come up. When 'our principal' cut short the discussion and imposed her decision, overruling the Viper, the latter got up and left the room, slamming the door behind her. Old Livy was quite relieved – not just for my sake but for his own as well, for he couldn't bear the woman.

It wasn't until the final exams that I saw Madame again.

Wearing a dark-blue blazer, a pleated green tartan skirt and low-heeled black shoes, she strolled slowly among the rows of desks where we were busy with our papers. From time to time, as the exam papers blackened with writing, she would stop and glance at someone's work; occasionally she gave what seemed like a hint or even pointed out a mistake. But she never stopped at my desk, didn't even come near it. I got the impression she was avoiding that whole row.

She looked blooming: tanned and youthful. She had probably gone to the mountains somewhere for spring break . . . with the director, perhaps? My heart constricted again and I couldn't concentrate. I took hold of myself. You've got to stop this, I thought. There's no point in it. You'll end up with a blank sheet and you'll fail.

I wrote my paper and passed. I even graduated with honours.

But that isn't important. What matters is what happened at the prom – on Midsummer's Eve, the shortest night of the year.

I went to it reluctantly and with no expectation of enjoying myself. Loud music and feverish dancing, accompanied by surreptitious sips of vodka or cheap wine, were not among my favourite forms of amusement. At best such events simply bored me; at worst I found them a trial. This evening announced itself as a bleaker prospect than usual, since relations with my classmates, at any rate those I had considered my friends, remained cool, and nothing augured their return to normal in the near future. I suspected I would spend the evening alone, not knowing what to do with myself, feeling foolish and out of place and rejected. Nevertheless I went – from inertia (because it was 'the done thing', because 'everyone would be there') but also, in some measure, from bloody-mindedness. I had a masochistic urge to prove to myself that I was indeed as isolated and estranged as I thought, incapable of normal relations with people and doomed to solitude for the remainder of my days.

As for Madame, I avoided thinking about her. I told myself it was over and done with, and tried not to wonder whether or not she would be there. At least, my decision to go had nothing to do with her.

The thing was supposed to start quite late, at nine in the evening, and go on until dawn. The proceedings included a formal supper, with 'licit' alcohol (a glass of champagne and one of white wine), followed by a dance in the big auditorium, with a hired band (vocal and instrumental) called The Howling Panthers and liberal quantities of 'illicit' alcohol (vodka and 'brand-X' wine, smuggled in beforehand and stashed away in the cloakroom and lavatories).

My predictions were soon confirmed. I was, and felt, left out. I wasn't deliberately cold-shouldered: no one turned his back or went out of his way to avoid me, but most people were in couples or well-defined groups, and preoccupied with their own enjoyment – dancing, drinking and having an all-out, uninhibited 'good time'. No one was in the mood for conversation or even for joking and clowning around. My fate was shared only by the ugly, boring girls and by that gloomy eccentric and know-all, the mathematical genius Roz Goltz.

I wandered aimlessly around the rooms and corridors where the party throbbed, playing – for my own benefit as much as anyone else's – the serious artist who 'suffered for millions' and was above the silly amusements of the common folk. All I lacked was a romantic costume to go with the part: a black coat or, better still, a black cape that I could fling over my shoulder in the style of Chateaubriand. But it would have made little difference, for almost no one paid me any attention, and those who did only gave me mocking or pitying looks that seemed to say, Won't drink, won't smoke, won't dance and hasn't got a girl. Pathetic!

I started to think about leaving. And then I noticed Madame. She was sitting at a long table in the teachers' room (the folding doors of which stood open, pulled all the way back), surrounded on both sides by members of the school board and the parents' committee. The table, covered with a starched white cloth, was set for coffee and dessert, and also held a number of shiny silver jug-shaped Thermoses and bottles of vermouth. Madame had on a tight cream-coloured dress, low-cut and sleeveless; around her neck was a string of small pearls. She sat in the centre and seemed to be presiding; when I noticed her she was just in the act of making a toast to the future of the school and . . . a good summer holiday.

I watched this scene from behind a bend in the corridor, unseen by the revellers at the table. She's drinking to her departure! I thought. This is her farewell toast, although they don't know it. This is the last supper!

I elaborated this thought into an internal monologue in the appropriate style. Farewell, then, divine and cruel creature; why did I ever set eyes on you! Too radiant and beautiful not to kindle fire, too distant and proud to quench it. Why did you have to enter my life! If you hadn't, if I had never beheld you, my fate would have been kinder: I'd surely be dancing with one of my peers, perhaps even with Lucy Rosenberg herself, at any rate with a girl of my own age, someone willing and eager, panting and red-cheeked and smelling of young sweat, and at the end of the dance I would no doubt manage to steal a juicy kiss. As it is, here I am, alone in the dark, suffering, a shadow of my former self, isolated, estranged . . . defeated. You've won. But what is that to you? Farewell, Ice Queen! *Adieu,* La belle Victoire!

I moved off slowly down the deserted corridor and returned to the auditorium, to haunt the revels there with my air of gloomy estrangement. In one corner, as far away as possible from The Howling Panthers, sat Roz Goltz, alone, hunched over a book. Feeling a sudden camaraderie, I sat down next to him. 'What are you reading?'

'*Islands of Physics*,' he replied, raising his head. 'Quite educational,' he added, in that strange way of his.

'What is it? It doesn't look like science.'

'It's not. It's a collection of stories.'

'Stories?' I looked more closely at the book. '*You*, reading stories?'

'What's so amazing about that? If they're true . . . I don't limit myself to fiction. Especially not that Polish rubbish they made us read here.'

'So what are these true stories about?' I asked, nodding at the book.

'Here, take it, see for yourself,' he said, getting up. 'I'm going to get something to drink.'

It was a newly published book by two Polish authors: a collection of stories based on the lives of the great physicists of the past hundred years, interwoven with accounts of their discoveries. The first of them, called *Miss Krüger of Hamburg*, was about Einstein, and presented his theory of relativity and the concept of space-time against the background of his decision to leave Nazi Germany.

It was well done. Abstract ideas about the constitution of the universe, its first laws and founding principles, were deftly embedded in a melancholy atmosphere of nostalgia and regret: sadness at leaving and parting, the anxiety of waiting for a piece of news on which much depended, bitterness and disappointment when at last it came and turned out to be bad. The cosmos against a background of human emotion: entropy, the flight of the stars; and here, on earth, another kind of flight – from a terrible, destructive madness.

It was engaging, beautiful and sad; before I knew it, I had reached the end. I went on to the next.

Suddenly the music died down and the deep voice of Carl Broda came over the screechy microphone. 'Friends,' he boomed, 'midnight has just struck: the crowning moment – the summit – of the evening has arrived! This will be our last exam, our final test. Our teachers, stern mentors that they are, want to call us out and test us for the last time. But not to worry, no need to be nervous. This time they want to call us onto the dance-floor – to dance! Come on, everyone! Music!'

'As long as it's something slow!' shouted the white-haired Livy.

There was laughter.

'Of course it'll be slow!' Carl Broda yelled back. 'The Beatles – "Yesterday"!'

There was a roar of approval and wild whoops of joy, and The Howling Panthers began strumming their guitars.

'My God, what a zoo!' muttered Roz beside me. I'd been so absorbed in the book I hadn't noticed his return.

'True,' I agreed absently, and went back to *Islands of Physics*.

'Look out: she's coming your way,' said Roz, in a strangely quiet voice.

I looked up and froze. Yes, it was she – Madame. My head spun. It's not possible, I thought; *such things don't happen in this world*. But before I could embark on a discussion with the spirit of Thomas Mann, whose voice had once again sounded somewhere within me, there she was, standing before me.

'What a pair of turtle-doves!' she said, her eyes swivelling from me to Roz with a look of playful mockery. 'All this one ever does is read!' she went on, nodding at me. 'But you won't get away with it so easily! I'm taking away your friend,' she announced to Roz, and then, seeing I hadn't moved, put on a stern face and said imperiously, 'Well, what are you waiting for? Will you refuse me this dance?'

Half-conscious, moving in a daze, I rose and gave her my left hand (as Hippolytus had given his to Aricia). She put her cool right hand into mine, and her left on my right shoulder (which sloped slightly). Then I reached out with my right arm and, my heart pounding like a hammer, touched her waist.

'Yesterday, all my troubles seemed so far away,' the sweet treble of The Howling Panthers' lead vocalist rang out *à la* Paul McCartney.

We moved off. Our first steps weren't a brilliant start. I was still dazed, and didn't know where to look. Her face, her eyes and lips, were no more than ten centimetres in front of me; I was intoxicated by her scent (not Chanel No. 5 this time, but something equally good), and as if that were not enough, with the fingers of my right hand I could distinctly feel, under the thin fabric of her dress, the strap and fastening of her bra. A black-and-white scene from *A Man and a Woman* flashed through my mind: the scene of their first, apparently innocent touch: the conversation in the restaurant, the back of Anne's chair and Jean-Louis's hand coming to rest there and accidentally brushing against her.

What kitsch! cried a voice inside me. You're drowning in kitsch!

'Pull yourself together!' she whispered through her teeth, 'and start leading! Everyone's looking at us. Do you want to make a fool of yourself? And of me as well?'

I grasped her more firmly, but my feet still stumbled.

'Well, well, this is a fine thing!' she went on, mocking. 'My favourite, best pupil, the one who wrote those essays for me – he can write essays like that, but he can't dance! And not just essays: he played the piano, he recited verse – he even performed on stage! He wasn't timid then.'

'Please, don't joke about it.'

'Joke? I'm not joking! I'm merely surprised. That *my* pupil, *mon élève,* my obedient subject' – she was enjoying playing the queen – 'should, deep in the dark night' – here I froze in terror, fearing that she knew about my January act of Acteon-like audacity – 'of the school year, beguile me with sweet words and then permit himself the extraordinary impertinence of reaching for my hand – more than my hand, my wrist! Was he not aware of the nature, the meaning of his gesture?' She looked into my eyes. 'And that this same pupil, a graduate, top of his year, a mature young man with a high-school diploma, now standing here under these bright lights, given unprecedented encouragement by me, should be so abashed and confused that I almost have to prop him up for fear that he might fall.'

'I'm not in the least abashed or confused,' I stammered, turning us around, 'perhaps just a little –'

'A little *what*?' she asked, smiling. 'You're trembling all over, like a rabbit!'

For a moment I felt a sort of helpless fury ('*Et tu, Brute?*'). But I stifled my indignation and, grasping her more tightly and trying to move with a confident step, retaliated with her own words that day in the office. 'You exaggerate. Highly,' I said, and was about to go on when she broke in.

'Well, that's a bit better. Now if you could try to keep some sort of rhythm, too.'

'We'll get to that, too, don't worry.' I was beginning to relax. 'I just wanted to say that if I seemed ill at ease at first, it was because I was a bit startled.'

'Startled? Indeed! And what was it, pray, that startled you so much?'

'How can you ask! Your choice of partner, of course. It's been almost six months since we talked in your office, and in all that time you haven't said a single word to me . . . you've ignored me, behaved as if I wasn't there . . . and now, all of a sudden, you appear out of the blue and ask me to dance. You must admit it's somewhat unexpected.'

'I admit no such thing. Stop talking so much!' Her tone was one of flirtatious reproof. 'Listen to the music and dance!'

'Yesterday, love was such an easy game to play,' crooned the lead vocalist of The Howling Panthers.

'Don't you think this is kitschy?' I asked, playing the hardened cynic.

'What?'

'Well, this sweet dancing of ours to these sweet words.'

'You may be surprised to hear it, but I don't know English. Besides . . . sometimes . . . kitsch can be quite pleasant. You shouldn't reject it so scornfully. Without kitsch there'd be no great art. Without sin there is no life.'

'And wouldn't that be better?'

'Oh, do stop it!' she snapped. 'Enough of these silly notions of yours! After this dance I'm leaving. My role is finished. My duties are done.' She seemed to be speaking to herself. '*Fini, c'est fini . . . c'est la fin.* I'm going home. To rest.'

'Oh I believe in yesterday,' The Howling Panthers' Paul McCartney finished up soulfully.

'And now' – Madame, too, was finishing – 'if this know-all, this beloved pupil of mine would like to be a gentleman and see his teacher, his . . . *maîtresse de français,* home, then he should wait for her,' she took her left hand from my right shoulder and glanced at her watch, 'in a quarter of an hour – at twenty past midnight. Outside the main gate, by the kiosk.'

I was stunned, and probably paled. At any rate I felt the blood drain from my face. She's arranging a tryst with me just as she did with the director, I thought, with a flutter of panic. She must have noticed my consternation, for she added skittishly, 'Unless, of course, he's enjoying himself too much here and prefers the company of his friend. In that case he should say so. Then I'll take a taxi.'

'He'll be there,' I said.

'That's very nice of him.' She gave a little curtsy and began to make her way to the door through the excited throng, which was now clapping and shouting.

'More Beatles! More Beatles! More Beatles!' chanted the Yankees, as the graduates of the so-called English stream were known.

The Howling Panthers started to play 'Ticket to Ride'.

In a complete daze I stumbled back to my seat beside Roz.

'Our headmistress likes you,' he observed, with a suggestive smile.

'Don't exaggerate,' I replied, but the effort of feigning indifference was enormous. 'She's just playing with me.'

'Well, that's not bad, either,' he remarked. 'Everyone was staring, did you realise?'

'Are you serious?'

'Their eyes were popping out of their heads. Even that little bolshevik creep Kugler. Admittedly, there was plenty to stare at.'

'What do you mean?'

'You make a nice couple.' He smirked.

'Oh, don't be ridiculous, Roz.' I felt myself going red. 'You're incorrigible. I don't know why you say these absurd things,' I said firmly and, with an air of weariness at his insinuations, went out into the corridor.

I stopped by a window and looked down at the dark, box-like shape that was the kiosk outside the gates.

Why are you so nervous? said the voice in my head. You should be happy. Things like this don't happen to many people. And there are some (I needn't tell you who) who claim that they never happen to anyone. Anyway, isn't this what you wanted? Didn't you do everything in your power to bring it about? You said to her outright (more than said: you announced it in writing!): 'Pray command me.' And it happened: she has commanded. It's your move. Face up to it.

I ran down the back stairs and left the building, or rather, I sneaked away, skulking along the walls and slipping out of the grounds through a hole in the fence at the back of the schoolyard. Then, taking a roundabout route, I made my way back to the kiosk by the main gate.

It was hot, but not oppressively so. There was a briskness in the air and the sky was clear, with a full moon. I looked up at the stars. There they were: Virgo, Aquarius and the North Star, in its place in Ursa Minor. For centuries they've kept their ancient places, and yet they're in flight, I thought, remembering a sentence from *Islands of Physics*. Then I heard a familiar click of heels.

I peered out from behind the kiosk.

'Oh, good, you're here,' she said. 'I was beginning to think you'd stood me up.'

'Me, stand *you* up? What an idea!'

'You never know . . . what ideas a student will get into his head.'

She was wearing a loose white linen jacket, and slung over her right shoulder was her bag, the one she used for school, bigger and more capacious than the bag she'd had at the Zacheta Gallery, the theatre and the Skarb Cinema. It was only now I noticed that her legs – unlike those of the other women teachers, even the older ones, and, of course, of the girls – were not bare but sheathed in thin, transparent stockings.

As we set off I cast an involuntary glance at the school. In one window, the one where I had stood looking down a quarter of an hour ago, I saw someone's silhouette. It was clearly male, but I couldn't tell, during that fraction of a second, if it was Roz or Kugler, and had neither the time nor the opportunity for more prolonged observation.

'So,' she said after we had walked a dozen or so steps in silence, 'you intend to study Romance languages?' She spoke as if she were returning to the subject of a recently interrupted conversation.

'How do you know?'

'How do I know?' she shot back at once. 'Don't all university applications pass through my hands, and do I not personally comment on, or at least sign, every single one of them?'

'I suppose so,' I admitted. 'Yes, those are my plans. What of it?'

'Nothing. You're doing the right thing. You'll get in, I'm not worried about that.'

'Then what *are* you worried about?' I asked, looking at the ground and seeing in my mind the image of my notebook with the essay, reposing in its plastic envelope in the shiny file on the Green-Eyed One's desk.

She gave a low laugh. 'One has to watch one's step all the time with you, can't relax for a minute. You latch on to every word.'

'I'm not latching on to anything. I'm asking.'

'And then, later – what do you want to do?' she asked, returning to the subject in a cool, offhand voice.

'When, later?' I feigned incomprehension.

'After university.'

The image of Freddy floated up in my mind. 'You mean, what are my plans for the future?' I said, quoting him.

'If you like.'

'Don't you know?' I muttered, with a note of disappointment. 'I want to write. To be a writer.'

'Ah, of course!' She nodded, smiling again. 'Virgo, with the goose-quill pen.'

'You have a good memory.'

'And that's what you intend to live on? Your writing?' She looked at me, raising her eyebrows slightly.

'Well, you know,' I said loftily, 'I don't think . . . in those terms. It's just what I *want*. Whether I'll succeed, and whether I'll be able to make a living from it, is another matter. It's not something I'm concerned with for the moment.'

'A maximalist,' she summed up. Her tone was one of ironic mock-respect. 'All or nothing.'

'You could say that,' I conceded. After a moment's hesitation I hazarded a more attacking move: 'Actually, my name really should be Maximilian. It's curious: even as a child I wanted to be called Max.'

She didn't even blink. 'Like Robespierre,' she said pointedly. 'And Gorky – wasn't his name Maxim?'

'No, not like them,' I replied. 'You can be sure of that.'

'I should hope so,' she replied emphatically. 'And what is it you're so eager to write about?'

'Oh, lots of things. Joanna Schopenhauer's journey across Europe, from England to Gdansk with the future Arthur in her womb, for example. Or Hölderlin, my favourite poet, and his journey home on foot from Bordeaux, across the Alps, where he saw Dionysus in a vision. Or the wanderings of the Marquis de Custine in Russia under Tsar Nicholas.'

'Well, well, quite ambitious,' she observed with what seemed like quickening interest. 'And you intend to write all this in Polish?'

'What else should I write in?'

'It would be even more ambitious to do it in French. Besides,' she added, with a sly smile and an oblique glance in my direction, 'I had the distinct impression that your notes, and all those quotations you've been gathering, were in French.'

'Tell me honestly,' I said, 'when you took away the notebooks that day to inspect them, was it because you wanted to see what I was writing when I sat there paying no attention to the lesson?'

'Why wouldn't I have taken just *your* notebook if that was what I wanted?'

'So as not to show me that you cared.'

'And you think I cared?'

'That was my impression.'

'Impression! The prerogative of the artist. But to return to the subject, what will it be, Polish or French?'

'I told you, Polish.'

'I thought you harboured dreams of fame and international recognition,' she said in a disappointed voice.

'What's that got to do with it? If what I write is genuinely good, sooner or later it will float out onto open waters.'

'Maybe, maybe not,' she persisted. 'If it does, it's liable to be later rather than sooner. Much later. Too late, perhaps?'

'What do you mean by that?'

'Nothing, really. Just that before your work floats out onto open waters, as you so eloquently put it, it has to appear in the original – that is, it has to be published here first, and *then* translated. And that's a long way to float.'

'And you think that if I were to write it in French from the start –'

'Do you remember,' she interrupted, 'what your friend said in a lesson one day?'

'Roz?' I laughed. 'He said all sorts of things. Mostly I remember what he wrote in his essay about Antek in Prus's novella.'

'And what enchanting aphorism was that?'

'A singular warning against the perils of overwork.'

'I mean that time he ran amok in class, when he said that the only writer of Polish origin who ever made it, and is read all over the world, is the author of *Lord Jim*, who didn't write in Polish. Do you know how old Conrad was when he left Poland?'

'About ten, I should think.'

'He was your age – a year younger than you. And he didn't know any English.'

'Have you read *Victory*?' I took advantage of the opportunity to ask.

'No. *Victoire*? *Non*.' She gave a wan smile, as if smiling at her own thoughts.

'Pity. Do read it.'

'I will, without fail, just as soon as . . .' She let the sentence trail off.

'As soon as what?'

'As soon as I get home.' She gave me one of her innocent, wide-eyed smiles.

We were approaching the familiar housing estate: it lay just beyond the blocks of houses ahead of us. For some moments we walked along in silence.

What is she up to? I thought feverishly. What is she getting at? Why this interrogation? She's never talked like this to me before – so seriously, despite all the irony. What's going to happen? What's going to happen now? And *how*? How will it come about?

'If I'm not mistaken,' she said suddenly, breaking the silence, 'in that prize performance of yours you recited something from *Endgame*. Is that right, or have I mixed something up?'

'No, that's right. How do you know?' She'd startled me again. 'If *I'm* not mistaken, you weren't there.'

'You're not the only one who knows everything,' she replied, with a meaningful look. 'I know a few things, too.' She gave me that sly smile again. 'But in this case the answer's quite simple: my deputy, Mr . . . Mr . . . oh, what *is* his name?' She snapped her fingers impatiently, feigning a temporary memory block. 'What do you people call him?'

'The Tapeworm.'

'*Voilà!* Well, Mr T. showed me your script.'

'Ah, so it was *your* doing!' I laughed bitterly. '*You're* the one who had it stopped! Well, well. The things one learns.'

'Me?' she cried cheerfully. 'I had nothing to do with it.'

'Nothing to do with it? You just told me he showed you the script.'

'Yes, and?'

'Why would he have done that unless it was to ask you to decide?'

'I did decide. In favour.'

'If that's the case, then why the refusal?'

'Oh, he tried to convince me that it was too gloomy . . .

not patriotic enough . . . not really the kind of thing we wanted, and so on. *Defeatist*, he called it.'

'And what did you say?'

'I told him, quite calmly, that if that was what he really thought, he should forbid it.'

'Covering your . . . back, in other words.'

'Possibly. On the other hand, sometimes it's better to give in, especially on a minor point, in order to get your way elsewhere – about something more important.'

'I wonder what that could be,' I challenged her.

'Co-operation and harmony,' she replied with a straight face. 'Not to mention,' she added severely, 'getting you out of the mess you got yourself into with that *maximalism* of yours, in other words your sheer stupidity with your biology teacher.'

'She was offensive!' I objected. The words came out in a hysterical sort of shriek. 'Besides, she was insulting about you,' I added sycophantically.

'So, my knight in shining armour had to stand on his honour!'

'Such is his custom,' I replied, mentally flinging my cloak over my shoulder.

'That means he hasn't read *Lancelot* carefully enough.'

'True,' I said. 'I wanted to read it with you.'

'Now *there* was a knight who knew when to swallow his pride. Well, but that isn't what I want to talk about now. Do you remember the play?'

'*Endgame*? A bit.'

'Did you read it in the original?'

'No, only in translation.'

'Yes, I see . . .'

'Meaning what?'

'Meaning that you *can't* know it – even if you know it by heart.'

'That's rather extreme. Is the translation really so bad?'

'*Pour en dire le moins*, to put it mildly.'

'Well, anyway, what about it?'

'I wonder if you remember any of the words spoken by . . . the only female character in it.'

'You mean Nell?'

'Very good! You know her name, at least. What about her lines, do you remember anything of them?'

I exerted my prodigious memory. It yielded nothing. Not a word.

There was a moment of silence.

'That's what I thought,' she said, breaking it finally. 'Of course! Who would remember the prattling of a woman, a crippled old woman at that! You only remember what the men say, don't you? Naturally – everyone does.'

'What about Phaedra?'

'It's generally agreed that Phaedra is really a man,' she replied with a dismissive smile. 'She wants the impossible. Just like Virgo in your Zodiac.' She glanced at me. 'But Nell – Nell is a woman. Not just nominally. Completely.'

Finally something did float up to the surface of my memory. '*What is it, my pet? Time for love?*' I recited.

The look of derision on her face gave way to one of pity.

'Did I get it wrong?' I asked.

'No, it was fine. Perfect,' she said ironically. 'And that's it, isn't it? That's all you remember?'

'I think I must have remembered it because it's the first thing she says,' I tried to explain, 'and because it's funny.'

'*Rien n'est plus drôle que le malheur* – there's nothing so funny as unhappiness,' she said slowly, looking into my eyes, as if she meant to suggest that the words applied to me, that my unhappiness was somehow comic.

'I'm sorry, was that supposed to be about me?'

'Of course not!' she protested. 'Just another quotation.'

'Is that the one you meant?'

'Not quite.' Her thoughts seemed to be elsewhere.

There was another moment of silence.

I felt a growing tension. By now we had entered the housing estate; a few short paths were all that separated us from the goal. Thoughtlessly, involuntarily, I quickened my pace.

'And where do you think you're going?' she asked, halting at a point where several paths diverged. I had automatically taken the one that led most directly to her building.

'I don't know,' I stammered, 'I've really no idea . . . absent-mindedness, I suppose. I was trying to remember the words and . . . I just walked on without thinking.'

She studied me intently for a moment, then set off down the path that led straight ahead. I followed.

'Now there,' she resumed, again as if she were returning to the subject of an interrupted conversation, 'there you have another writer who chose a foreign language.'

'Who?' Still not quite recovered from my slip, I was momentarily lost.

'Who! The author of *Endgame,* of course.'

'Ah, yes. Well, what of it?'

'Nothing. I'm just telling you.' She shrugged. 'You asked me for extra coaching . . . for what the physics teacher gives Roz Goltz. So I'm fulfilling your request. I'm giving you a special lesson. In the theory of relativity – of languages.'

'Well, here we are,' she announced with a smile. (Her house was another hundred yards away.) 'Thank you, my knight. And here's a *cadeau* from *Madame le professeur.*' She opened her bag and delved inside.

My eye was immediately drawn to something green protruding from an inner pocket, a small booklet with the words 'Special Passport' on it.

Madame's hand, meanwhile, had emerged from the bag holding a small book with a white cover which she handed to me.

The title, printed in light blue under the author's name, was arranged in a sort of pyramid:

FIN DE PARTIE
suivi de
Acte sans paroles*

On the bottom it said 'Les Editions de Minuit' and in between was a five-pointed star intertwined with a lowercase *m.*

'It's like a description of the scene with Paolo and Francesca,' I said in an undertone, staring at the cover.

---

*ENDGAME, followed by Act without Words

'With whom?' She snapped the bag shut.

'I told you about them once. They're the ones who were reading about Lancelot, and then they stopped reading and . . . "*read no more*".'

'That's what usually happens,' she said, spreading her hands as if to say, That's how it is! *C'est la vie!*

'Would you inscribe it for me?' I asked, searching desperately for a move that would prolong the game, even if only for a moment. 'A book without an inscription . . .'

'Who said there wasn't an inscription? It's there; everything is as it should be.'

I peeked inside the cover. On the title page were four pencilled lines:

> See page thirty-two, Nell's last word.
> An adjective? or a verb in the imperative?
> Your French studies are ended; this is the last question.
> *Pour mon meilleur disciple.*
> 24 June.

'In pencil? And unsigned?' I looked up at her.

'Is there anyone else who could have written that to you?' she asked flirtatiously.

'No – I suppose not.'

'Well, then. And it's in pencil because . . . well, who knows? You might want to erase it one day.'

'The form of this inscription,' I began enigmatically, 'even its rhythm' – I paused, maintaining the suspense – 'seems somehow familiar.'

'How so?' she asked matter-of-factly.

'I read a similar inscription written to someone by' – here I paused and looked into her eyes, but at the last minute swerved from my course and finished calmly – 'Joanna Schopenhauer.'

'I assure you I don't know it.' She held up her hand in oath.

I leafed through the book, looking for page thirty-two.

'Not now,' she said, with a restraining touch of her hand on my arm. 'Later. When you get home.'

Now! said the voice in my head. Not later, now! *Now* is the time to swallow your pride!

I took hold of her hand and looked into her eyes again.

'We've had the *Fin de partie*,' I began. My heart was pounding. 'And now it's time for *Acte sans paroles*.' And slowly, in the way I had seen it done in countless films, I approached her lips with mine.

'*Non*,' she said, and stopped me, literally at the last moment. 'That would be terribly kitsch. And you don't like kitsch.'

I swallowed nervously and hung my head. So it's not to be, after all, I thought.

Then she said, '*Non . . . pas cette fois . . . pas encore. Et pas ici, bien sûr.*' After a pause she added, '*Un jour . . . ailleurs . . . peut-être. Quand ton oeuvre sera finie.*'*

I raised my eyes to her face. She ruffled my hair affectionately. Then she turned and walked briskly away. She reached another fork in the paths, turned down one of them and disappeared from view around the side of the building.

I raised the book to my eyes and found page thirty-two, and on it Nell's last word.

The word was: '*Déserte*.'

L'âge viril

There is surely no need to describe my feelings after the events of that Midsummer's Eve – my 'Walpurgisnacht', as I thought of it. Sleep was out of the question. And the following day a kind of choking weight oppressed me. All the questions and anxieties that had plagued me for the past months resurfaced with renewed urgency.

What did it mean? What did she know about me – and about what I knew about her? What did she really want? How was I to read her, with her oscillations between extremes, her

*No . . . not this time . . . not yet. And, of course, not here. One day . . . elsewhere . . . perhaps. When your book is finished.

'ice' and her 'fire': one moment treating me with disdain or behaving as if I simply wasn't there, and the next bestowing those special attentions, and sometimes those suggestive, disturbing expressions of affection? And that final meeting: the dance, the memento, the inscription. Regardless of its message, it *was* very like the one her mother had written for Constant in the Gdansk edition of Joanna Schopenhauer's memoirs. Did she know of it? Did she know anything at all? If she did, why should she want to play these games with me? And those last words of hers, those words she'd spoken in French when, 'plummetting from the heights', I'd lowered my eyes and bent my head – had they been serious or in jest? Spoken in good faith or just carelessly thrown out? Did they express a kind of hope, and a desire to keep it alive, or were they just words – meaningless phrases, cheap, stale clichés snatched at random from the standard repertoire of casual flirtation?

Now, as before, my conjectures and attempts at analysis came to naught. I reached no convincing conclusion I could hold on to. But this time the thorn that pricked my heart was so deeply embedded I couldn't bear the pain. I had to do something.

Phone her, I thought the next morning. Make some use of the phone number I had found that day so long ago. Ask her to meet me and demand an explanation. And if she finds an excuse to avoid a meeting, turn up at her door.

In my mind I began composing the speech I would make to her. 'I've come. I had to see you,' I would say. 'We have to talk. Please tell me, tell me honestly and without hedging and beating about the bush, what you know about me and what you think of me and what you want from me. You can't leave me with these questions unanswered. What did you mean by telling me to run away – to desert? Where to? When, and how? And why – what are *your* motives in telling me this? And what did you mean by that "one day" when my *oeuvre* is finished? Do you really believe that? Did you mean it seriously or was it just empty talk? It's important to me, I've got to know.'

I snatched up the phone and dialled her number. No answer. I kept trying, at first every half hour, and then every few minutes. Still nothing. Silence.

I gulped down a double shot of vodka and set off for her flat.

It was about one o'clock in the afternoon, and the weather was hot and sunny. The blinds in both windows were down. My pulse quickened. She's asleep, I thought as I climbed the stairs, sleeping off last night. She's unplugged the phone. She's undressed. Is she naked? In a nightgown? A dressing-gown, perhaps? A push on the bell (of the 'ding-dong' type) brought none of the expected results. No footsteps, no 'Who is it?', no opening of the door; not a sound. Complete silence. I pressed my ear to the door and kept it there for a long time, trying to detect some sign of life, to see if perhaps she was skulking inside, pretending to be out. Not a murmur.

Like Jean-Louis racing back to Deauville after not finding Anne at home, I jumped on the bus and went to the school.

I found people in the process of cleaning up after the prom. Madame's office was locked. Making up some story about a missing signature on my university application, I asked the secretary in the horn-rimmed spectacles where the headmistress was.

'The headmistress,' she muttered indifferently, not bothering to look up, 'is not here. She's gone away on a training course.'

'Not here?' I blurted out, unable to control my voice or even what I said. 'But she was just here –'

'Yes, but now she's gone,' observed Horn-Rims with a sour smile.

'But . . . what am I going to do now?' I said helplessly.

'You could go to the train station, if it's really so important,' she advised with a sneer. 'Maybe you can still catch her.'

'Are you serious?' I clutched at the suggestion like a drowning man at the proverbial straw. 'Which station? When does the train leave?'

'How should I know?' She shrugged. '*I'm* just the menial around here; no one ever tells *me* anything. Such information is not for the likes of *me* – a mere secretary. I only *happened* to overhear that it was the Gdansk station, apparently. Sometime in the afternoon. Around now.'

I ran out of the secretary's office and raced to the train station.

From the viaduct I saw a long train made up of various carriages, both European and Soviet. Moscow–Warsaw–Paris, 15.10, announced the sign on the departures board. But this time the scene was like something from a bad film: when I ran onto the platform the train was just pulling out. I stood there as the different carriages passed me: first the green Soviet ones, then the French and German ones – the Western ones. Each displayed a board with the name of its destination. The one that rushed by most often said *Paris-Nord, Paris-Nord, Paris-Nord* . . .

The melancholy that weighed me down in the days that followed did not dissipate until the university entrance exams. Being forced to concentrate on achieving a specific goal was a blessing: there were tasks to be accomplished, things to be done and seen to, new people to meet, the competition to be contemplated – all the excitement and flurry of being part of the 'market'. The cloud lifted a little. But when it was over, when, in mid-July, my promotion to the status of university student had been confirmed and the prospect of summer holidays stretched before me, my 'disorder and early sorrow' threatened to return.

To escape it, I decided to go away. But not, as in recent years, to the Tatra mountains. This time I would go to the Baltic coast – to Gdansk, where I had spent childhood summers and still had a childhood friend, a boy slightly older than I was whose company I used to enjoy. I had found it both stimulating and soothing, and hoped that it would have the same effect now. Andy, for that was his name, inhabited a world completely different from mine. It was a world both useful and quantifiable, a world of technical problems and practical concerns: he was a ham radio operator, a model-maker, an angler; he owned a bicycle and a motorcycle; he was studying shipbuilding. Art and literature had never much interested him. I hoped we could recapture the old, carefree atmosphere of the holidays of our boyhood; perhaps an immersion in his simple, practical life might allay some of my restlessness and repair my shattered nerves, even bring about a complete cure and make me forget Madame.

I was not disappointed. The older, taller and more manly version of Andy was not so very different from the little boy I had known. He was still the 'good, reliable lad' he had always been, cheerful and down-to-earth, untouched by the poison of disenchantment. He greeted me as before, as if there had been no break in our summer meetings, as if time had stood still. Once again we were 'mates', 'best friends', schoolboys playing together; cheerful, open, pure-hearted little boys with innocent boyish dreams and untainted boyish souls. We played tennis, we went to the beach, we took long walks in the forest; everything was just as it had been all those years ago. Andy was putting together a radio of his own devising ('from the best transistors'); in the evenings we listened to 'Western' stations and Radio Luxembourg. We also rode, on his motorcycle, to the port and the shipyards, where from various spots on the jetty we could look at the ships – in the docks, sailing out of the harbour, on the horizon.

It was a pleasant time, carefree and nostalgic, like a miraculous and unexpected extension of childhood. A kind of coming back, to things and experiences I had thought beyond recapturing.

And then, one hot Sunday, when we were wandering aimlessly, 'as in the old days', around a quiet and remote part of the city, a strange thing happened. On Polanki Street Andy suddenly stopped, pointed to some old, dilapidated buildings horribly deformed by an ugly grey barracks and walls with barbed wire that had been built around them, and said something I would never have expected of him: 'Look, that used to be the summer house of the Schopenhauer family. You know what it is now? A kind of prison: a reformatory. Interesting taste our government has.'

I nodded, digesting this information in silence, betraying no interest, no hint that I knew the least thing about Schopenhauer. But the moment – the unexpected sight of that legendary house, its disrepair, the use currently being made of it – made an impression on me. I was strangely moved.

I began to go back there, without Andy, just to stand and look – at the house and the surroundings. Then I went to the

Old Town to see the house on the south side of Holy Spirit Street – the one in the frontispiece photograph of Joanna Schopenhauer's memoirs. I didn't find it, however. I learned later that it had not survived the war. There was nothing where it had once stood: just a flight of steps leading nowhere.

I don't know when the bubble burst, but suddenly the magic atmosphere of childhood regained was gone. Life was no longer cheerful and carefree. Andy's company became wearisome. His way of thinking, his interests, his sense of humour – all the traits once so soothing to my aching soul – now irritated me, seemed merely childish and naïve.

I wasn't sure what had caused the change. The unexpected sight of the Schopenhauers' house, presumably, but why? What did that old ruin have to do with me? Was it because somehow, by a very tortuous route, it was connected with Madame and by some strange alchemy had rekindled thoughts of her? Possibly. But it was more complex than that, and it wasn't until much later that I came to understand it fully. For the moment I wandered about in a fog, allowing myself to drift on the wave of thoughts and emotions which this strangely compelling atmosphere evoked.

I returned to Warsaw in an odd state of abstraction and excitement. My head teemed with ideas and images, phrases and dialogues that seemed to be forming themselves into fragments of a story. I lay on my bed, surrounded by books about Schopenhauer (mostly about his life), going over various details in my mind and developing them into scenes and conversations. Finally I began to write.

The idea was very simple, almost banal. Of the dozens of events in Schopenhauer's life that I had read about, I picked the two most influential ones – the 'load-bearing' ones, as it were: the death of his father, probably suicide, although the motives were obscure; and his violent breaking-off of relations with his mother, in the 1810s, in Weimar.

Both were tragic events, suffused with bitterness, disappointment and anger. The father departed this world a triply defeated and resentful man: because he had left Gdansk after the second partition of Poland, when that part of the country was occupied by the Prussians, and had never been able to get over it; because his marriage was not going well; and because his son Arthur, despite all efforts to make him a worthy successor at the head of a great merchant house, had failed to fulfil the hopes vested in him, and spent his time dreaming about . . . philosophy. After the father's death, the mother, Joanna, by then a woman past forty who had somehow managed, despite successive blows of fate, to maintain her high position in the world and reconstruct a life for herself (entering into a relationship with a man who was both town councillor and writer, and establishing a literary *salon* frequented by Goethe himself), found herself suffering dreadful humiliations at the hands of her wunderkind son, in the two (in this case equally delicate) spheres of finance and morals: Arthur destroyed her reputation, calumnied her in public, demanded that she break off relations with 'that man', and finally gave her an ultimatum: 'him or me'.

My description of these events, reconstructed from the available accounts, was interwoven with the thoughts and memories of the two protagonists, flashbacks to the time of that memorable trip through Western Europe: the time that began with Joanna's discovery of her pregnancy and ended with their return to Gdansk, her labour and Arthur's birth.

I created a sharp contrast between the dark, overcast mood of the present and the bright, sunny memories of the past. Arthur's father, gnawed by bitter resentment and regret, weary of life and convinced that his death would be a relief to everyone – his wife, who has grown cold towards him, and his son, who finds the idea of trade repellent – cultivates thoughts of putting an end to his life. And we see him standing by the crane of the grain silo from which the next day, in circumstances which are to remain obscure, he will fall to his death, gazing for a long time at the waters of the harbour canal and letting his thoughts wander to that night in Dover when he stood on the ship's deck, stood just as he is standing now, high up above the wharf, and, leaning over the railing, watched in suspense as the armchair containing his wife in her seventh month of pregnancy glided slowly upwards on its ropes. And he recalls the feeling and atmosphere of that moment: one that was, despite the suspense, cheerful and full of hope.

He remembers the words in which he had expressed that feeling: 'This is the most precious cargo I have ever transported,' he had said then, with a shade of irony. 'Well, he won't be born in England, as I wanted him to be – never mind. He'll be born in Gdansk. I'll give him the best life and education I can. I'll make him travel the world as early as possible; he'll learn foreign languages and foreign customs. I want him to be more of a man of the world than I. I shall call him Arthur.'

And we see Joanna after another round of 'family negotiations' devoted to abuse and invective from her ungrateful progeny, who treats her as if she were some vile Gertrude, hurling accusations of wanton shamelessness and betrayal, as she bursts into violent sobs and runs from the drawing-room, flees to her bedroom, and there, weeping, recalls the night in Westphalia when their carriage axle broke on a pothole and she was carried across the fields in the arms of an asthmatic giant who kept stopping and plumping her down unceremoniously every few steps to catch his breath.

'Oh, I should have miscarried then!' she cries bitterly. And when her daughter Adela, a kind-hearted but plain girl, reacts with a cry of shocked protest ('Mother, how can you say such a thing!'), she remembers that spring soon after their return, when she felt, as a new mother, happier than she had ever felt in her life, and her newborn son seemed the most beautiful, wonderful child on earth.

In short, it was a novella about the illusory nature of human hopes and dreams, darkly pessimistic and permeated by an unrelieved scepticism about the possibility of happiness. Happiness does not endure, the narrator seemed to be saying; it does not breed happiness. It can only be fleeting. Life's melody is a sad one, and if it is sometimes heard in a major key, it always ends in minor. A joyful, hopeful beginning must always be viewed from the perspective of the end.

I enjoyed writing it, and the process of writing brought a certain relief: it liberated me from something. It fulfilled an obscure longing. I seemed at last to have found the form in which I could assimilate love.

It didn't matter that what I wrote about had little to do with either my life or Madame's. Through a certain twist of fate, a concatenation of circumstances, writing about the Schopenhauers gave me access to things that were otherwise unattainable. It released thoughts and emotions I could express in no other way, and gave new form to that first, uncertain leap of the imagination I had made at the cinema the night I'd watched Madame from behind the curtain and suddenly seen her whole life in a flash, encapsulated in one brief paragraph.

I gave my novella the ironic title *The Shape of Hopes Fulfilled, or Two Scenes from the Life of Arthur Schopenhauer,* and realised suddenly that I was cured. Thinking of Madame no longer caused me pain. If I still desired anything, it was perhaps only that she should read what I had written.

With the start of the new academic year, therefore, I went back to the school to see if she had returned. I rather doubted it, but I wanted to make sure. It was as I had suspected: the school was in chaos; the Tapeworm had taken over the reins of power. Whether his accession was permanent or merely an interregnum was unclear. The 'ex-headmistress' was not a subject anyone was eager to discuss with me.

I showed my novella to Constant, who was pleasantly surprised. He suggested a few corrections and pronounced it publishable. It appeared in print about six months later, in a literary journal. By the end of my first year at university I had made my début on the literary scene.

The summer holidays came round again. And then, in September, something happened to disturb my peace once more.

The day after my twentieth birthday a package came from France. Although it was a small package, it was delivered by the parcel service, not by the postman. I even had to pay a charge before I could claim it. My name and address, both on the label and on the parcel service form, were not handwritten but typed, and the space intended for the return address bore the stamp and logo of a firm whose name meant nothing to me. I had not the faintest idea, as I unwrapped it, who it was from or what it could contain. Even when I had removed the brown paper and saw the object within – a flat black box with a coloured picture of Mozart as a small child and the words '*Hommage à Wolfgang Amadeus Mozart*' engraved in flowery gold letters – even then I still didn't know.

It didn't hit me until I opened the box.

Inside, held fast in a decorative support and cushioned on a bed of velvet, was a fountain pen. It was black and extremely elegant. On the narrow gold band encircling the cap were three words: '*Meisterstück*' and '*Mont Blanc*'.

I gazed at it motionless, still unbelieving. After all, there was no evidence.

Then I found it.

There was an envelope stuck to the bottom of the box, and in it a colour postcard of Mont Blanc. On turning it over, I found a few lines of writing. Inscribed in pencil, and in a familiar hand, were the following words:

> *Tout ce qui naît d'une source pure est un mystère.*
> *A peine si la poésie elle-même ose le dévoiler.*
> Have you found the answer to my last question?
> Instructions inside.

Shakily, I examined the box to see where else, apart from the velvet bed on which the pen reposed, 'inside' might refer to. Finally I found it. The box had a sort of false bottom: the black velvet covered a removable cardboard *passe-partout*. I removed it. Underneath was a gilt-edged card on which, neatly centred and in beautiful calligraphy, were six short, black lines of writing, in ink this time, in Madame's hand. They read as follows:

De la part du Verseau dans la force de l'âge
pour la Vierge à l'âge viril
(depuis le dix septembre)
au lieu d'une plume d'oie

avec les meilleurs souhaits
de courage et de . . .
*Victoire**

I stared transfixed at this signal, this complex construction of words and objects, mentally unwrapping it further, peeling off successive layers of meaning to find deeper and deeper ones as its significance seeped in. There were so many implications to consider! There was the 'first cause' itself – the fact that she had sent this at all, that she had remembered my twentieth birthday and decided to give me a present. There was the embodiment of that idea, the object – a Mont Blanc pen from the '*Hommage à Mozart*' series. Finally, there was the message – the inscription on the gold-edged card.

She knew when my birthday was – and had remembered it. She knew my address. How? She may have found it in the school records, but in that case she must have written it down and taken it with her – and why would she have done that? On the other hand, where and how else could she have got it? Then there was the message: she remembered that 'last question' in her inscription and she remembered my essay – remembered it well. The underlining of those three letters was a subtle allusion to a tiny detail: my grotesque, pseudo-scholarly argument that the word '*virginité*' supposedly comes from the Latin '*vir*'. '*Vir*', she was saying by that underlining, 'is the root of *viril*, the adjective which properly qualifies your current condition – not of *virginité,* as you insisted then.' And her choice of gift was a double allusion: to the way I had interpreted Virgo's occupation and to my avowed desire to be a writer.

In the extraordinary memory, the precision, the attention to detail, I saw a trace, a distant echo, of her father, the Max Constant had described to me. I remembered the story of their meeting on the sixth of August, at noon, in front of the railway station in a little Swiss mountain town, as arranged, on Max's

---

*From Aquarius in his prime to Virgo in the age of virility (since the tenth of September), instead of a goose-quill pen, with best wishes for courage and for . . . victory.

initiative, eight months earlier, on the spur of the moment in a Warsaw street.

But there was more. Embedded in the mosaic she had sent were pieces of rock from geological strata of her life about which 'officially' I knew nothing. The postcard with the view of Mont Blanc, the phrase '*la force de l'âge*', and that final 'Victoire', with its capital letter and dual function – as the complement of '*souhaits*', but also as a proper name – her signature. Of course, it could all be explained differently: the postcard of Mont Blanc could have been picked simply because it made a nice allusion to the pen; it wasn't necessarily a reference to her father's hopes and dreams about her birthplace. The phrase '*la force de l'âge*' was a common one; it needn't be an allusion to Simone de Beauvoir. That final 'Victoire' could, after all, be an allusion to the last words of my essay or to Conrad's *Victory,* which my *Cahier des citations* had copiously quoted.

But I didn't believe it. I believed these were signals connected with the deep currents of her life. But if so, if they were indeed references to her 'personal data', then several questions arose. Should I conclude that she was aware of how much I knew about her? Yet how on earth could she have found out? Who could have told her? And why was she letting me know it now? What was she playing at, and why? What did she intend? What did she want to achieve?

And the last, crucial question: did this whole surprise have any connection with my *oeuvre* – my recent literary début? Could she have read my story? How? Where? And what, in that case, did it mean? 'You write nicely, my knight. So now . . . now write something for me. As a token of your love, a tribute to your Mozart'?

I went to see Constant and asked him straight out whether he'd talked to anyone about my novella. He said yes, he'd mentioned it to a few friends. Had he sent it to someone abroad, by any chance? He stared at me in surprise. I took the postcard of Mont Blanc and my new fountain pen out of my pocket, handed them to him, and said 'These just came for me from France. Through the post. Have you any idea who they could be from?'

He examined the pen, nodding appreciatively, then glanced at the postcard and gave a faint smile. But when he turned it over and saw what was written on the back his whole body tensed. He gazed at it in silence.

'Well, what do you think?' I asked finally.

'I don't know what to think of it,' he replied, his voice strangely changed.

'Of what, exactly?' I persisted, feigning bafflement.

He went over to the little shelf with the lamp and again took out the old, paper-covered book; again he opened it to the title page. Then he placed the postcard with the view of Mont Blanc alongside the faded lines inscribed there, and for a long time studied the two texts thus juxtaposed.

'You know where this quotation comes from,' he said, pointing to the two lines of French. It was a statement, not a question.

'Yes, of course,' I replied, smiling inwardly at the sight of my mentor falling victim to his own boomerang, which he had thrown at me almost two years earlier. 'From Hölderlin's *Rhine* hymn.'

'Yes,' he muttered absently, 'but from which bit exactly?'

As the question fell, my self-confidence suddenly left me; in that one moment, the feeling of being in control, of performing, like a magician amusing himself with his tricks, ebbed away and dissolved. For it was a question I had never thought to ask myself. Absorbed in reading between the lines and deciphering the message's subtle allusions, I hadn't paid much attention to the quotation; my eyes had slid over it, noting it but for some reason treating it as something obvious, not needing interpretation or analysis. After all, it was in my *Cahier des citations*, which she had read – or at least kept, for some days, in her possession. My mind must have decided that this was explanation enough, and passed on. Now, belatedly, I saw that it was far from adequate. The quotation in my *Cahier des citations* had been in German, and it had not been among the lines I had singled out as the most 'significant' by underlining them and writing out Constant's translation alongside: the lines her mother had inscribed in Constant's copy of the memoirs. Why, then, had she picked *this* particular quotation and not any of the others? Because it went well with the photograph?

But there was no spring, no source, on Mont Blanc! Those lines were about the mystery of the Rhine, which flows from elsewhere. And finally, how had she come by the French version? Had she gone to the trouble of digging up a translation (as I had done at the Centre)? Or had she translated them herself? In both cases she would have to know German. But did she? Where was the truth in all this?

Trying to disguise my confusion, I asked casually, 'What does it matter which bit?'

'What does it matter?' He gave an odd smile. 'Listen: "The pure of source is always a mystery. Even song can scarcely unveil it." This,' he said, tapping the postcard with his finger, 'comes directly before the passage inscribed here.' He tapped the book. 'These are the next lines . . . how does she know that?' he added, almost in a whisper.

'How does *who* know?' I asked, still feigning innocence.

'Oh, come on, stop playing around,' he muttered impatiently. 'Honestly, I don't know why you persist in this charade.'

'Because I don't understand it myself,' I admitted, discarding my mask. 'I thought you might have something to do with it. Now I see I was wrong. I take it you don't know her address in France?'

'Wasn't it on the envelope?'

'If it had been, I wouldn't be bothering you with all this.'

'No, I don't,' he replied. 'I believe I told you she'd broken off all contact with me.'

'She could have renewed it.'

'She could have. But she didn't.'

'And Mr – Freddy, I mean – does *he* know anything?'

'About what?' His mind was clearly elsewhere.

'What's become of her. Where she lives, and so on.'

'I doubt it. But I don't really know.' He shrugged and put the worn, paper-covered *Jugendleben* back in its place on the shelf. 'Why don't you ask him? Ask around; ask the people at the Centre.'

I asked him. I asked around. I asked everyone I could think of.

They all shook their heads. No one knew.

SEVEN

Classroom Experience

Should I go on? Well, the story doesn't end here. So I'll go on.

My university days were exciting and turbulent, but they were also depressing. Turbulent because many things happened in my life during that time, and depressing because the authorities, after some years of relative moderation in their harassment of citizens and devastation of the country, again bared their claws and showed their uglier side.

I read, I studied, I perfected my craft. I discovered various pleasures of life, availing myself of the freedoms that come with maturity. I conspired with an innocent and hopeful heart against the regime and gradually became a fully fledged participant in the dissident movement. Around me, in the meantime, things were worsening: the government indulged in ever harsher and more despicable acts of repression; it grew violent and unrestrained. In 1968 there was the campaign against Jews and the intelligentsia; then Czechoslovakia, and Poland's part in the provision of 'fraternal aid'; finally plain slaughter, in good old Moscow style, in Gdansk and especially in Gdynia.

Well, I had what I wanted: vivid experiences! Strong emotions! Thrills and chills! History with a capital 'H': here it was, in the making. I certainly couldn't complain that life was bland or boring. My dream of 'living in interesting times' had been fulfilled, with a vengeance.

The manner of its fulfilment was bitter enough, but the irony was that my experience of its 'inspiring' and 'uplifting' power was not confined to what reached me, in the safety of my armchair, through the press, the radio or the television news: as a student, and especially as a fledgling author, I felt its effects more directly.

After the purge at Warsaw University, the standard of lectures and seminars fell dramatically; at the same time the number of restrictions rose and discipline became draconian. The infamous Dr Dolowy became chairman of the department; Professor Levittoux emigrated; Freddy, who in any case had for years been relegated to the margins of departmental life, now found himself completely shunted aside. Mediocrities triumphed; opportunists and sycophants, envious and frustrated second-raters had their day. It became clear to me that there was nothing to be hoped for there; I would have to look to myself and forge my destiny alone. Which in fact accorded perfectly with my aspirations.

So I wrote. I lived in a world of imagination and form. I felt independent and free. But this solution had its limits. After all, I wanted to be a writer: sooner or later, if I considered my writing not – at least not mainly – as a means of self-defence but as an attempt to create art, I would have to go out and present it to the world. And that was where the awful madness began: the attacks on one's dignity, the injuries to one's pride, the agonies of humiliation. For although my work had little to do with current events and nothing at all with the world of the 'leading political system', the censors always found grounds for suspicion. They made constant demands for changes, cuts, or at least so-called negotiations, which could end only in so-called compromise, even if it was just over a minor detail. I got the impression that their true purpose was not so much guarding and preserving purity of thought as systematically breaking the will of authors: making it abundantly clear to them that they were insignificant, superfluous creatures who, if they refused to agree to the conditions of the game, would cease to exist as authors altogether.

The censors seemed to be negatively predisposed from the beginning, whatever was brought to them. Every writer lived in fear of them, even if he had only composed a little poem about flies and insects. 'Why flies?' they would say. 'And insects to boot! Are you implying something about dirt and disease? Is that what you meant? No, no, we can't have that. If you really want to write about the beauty of nature in our country, then go and write about butterflies and ants – industrious creatures, ants.' But if you came in with a poem about butterflies and ants, they would say, 'Why ants? Are you implying our country is an ant colony, some kind of giant machine in which our citizens are interchangeable robots? That the individual doesn't count, is merely a cog in the wheel? No, no, that's unacceptable. These aren't Stalinist times! The day of errors and distortions are long past.'

When I finished my second novella, *An Encounter with Dionysus* – about Hölderlin's journey on foot across the Alps, his vision of Dionysus and his ensuing madness – and submitted it for publication, I was asked (the question would have been typical of the Tapeworm) why I had chosen as my hero a man heralded by Goebbels as the 'standard-bearer of the Third Reich'. My explanatory efforts, backed up by voluminous documentation (naturally from books published in East Germany) attesting unequivocally that this was a sacrilegious act of slander on Goebbels's part, were received reluctantly, with suspicion and mistrust. After raising endless objections and difficulties, the all-knowing censor, clearly a philosophy graduate, eventually passed the text but made it clear to the editor of the journal where it was to appear that he knew perfectly well 'what was really going on here': it was a blatant attempt, he said, to 'propagate Western intellectual trends, existentialism among others', since 'that notorious fascist, Heidegger, one of its pillars', had been interested in Hölderlin.

But this was nothing compared to the battle I had to wage to publish my third story in this cycle about journeys (the idea that had germinated at school), a novella entitled *Monsieur le Marquis*, about the Marquis de Custine in Russia in 1839.

I was fully aware of the risks involved. For although the target of Custine's literary thrusts and the object of discontent of the 'Russian masses' and 'Great October' revolutionaries were one and the same, namely the rule of the tsars, that 'despicable system of exploitation and humiliation', the Marquis was looked upon with great disfavour in the 'motherland of the proletariat'. What was sauce for the masses, especially for the Bolsheviks, was not necessarily sauce for anyone else, certainly not for a Frenchman of the minor nobility. It was not Custine's blue blood, however, or the fact that he was French, or even his breathtaking insolence in daring to violate the carefully guarded Bolshevik monopoly on criticising the tsars, that inspired such loathing. What really rankled was that his vision of Tsar Nicholas's Russia was unflattering to Russia in general (this by itself was blasphemy); worse, he had managed, quite unintentionally and from beyond the grave, to sow seeds of doubt about the claim that the Revolution had brought liberation and that communist Russia was the embodiment of the greatest freedom in the history of the world, and to expose this claim as the complete and monstrous lie that it was. When one read his 'Letters' – accounts of customs at the Romanov court, of human relations, of city and country life – one could not shake off the persistent impression that one was reading a report about the Soviet Union; one even found oneself harbouring the germ of an even more outrageous, truly criminal suspicion, namely that the days of the tsars were child's play compared to life under the communists, that the latter by far surpassed in cruelty, oppression and destruction the worst excesses of the former.

The Marquis de Custine's wonderful account did not exist in Polish (it could have been published in Poland in the interwar period or by a Polish press abroad, but it hadn't been). So my approach was rather different from the one I had taken in my previous two novellas. This time the facts themselves occupied the foreground, not my imagination or my interpretation of them. I saw it as my task to revive the memory of the marquis and his journey by sketching a few of the episodes described in his account and quoting from selected passages; I kept myself in the background. Here my aim was to render a service to history by smuggling into my novella a small glimpse of historical truth which otherwise would never be permitted to enter the consciousness of the people living in the People's Republic of Poland.

I had barely submitted the text before the difficulties began. 'You haven't got a hope in hell,' pronounced all the editors, even the braver ones, whose support I could usually count on.

'What on earth were you thinking, choosing a subject like this? Don't you know where we are?'

But I was obdurate. I insisted on taking the risk of sending it to the censors. And so, in the end, it was sent. The answer, when it came, was not the categorical 'no' I had feared, although substantial changes and cuts were demanded. Mostly these concerned the quotations from Custine that I had translated and incorporated, but a few remarks of mine, too, had been found objectionable.

The negotiations began. And that was when I had my first taste of defeat. Psychologically, the battle I had embarked on was rather like gambling: addictive in a similar way. And the strange thing was that as one gave in and bowed to the censor's demands, the desire to see one's work published, instead of weakening, became progressively stronger. Tempting voices, internal and external, whispered, You've already given way on so much; why are you suddenly digging in your heels about this trivial little detail? It's only an ornament, after all; what does it add? Nothing! Do you really want to risk forfeiting everything because of *this*? But if you agree to take it out or substitute another word, we'll pass it, and you've got another publication to your credit.

I cut, I made changes, I hedged; I tried to be as devious as I could. I succumbed to the illusion that I was cleverer than they were. The process went on for weeks. Finally the thing appeared in print. It was changed beyond recognition – a different text. I felt wretched, disgusted at myself for what I had done: it was vile, despicable. I was a nervous wreck. The praise of friends, the signs of appreciation from university colleagues, brought me no relief, let alone satisfaction. The opponent had won: I had allowed myself to be drawn into the game and to become dependent on him. I had given in; I had been broken. My self-respect was in shreds.

Yet the compromise turned out to be beneficial, for the Custine novella speeded up the appearance of my first book. (This in itself, of course, was instructive: an excellent lesson in the do-it-yourself method of degradation.) As I neared the end of my fourth year at university I had a volume of stories to my credit. It bore the old-fashioned title *Romantic Journeys*.

And that was when the Flausch affair erupted.

Dr Ignatius Flausch was head of the departmental section that dealt with methods of language teaching. Academically the section was poor and the people who taught the subject mediocre, but for reasons of politics or ideology it was considered important. In a socialist state ('by definition in every way superior to bourgeois states'), university departments of Romance languages (or any other 'Western' languages, for that matter) existed principally in order to train 'language personnel', not to produce scholars in literature and the humanities. The latter were considered marginal: after all, what use were they? What were they *for*? What we needed were people with a knowledge of foreign languages who could be useful in the diplomatic service and in foreign trade, or who could give courses and lectures and teach in schools.

For this reason Dr Flausch, along with his subordinates, however incompetent he was at the task assigned to him (the teaching section had the lowest reputation), was able to throw his weight around the department and interfere in everything.

He was no longer a young man (Freddy called him a 'prewar mediocrity'), and his personality was reminiscent of the Eunuch, the Tapeworm and the Viper. In other words, he was irritable and neurotic, suffered from an inferiority complex and at every turn demanded tributes and expressions of respect for his high position.

To his chagrin, his lectures, excruciatingly boring and a complete waste of time, were not obligatory but merely 'recommended'. In spite of this, everyone meekly went to them, for word had gone round that Flausch mercilessly revenged himself on absentees by withholding credit for the course. At the beginning I, too, succumbed to the mass psychosis and took my seat in the lecture room. After a while, however, my capacity for boredom and boundless idiocy had been surpassed, and I could endure no more. Trusting to the letter of the law (which clearly said: 'not obligatory') and to my own strong position (I had a high average in the main subjects), and believing, furthermore, that all I needed to do to pass the orals was read the good doctor's *magnum opus* (a thin booklet entitled *A Short Course in Methods of Teaching French*), I stopped attending.

At the orals I stood before the severe visage of the Great Methodist for the first time. I was fairly confident. I had familiarised myself with his 'fundamental work', a mishmash of the obvious and the ridiculous; I could have reeled off whole passages by heart, it was so simple-minded. And I had already passed (with flying colours) the final exams in all the other subjects, which strengthened my position. In addition, I was in the midst of my first literary triumphs, which I would have thought indicated well enough my interests and ambitions for the future.

I was wrong. The local lore proved true. The price of failing to bestow upon the good doctor the respectful attentions he considered his due was indeed as high as all the tales claimed.

He questioned me at length, intensely, maliciously, on subjects that were not covered in the syllabus. At the end he pronounced ceremoniously that I was unfortunately not yet ready to teach a foreign-language course, certainly not in a school. I assured him, half-joking, that I was not shattered by the news, for I entertained no plans of doing so. This innocent reply clearly provoked him. He smiled acidly and said with insincere concern, 'You never know': I might be convinced *now* that I could become God Almighty and conquer the world, but I might end up as an ordinary schoolteacher. And it was he, Dr Flausch, who bore the responsibility for how well I fulfilled this honourable but difficult role. It was hereby his duty to declare that I would fulfil it exceedingly ill.

This was too much. The soul of the artist in me rebelled. Here I was, the darling of the department, fresh from my literary début – the affront to my pride was too great. I rose, said I would survive the blow somehow, and wished him luck with students more adept than I.

Of course a monstrous row erupted. Flausch demanded a disciplinary hearing and refused even to consider the possibility of my being allowed to retake the exam. I was locked in a head-on conflict – just like the affair with the Viper years ago.

My God, I thought; will my schooldays never come to an end?!

Frankly I'm not sure how it would have ended had it not been for Freddy, who at some point leapt into the fray and helped me disentangle myself. He summoned me for a talk and advised me in the strongest terms to go through the obligatory period of teaching practice, even though I hadn't been given credit for the pedagogy course, and try to make a good impression on the senior teachers. He would see to the rest: have a 'suitable talk' with Dolowy – *Dr* Dolowy, our honourable chairman – and persuade him to let me have someone other than Dr Flausch as my examiner in this wretched subject, 'given the regrettable misunderstandings that have accidentally arisen'.

This plan was my only salvation. But what did it mean in practice? It meant that in September, instead of enjoying a peaceful holiday, as in recent years, I'd have to go back to school; and that there was hard work ahead. I'd have to put my nose to the grindstone if I wanted a favourable evaluation of my pedagogical skills. I rebelled at these prospects. The thought of poring over textbooks, drawing up lesson plans and learning how to teach grammar and pronunciation was nightmarish.

I started to look for ways of avoiding this reef. How could I chalk up credit for classroom experience and get good marks without too much effort – just for my pretty face, as it were? Then it struck me: my old school! Do it there. It was the obvious way. Walk in with a smile and play the prodigal son returning to the bosom of his old family; a clever performance would win me the favour and sympathy of my old teachers. As for the language teachers (doubtless complete mediocrities), I could dazzle them with my accent, my erudition and my memory. I could twist them all around my little finger and walk off with an A.

I submitted the necessary forms, and at the beginning of September again found myself in the place where almost half my life had been spent, and where I had last set foot five years ago: back at school, within the old, familiar walls.

* * *

As I set off on the first day I felt a little like Jozio, the hero of Gombrowicz's novel *Ferdydurke,* abducted at a mature age by Professor Pimko and forcibly installed in the temple of Immaturity. For it did feel like something out of a bad dream. Here I was, a twenty-three-year-old Spirit, soon to be Master of Arts, an Artist, Author of a Published Book hailed by the critics as a 'brilliant début' – back at school! In principle as a trainee teacher but still, in a way, as a pupil. At any rate a degraded creature, thrown back into a world of immaturity and childishness, embodied both by the 'ancients' (the teachers) and by the 'young' (the pupils).

'I'll be squashed,' I thought, in Jozio's words at the beginning of the book, 'humiliated and crumpled and crushed.' Reduced once more to a blushing, shamefaced child.

In the event, things turned out incomparably better than I'd expected. My old teachers received me with ordinary, respectful politeness, even some affection; there were no embarrassing remarks or patronising jokes. The new ones, particularly the French teachers, who were supposed to be doing the evaluating, seemed quite sensible, and appeared to treat my training period purely as a formality. And the pupils, especially the older ones, weren't all that trying: not insubordinate, insolent or difficult. If anything, they were overly bland: polite and submissive, without verve, initiative or humour. There was no fire there, no imagination, no spark. Finally, the classroom training itself was far less taxing than I had feared. It consisted mostly in my being present at lessons and taking notes on how they were run and the material they covered. I only had to teach four lessons myself – at four different levels – and that wasn't until the very end, after a month of passive observation.

Boredom, rather than any threat or insult to my new maturity and dignity as an 'artist', was my main complaint. And this was probably why, sitting there in the last row, as I had sat five years before, listening to the lessons, I found myself going back in time. Old thoughts, old dreams came floating back; old passions were rekindled. And at some point, insidiously, without my being aware that it was happening, Madame revived in me: her mystery and her magic, her beauty and her power, and that obscure longing she inspired.

The memory of her pulled me deeper and deeper; it drew me like a drug. After school I would wander listlessly about Zeromski Park in the golden autumn sunlight, and my heart was again painfully alive. Where was she? What was she doing? What would it be like if we met now? If she were still teaching?

I would come home gloomy and restless, take out the postcard with the view of Mont Blanc, stand it up on my desk and in front of it, as before an altar, place my three relics: the copy of *Fin de partie*, the '*Hommage à Mozart*' fountain pen, and a folded handkerchief with a label that said 'Made in France'. The scent of Chanel had long evaporated; only a few blackened spots of blood remained.

I don't even have a photograph of her, I thought sentimentally. Who was she? Who *is* she? I'll never know. *Can* one ever know such a thing about someone?

Then I had an inspiration. It was a sort of twist on Schopenhauer's idea that by treating oneself as a thing-in-itself one can come to know from the *inside* what is unknowable objectively, from the outside.

I *can* possess her, I thought; I *can* penetrate her mind. I can *become* her, and by becoming her know her at last. It would be a sort of embodiment.

Again, as so many times in the past, I set about preparing for lessons. My preparations, however, had little to do with accepted methods of teaching. I was writing a script and learning a role.

At last the time came for me to make my entrance on the stage of the classroom. I assumed my role; and I acted as I had never acted before. It was a brilliant performance. The passive, silent observer, the unremarkable student, was suddenly transformed into a star – a magician. A stream of pearly, perfect French issued from my lips; Polish was forbidden; the lesson whizzed along at a dizzying pace. Everything was *presto*. Conversation period, exercises, tests – not a moment's pause, not a moment's silence. If someone didn't know the answer, or made a mistake, or started stammering, I would cut him off and finish for him. I was like conductor and orchestra rolled into one, or like a virtuoso soloist who plays on regardless when the rest of the ensemble can't keep up or has lost the place. I deluged them with anecdotes, quoted passages of verse and plays (including Racine, naturally) from memory, dazzled them with my acting, my erudition, my wit. When they floundered or relapsed into dumb unresponsiveness, I knew how to prick them with just the right amount of biting irony. I held them spellbound. I was Prospero: a vision from another world – a 'world apart'.

And there was a message in the part I had created. I was saying to them, Look – you see? *This* is what a lesson should be; this is what teaching, and learning, can be like. This is what *life* can be like! *Your* life: you, too, can soar; you, too, can be like this! Of course, not all of you. Not everyone succeeds. But you have to try; you have to persist, make the effort to seek happiness. How? Very simply: by learning foreign languages; by mastering the art of speech, the art of using words. If you know how to *speak* – to speak intelligently, fluently and well – your poor, grey world will be illuminated. At least, it will become a little more colourful. Because it's from language that everything flows; it's on language that everything depends. Because, as the Scriptures say, in the beginning was the Word.

Thirty-odd pairs of eyes gazed at me with awe and devotion, as if I were a divinely inspired prophet. And sometimes, here and there, there was longing in their gaze – an obscure, blissfully painful longing. And sadness, because I would soon leave, and their holiday would come to an end. I was like a rarely seen comet that had passed the earth and was receding into the depths of the universe, perhaps never to be seen again.

I had succeeded: I had become Madame. I knew what it was like to be her; I felt her – through myself. I understood who she was and how, perhaps, she had seen me.

In the staff room, surrounded by my old, embittered teachers (the Tapeworm and the Viper among them), the French teachers were full of praise. 'Such talent! It's a gift! You're a born pedagogue! You should be teaching! Join us!'

I would smile sadly, as if to say, I'd like to, but I'm afraid

I can't; I have other plans, different ambitions, which call me. My place is elsewhere.

Then they would say, 'Oh, it's such a pity. Really, it is. You might be missing your true vocation.'

But the most extraordinary scene, at once funny and touching, took place on my last day – when, having finished my last lesson (with a final-year class) and duly received, from one of the French teachers, an enthusiastic evaluation of my performance, I was on my way out, bidding farewell to the school for the last time.

Those were the Days!

At the gate a member of my 'audience' was waiting for me – a boy in his final year, from the class I had just finished teaching. He was a thin, frail-looking boy with a pleasant face and dark, sad eyes. I'd been aware of him from my first class. He stood out not just because of his looks and his proficiency in French, but also because of his behaviour: he was clearly studying me with great attention and constantly tried to catch my eye. His answers, and especially his fluency in reading aloud, earned him an A – the only A that I awarded. So I smiled inwardly when I saw him approach, thinking he simply wanted to thank me and flatter me a little, as pupils sometimes will.

I was wrong; that wasn't what he wanted at all.

'Are you . . .?' he began hesitantly, pronouncing my name.

Somewhat surprised, I admitted my identity.

'Could we talk?' he asked, looking serious.

'Of course,' I replied.

'No, not here; not in school,' he said, grimacing with distaste. 'This is no place to talk.'

'Well, where, then? What do you suggest?' I shrugged.

'How about a walk? In the park.'

'Zeromski Park?' I asked, smiling again, but openly this time.

'It's quiet there. It's a pleasant place to talk. We could sit on a bench.'

'All right,' I said. 'Let's go.'

We left the building. For a while we walked along in silence. Finally he spoke. 'I've read it,' he said.

So that's what this is about, I thought, with some irony. Literature. Poetry, perhaps. He wants to be a writer. Maybe he's already written something and wants my opinion.

But here again I was wrong.

'I've read it,' he repeated, more loudly this time. 'Your book. I liked it. Particularly those *Two Scenes from the Life of Schopenhauer*. But that's not what I wanted to talk to you about. It's something else.' He looked at the ground as he walked, his head bent.

'Well, what is it?' He was beginning to intrigue me.

'You went to this school, didn't you?' He gave me an oblique glance.

I nodded. 'Yes, I did. Did they tell you that?'

He smiled enigmatically. 'The Modern Jazz Quartet, is that right?' he asked, and the mysterious expression on his face dissolved into a dreamy look.

'What do you mean, is that right?' I asked, feigning incomprehension.

'Well, there *was* a group called that, wasn't there?'

'Yes, that's true. What about it?'

'Didn't you . . . play the piano . . . and sing . . . like Ray Charles?'

I couldn't believe it. It had actually happened! A legend had been born: a classic example of the school myth. I had finally done it – I had become the hero of a myth!

And the thin, sad boy went on, a fever shining in his eyes: 'You had a jazz club down in the workshop – the woodworking room . . . you used to play there in the evenings, wreathed in clouds of cigarette smoke . . . and a few times a year you had jam sessions . . . they say you even had university students who came down there . . . Isn't that how it was? Please tell me!'

I looked at him with friendly condescension. 'What a dreamer you are! That's how it was *supposed* to be, yes; but it's not at all how it *was*. There was no club, and there weren't any jam sessions; we rehearsed in the gym, after school, in a nauseating fug of sweat and the stench of unwashed feet. There were clouds of cigarette smoke, that's true, but alas, only in the lavatories. We did play Ray Charles's "Hit the Road Jack" – once. And we played well. But it was our swan song: the next day the school authorities swooped down and officially dissolved our ensemble, and my irreverent behaviour earned me a D in discipline.'

He listened to this utterly absorbed, as if I were revealing some fascinating secret, and when I had finished he muttered, half to himself, 'Yes, yes . . .'

For some moments we walked in silence again.

'And what about the Shakespeare Theatre?' he asked suddenly, in a low voice. 'You're not going to tell me that didn't exist either?'

'The Shakespeare Theatre?' I snorted. 'What Shakespeare Theatre?'

'The one you directed,' he explained, unperturbed. 'You got the first prize for your production of *As You Like It* – you're surely not going to deny *that*! There's a framed certificate hanging on the wall of the auditorium to prove it.'

'It doesn't say that it's for *As You Like It*.'

'Oh, all right then, it says that it's for *All the World's a Stage*, if you prefer. That's a line from *As You Like It*. All right? Do you admit that, at least?'

'Yes, *that's* true enough,' I said, 'but we didn't do the whole play, and our little drama circle certainly wasn't any kind of Shakespeare Theatre.'

'They say you know dozens of monologues by heart . . . and that you can even improvise in Shakespearean style . . . talk in heroic iambics on any subject.'

'Oh, that's not so hard,' I said dismissively, echoing Constant's casual response to my expression of awe when I heard that Claire, Madame's mother, could read Gothic script with ease.

'Not so hard?!' He laughed. 'Don't be coy. Even for the great man himself' – he mentioned S.'s name – 'it was an effort to keep up with you.'

'You exaggerate. Highly.' I shook my head. 'But the main

thing is that you should know the facts, and they are as follows: the life of our drama circle, which, by the way, I put together with the greatest of difficulty, was poor and short. We gave just one performance, and it was a very humble one: no stage set, no props, no costumes. That was the *All the World* thing. And it wasn't a play; it was a sort of collage, bits and pieces of different plays woven together. And as for the prize, yes, we did win the first prize at the Festival, but I wouldn't wish my worst enemy that kind of success.'

'Why?'

'It's a long story. But to sum it up: how would *you* like to be rewarded for a Work of Art with . . . a Ruhla watch? Presented to you on stage by a prancing idiot? In the municipal community centre? In front of a bunch of adolescents who'd come to have a good time at the dance? And have to recite Jaques's speech about the seven ages of man in front of them?'

'I'd rather not.'

'Well, then. But I had to.'

'Yes, yes . . .' he muttered to himself again.

We entered the park. The sun shone brightly on the changing leaves; shrubs and trees shimmered with colour. Here and there a gossamer thread floated in the warm, still air of early autumn.

'Can I ask you one more question?' said the Sad Boy.

'What is it? Ask away.'

'You won't be offended?'

'That depends on the question.'

'When you were at school,' he began hesitantly, 'the headmistress was a Frenchwoman, is that right? Or was she half-French? Something like that – I don't really know.'

I froze. But I had no glimmer of where he was headed. 'She was Polish, actually,' I replied, 'but bilingual. She spoke French like a Frenchwoman.'

'Oh,' he said quietly. 'And who was she, this . . . lady?'

'I'm not quite sure what you mean,' I hedged, pressing him for more. 'What is it exactly that you want to know?'

'Well, I mean, what kind of person was she? What was she *like*?'

I cast about for a suitable answer. At length I said, 'She was different from the rest. Well dressed. She was . . . an interesting person. Very intelligent.'

'And very good-looking, I'm told,' he put in, with an oblique glance.

'Yes, not bad,' I agreed casually.

'Ah . . .' He gave a shaky sigh. 'And is it true –' he began, and then stopped. He swallowed nervously. 'Is it true,' he began again, stammering, 'that she . . . that is, that you . . . how should I put it?'

'Clearly and simply would be best,' I replied, echoing one of Freddy's gently ironic replies. But my heart began to beat faster, for I could already hear the next part of his sentence: '. . . that you were terribly in love with her.'

But the words he pronounced, when at last he found the courage to spit them out, had quite a different meaning. 'That you and she had a passionate love affair,' he said.

It was a struggle to conceal my astonishment and stifle the hollow laughter that welled up within me. I made an effort, however, and walked calmly on, head down, slightly stooped, arms plaited together behind my back, to all appearances deeply absorbed in thoughts of the distant past.

How vast, I thought, amused and a little awed, how extraordinary, is the power of the Imagination and the Will, that it can give birth to such myths, and pass them down through generations! That hand, that scene from *Phèdre* in her office, glimpsed by Mephisto and Prometheus; the dance; the meeting by the kiosk, observed by Roz (or had it been Kugler?) from the window – that was all it took to give rise to the myth, so much more powerful and enduring than the reality! But in that case, perhaps Madame herself was a myth of my own making? Perhaps *her* life, too, was quite different from what it seemed to me? Perhaps *I* had created it all – with the help of Constant, who had been in love with Claire?

But what *is* truth, after all? Is it the thing-in-itself, the thing-for-itself? Or the thing as it seems to us, as we imagine it? Or perhaps it's both? But then how do we choose? Which truth is the right one? The hidden? Or the apparent, however relative?

And had it not, in a sense, *been* a 'passionate love affair'? Didn't this banal story of mine have all the typical characteristics of one? All the elements were there: the curiosity, the desire to know and possess the other, the obscure longing. The love letter in the form of a school essay about the stars, the pinch of innocent mysticism, the surveillance, the jealousy, the 'Golgotha' under her window that January night. The 'resurrection': Phaedra's confession – the hand – the two hands joined in the 'ritual of marriage'. The 'Walpurgisnacht': the dance; the midnight tryst; that mysterious, urgent plea; the promise of a 'second coming'. And then that last message, like a sign 'from the beyond' . . .

I went on walking in silence, analysing my life. Had I experienced anything like that since? There had been flirtations, flings, brief romances; encounters of one kind or another; cold affairs of the flesh. But nothing like that. Those things had been ordinary – 'earthly'; there was no fever in them, no passion, no poetry. They also had little to do with what people call 'happiness'. For Tonio Kröger was right: happiness 'lies not in being loved; that merely gratifies one's vanity, and is mingled with disgust. Happiness lies in loving, and perhaps snatching brief, illusory moments of closeness to the beloved object.'

'I knew it,' my disciple said into the silence. 'I've offended you.'

'I'm not offended,' I replied, still absorbed in my thoughts. 'I'm just wondering what to say.'

'Tell me the truth.'

'Ah, the truth! But what is truth, as Pontius Pilate said?'

'Well, you're probably the one who knows best,' he said sadly.

Puisque ça se joue comme ça . . . I thought, remembering a passage from the end of *Fin de partie*: 'Since that's the way we're playing it, let's play it that way.' I made up my mind.

I halted suddenly, looked my interlocutor straight in the eye (as Constant had a habit of doing), and said, 'A gentleman, as you know, doesn't normally speak of such things, even if they belong to the past. I'm going to diverge from this sacred principle because I like you. But you must promise me not to tell anyone.'

'I won't, I promise!' he assured me earnestly.

'You give me your word?' I raised the bar a little, calculating that the more I insisted on his discretion, the quicker he would blab it all out.

'Word of honour. Honestly.'

'All right. Here we go. It's true: she meant something to me. She fascinated me. I wrote elegant essays for her, and she entered one of them, an essay about the stars and the Zodiac and Nostradamus, in a competition organised by the French Embassy for schoolchildren learning French. It won a prize, and I got to take part in a summer course near Tours, on the Loire. The idea was that you went with your teacher, who would also take part in a course there – a training course for teachers. So we went together, she and I, teacher and pupil. At the end of the course there was a competition in declamation, which I entered. I recited a passage from Racine – one of Hippolytus's speeches. I won first prize: a trip to the Alps. To Chamonix. I went there alone, but a few days later – on the sixth of August, I remember – she came out to join me. We met at the train station and went up Mont Blanc together. She told me she had been born there – well, not right at the top, but in that area, near the "roof of Europe". And when we got up to the Vallot refuge, she recited a poem that her mother had liked, and used to read to her in her crib.'

I tilted my head slightly upwards, half-closed my eyes and, pretending to be imitating *her*, while in fact becoming the embodiment of Constant, recited (I give the poem in translation):

A mystery is the pure of source.
Even song can scarcely unveil it.
For as you are born, so will you remain;
Stronger than hardship
And education
Is the moment of birth,
The ray of light which greets
The newborn.

'Did you get that,' I asked, like Freddy, 'or shall I translate?'

'No, that's fine,' he said, echoing my own reply from long ago.

'I'll go on, then. The emotion, combined with the rarefied air,' I continued, carried along on a wave of inspiration, 'made her faint. I tried to revive her.

'"What do you think you're doing?" she asked skittishly, when she had come to.

'"I'm presuming to come to your rescue," I replied with a smile.

'"Careful," she said, wagging an admonishing finger. "Your devotion seems a trifle excessive."

'As a memento of this whole extraordinary adventure she gave me a pen – look, here it is. A Mont Blanc.' I took the *Hommage à Mozart* out of the inner pocket of my jacket and showed it to him.

He took it with trembling hands and gazed at it reverently. Then, in an undertone, he read out the words engraved on the little gold band which encircled the cap: '*Meisterstück*,' he whispered; '*Meisterstück . . . Meisterstück*.' He handed it back and raised his eyes to my face. They were huge as saucers and filled with a boundless longing.

'That's it,' I said, shrugging. 'That's all there was. There's your *passionate love affair*!'

He lowered his head slowly. He didn't know what to do with his hands. After a long moment of silence he whispered, half to himself, 'Those were the days!'

I made no reply. But the thought flashed through my mind, as I replaced the pen in my pocket, that perhaps I hadn't been born too late after all.

POSTSCRIPT

My story is ended.

I began writing it on the twenty-seventh of January, 1982 – a year and a half ago. By then ten years had passed since its closing scene – my conversation with the Sad Boy – and almost fifteen since the June night when I saw Madame for the last time. Poland had been under martial law for a month and a half. Once more people were being brutally crushed and broken; once more their dreams of freedom and a life of dignity were being beaten out of them. The Solidarity 'uprising' was quelled, and communication with the rest of the world was cut off. Tanks rolled around the cities; soldiers patrolled the streets; there was a curfew. Food and other goods were rationed, and you needed a pass to leave the city.

I had long been disabused of any illusions about where I lived and the nature of the regime in power here; ever since deciding to publish my work in Polish presses abroad rather than entangling myself in further 'arrangements' with the censors, I had felt the touch of the 'severe, reproving arm of the people's justice' in my own life. Its attentions were particularly unpleasant in the 1970s, after the publication, in the West, of my novel *Defeat*, about the tragic fate of Madame's father. Described by expatriate Polish critics in the West as a 'dark and powerful novel in the style of Conrad', it was a denunciation of communist Russia as the power responsible for the Spanish civil war – the manipulator that had deliberately planted the seeds of madness and destruction in Spain and cold-bloodedly planned the fall of the Republic. It was also a challenge to writers who had allowed their brains to be addled by left-wing propaganda and distorted, in their work, the true picture of that war. In my account I followed George Orwell – a writer dear to me for many reasons, and certainly unparallelled in his treatment of the Spanish civil war.

The book caused a stir and infuriated the authorities. I was vilified by the Party newspapers, denounced as a fascist and the 'posthumous progeny' of Franco, sneered at and ridiculed as a writer: I was a nonentity, a nothing, a 'pathetic, hopeless scribbler greedy for his thirty pieces of silver and hoping for the applause of the extreme Right'. When the press had dragged me through the mud I was subjected to more concrete methods of harassment: a total ban on the publication of my work and the refusal of a passport. Then came harsher reprisals: direct acts of repression in the form of constant police surveillance, house searches, interrogations and arrests. The circle began to close.

It was clear to me that I had ventured into forbidden territory, raised a subject that was taboo. I had touched a deep nerve – the very root of the leprous demon's sore spot. Central Office didn't let such things pass unpunished.

'Spain' seemed to suck me in like some sort of Bermuda Triangle. First it had swallowed up the man on whose life my book was based; then it had engulfed his wife. Then, for years, it had wrought revenge on their daughter. And now, all these years later, I, too, had been drawn into its vortex – only because I had dared to touch on the subject. Constant had been right when he'd warned me about it and made me promise to keep my mouth shut.

I was out of town on the night of the thirteenth of December, when martial law was declared, and this saved me from the wave of internments. I went into hiding. Various friends took me in. Then, on New Year's Eve, I took advantage of a momentary lapse of vigilance on the part of the police and slipped away to Gdansk, where the unfailing Andy found me a permanent place – one that was both comfortable and safe. It was a little attic room in an old German house, with a so-called kitchen nook and a view of the sea.

It was there, in that little attic hideaway, that I began to write, and what emerged was this story. I had to find some occupation to fill the time, and I wanted to immerse myself in something clean and untainted, or at any rate remote from the world around me. At the beginning the writing was merely therapeutic; I viewed it as a kind of purifying cure, hoping it might disinfect me from within and help me regain my balance. With time, however, the wind caught my sails; the writing developed a momentum of its own and gradually carried me with it. I stopped regarding it as mere therapy. I was no longer simply writing; I was *creating*. With full deliberation I began to compose and hone, to structure and to shape: seven 'large' chapters, for the seven days of creation; and thirty-five 'small' ones, for the moment in our 'heroic age' when Madame came into the world, and also for my own age now – for today I find myself 'at the midpoint of the journey of human life'.

My diaries from those years, blessed, miraculous survivors of the ravages inflicted upon my flat by innumerable police searches, were immensely helpful. If I hadn't kept diaries then, or if they had been found and confiscated, the book would be considerably poorer in detail.

I should add that I wrote it with my *Hommage à Mozart*, in a series of school notebooks with ruled pages.

Publishing it in Poland is out of the question. Not only because I am on the index of banned authors but also, indeed mainly, because of its content. The 'war with the nation' is still going on, and nothing heralds changes in the foreseeable future. The authorities, under the leadership of a loyal servant of Moscow, a man sick with ambition and greedy for glory, a man who takes his orders from the East, have the country in a tight grip. Everything is controlled; all resistance is smashed.

I shall give the manuscript to someone I can trust, and it will be smuggled out to the West in the diplomatic bag. It should be published in six months at most.

As for me, I don't know what happens next. Practically everyone from my circle is gone. Constant is dead; Freddy has emigrated. Most of my friends from university are abroad. Roz has been a professor at Princeton for some years now.

I feel it would be dangerous to remain any longer on this sinking ship. It's not that I think my life is at risk; it's life here I'm afraid of – what it would do to me. I think it would destroy my soul. I am afraid of internal devastation: of rotting away inside. More and more often, more and more clearly, I hear a familiar voice calling to me, urging me in the words of that memorable cry: '*Jump, George! Jump! Oh jump!*'

Would it be a leap 'into a well' – into an 'everlasting deep hole'? Or into something that would one day lead me to the summit, and let me see 'the sun and the other stars' again?

I don't know. But something tells me I have to do it. I must set off.

I wish I could repeat Hippolytus's sad parting words: 'My mind's made up, Theramenes; I leave today.' But I can't, for I am not fully master of my own fate.

Voici l'oeuvre finie. I cast it out into the world like a message in a bottle onto the waters of the ocean. Perhaps one day you will come across it; perhaps you will fish it out, and give me some sign – my North Star, my Aquarius, my Victoire.

Warsaw, 10 September 1983